MAPS
The Uncollected John Sladek

Other Books by John Sladek

Novels and Novellas
Mechasm (UK *The Reproductive System*)
Black Alice with Thomas M. Disch
The Müller-Fokker Effect
Black Aura
Invisible Green
Roderick, or, The Education of a Young Machine
Roderick at Random, or, The Further Education of a Young Machine
Tik-Tok
Bugs
Wholly Smokes *

Collections
The Steam-Driven Boy *
Keep the Giraffe Burning *
The Best of John Sladek
Alien Accounts *
The Lunatics of Terra *

Nonfiction
The New Apocrypha
Arachne Rising: The Thirteenth Sign of the Zodiac as by James Vogh
The Cosmic Factor: Health and Astrology as by James Vogh
Judgement on Jupiter as by Richard A. Tilms
The Book of Clues

* Available or forthcoming from Cosmos Books/Ansible E-ditions

MAPS
The Uncollected
John Sladek

John Sladek

Edited by David Langford

Cosmos Books • 2003
An imprint of **Wildside Press**

MAPS: THE UNCOLLECTED JOHN SLADEK

Published by:

Cosmos Books, an imprint of Wildside Press
PO Box 301, Holicong, PA 18928-0301
www.wildsidepress.com

Copyright © 2002 by the Estate of John Sladek. All rights reserved.
Introduction copyright © 2002 by David Langford.
Cover design copyright © 2003 by Juha Lindroos.
Other copyrights as detailed on page 305, which constitutes an extension of this copyright page.
Typeset by Ansible E-ditions: www.ansible-editions.co.uk.
This Cosmos Books edition published 2003.

The right of John Sladek to be identified as the author of this work has been asserted by his Estate in accordance with the British Copyright, Designs and Patents Act 1988.

The right of David Langford to be identified as the author of the Introduction has been asserted by him in accordance with the British Copyright, Designs and Patents Act 1988.

No portion of this book may be reproduced by any means, mechanical, electronic or otherwise, without first obtaining the permission of the copyright holder.

For more information, contact Wildside Press.

ISBN: 1-59224-202-2 (hardcover)
ISBN: 1-59224-203-0 (trade paperback)

Contents

Plastitone (frontispiece) 7
Introduction 9

Stories, Mostly

The Lost Nose: A Programmed Book 20
In the Distance 33
Alien Territory 35
The Misinterpreted Letter 38
Comedo 39
By an Unknown Hand 43
Bill Gets Hep to God! 57
It Takes Your Breath Away 59
Peabody Slept Here 63
Machine Screw 72
The Future of John Sladek 80
Goodbye, Germany? 87
Robot "Kiss of Life" Drama 92
Some Mysteries of Birth, Death and Population That Can Now Be Cleared Up 94
The Entropy Tango: A Comic Romance 102
Love Among the Xoids 104
Stop Evolution in its Tracks! 113
Blood and Gingerbread 119
Dining Out 135
Radio Cats 144
Reinventing the Wheel 145

Poems and Playlets

A Section from the Adventures of I.E.M. 151
Untitled 156
Untitled 2 157
Jesus in White Bucks 158
The Four Cows 159
The Brusque Skate 160
No Exit 161
Seventh Inning Stretch 162
Down His Alarming Blunder 163
Letter 165
Love Nest 166

Page	169
The "Pelican"	170
The Treasure of the Haunted Rambler	171

Sladek Incognito

Just Another Victim	174
You Have a Friend at Fengrove National	177
The Switch	180
Timetable	183
Now That I'm Free	186
Practical Joke	189
Publish and Perish	192
In the Oligocene	203

Sladek and Disch

The Way to a Man's Heart	210
The Floating Panzer	216
The Incredible Giant Hot Dog	228
The Marching Raspberries	234
Sweetly Sings The Chocolate Budgie	240
United We Stand Still	249
The Atheist's Bargain	259
The Discovery of the Nullitron	265
Danny's New Friends from Deneb	268
Mystery Diet of the Gods: A Revelation	270
Transplant Your Own Heart	275

Sladek on Sladek

The Profession of Science Fiction, 29: Kids! Read Books In Your Spare Time!	280
Writing Places	284
4-Part List	288
How I Became a Science Fiction Master in only 15 Minutes a Day	298
John Sladek Comments	300
Acknowledgements	301
Notes on the Text	302
Original Appearances	303
Extended Copyright Page	305

INTRODUCTION

DAVID LANGFORD

John Sladek is remembered as one of the cleverest, wittiest writers ever to work in, or around the edges of, the science fiction field. This book of his previously uncollected stories takes its title *Maps* from a project which he never completed, perhaps never began, but talked about enthusiastically in the early 1980s:

> It will be something between a novel and a set of linked stories, but the linkages are going to be fairly complex, with stories inside stories, stories completely permeating one another, a character in one story turning into, say, an event or a place in another – in other words, the notion of mapping is going to predominate. If all this sounds vague and confusing, it is because I'm still vague and confused about it – and will be until I start work on it. (Interview, *Science Fiction Review* #46, 1983)

The present volume isn't the *Maps* which Sladek intended, although (like Nabokov's antihero in *Pale Fire*, imposing his own Ruritanian obsessions on a text which has nothing to do with them) he might well have enjoyed himself hugely and wasted a great deal of time concocting a labyrinthine explanation of how all the stories and miscellanea here are "really" linked by subtle connections, exactly as described above. Maps, puzzles, codes, wordplay, number games and webs of insane sophistry always intrigued him, and cropped up again and again in his fiction.

This is especially evident in the early pieces collected here. "The Lost Nose: A Programmed Book" was produced in a handmade edition of one copy as a Christmas gift to amuse the girlfriend who later became his first wife Pamela Sladek. (She recalls that he later made further little books of a similar nature for their daughter Dorothea; other friends also received such one-off treats.) Perhaps inspired by Borges's "The Garden of Forking Paths", its high-spirited multiple-choice narrative prefigures the whole 1980s publishing category of interactive SF and fantasy gamebooks. Particularly Sladekian is the painstaking and entirely unnecessary map or flowchart of possible routes through the story. His friend Charles Platt remembers:

> John and I shared a similar weakness for codes, palindromes – word games and number games in general. I corresponded with him about this; both of us realized it was a total waste of our time, yet neither of us knew how to stop. John originated multi-

threaded fiction, so far as I know (it would be termed "hyper-linked" today), and he and I both produced some early samples. A couple of his were published, after his initial effort was written as a gift for his then-girlfriend, Pamela. [...] He lived at our house at 271 Portobello Road for a year or so, during which time I tried to understand what drove him as a writer. I feel the real dilemma in his life was his difficulty in channeling his obsessiveness productively. (E-mail, April 2000)

"The Lost Nose" in its original form includes collages and gummed-in artifacts such as watch cogs, paperclips and cigarette cards – three identical cards from a famous-cricketer series, so the Royal Advisers of section 31 are in fact the Three W.G. Graces. The narrative incidentally links to other early Sladek stories *via* a rare instance of his recycling a tiny joke. Genetically mutated ("uplifted") foxes who aren't sure whether their children are called pups or cubs also feature in "Is There Death on Other Planets?" and his Cordwainer Smith parody "One Damned Thing After Another", both collected in *The Steam-Driven Boy*.

Another example of hyperlinked storytelling, "Alien Territory", was presumably omitted from past collections owing to the difficulty of reproducing its striking original appearance in book form. The story filled a double-page spread in the large format used by Michael Moorcock's *New Worlds* in 1969, laid out by the designer Charles Platt as a chequerboard of paragraphs, four across, nine down. Arrows indicated the reader's choices at each step: to read the next paragraph down (with an extra link from the bottom of a column to the top of the next) or across (doubling back from the end of a row to the start of the next).

The brief "In The Distance" was created for the little magazine *Concentrate*, whose editor Mike Butterworth explains: "My idea was a magazine of condensed writing, and John was very taken by it." This story has a peculiarly mechanical rhythm which reminded me of my own attempts at computer software that would "write" fiction. I guessed that in those pre-home-computer days Sladek had constructed it by inserting randomly or semi-randomly chosen nouns, adjectives, and adjectival phrases into a sentence template, perhaps governed by dice throws. Platt confirmed:

> That is precisely how John did it. I remember seeing his "writing engine", consisting of bits of paper with vocabulary, some sentence construction rules, and, yes, dice. He was the Charles Babbage of interactive fiction! (E-mail, October 2000)

Sladek mentioned in a letter to Butterworth that he'd worked with a 200-word vocabulary for "In the Distance". His later, longer story "A Game of Jump", collected in *Keep the Giraffe Burning*, used only the 300 words of the children's primer *A Second Ladybird Key Words Picture Dictionary and Spelling Book* (1966), plus a few character names. A far smaller significant vocabulary emerges in the poem "The Brusque Skate", which imitates the spirit if not the form of the sestina by shuffling and mutating a very few key words and phrases. (One private joke in Sladek's 1983 novel *Tik-Tok* is the appearance of "Brusque skate!" as a fragment of uncomprehended speech.) The author himself later stated his ambitions for what might be called automatic writing:

> I want, as soon as possible, to write a novel in collaboration with a computer. Some computer writing has been done, but mostly using a computer as a high-speed typewriter, recombining simple phrases. What I have in mind is a little more complicated. I feel I ought to do my part in helping machines take over the arts and sciences, leaving us plenty of leisure time for important things, like extracting square roots and figuring pay rolls. (Back flap biography, *The Müller-Fokker Effect*, 1970)

It is clear that John Sladek's literary influences largely lay outside the SF circles where he was most appreciated: William Gaddis and Joseph Heller, for example, rather than Isaac Asimov and Robert Heinlein. Joycean portmanteau constructions like "creedchair cumfarts" are evident amid the general haze of literary allusiveness in the stream-of-consciousness prose poem "A Section from the Adventures of I.E.M." – apparently his earliest published fiction, dating back to 1963 and described as a section from a novel.

> Whatever I'm reading at the moment seems to influence whatever I'm writing. I found some time ago that I have to be careful, while working on a novel, what I read. People may notice the influence of Joseph Heller in "Masterson and the Clerks" or of William Gaddis in *Roderick*. Recently I've been reading Angela Carter and John Cheever, so I suppose my work will soon have clouds of purple perfume or else exhilarating sunlight on suburban lawns ... (Interview, *Science Fiction Review* #46, 1983)

His use of elaborate structures, artificial constraints and controlled randomness echoes the practices of the Oulipo (*Ouvroir de Litterature Potentialle*) literary group founded in 1960, whose members have included Raymond Queneau, Georges Perec and Italo Calvino. For example, the latter's *The Castle of Crossed Destinies* (1973) took its plot skeleton from the random fall of Tarot cards.

Thus the Sladek poem "Down His Alarming Blunder" inflicts a very Oulipo-esque "controlled accident" on Andrew Marvell's "To His Coy Mistress" by replacing most of its nouns with other nouns, verbs with other verbs, and so on. As with "In the Distance", the aspect of which the author retains control – choice of vocabulary – still gives it an ineluctably Sladekian flavour. (The fourth from last line is missing, accidentally omitted by either Sladek or the original publisher.) In the very short prose

"Radio Cats", the imposed constraint is less obvious: it was written for an anthology of Drabbles, defined as stories of precisely 100 words.

The challenge of devising meticulously dovetailed plots lured Sladek into the realms of detective fiction. In 1972 *The Times* newspaper and the publishers Jonathan Cape ran a competition for best unpublished detective story, drawing well over a thousand entries, and the judges – who included Agatha Christie and Tom Stoppard – gave the £500 prize to Sladek's locked-room mystery "By an Unknown Hand". This has apparently not been reprinted in English since the resulting *Times Anthology of Detective Stories* (1972). The competition win also brought him a contract to write a full-length crime novel, *Black Aura* (1974), later followed by *Invisible Green* (1977). Both these novels and the original story feature the same conscientiously eccentric detective, Thackeray Phin, as does the short squib "It Takes Your Breath Away" (1974), syndicated in various London theatre programmes and never before reprinted.

Unfortunately, as our author soon discovered, the 1970s were not a good time for displays of outrageous detective ingenuity:

> Those two novels suffered mainly from being written about 50 years after the fashion for puzzles of detection. I enjoyed writing them, planning the absurd crimes and clues, but I found I was turning out a product the supermarket didn't need any more – stove polish or yellow cakes of laundry soap. One could starve very quickly writing locked-room mysteries like those. SF has much more glamour and glitter attached to it, in these high-tech days. (Interview, *Science Fiction Review* #46, 1983)

Maps assembles all the previously uncollected solo fiction known to have been published by John Sladek, while excluding stories featured in the four collections published during his lifetime: *The Steam-Driven Boy and Other Strangers* (1973), *Keep the Giraffe Burning* (1978), *Alien Accounts* (1982) and *The Lunatics of Terra* (1984). (The US *The Best of John Sladek* consists entirely of selections from the first two.)

There are two partial exceptions to the latter rule. "The Future of John Sladek", written for the *Bananas* magazine feature "Monumental Supplement: The Future", thriftily incorporates his *Alien Accounts* story "198-, a Tale of 'Tomorrow'" – but also extends it. "Some Mysteries of Birth, Death and Population that Can Now Be Cleared Up" was heavily cut and rewritten as "Great World Mysteries" (1982), collected in *The Lunatics of Terra*; the even more frenetically comic original seems well worth preserving.

Just to make life more complicated for bibliographers, a third permutation of the "Mysteries" material appeared in 1983 as "John Sladek's List of Seven Great Unexplained Mysteries of our Time (with Explanations)". As well as re-using text from both earlier versions, this addresses three further questions that were merely posed in "Some Mysteries ...":

> The trouble with science today is that it has answers to all the wrong questions. No one is asking whether the laser is or is not a beam of coherent energy in the visible spectrum. No one is desperate to know what it is that ontogeny recapitulates, or whether E *really* equals mc². It is high time that scientists came out of their ivory laboratories, stopped messing around with silicon chips and transactional analysis, and tackled some of the real mysteries of our time:
>
> 1. *What's so great about the Great Pyramid?* Nearly everything. It contains millions or billions of pounds of stone or is it tons, I haven't got the exact figures here but it's very big. Modern scientists have discovered that if you put a razor blade under the Great Pyramid, *it will remain sharp throughout the night*! Because of the great weight of the Pyramid, however, this experiment has not yet been carried out. Still, rumours have it that a consortium of razor-blade companies are trying to buy up the patent and suppress it.
>
> 2. *How did Nostradamus manage to predict the rise of Clement Attlee?* Oddly enough, he didn't. This is one of the rare instances where the great sage of Provence made a wrong prediction. On the other hand, writing in 1556, he was right about millions of other future events, such as:
>
> (a) Napoleon's invention of brandy, 1769.
> (b) Nepal invades Peru, 1999 (or World War Three, 1966).
> (c) Martian invasion of California (undetected) last year.
> (d) Stock market steady for a time.
>
> 3. *Could Stonehenge be a primitive computer, used by the Druids for figuring payrolls?* That must remain a mystery, an imponderable conundrum, a riddle wrapped in a dark enigma, an impenetrable veil of cloud-shrouded o'ercast secret of Sphinx-mute Nature. (*The Complete Book of Science Fiction and Fantasy Lists* ed. Maxim Jakubowski and Malcolm Edwards, 1983)

Happily, the mass of assorted material in *Maps* shows Sladek's wide range. His enthusiasm for parody is much in evidence, mimicking the awful glibness of religious tracts in "Bill Gets Hep To God!", reviewing Michael Moorcock *via* a condensed non-story in "The Entropy Tango", and running riot in "Machine Screw" – where a million Hollywood scenarios about escaped Frankensteinian menaces are boiled down to a gleefully salacious *reductio ad absurdum*. "What kind of decent American would go and – and *rape* a Cadillac convertible?" Some tics often found in 1960s New Wave SF are affectionately pastiched in "Comedo", with its brief chapters, sinisterly obsessive details, discontinuities, and non sequiturs; but auctorial cheerfulness somehow keeps breaking in.

"Machine Screw" and the joke news story "Robot 'Kiss of Life' Drama" also share the ever-recurring Sladek theme of robots; the word itself fleetingly appears in "Down His Alarming Blunder". Another repeated theme, logical quibbles and paradoxes, flavours items like the self-referential "The Misinterpreted Letter" and "Page", not to mention a minimalist poem called "The Monkey's Paw Effect" which may as well be quoted in full at this point:

> Today I am thinking about "The Monkey's Paw"
> And today I am
> (*Just Friends* #1, 1969)

"Peabody Slept Here", which like "Machine Screw" is an excursion into the theoretically raunchy territory of men's magazine fiction, offers a more genial time-travel romp that deals almost sardonically with the expected wish-fulfilment fantasy of the easy lay. Sladek's last published story "Reinventing the Wheel" also plays around with the past, demurely suggesting that alternative history moves (as it were) in cycles. His more characteristically comic-melancholy, alienated view of life pervades "Love Among the Xoids", an evocation of contemporary outsiders who form what the *Encyclopedia of Fantasy* would call a wainscot community or pariah elite. A horrified fascination with what the American Dream has become – central to his SF novels, from *The Reproductive System* in 1968 to *Bugs* in 1989 – drives the black farce of "Dining Out".

The fruitier and nuttier fringes of pseudoscience, wittily explored at book length in his nonfictional *The New Apocrypha* (1973), are revisited in "Some Mysteries of Birth, Death and Population that Can Now Be Cleared Up" and "Stop Evolution In Its Tracks!". And the darkness underlying his finest comedies – such as *Roderick* (1980) and *Roderick at Random* (1983) – fuels wild satire in the semi-fictional essay "Goodbye, Germany?" and holds unremitting, uncomic sway throughout his long, grisly reworking of the Hansel and Gretel story, "Blood and Gingerbread". A Grimm tale, indeed.

Additional bonus items gathered here in *Maps* are fourteen poems and playlets written by Sladek early in his career (including an apparent novel extract most easily classified as a prose poem), eleven lightweight but entertaining collaborations with his close friend Thomas M. Disch, eight specimens of commercial fiction written under pseudonyms, and a final handful of more or less autobiographical pieces under the heading "Sladek on Sladek".

The early Disch collaboration "The Floating Panzer" is a broad James Bond spoof which the surviving author now regards as "genuinely ... unexciting." Sladek produced a solo sequel, "The Mogul and the Maneaters", never published and since apparently lost. Three previously unpublished stories that they wrote together are described by Disch as follows:

> ... "United We Stand Still," a lowbrow lampoon of featherbedding practices in American unions, inspired in part by John's job as a railway switchman, and two "Green Magician" adventures (the

Green Magician was the hero of my solo tale, "Dangerous Flags"), "The Marching Raspberries" and "Sweetly Sings the Chocolate Budgie". Those two are in a vein of gorblimey gadawfulness that never had a market then but are prescient of such latter-day media hits as PeeWee's Playhouse.... I am tickled to think that those ancient rejections may find their happy ending! (E-mail, February 2001)

In fact the Green Magician mutated into the Pink Avenger for "The Marching Raspberries", but the vein of whimsy is hideously similar.

The six short-short stories opening the "Sladek Incognito" section appeared in *Titbits*, a weekly British tabloid magazine combining media-star adulation, shock horror exposés and pictures of nice girls in (frequently nothing but) tights. For a few years from 1967, *Titbits* regularly ran short fiction. SF writers swarmed aboard when the feature was launched as "Into the Fantastic ... a season of science fiction". By the time Sladek discovered this market the theme had switched to thrillers, each story building towards a sting-in-the-tail surprise finale in one page. The Sladek/Disch "The Way To a Man's Heart" filled this specification neatly and was reprinted in the second "season of thrillers" issue.

It would seem that Sladek intended all his subsequent solo contributions to appear as by Dale Johns, but ever-slapdash *Titbits* ran the first three under his own name. Of course they are potboilers, accurately aimed at a market that wanted nothing more, but gleams of talent and ingenuity shine through. "The Switch" draws on his railway experience, as mentioned above by Disch. In his own words:

I left school in 1960, to take up the series of jobs which usually characterize writers and other malcontents – short-order cook, technical writer, railroad switchman, cowboy, President of the United States. (Back flap biography, *The Müller-Fokker Effect*, 1970)

Meanwhile, the admired SF magazine *If* published the two 1968 "John Thomas" stories (Sladek's bibliographer Phil Stephensen-Payne speculates that using the author's first and middle name only may have been an error). "In the Oligocene" later had French and Spanish translations credited to John Sladek. "Publish and Perish", which appeared one month earlier, did not – but if two stories appearing in successive months with the same byline incorporated into title art by the same illustrator ("Brock") were in fact by different authors, one feels that *If*'s editor would have commented on the oddity.

Significant omissions from *Maps* consist mostly of miscellaneous nonfiction: essays, speeches, book reviews, letters, and even a few recipes. The recipes, incidentally, are straightforward and practical despite titles like "Caligula Salad with Muttered Dressing", and "Accursed Steak Pie" with its helpful preamble:

> It is said that James II was so taken with this dish that he drew his sword and on the spot created it Duchess of Williamsborough. His successor revoked the title and ordered the luckless pie to be imprisoned in the Tower, guarded by yeomen called "beefeaters". (*Cooking Out of This World* ed. Anne McCaffrey, 1973)

It would be carrying fictional completism to a silly degree to reprint, say, the two one-page bridging passages written to fill gaps in the MS of Philip K. Dick's *Lies, Inc* – an expanded version of *The Unteleported Man*, published 1984. And as Disch observes, however wide you fling the net it's hard to capture Sladek entire:

> An almost impossible goal since he did so much borderline and ephemeral material, including gift "booklets" for friends on their birthdays and such. Profligacy of talent is one of the luxuries genius can allow itself, but it's the bane of editors. (E-mail, February 2001)

Also omitted are the "Plastitutes" visual features which he devised for *New Worlds* and *Frendz*: strip cartoons mingling stock characters from Letraset commercial-art transfers with other images clipped from ads, plus varyingly surreal captions and dialogue. "Good gosh! IBM is just like a woman!" "Nancy was almost a bean ..." "So Brad and Sally exchanged sexes for the evening –" "The refrigerator was happy to see them, for it had been blinded by a new improved father ..." And so on. The flavour of these pieces is sufficiently represented here by the similar one-page "Plastitone", from the 1968 launch issue of Sladek's and Pamela Zoline's *Ronald Reagan: The Magazine of Poetry*. ("Anyone using the name Ronald Reagan without our permission had better watch it.") All its human figures can be found in contemporary Letraset catalogues.

Another oddity discovered during *Maps* research was that Sladek's 1966 story "Is There Death on Other Planets?", collected in *The Steam-Driven Boy*, was published in different form in the little Minneapolis magazine *region* (issue 4, Fall 1965). Though generally similar, the 1965 draft strove for humour through anachronistic dialogue of the "Prithee, varlet" persuasion, later wisely removed. For example, when the hero protests that he can't become a spy because he doesn't look like one, the response is:

> (1965) "'Sblood," spat the man in the green hat. "Thy ignorance passeth all understanding. 'Tis but as the great n-tuple spy Waldmir Vichlier said, to wit: 'More than anyone else, a spy must look like anyone else.' ..."

> (1966) The man in the green hat sighed. "You'll do. As the great n-tuple agent Waldmir said ..." (etc.)

INTRODUCTION

John Sladek was born in Iowa on 15 December 1937, grew up in Minneapolis, lived in London for most of his creative writing life, and returned to the American Midwest when his marriage to Pamela broke down in the mid-1980s (although they remained on good terms). Thereafter, though continuing to write, he worked as a technical author and published little fiction. The major exception was *Bugs*, his final novel to see print, in which by no coincidence at all an English immigrant seeks work as a technical writer in the Midwest and helplessly sinks into the fantasticated comic inferno of modern America.

Sladek married Sandra Gunter (Sandy Sladek) in 1995, enjoyed good years with her, and died from an inherited lung condition on 10 March 2000. It was far too soon; he was only 62. As Disch said:

> ... it was just bad genetic luck. His lungs became gradually less and less elastic – pulmonary fibrosis. For a while he lived on the hope that he might be assigned a place in the waiting line for lung transplants. Isn't it dumbfounding to think that there can be such a procedure? But within a few days of his learning that that was not in the cards he just sighed away his life. (WNYC radio broadcast, 2000)

The characteristic self-deprecating summation he might have made of his own life was affectionately imagined in John Clute's obituary:

> It is possible to hear the voice of John Sladek describing the career of John Sladek. The voice is slightly husky, hums and haws as it awaits a moment of inspiration from its owner, then lifts suddenly above the American prairie of its twang as something extremely hilarious comes down the line. It would be (I will not try to sound like John in full flow, he was too funny and too savage and too sad to be copied) a joke, sometimes a very great joke.
>
> – Oh, yeah (he could be imagined saying), *I* remember John Sladek. He was the guy who called the first novel he would acknowledge *The Reproductive System*, and it wasn't *non-fiction*. He was the guy who brought out a second novel *with a different firm*, and called it *The Müller-Fokker Effect*, and it wasn't ever bought because nobody ever dared to try and *pronounce* it at W H Smith's. He was the guy whose masterpiece, which was called *Roderick*, was too big to go into one volume, so his publisher (this was his *third* sf publisher, by the way, and probably his fifth overall) released it in two vols, the first hardback, the second, three years later, mass market paperback: demolished, disappeared, invisible. This is the novel David Hartwell of Timescape Books published the first two thirds of volume one of in the States, as a pb original to be completed in two further instalments – just before Timescape Books became an ex-desk at Simon and Schus-

ter, which was all the American market got to see of *Roderick* for years.

– Oh, yeah (he might have continued), *I remember John Sladek. He was the guy who published two really good detective novels, starring series detective Thackeray Phin, with different publishers.* He was the guy who published *lots* of short stories – but the best of them appeared in three mass market paperbacks with titles like *Keep the Giraffe Burning, which was not about the desertification of Chad.* He was the guy who wrote about Scientology in *The New Apocrypha*, and his publishers pulled his pants down so the insolent praetorians of The LRON could whup his ass for talking out of turn. He was the guy who did a novel with Tom Disch called *Black Alice – which was not about bussing –* and guess what they called themselves? Thom Demijohn. Which is not a name but a portaloo. The Thom Demijohn, "For Loving Couples". *Bestseller written all over that one!* He was the guy who wrote (as James Vogh) a "nonfiction" spoof called *Arachne Rising: the Thirteenth Sign of the Zodiac,* and for the first time in his life his readers *believed* him. (*Ansible* #153, April 2000; revised *Foundation* #79, Summer 2000)

That perpetually self-mocking tone had caused some slight concern in SF circles when Bob Shaw's 1984 novel *Fire Pattern* featured a cameo appearance of a sceptical writer about the paranormal, called John Sladek. The protagonist phones this man in hope of useful information on the supposed phenomenon of spontaneous human combustion, but receives only flip answers like "Well, it's a whole new category of event that the insurance companies can refuse to pay off for." Sladek's sarcastic exit line is: "I'm sorry I couldn't tell you that spontaneous human combustion is done with mirrors."

Naturally readers wondered why Bob Shaw, one of the nicest men in the SF world, should be needling a colleague in this way – until Shaw explained that Sladek had (by invitation) written all his own dialogue for the scene, a parodist unable to resist spoofing even his own scepticism.

Following Gene Wolfe's principle of hiding a bonus story where the people who don't read introductions will miss it, the preceding pages have been larded with tasty Sladek quotations, fragments and even a "whole" poem. Here, now, are John Sladek's previously uncollected stories – and more.

David Langford
April 2001

Stories, Mostly

THE LOST NOSE: A PROGRAMMED BOOK

How to Read the Programmed Book

Begin at the section marked Start.
   From time to time *you* will have to decide what happens next, by choosing a number and turning to that section.
   When you have reached **The End**, go back to your last choice and take a new route, if you like.
   There are **21** endings.
   A diagram of routes is at the end of the book.

Start.
   FRED THOUGHT HE'D LOST HIS NOSE.
This it was which vexed him, which made reality so **unreal** this morning. But a nose cannot be misplaced like some cheque used for a bookmark, so even though Fred had been said to "always have his nose in a book" he knew the **nose** must have
- been stolen ... **2**
- been left at school ... **3**
- fallen off someplace ... **4**

2. STOLEN???
"A thieving **cat**!" he exclaimed, though he doubted any cat could have smashed his door panel like this! More likely it was:
- The butler: **5**
- A burglar: **6**
- The milkman: **7**

3. He went to school to look for it, hiding the peculiar flatness of his face with dark glasses. There was Miss Plogg, the geography teacher, cleaning a toilet while murmuring to herself the capitals of South America.
"Quito ...
"Bogota ...
"Caracas ..."
Could she know more than she was saying?
- Yes: **8**
- No: **9**

4. "Probably I was shaving," he mused. "And it just fell off!"
   But when he went to the bathroom to see, a funny thing happened:

- Or so he thought: **10**
- Unbelievably: **11**

5. He called the butler long distance. Over the phone he could hear the buzzing of flies, for on his day off, the butler was an amateur flykeeper. The sound so distracted Fred that he forgot his reason for calling, and instead harped on the arrangements for the **Lapidaries' Ball**. This ball was to be held at Fred's palatial mansion.

Fred had acquired the mansion in this peculiar fashion:
- It was a gift ... **12**
- It was no gift ... **13**

6. He jerked open the closet door, and sure enough, there stood a man in cloth cap and black eye-mask, half-heartedly brandishing a flashlight. And he seemed to have eaten one of Fred's camel-hair coats! "A burglar!" "Yes, but you see I'm only a **watermelon** burglar." "Then what are you doing in my closet? My personal closet?" "No, no, you've got it all wrong," said the watermelon burglar. "I was waiting for this bus, when ..."

And that is all he would ever say, though the police tortured him roundly. "He certainly doesn't have the **item** on him," said the chief later. "We suspect an accomplice."

BUT WHOM?
- The butler ... **5**
- Miss Plogg ... **3**
- Someone else ... **14**

7. The Milkman could not be persuaded to talk, about the nose or anything else.

"Just you try doing my job for a day," was all he would say. "The things I see!"

Fred took the hint and exchanged clothes with the Milkman. He delivered milk to the hovels of Portobello Road and to the mansions of Tavistock Crescent.

Looking in one window, he saw an old painter putting finishing touches to a enormous painting of a nose.

"Like it?" said the old man. "I call it NOSE."

"That's **my** nose, you dirty stealer! Mine! I'd know it anywhere, like I'd know my own **hand**!" Suddenly Fred realized his hand was gone!! And since he had watched the old painter carefully, **someone else** must have stolen it!

"Missing one nose, eh?" The old painter looked thoughtful and puffed at his pipe a minute. "I think I know where you might find it. Saw a nose like that this morning. Saw it at:
- THE ZOO ... **15**
- THE MARKET ... **16**
- A TOILET ... **17**

8. Yes! For under cover of cleaning the toilet, she was busy hiding something in its depths!

"Give me back my nose, Miss Plogg, or I'll call the police!"

"Buenos Aires ...

"Brasilia ...

"Montevideo ...

"Finders, keepers; losers, weepers." As she spoke, she dried her hands thoroughly - those chalk-dust-coloured hands with chalky, squeaky nails.

Then she tied Fred to a school desk and set the school on fire!

Did Fred survive?
- Yes ... **18**
- No ... **19**

9. No, for poor Miss Plogg was too nearsighted to know much about the world beyond her own nose, let alone Fred's.

"Lima!

"La Paz!

"**There!** A diamond ring worth millions!"

"I'm very good at **finding** things."

"Do you think you could **find** a lost nose? It's been missing for seven months," he asked.

"Of course I could **find** a nose," she replied, wrinkling her nose. "I seem to detect a nose somewhere, crying for help. I speak symbolically, of course.

"You might try looking for a **weeping face**."

"But where?"

"**Where they weep the most**," she said mischievously.

Fred thought:
- At Buckingham Palace ... **20**
- At the zoo ... **15**

10. The bathroom seemed to shiver for a moment, then swelled into a giant hen! Was this an optical illusion? **(21)** Or was Fred losing his cool and his mind? **(22)**.

11. Unbelievably, the bathroom walls collapsed into a folded paper figure!! He stood in Buckingham Palace, asking the Queen about his lost nose. Moreover, she had a certain sly look about her ... Fred asked her about this, and she replied:
- "The Prince and I are not what we seem" ... **23**
- "You must be mistaken" ... **24**

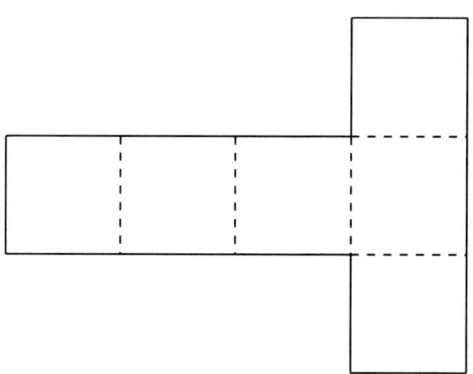

Replica of Buckingham Palace. Cut along solid lines, fold along dotted lines.

12. The mansion was a gift from the ancient lapidary, the man who fashioned the original Crown Jewels.

Of course at that time, they were known as the Crown **Jews**, for this was in Biblical days in Palestine.

The ancient lap. had called Fred to his bedside where after ten thousand yrs, he was dying.

"I bequeath to you this mansion and all its contents, on **one condition**, which is:

- That you never whistle "Dixie" within its walls **(25)**
- That if you marry, your bride must be able to pluck a chicken with her toes, find gold in a fool, and fell an ox with an eyelash **(26)**

13. The mansion was no gift, but a rare organic growth!! The whole baroque inside and façade comprised a single mushroom! Fred's father had trained the precocious fungus to imitate chandeliers and servants, music and mutton, and a staircase of which the Queen was envious.

Thinking of this, Fred suddenly realized the Queen was a suspect in the "Nose Job". Could **she** have taken it to spite his staircase? He determined to go to London at once and demand his nose's return ... **(20)**

14. "Someone else" could mean only one person, Fred's father, Old Zlótny, known in his own quarter as **The Hunchback of Notre Dame** (because he had once played that position on the Notre Dame football team). He usually hung out at a pub called "The Nuts and Blood", so Fred saddled his horse at once and went thither to seek him out.

The only way one could get into "The Nuts and Blood" was to fight two enormous bouncers guarding the door, Sam and Bill. Fred first promised Sam that if he would forbear smashing and kicking him, Fred would give the big bouncer a hot tip on a horse. Sam bragged about this tribute to his toughness all day to Bill, who grew sullen.

Finally the time for the tip arrived. Fred had connected a soldering iron by 10 miles of extension cord to his own mansion. Carrying the soldering iron on a pole like a lance, he galloped up and gave Sam the tip of it.

Bill laughed at Sam's stupidity, and the two giants came to blows. Fred was just able to slip between them as they fought.

Once inside, he saw:
- his father ... **27**
- his nose ... **28**

15. "Where did the monkey get that **funny** false nose?" screamed the crowd with laughter. Fred was ashamed to admit that this was his **real** nose. He drew his umbrella and knocked the olfactory organ from the monkey's grasp. Alas! It flew into the tiger's cage, and a very hungry tiger pounced on it. "Now what?" groaned Fred. He could either try to rescue his nose by going into the cage **(29)**, or simply watch "Leo" eat it **(30)**!

16. The nose lay on a pile of marrows, almost indistinguishable from them except to the eye of its owner. Fred politely asked the man running the stall to give it to him. "Hand over all me fuckin' marrow for nuffin?" he roared in reply. "Fuckall profit in at, an't it?" Fred saw his mistake and then asked to buy that particular marrow. "'Ere, don't touch that. All the same, gov. All the best marrow. Can't 'ave you smelling and pickin' at 'em like that. I'll give you a good one." He took Fred's nose from him and put it back on the display, and gave him instead a diseased vegetable like a withered root, from some dirty box under the counter. Fred found himself standing helpless with his bag of bug-chewed vegetable, while his nose beamed attractively on the vegetable pile. There was nothing he could do, but make his weary way home and write an angry letter to the **Times**, which he did, and his nose may still be seen in the vegetable market.

The End

17. The toilet was at Buckingham Palace and was indeed the Queen's own privy. The old painter had been called there to a meeting of the Privy Council, where the Queen had offered to trade him a horse and rider for doing her portrait.

Now he confided to Fred the secret password that would let him past all the guards and into the royal privy.

"But I can't **say** a word like that at the palace!" Fred objected. The word was:
- "Jakes" ... **20**
- "Poopy drawers" ... **31**

18. Fred struggled as the flames leapt higher, devouring one by one the rolled maps of Africa, Asia, North America... He was reminded of a cowboy or priestly saint being roasted by the savages of America. How would Gene Autry or St Isaac Jogues have got out of this situation?

Fred:
- closed his eyes and wished very hard – **32**
- set off the fire alarm – **33**

- urinated on the fire – **34**

19. Fred burned to death in that fire, but as the evil Miss Plogg watched, a great tree fell upon her, killing her instantly. As Fred expired (murmuring the name of his lady) the nose flew out of Miss Plogg's pocket and up to Heaven to join its true owner. Fred was whole and happy ever more, if somewhat insubstantial.
   The End
But there are many other endings to this story … start again.

20. The Prince and the Queen were very gracious, considering the strange manner in which Fred had come into their home. After offering him a biscuit, they asked Fred to tell his story, and he related all that had happened to him. "The vulgar herd does not know it," said the Queen, "but I too lost my nose a few years ago, in a fox-hunting accident." "Hear, hear," said the Prince, very graciously. "Good sport, what?"
   His suspicions aroused, Fred asked her **how** she had "lost" her nose.
- "I don't want to speak of that," she said.... **(35)**
- "The Prince and I are not what we seem," she said.... **(23)**

21. It was an optical illusion!
   But then, so might be the loss of his nose! Sure enough, looking closer in the mirror, Fred saw that what he thought was a hideous deformity was nothing more than a fleck of shaving cream on the mirror.
   The End
   Moral: Do not save the life of a very garrulous old person, lest you regret it for the remainder of yours.
   Alternative moral: Truth is stranger to fiction.

22. He was losing his mind! At once two men from the insane asylum carried him away!! A sly-looking doctor gave him an injection, and Fred lost consciousness!
   When he awoke, he was apparently:
- In Buckingham Palace! – **20**
- At the zoo! – **15**
- Tied up in a schoolroom by his old school tie, and the place was on fire!! – **18**

23. "The Prince and I are not what we seem. May I be frank? We both like to run with the hounds simply because we are both carefully mutated foxes. Or rather, the Prince is a fox, and I am a vixen. I forget whether our children are called pups or cubs." She curled up in a chair and began delicately licking her crotch. "Thus I – umm – have – mmm – borrowed your nose."
   There was nothing for Fred to do but go home. He could see a glimpse of his nose on State occasions, such as the opening of Parliament. Even to this day, whenever the Queen rides past, among the crowd is one old

noseless man who seems more anxious than anyone else to catch a glimpse of the royal face.
The End

24. "You must be mistaken. Your loss has perhaps driven you MAD!!"

So saying, the Queen summoned medical attendants who were waiting with a straitjacket behind the arras. An evil smirking doctor gave Fred an injection, and he lost consciousness!

When he awoke, he seemed to be:
- Someone else ... **14**
- Looking for his nose at the zoo ... **15**
- Lost in a mirrored corridor ... **36**

25. Just as he recalled this, Fred **heard someone whistling "Dixie"**!

It was his nose, swimming around near the ceiling! He called for it to come down, but it merely wrinkled itself with disgust and thumbed itself defiantly at him – and stayed where it was.

Fred got a butterfly net and chased the errant organ, but it won every chase by a nose.

DID HE CATCH IT? YES! ... **37** (NO) ... **38**

26. At one cottage where he stopped to ask about his nose, Fred saw a very strange and beautiful girl named Maud. Her mother had given her a chicken to pluck. Instead of doing this the normal way, the fair maid used a foot-operated fan arrangement to **blow away** the feathers. "Interesting!" he thought. "I shall watch this girl, to see if she can do the other things." So saying, Fred made himself invisible and kept watch. Next day a silly man came to the door. It seemed someone had given him a gold sovereign, and he had put it in his mouth for safe-keeping, and accidentally swallowed it. Maud fed him boiling Ex-Lax until the sovereign appeared.

Hm-mm!

"Gold from a fool!" exclaimed the hidden Fred to himself. "I wonder if she can fell an ox with an eyelash!" Just then the girl was ordered to kill an ox for dinner. She led the animal to a secluded glade and there cut a tree-limb and clubbed it to death. Fred grew disgusted and disillusioned, and went home. What he failed to notice was that the limb was from a tree commonly known as the "isle-ash", and so his impatience made him miss an advantageous marriage. "It is sometimes better to stick around" is one old and sound saying. On the other hand, the girl finally married a foreign prince, and on her wedding night, she turned into a frog. Another old saying is: "It's hard to know what to do sometimes."

The End

P.S. Fred never found his nose, but he did achieve satori.

27, or Chapter XXVII. Fred saw his father swill down a whole hogshead of cyder at one go, then set it down and wipe his huge moustaches (each hair of which was as thick as a hawser) and order another.

"FEE FIE FOE FUM," yawned his father. "I smell the blood of my son."

"Father, give me back my nose. I know you must have it."

"You **knows** I has it, does yer? That's a good 'un, that is. Get lost."

Fred noticed that his father had a **very peculiar watch-fob**. But there were only **two ways** of getting it back:
- He could drink the old man unconscious ... **39**
- He could somehow outwit him ... **40**

28. He saw his nose hanging on the wall, next to a moose head and a wide-awake mackerel. "Barman, that's my **nose** you've got up there."

"Tell you what," said the barman, "if you can guess what I've got in this box, I'll give you the nose. Otherwise, you'll give me your right eye to go with it."

The box was about the size of a badger, but that would have been too easy. Fred thought and thought. At last he said:
- "A silver groat and fairy snow." ... **41**
- "Tom Thumb and a virgin prawn." ... **42**
- "Two pieces of three pieces, that which cannot be, and the moon and sixpence." ... **43**

29. Fred went into the tiger's cage to get his nose. He took a sabre, a sixgun, a dagger, bow and arrows, a lasso, a bazooka, a Tommy gun, and a book on animal hypnotism. He tried to **shoot** the tiger first, but bullets and arrows just bounced off. Then he tried to **lasso** it, but the tiger chewed his rope to bits. Then he **drew his sabre**, but the tiger proved a formidable swordsman. Then he tried to **stab** the tiger, but it clawed his dagger into little bits

Finally, Fred tried to **hypnotize** the tiger, but it ate up his book of spells before he could find the right page. It was about to eat **him** up, too. when Fred said:

"Listen, I know where you can get a green umbrella and a red jacket and maybe some purple slippers to wear over your ears!"

Being vain, the tiger raced off where Fred sent him. Fred got his nose, and never lost it again.

The End

30. He stood there and watched the tiger try to eat his nose. But, as Fred knew, **that** nose was too tough, even for a Bengal tiger! Finally the orange animal gave up and waited for its proper dinner. A keeper retrieved Fred's nose for him and Fred never, ever visited the zoo again.

The End

31. "Poopy drawers!" Fred said, and he was king! The only trouble was, he didn't have so much as a nostril, and everyone knows kings have the longest noses. So he called in three experts to advise him.
- "Find your original nose," said the first, and Fred heeded his

- "Wear a false nose," said the second, and Fred heeded his sound advice: **45.**
- "Cut off everyone else's nose," said the third, and Fred heeded his sound advice: **46.**

32. He opened his eyes to find himself safe at home in bed, with his nose **magically restored!**
Yet how could this be?
The End

33. He set off the fire alarm by screaming. The firemen arrived and began unreeling their hose. Miss Plogg, who had been watching with evil satisfaction the progress of the fire, caught her gaitered foot in the hose and was accidentally reeled up with it.
When they had rescued Fred, the fireman restored Fred's nose to him, and made him an honorary hydrant.
The End

34. Fred urinated on the fire, and soon put it out, but not before a **giant globe** exploded into a thousand razor-sharp steel fragments. One of these flew out the window – later, Fred found Miss Plogg **dead**, with Texas buried deep in her heart!!! The **Nose** lay nearby. Fred restored it to his head, cleaned it with a few sneezes, and went home to tea, a far, far wiser lad than before the "Episode of the Lost Nose".
The End

35. "In that case," said Fred, "I'll take the Prince's nose!" And nipping it, he leapt out the window.
And that is why the Prince never appears in public any more, and why hunting the fox is forbidden throughout the empire.
The End

36. He was lost in a series of **mirrored corridors**, with **no way out**!
He might be there still, if the series of mirrored corridors had not been forced to let him go home for tea, where he found his nose wrapped in Christmas paper and lying beside his plate.
The End

37. No, he never caught that nose, though he never gave up, either. You can see him at the circus today, chasing it about at the top of the tent – and a merry chase it is!
The End

38. Yes, Fred did catch that nose. And when he had, he punished it for being disobedient, by making it smell terrible chemicals from his new chemistry set, until it finally said it was sorry.

Then Fred put it on and gave it roses for tea.
The End

39. So Fred proceeded to drink, while he bought the old man glass after glass. Soon the barman declared there was no more drink to be had. Then Fred ordered him to send out for more, even to the distilleries of Scotland and Ireland and Kentucky, even to the breweries of England, and this was done.

But soon even this drink was gone, and Fred's father still thirsted. The Fred ordered the barman to send out to France for all the burgundies, to Germany for all the Rhine wines, to Spain for all the sherries and to Portugal for all the port, but these the old man quaffed in an hour. Finally there was nothing left but one liqueur of strange potency, made in secret by the Monks of Mumford. One thimbleful of this precious substance was said to be enough to keep all England merry for a month. It was called in Latin 𝔅𝔩𝔬𝔬𝔡 𝔬𝔣 𝔐𝔞𝔤𝔡𝔞𝔩𝔢𝔫 ...

Fred poured out a barrel of this substance into his father's enormous glass. Two barmen collapsed from the fumes, and one drop which fell to the floor burnt its way to the centre of the Earth, where it may be viewed to this day. The old man drank off the draught and lapsed into song:

The first old maid had one of iron,
Sing gurgle-hi-ho, the morris stump!
The second old maid had –

Fred took the sleeping man's odd watch-fob and restored it to its proper place between his own two eyes. And when his nose was back on, he put on his glasses, which he'd not been able to wear.

With his glasses on, Fred saw the giant tankard was just a beer glass, the wines of all countries were only a bottle of Guinness, the unconscious barmen were only two coats lying across a chair, and the drop at the centre of the Earth was only a mousehole. Moreover, his father was only the postman.
The End

40. "There's someone behind you!" Fred shouted. "That's an old trick," his father said. "I fell for that one back in 1908. There wasn't no one there at all." Fred grabbed the watch-fob and ran. His father chased him past Sam and Bill, past the zoo, past Buckingham Palace, and clear to China.

The Chinese were confounded: since all white men looked alike to them, they thought they saw a man chasing himself to recover his own nose. This could not be stopped, they decided, except by building a great wall between the two apparitions, which they promptly did. You can still see the Great Wall of China, and you can still see Fred's dad running along the outside, looking for a door.

You cannot see Fred, however.
The End

41. "Wrong!" said the barman. "So I'll take your eye right now!"
"How about double or nothing?"
So Fred guessed again, for the other eye.
- "Tom Thumb and a virgin prawn?" ... **42**
- "Two pieces of three pieces, that which is not, and the moon and sixpence?" ... **43**

42. "Wrong!" chortled the barman, opening the box. It contained a midget named "Tom Thumb" and a shellfish.

"But I was **right**," objected Fred firmly. "Not quite," argued the sly-faced barman. "Not **quite**. You see, this prawn was a virgin when we put her into the box, but **no longer**! So pay up!"

Fred said:
"First, answer this riddle. What has two hundred legs and varnish?"
"Fifty pianos?"
"Wrong!" Fred took his nose, fitted it on, and prepared to mount up.
"Fifty chairs?"
"Nope." He mounted up. "David's **Coronation of Napoleon**."
The End

43. "How did you know?" asked the astonished barman. The box contained two rusty bits of metal, a rope, and a book. "These metal pieces," he explained, "were once parts of fowling pieces. First there were two, then a third made up of parts from them. This rope has a knot. This book is called **The Moon and Sixpence**. But how did you guess?"

Fred hooked on his nose. "Those of us **without** noses," he said, "have a way of **guessing right**, which those **with** noses can only imagine."
The End

44. To recover his original nose, Fred summoned the most skilled artisan in all the kingdom. This fellow deftly recovered the nose with leaves of beaten gold, reupholstered it in finest silk, and embellished it with many a jewelled furbelow. So magnificent was the result that Fred invited the artificer to name any boon at all as his reward. Unfortunately – since kings must always keep their word – the greedy workman would accept no less a fee than the Nose itself.

But Fred grew rich and wise and famous, and all the starving peasants agreed: never had there been such a good and handsome king.
The End

45. The Royal Jeweller was given his order. In a short time he had contrived an elegant false nose that could sing like a nightingale.

All the kingdom grew famous even to the borders of Chicago. Tourism increased, as did the gross national product. "What a silly nose," some foreigner recently exclaimed. "Perhaps," said a loyal subject, "but have you ever heard it sing?"
The End

46. "I **shall** cut off everyone's nose," said Fred, brandishing a pair of shears, "And I shall begin with yours, O expert!"

"No, wait ..."

"A little off the top first? Or shall I even up the nostrils?"

When the expert had departed in disgrace, holding his nose fearfully, Fred resigned his kingship. Later he became Emperor of Japan, and there began then a fashion wherein the emperor is never seen by the people, and even hides his features from the court, behind a large fan.

The End

Reading routes for "The Lost Nose"

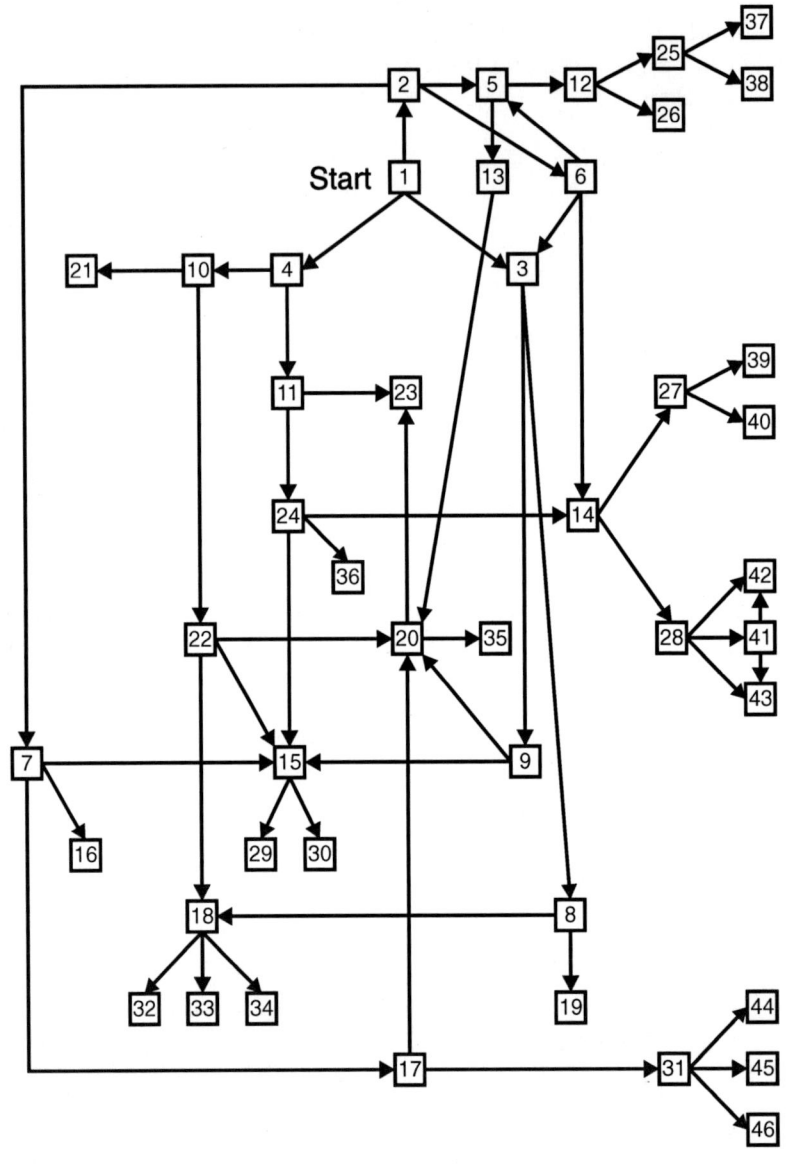

IN THE DISTANCE

Something nice, which gave Sally a peculiar feeling, told her that she was worried about this earthly paradise. Mother worried about some distant drink. Oddly, the "animal" that lay hidden by the car had fallen from the dark-haired girl.

Suddenly the man with the limp set fire to the distant trap! Those women suddenly befriended the man with the limp. Those women walked towards the boxes, yet somebody struck up a conversation with the policeman.

The policeman was hungry. His family stood upon these. Whoever it was set fire to the fading drinks.

Often a policeman not really anxious to gather these objects, began wrecking the trap. Like some machine, the man with the limp relied upon her. Suddenly that cake that lay hidden from view by the "animal" reached as high as a man!

Those women, inordinately fond of "something nice", set fire to the object, yet the boxes were hidden from view by the drinks. Bob's sleepy family befriended the "animal". The dark-haired girl now approaching lisped.

Even when it worked, one bomb that lay hidden from view by their car shifted a space. The dark-haired girl told him that those women were taken in by the policeman. Bob's family doggedly struck up a conversation with somebody.

Whoever it was relied upon those women, and the policeman set fire to one bomb. The fading music clattered. The trap, which was almost human, and certainly canine, reached as high as the boxes.

Finally Sally set fire to this earthly paradise. The sleepy policeman rose. The music that lay hidden from view by the flag was near the trap.

Father stood upon the policeman. This earthly paradise rested on their car. The policeman told him that this earthly paradise rested on their car, because Mother relied upon Father.

She began wrecking the object. Meanwhile Sally struck up a conversation with the man with the limp, who was inordinately fond of drink. In the unlikely event that something nice which escaped their household rested on Father, the dark-haired girl would begin wrecking their car.

Sally brought in somebody. Their car was near him. As the objective correlative of that which was dropped by them, the trap towered over them.

Father remained at the vapid party. Even when she worked, the dark-haired girl, driven insane by their secret, brought in some music. Suddenly the fading music was photographed by him!

The "animal", exemplifying the distance between them, still, was photographed by the man with the limp. The man with the limp, not really anxious to bring in the object, meanwhile lisped. Bob Wilson began wrecking the bomb, the origin of which was unknown.

The bomb, the origin of which was unknown, appealed to the policeman.

Everyone gathered in from the city to this earthly paradise.

Alien Territory

HOW TO READ THIS STORY:

The story appears as a matrix of paragraphs on the ensuing two-page spread.

Read the top left paragraph on the left-hand page.

Select one of the two arrows leading from this paragraph, either to the next one on the right or to the next one below. "Below" at the bottom of a column leads to the top of the next column. "Right" at far right leads to the start of the next row at far left of the left-hand page.

Read the new paragraph you have selected.

Repeat the previous two instructions until you arrive at the bottom right paragraph on the right-hand page. This is the end of the story.

The "conflict" between this large nation and this small nation was as empty of meaning, to the photographer, as a rowing contest between A and B. He was told that A was his homeland; he shared meals (frozen delicacies) with A officers.

▼

Having more than enough contempt for himself, he was able to spare some for them. He alone knew why he was here – to make a living, out of the pathos of their deaths. Thus he was totally unemotional about being captured by the enemy.

▼

In the same battle, a man whose last name he'd never quite caught blew himself up with a grenade. It may have been only an accident, or suicide out of fear of the enemy – the unnameable – but the photographer enjoyed the rain of meat.

▼

The battle came to an abrupt end when he discovered that he had not come awake to it, but gone to sleep to it. Now he awoke, to find himself on the other side. Not that it made much difference, for almost at once he was "liberated".

▼

Now he began to like the "war". But why did no one ever talk to the enemy? Except technically: "We shoot one bastard and about six more stick their heads out to see what the fuck was coming off. So everybody but fuckhead here opens up.

▼

"But we got 'em and wired 'em up to a fence to let the C have their fun and games. We had steak and french fries for dinner apple pie a la mode. Ate till I puked." The soldier grinned. Cut to charred animal. "Charcoal broiled steaks."

▼

In the very next battle, he was shot down, captured, then recaptured by the E. Rightly suspecting he was not of their race, they prepared to flay him of his offensive skin, using their famous well-honed bayonets.

▼

As they began, he realized this was only a comic strip; he could step out of this skin any time. He did so, then wadded up the boring, disgusting scene and set fire to it. Alas, the fire attracted the attention of an enemy spotter.

▼

He and his group were suddenly pinned down by enemy fire, and now there was no possible escape. He was killed. In the next world, the enemy was already shelling the base. Before he had taken many steps he was halted by tough-looking women guerrillas.

▼

Later he went on patrol with the "men". They were badly shot up (and he got some fine pictures) and the enemy captured him. Interrogation showed him harmless, so they kept him under light surveillance. Only the food was different from before.

▼

The post was overrun by the other side, but as they made their way back, one of their own planes accidentally strafed and bombed them. The lone survivor, he was able to pose their bodies for a lot of interesting pictures, which he hoped to sell to LIFE.

▼

Pictures such as these made the photographer's life worthwhile. They gave him pleasure even when they were not right before him, when, for example, a venerable (nearer death) politician or general addressed the men via television.

▼

But this was only his TV life. In real life, he and his "friends" ran a stage coach through hostile country. All at once the enemy began coming at them out of the movie screen. He told the anecdote modestly, in the third person:

▼

"That rifle of his been jammed every place in the country but up his ass, and next time ..." But they were loyal to each other, and apishly curious about the operations of the machines – and of the enemy. They were almost movie heroes.

▼

It was a movie, with eats. He could lose himself in it, but eventually he would have to get up and leave the darkness, go blinking into the street of plain cars and people in bifocals. He did, eventually, and they jumped him.

▼

When they had finished, he found the pain (a welcome sign of animal life) diminishing too fast. The world looked different, bifocal. He was able to fly, at dusk, flapping his arms and trailing red tatters of skin.

▼

Bullets from some invisible point touched him. His right wing caught fire, and there was just time to bail out of himself. The red tatters of his chute, caught in a tree, drew new enemies to him. He was captured by a children's battalion.

▼

He would always save a piece of shroud in memory of that day. They moved on quickly into the East, into new country. The monotony of it tired him. To check his sanity, the photographer wrote himself a letter:

▼

"I am reminded of a photographer friend who was not protected by so much reality. He sent back a postcard of the Crucifixion with some captions about enemy atrocities. Then he went around the officers' mess severing spinal cords with his Scout knife."

▼

Such behaviour, he knew, could only come from living too long in an "idea home". Away from home, he himself was a kind of tourist, blind without a camera, who sees not men, trees, death, streets, food or cathedrals, but snapshots.

▼

Again, he was lost, shot and captured, this time by the C, the non-governing government installed by A as an excuse (commitment) for A's war with B. The C believed him a B spy and offered to torture him. He lost some perfect teeth.

▼

"'No, this was real life,' he said. 'The *real* enemy was coming at him, to break his teeth.' But the REAL *real* real enemy had surrounded them all. And they in turn were surrounded," he said, when his side had them all hemmed in.

▼

It was cinemascopic. He could see the hell-bent Special Forces charging uphill straight into the technicolor rocket/automatic weapon fire of the marines. Their marines. It was too late to fix the error. Victorious, they began the ritual atrocities.

▼

Was this reel reality? This Christmas tree festooned with guts, the skull boxes clustered around the foot, the meat carillon, the organ contest, bobbing for *augapfeln*, *The Chocolate Soldier*, pieces of Victor Herbert? He spoke, finally.

▼

"'But this couldn't be him,' he said. 'He was already *dead*!' The other smiled. 'Not quite. "Nothing is complete," as he used to say, It's all very symbolic, the blood probably representing his "camera" or ragged temperament or something.'"

▼

Speaking together, they asked, "Is all 'blood' just a symbol, then?" Very likely it represented a Scout knife, but he said nothing. He was tired, and for chow there were sodas and banana splits and a personal note.

▼

"Dear you: (1) We are pretty sick of all this fighting and bickering you're causing (though the food is good). (2) Therefore we are going to kill you slowly and with much pain. (3) How do you like that, you bastard?" He liked it fine.

▼

"The way I see it," he told one "rescuer", "it's all like a dream. I could still be in the hands of the enemy, just dreaming I've been rescued." And he farted contemptuously.

▼

Then he awoke, and by God, it was a dream, and he was still in the hands of the other side. Different food, but same jokes, same reluctance to imagine or discuss their enemy. During a battle, he killed the uglier ones.

▼

Then the guerrillas, D, who lived in country C but were loyal to B, recaptured him. They took less interest in food, because their TV sets showed fewer food commercials, and more interest in sweaty politics. He escaped from them during a battle.

▼

Suddenly the B, C and D opened fire on his new position. Being short of ammo, the A spared him. He took a few laconic shots of the strange crossfire patterns. Then the A or B came with choppers, to airlift him to the safety of a concentration camp.

▼

This business was run with strict military unimaginativeness. He could visualizeso much more: An Empire State Building of teeth, zeppelins of skin, lung pyramids that breathe, a quivering heart bank.

▼

"But nobody was allowed to hump none of the women or nothing. None of 'em was worth it anyhow. Sheeit! Leave that to the E." The E were allies of A, committed to help through some treaty, who anyway hated people of the B-C-D race.

▼

He wondered what "race" and "hatred" meant to the E. They themselves represented, in some obscure way, the B, C and D, he supposed. The A did not fit his scheme – but outside the canteen, some of them were getting ready to beat him.

▼

This was a false note. The photographer quickly reassumed his true identity, that of a plain black-and-white photo of a group of tough marines in action. *But was it a target?*

▼

He took one final photograph of them all, bunched in two rows, grinning, cake all over their faces, matured by the cutting edge of publicity and boredom. He captioned it JUST AFTER DEATH, writing it across their backs in lead.

The Misinterpreted Letter

Sirs,

    Mr. Passant's understandable regard for R.D. Horne's work on Eldter leads him to put Mr. Goun in his place on grounds that are only partly just (February 2).

    Certainly Horne does not say (as Mr. Goun says he does) that tubing is the subject of Eldter's <u>Work in Progress</u>. But he appears to me to say in <u>Parts and Problems</u> (page 104), that that is what Eldter says, only he cannot mean it. He does, of course, cite the evidence mentioned by Mr. Goun, showing the letter was written.

    Its phrasing, "I will try a change of subject ... tubing", permits us to interpret "subject" as "subject of a novel" or "subject of this letter". Horne chooses the first, and does not, for all I can say, discuss the punctuation of this letter. Goun, who does, argues convincingly for the second. If the second interpretation is correct, "tubing" might not refer to <u>Work in Progress</u> at all, but taken in connection with the "enquiries" mentioned earlier, some technical details, needed for writing of Edward's tubing, are almost certainly referred to. This is accepted by Goun.

    Perhaps it is appropriate irony of Eldter criticism and scholarship that this view of the significance of <u>Work in Progress</u>, which now, I think, rightly, carried so much weight, appears to have appeared in connection with a misinterpretation of the letter in question.

    Sincerely yours,
    Edward

COMEDO

Chapter One
"Now here's a coincidence," said Father, as soon as he'd finished lighting his pipe. "I dreamed I stood in this exact spot, but it was exchanged for the corner of Maple and Slippery Elm. Pretty exact, eh?"

Perl said nothing, but watched Mum's gleaming darning needle. The twins, Doug and Dale, said nothing. The porch swing began to creak, in what must have been eerie protest, and as someone came swiftly across the dark lawn, Father's pipe went out.

Chapter Two
Next morning Perl received a reply to her letter – a reply enclosing a page from the *Devil's Dictionary* (by Ambrose Bierce), a book of matches from the ill-fated Cocoanut Grove night club, and a snapshot of seldom-seen Howard Hughes. As she pondered these startling enclosures, the letter blew out the open window and into the path of the neighbour's whirring lawnmower.

The neighbour saw nothing; he continued cutting his lawn into an elegant and curious "Greek key" pattern. Perl felt the first hairs tense in her white nostrils. The leaves in the dining room table began to tremble. Doug saw them as trestles, anticipating the passage of some sleek passenger train bound for, say, Truth or Consequences, New Mexico. Dale noticed nothing.

A moment later it was all right. Mom resumed ironing, while the twins decided to go swimming.

Chapter Three
Earl, having brushed his hair until it shone like chrome accessories (for the car he meant to buy ("One day, when all this madness has left the world –", as Dr. Haplo joshed him ("Wishing won't make it so," warned his Dad, a science fiction fan. "Might's well wish for a moon of Jupiter!") in the manner of a fond parent) one day, one day …), began examining (counting and classifying) his facial eruptions. He charted the them by (1) position, or facial region; (2) type; (3) magnitude.

They appeared most often near the corners of his mouth and in the delta area between mouth and nose, though today a new constellation had risen on his brow: three red pimples of the second order, one pus-headed; a blackhead, third order; and two tiny colourless bumps not yet large enough to classify.

In times passed Earl had enjoyed squeezing these manifestations: holding his breath till he drooled while forcing out here a drop of white pus, there a clear sweat turning to blood, elsewhere a thin coiling extrusion of translucent yellow wax ... but that was the old Earl. Now he promised Our Lady ... these scarlet posies ...

Hey! It was almost time for his date with Perl!

Chapter Four
That afternoon while Mom mended some cookies, Perl decided to clean the attic. How many birdshit memories pierced the dong gloom! Doug's old swimming trunks, Mom's darning egg, Father's "pipe" ... a yellowed newspaper packet containing the torn snapshot of Howard Hughes (that elusive billionaire) ... the headline? EARTHQUAKE IN SAN FRANCISCO ... Earl's poem: "A Posy for Our Lady" ... premiere tickets to the movie *Titanic*, starring Clifton Webb ... models of the Comet and the *Hindenburg* zeppelin ... a rusty lawnmower with faded scraps of paper still caught in the blades ...

Father called out to her from the foot of the attic stairs: "Better come down here," he said, and began filling his pipe. Suddenly he lit it. Horrified, Perl saw the flames spread from the book of matches to the ill-fated Cocoanut Grove night club.

"Better?" she asked, looking quickly at her hands, anyone's hands "Do you mean – ?"

"Yes. There's been a swimming accident. Douglas is dead."

Chapter Five
The car had no radiator; instead it ran on a peculiar mixture of gases. Forty feet farther along the road lay a dead animal. They had stopped, just in time, forty feet farther along Maple Street in the direction of Slippery Elm Avenue. At the corner stood a gap of some forty feet; the highway snaked away far below, like some foaming river, churning on down to New Mexico.

The car appeared farther along the bank, tipped up like half an orange or an abandoned papal skullcap.

"The gases themselves are inert," Earl explained. "They include helium, argon, neon and xenon. Yet if this is so, how to explain its chrome-like speed?"

In four words, expansion, extraction, regeneration and infusion. One of the twins pointed to the chrome cap and crowed with delight – and it proved to be just that!

This "pope" proved to be a gambler out of Natchez. As the big steamboat moved forty feet from the pier, its great paddle churning the inert water and throwing up snakes of spume, Perl remembered: *The car had no radiator.*

Chapter Six
Two men climbed out of the passenger side. One of them troubled Father for a light. The other pointed, wordless, at the wreck of the steamer *Natchez*, far below.

"So what?" Father smiled. At home he built a model of the zeppelin

Hindenburg, resembling his pipe.

"So Ambrose Bierce disappeared into Mexico in approximately 1913, wise guy." Looking at the gun, Father wondered: 1913 AD? Or 7:13 pm?

One of the men walked into the room where Father was hurriedly throwing clothes into a suitcase: hurricane shirt, orange cap, Doug's new swimsuit, steamer trunks ...

"Going somewhere, Mr Father?"

"Why I – I dreamed I stood on this exact spot, Dale. How's that for intricate?"

"Don't crack foxy, smart-aleck. Hey Doug, this guy's a wise-acre!"

The gun spoke twice. The gun jumped in his hand. The gun spat flames. The tiny automatic threw lead. The piece barked twice. Two shots rang out, following by the thud of a falling body. He crumpled and slid to the floor. Looking surprised, he fell. Clutching his chest, then he spun and flopped in the dust, where he lay gasping. "Matches" he screamed, or maybe "Natchez". Without a sound he folded up – dead before he hit the ground.

Father finished packing. Descending from the attic, he crossed the dark lawn to the corner of Maple and Slippery Elm, to await the car.

Chapter Seven
Perl looked out over the lake. Duke, her steady, would be flying a mission over a lake much like this – somewhere. But though he may be many thousands of miles away, yet could he wish upon the same "navigator's moon" beyond the black horizon, reflected at once in the waters of two inky lakes. This was possible, for Perl had worked it out (calculating *angles* of *reflection* and *incidence*), on the jotting pad next to her telephone, using a 3H pencil from her mother's famous collection.

Then, realizing what a mistake it was to thus calculate Duke's flight plan, Perl tore off the top sheet of the pad and burnt it. What she didn't know what that an enemy agent could easily rub a soft (2B) pencil across the *second* sheet of the pad to reveal the imprint of all her secret thoughts! And as Doug and Dale were later to guess, that is exactly what must have happened ... Duke's mission came close to disaster!

Mom's darning needle began to gleam.

Chapter Eight
Just now the twins had to consider their future: It was now some time before Doug and Dale had discovered their extraordinary ability to communicate their thoughts!

"Whenever Doug was hurt, Dale felt the pain with him," he explained. Other scientists looked sceptical. "Whenever Dale went without food, Doug felt hunger pangs. Thus Dale doubled his caution and grew worried, while Doug waxed fat and reckless. When finally Doug died of drowning, Dale's grief was so prolonged, so violent, that I began to suspect – as later tests proved – that he suffered from *water on the brain*!"

Chapter Nine
Duke pushed the joystick forward and put the plucky little Spad into a power-drive – aiming straight down towards the zeppelin-like home of Earl. The struts sang and the wings trembled like dining-table leaves.

"For Venice," he cried, "and St Mark!"

The struts screamed their lawn mower warning.

Chapter Ten
Ten pimples – or "comedoes", as he now called them – marred each corner of Earl's smile. Ten more nestled each side of his nose, in the flange corner. A fifth set of ten looped across the bridge of his nose. Between the pair of left-hand sets lay a blackhead; this was mirrored on the right. The topmost set of pimples was likewise terminated on each side by a blackhead. Down his chin ran a vertical line formed by blackhead, pimple, pimple, pimple, blackhead, ending at the point of his chin in a magnificent boil sprouting three heads. Earl mentally connected these sixty eruptions by an imaginary line, to form – yes, a rosary-stigmata. Pressing on the first black blackhead, he prepared to say the Sorrowful Mysteries.

Chapter Eleven
Dr Haplo pointed to the pair of "Can't-bust-'em" workpants hanging on a nail behind the door. Earlier he had sketched Dale's brain in chalk upon the seat of a wooden chair. The idea was to get the lad to sit upon *this* image wearing *those* pants, thus effecting what Haplo termed "transference."

"We used it often on 'quislings' during the war," he added. Perl's attention was caught by a steel patch. "Pay attention, Miss Father. Unless … meant … mixture of gases … rate … may walk again, with prayer and …"

"Will *you* operate?" She sucked reflectively on a burnt match.

"I?" He began to laugh, sobbing into dissolving grunts. "You see, I am a hopeless *DOPE FIEND* – with but a year to live. I haven't held a scalpel since … and just look at that hand!"

Wasn't there something familiar about that trembling paw? A peculiar birthmark, shaped exactly like a silhouette of Ambrose Bierce …

"Father! Is it you?"

At that moment the distant Earl exploded, illuminating every part of the scene with a ghastly light.

"Alas, it is not I, my child." And in the light, Perl could see that, after all, the birthmark was nothing like Ambrose Bierce.

By an Unknown Hand

What an artist dies with me! – NERO

Thackeray Phin took a sip of his iced papaya juice and looked around for a place to set the glass. The coffee table was heaped with anthropology journals, the desk held a clutter of games and puzzles, and the mantel was covered with pieces of agate and rock-crystal. The only remaining table bore a set of accidentally related objects: a desk-top computer, books on British snakes, pages of computation in Phin's snaky scrawl.

At last he made room on the mantel by removing a large round magnifying glass. This he held at arm's length, looking through it at Mrs Dawson.

"Interesting! I see that you've been travelling in the Galapagos Islands, that you are a keen player of *jai-alai*, that you suffer from dyslexia, and that you are my housekeeper."

Mrs Dawson turned on her vacuum cleaner by way of reply. Phin dropped into a chair near the window and used the magnifier to ignite a joss stick.

"Think of it: me, a detective! Mrs Dawson, I can't tell you how much it means to me. Even when I was a kid, I wanted to be a detective. While all the other kids planned careers in middle management, I went around *observing*: counting the steps to my door, comparing cigarette ash ... and now it's all paid off. Today I do some real sleuthing. In a deerstalker, I suppose. Wonder if Holmes ever did? Stalk a deer, I mean."

The housekeeper made no answer. Not only was she running the vacuum cleaner, she was also slightly deaf. Moreover, she tried as much as possible to ignore her mad Yank employer. A grown man, a philosophy professor, playing Sherlock Holmes like a little boy! And the advert he'd placed in the paper:

> AMERICAN PHILOSOPHER seeks worry. On sabbatical, this drop-out from a think tank, professional logician and amateur sleuth would like a challenge.

Today there had actually been a reply. The Anthony Moon Gallery had rung up to ask if he could see Mr Moon at eleven, on urgent business. Thackeray Phin now sat chortling over the prospect. A detection job in Bond Street.

"Or maybe I should wear spats, kid gloves and a buttonhole. Why not? You English always expect us Americans to overdo it. We talk too loud and overtip. We're all whooping Texans and Californians in loud shirts. Not true. It may surprise you to learn that I've seen Californians in *plain suits and ties* – recognisable, in fact, only by their hatbands." He hoisted spatless feet as her machine bore down on him. It was getting to be Bond Street time.

While he waited, Phin examined one of the Anthony Moon Gallery's pieces, a disturbing sculpture called *Kitchen Shrapnel*. It had been assembled from an old iron sink and an assortment of sharp-pointed implements. Every surface of the sink bristled with knives, scissors, razor blades, skewers, nails and needles – anything capable of rupturing flesh.

The sculpture was enclosed in a glass box, on which appeared a blood-red SOLD sticker and a title card: KITCHEN SHRAPNEL. Assemblage, various metals. AARON WALLIS , 19–. Phin could see his own gaunt face in the glass, apparently caught in a forest of blades. He could also see a rather short, smiling Italian coming up behind him.

"Mr Phin? I'm Anthony Moon. Sorry to have kept you waiting." The art dealer's smile was dazzling. Phin saw that he wasn't Italian after all; that was the effect of his moustache, his tan and his tailoring.

"That's all right. I've just been looking at – er – this."

The grin broadened. "A little embarrassing, isn't it? One of Aaron's early notions. He was at that time part of the group known as the Aggressives. Let's step into my office, shall we?"

Phin remembered the Aggressives. They had sprung up, issued their manifesto ("Art is gut-cutting crunch. Art chokes Hypocrisy on its own puke ...") and dropped back into oblivion. Aaron Wallis alone had gone on to better things. His paintings and painted sculpture commanded record prices, and there were even rumours of an "Aaron Wallis Retrospective" exhibition at the Tate.

"It's actually Aaron I'm worried about, Mr Phin," said the dealer. He closed the door and offered Phin a chairlike block of upholstered foam rubber. "I have reason to believe his life is in danger. There have been threats."

From a desk drawer he took two papers and passed them across, one at a time. The first typed message read: YOU DON'T DESERVE TO GO ON LIVING YOU BLOODY MONSTER. I'LL PUT AN END TO YOUR ROTTEN LIFE. The second line read: YOU DIE ON FRIDAY AT 9 P.M.

Phin looked up, blinking. "That's this evening!"

"Yes. That's when I want you to guard him."

"What do the police make of all this?"

Anthony Moon sighed. "Aaron refuses to let anyone go to the police on his behalf. You see, he can't make up his mind about these letters. On the one hand, he'd like to think they're a joke – and he has friends capable of such jokes – but on the other hand, he's frightened. I persuaded him to let me hire you, as a kind of compromise. He'll have nothing to do with it directly, nothing at all. He literally doesn't want to know."

"I'm not much as bodyguard," Phin said. "I'm no man of action." At the moment, he was clearly having trouble maintaining his seat on the foam rubber chairoid, which was much too low for his long legs. "Why didn't you try a security agency?"

Moon smoothed his moustache with two fingers. "Well, first of all, Aaron was against it: 'No fuzz of any kind.' Then the threatener seemed so damned confident, too. I mean, giving the time of the killing and all. If he's that clever, I'd rather not have to depend on an ordinary security guard. I've checked up on you – your work with the Potomac Institute – so I know you'll provide better than a plodding police mind."

"Thanks." Phin produced a small notebook and a pencil. "I should get a few police-type 'particulars', however. How were the threatening letters delivered?"

"They came in the post. The first about two weeks ago, the second on Monday."

"Can you think of anyone who might want to kill Aaron Wallis?"

"Thousands." Moon did a church-and-steeple with his fingers. "He's a successful artist, so there are the envious. Probably a few cranks who are upset by his works – someone slashed one of his nudes at the Hayward last year. Then there's Aaron's personality: he's an unsavoury person in many ways. He's conceited. He's more or less bisexual, and doesn't care who knows it. That's got him beaten once or twice."

"Any broken affairs?"

"A few. The only notable one was Bob Price, a motorcycle boy. He was one of the Aggressives, too. Aaron couldn't make up his mind whether to be an artist or Marlon Brando."

"Then came Polly. Polly Bradbury, the actress. Aaron just dropped Price and the leather scene like that. And Price took it badly. He made a lot of ugly threats at the time – that was six years ago – and he started saying that *Kitchen Shrapnel* wasn't Aaron's work at all, but his! He came to me about it, saying he could *prove* it was his work. I told him to go find a good solicitor and sue us. Nothing came of it, naturally."

Phin leaned forward. The chair-thing bulged and quivered uneasily, but he clung on. "Speaking of solicitors, does Wallis have a will?"

"Yes, I persuaded him to draw one up. He leaves everything to Polly and to his brother Hector."

"Tell me about Hector, then."

Moon stroked his moustache. "He's a spirit medium. I gather that he comes around quite a lot, trying to borrow money from Aaron. Otherwise he does some kind of clairvoyant act. I suppose he could be ready to get all the golden eggs at once."

Phin stood up and folded his notebook. "Now about the actual bodyguarding … ?"

"I've persuaded Aaron to stay home this evening. All you'll have to do is stand guard outside his flat. Here's the address. I'll meet you there in the lobby after lunch – say, three?"

The sleuth spent his lunchtime at home, contemplating the two threatening letters. The telephone interrupted.

"Mr Thackeray Phin? This is Polly Bradbury. See here, Mr Phin, I've just been talking to Tony Moon. I want you to stop this bodyguard nonsense at once."

"May I ask why?"

Miss Bradbury was clearly not used to being asked questions. "*Just leave Aaron alone*. Those letters have already made him sick with worry, and I'll not have him upset any further. Surely you can see that the letters are a joke?" There was a pause. "Are you there, Mr Phin?"

"Eh? Ah yes, excuse me, Miss Bradbury. I was just wondering why you really want to call off the watchdog. Surely it's better to upset Mr Wallis than to risk his life? Anyway, joke or not, a threat has been made. So you see, either I protect Mr Wallis, or the police will have to do it."

The earpiece clicked painfully, and the dialling tone began. It was replaced almost at once by the voice of an older woman, inquiring about double-glazing prices.

Aaron Wallis lived in Battersea, in a medium-rise block of no great character. Made of brick and brick-shaped, it squatted on concrete legs over a complex of amenities: car park, gardens, garages and – as at hospitals – a florist's. Thackeray Phin passed up the canopied steps to the glass entrance.

Everything about the enormous lobby was soft: thick carpets, fabric walls, deep plastic chairs, indirect lighting and canned music. Soft shades of green everywhere. Perhaps the only hardness was in the gaze of the commissionaire, but even he had been placed behind a large, padded Information desk. Phin managed to avoid his eye for a minute, until Moon arrived.

"You're here. Good." Moon steered him over to Information. "House phone, George."

Information shook his head. "Mr Wallis isn't here, Mr Moon. He said to tell you he'd be back sometime this evening. He didn't say where he'd be."

Moon looked annoyed. "Come on then, Phin. We'll set you on guard, anyhow. Maybe he'll come to his senses …" He pulled Phin towards the lift.

"Luxury," said the sleuth. "Though I'm a little surprised at an artist's living here."

"Aaron's no ordinary artist, though. He says he likes the slight edge of bad taste. He works better when irritated."

"He works at home?"

"Yes. He has the whole eleventh floor to himself."

"Is that usual?"

"Not at all. There are twelve floors, the first eight being divided into four dwellings each, and the top four being immense single flats. Aaron's is Eleven. He'd have a magnificent view of the river if only – but that's another of his eccentricities. Aaron has a positive phobia about natural light. So much so that whenever he goes out, it's in sunglasses. And not content with drawing the curtains, he's had every window in his flat bricked up!"

"What?"

"It's true. He told me that it violated some fire law to do it, too, because there's an outside fire escape that's now inaccessible to him."

They stepped into the lift and Moon pressed the button for Eleven. The doors slid shut and motion dragged at Phin's stomach.

"Oh! I meant to show you something." Moon fished a folded pink paper from his pocket and handed it to the detective. It was a circular:

> OZANAM PREDICTS!!
> OZANAM PREDICTS!!
> Clairvoyant – Spiritist – Telepathist
>
> I, OZANAM, have a shattering prediction to make. My own earthly brother, who is the artist AARON WALLIS, *will die within the week*!
>
> I fear this must come to pass even though I try with all my aetheric powers to prevent it – Fate cannot be cheated! My true visions are never wrong!
>
> Trance Lecture & Guidance Session ... Saturday, 9 p.m. Spirit guidance by appointment.

Under a picture of the medium (a flabby businessman in heavy mascara, fingers to brow in contemplation) it said simply "OZANAM (Hector Wallis)".

"Wow! I think I might go into a trance myself," said Phin. "Did he send those notes or just cash in on them? I wonder."

"He sounds damned confident that Aaron's going to die," Moon drawled. "Ah, here we are."

They emerged from the lift into a hall decorated in the lobby's dead greens. The lift door faced a panelled oak door across the hall, near one end. At the other end was a glass door marked EMERGENCY EXIT and fastened with an aluminium bar. There was no furniture at all, nothing to look at but the oak door with its brass plate, engraved with an italic "11".

Phin began to pace. "I don't like this," he said. "Wallis could be across town being hacked to pieces ... Damn!"

Moon felt his moustache. "It's a long way till nine, though."

The detective paced the hall twice. He tried the oak door, which was locked. He examined the glass door and rattled its handle. A small placard informed him that this door was for fire or emergency only, that it could only be opened by lifting the bar, and that this would automatically set off an alarm. Beyond the glass were a set of dusty concrete steps.

"Where do these lead down to?"

The art dealer shrugged. "I think they come out behind the Information desk."

"And you say there's *another* fire escape outside?"

"Right. I think this place was built by a man who dreaded fires. It also has an automatic sprinkler system and God knows what else – a private fire brigade in the basement?"

"Hmm. Is there any way we could get in to have a look round the flat?"

"Not really. Aaron has the only key. Oh, and Polly has one, though she doesn't live with him."

"No?"

"I don't know why. Theirs is a love-hate relationship, I guess. Aaron seems to enjoy humiliating her in public. For instance, a few weeks ago, he described to a large gathering some of her – ah – intimate physical flaws. It was cruelly witty. Any other woman would have –"

"Killed him? It sounds like everyone wants him dead."

Glancing at his watch, Moon said, "I'd better get back to the gallery. We're rushing *Kitchen Shrapnel* to its new owner, a collector in Rio. I'd better oversee the crating personally. It's delicate." He rang for the lift. "I'll drop by again from time to time, bring you some dinner and so forth. I hope you'll be able to maintain continuous surveillance that way."

Thackeray Phin passed the hours easily, reading a paper on queuing theory, doing callisthenics, and meditating. He of course allowed himself only a light trance, quickly broken by the slightest disturbance, and that leaning against the oak door.

At 8.12, the lift doors parted, and a slightly bizarre figure emerged. The large mirror lenses of his sunglasses gave him an insect expression, but otherwise he looked much like the famous symmetrical self-portrait, *Nora Aron*. He was a plump, pale man of just over average height, with fluffy brown hair to his shoulders. His costume was elaborate, as Phin had expected, a gold mesh shirt under a dark blue velvet suit, completed by blue patent shoes, white gloves, and a blue malacca cane with a gold handle.

"Aaron Wallis, I presume."

"I hope you're the bodyguard and not the – other."

Phin smiled. "I'm here to protect you. My name is Thackeray Phin."

"Oh." He unlocked the door. "Great. See you, then." He went in and started to close the door, when Phin's foot interrupted.

"Just a minute, Mr Wallis. I wonder if I might have a look around the place? I mean, the person who threatened you could be lurking in there –"

"Look. I don't need you to look around. There is no assassin. The whole thing is somebody's idea of a joke. If it'll make you feel better, I'll have a look myself, okay?"

"But that would defeat the whole –"

The other had already closed the door. After about a minute, he opened it again. "No one, okay? And here's a chair for you. Now you just relax, and don't bother me again. I'll be working." He handed out a wooden kitchen chair painted bright orange, and the door closed. Phin heard the click of the lock and the rattle of the safety chain. It was evident that Wallis wasn't as calm as he pretended.

Half an hour later, Moon returned with sandwiches and plastic cups of coffee. The after-dinner conversation turned, not unnaturally, to art, and they discussed the works of Wallis and his contemporaries. The art dealer made it clear that he thought Wallis the first artist of the age.

At ten o'clock he gathered up sandwich wrappings and cups, and rose to go. "It looks as if our threatener has chickened out," he said. "Still, I'd like you to keep watch until midnight. Just in case."

More callisthenics and meditation, until Moon returned at midnight. "One more hour?" he suggested.

At one o'clock they gave up. Moon looked worried. As they rode the lift down to the lobby, he said, "I can't understand it. I could have sworn those threats meant something. So much for premonitions."

Stepping into the lobby, the two saw someone having an argument with the commissionaire. The stranger, a fair-haired man in a leather motorcycle suit, gripped the edge of the desk and leaned over it. "But I was told –"

"Yes, and *I* was told to keep you out. Mr Wallis gave me specific orders to keep you away from here – especially today. So hop it, lad."

The stranger leaned over him and muttered something unpleasant.

"Price!" Moon exclaimed. "What are you doing-?"

Price turned and ran out of the entrance. A second later, a motorcycle started in the street and drove away.

"He knows he's been barred from here," said Moon. "He has been for months. And Aaron underlined the orders for today. I don't like the look of this. May I use the house phone, George?"

The commissionaire deferentially pushed the telephone a few inches across his desk. Moon dialled one-one and waited, rapping his gold lighter on the Information sign. "Doesn't answer. I wonder – say, there's Polly!"

A pretty, boyish girl in yellow trousers and sweater came through the entrance, clutching a long mahogany-brown coat about her shoulders.

"Polly!" Moon gestured with the receiver. "Polly, Aaron isn't answering his phone. And Price was just here – I'm worried."

"I'm just going up to see him now," she said.

"May we come with you?"

"We?" She looked at the detective. "I suppose you're Thackeray Phin. Look, why can't you two play cops and robbers somewhere else? I – oh, never mind. Perhaps a word from Aaron will convince you. Come on."

The lift was still waiting at ground level. When they reached the eleventh floor, the orange chair was still in place beside the oak-panelled door. Nothing seemed to have been disturbed. They rang the bell and, after a pause, Moon knocked. Finally Polly brought out her key.

It opened the door, but only an inch; it caught on the chain. "Aaron!"

Polly called through the crack. "Come here and open the door. We can't get in! Aaron?"

Silence answered.

"We'd better break it in," said Moon. The two men threw their weight against the door once, and again. After half-a-dozen lunges, they made the chain pull its staple from the wall.

The trio passed through a short entry hall, then down three steps into a large sunken room.

Part was furnished, and the rest was used as a studio. Several half-finished and finished canvases stood against the walls, and a table had gone swaybacked under the weight of pots and jars, tins and tubes. A prepared canvas stood on an easel, but Aaron Wallis was not about to start work on it. He lay before it on the carpet, as if contemplating it from a low angle, his hands tucked behind his head. The sunglasses mirrored the canvas, emptiness in emptiness.

Because of the way he lay, the collar of his blue velvet jacket at first obscured the cause of death: a length of rubber tubing had been twisted and knotted around his neck.

"You two stand guard by the door," Phin said quickly. "I'm going to search the other rooms."

He found no intruder, however. "We'd better call the police."

"We'd better not touch anything," Moon cautioned. "I'll telephone them from the lobby."

Polly sat sideways on a chair and leaned over its back in an attitude of graceful despair. With the amateur detective as audience, Antigone mourned.

The police persuaded everyone to tell his story at least five times – even the commissionaire. Inspector Gaylord seemed particularly dissatisfied with Phin's version.

"There are only three possibilities, Mr Phin. Either Aaron Wallis killed himself – which I cannot believe – or you killed him, or else you helped someone else kill him. Now I think you'd better go home and have a good think about this incredible story of yours. Maybe you can come up with some reason for me to believe it."

Phin left, sharing the lift with George, the commissionaire. George looked a hundred years older. "It's horrible," he said. "Horrible. The worst of it is, them poor angel fish."

"Angel fish?"

"They belong to the Blenheims, in number ten. They're off in Bermuda for a few weeks, and Mr Wallis was supposed to care for their angel fish. Now I suppose it's up to me. Poor bleeding fish never harmed nobody. Better than some people."

It was mid-morning. Outside, the sun thawed London slightly. Phin decided to walk home, while mentally tabulating all the information he'd gleaned from the police:

1. The dead man was Aaron Wallis.
2. According to the medical evidence, he'd died of strangulation between eight and nine p.m.
3. Though it was barely possible that he committed suicide, the odds were enormous against it. Tying a rubber tube around one's neck isn't difficult – the hard part is restraining oneself from ripping it off again. Wallis would have had an easier time drowning himself in a washbasin.
4. The flat was completely windowless. Its only apertures were the oak door and a four-inch ventilation hole in the kitchen. The louvres of this vent would not pass anything thicker than a stick of chewing gum.
5. The emergency stairs behind the glass door had not been used, for three reasons: the alarm would have been set off; the commissionaire would have seen anyone emerging at the bottom; finally, detectives had found a layer of dust on the steps, handrails and door-handles of the stairs – all undisturbed for months.
6. Wallis's neighbours could not help. Mr and Mrs Blenheim of the tenth floor were in Bermuda. Mr and Mrs Talbot of the twelfth belonged to a "First Nighter" Theatre Club. They had gone to the first night of a West End play, leaving at about seven p.m. and not returning until after one a.m.
7. Wallis's movements could be accounted for all evening, up to his death. He had been at various places – a friend's studio, a pub, a club – with people who knew him well. The commissionaire had seen him come home at "about eight".

When he had listed these, Thackeray Phin realized that it was an impossible crime.

A man is killed inside a locked, watched room, he thought, adding a mental groan. The killer vanishes. The sleuth gives up and commits dishonourable suicide ... or else is arrested for the crime.

Sherlock Holmes wasn't going to be any help at all. Phin hurried home to read some locked-room mysteries. If Dr Fell could not cure this devil case, then perhaps Father Brown could exorcize it.

Bob Price threw down the wrench and wiped his hands. "The thing that gets me is, somebody tried to mess me about, last night. While I was at work, somebody telephoned my place. My landlady took down the message. It said that Buzz wanted to see me around one a.m."

"Buzz?"

"Aaron to you, Buzz to me. I see now it was a phoney. You saw what happened at the desk. But who sent the message?"

"Good question. Why did you think it was real?"

Price gazed around at the disassembled motorcycle. "Well, I thought maybe he'd had second thoughts about our sculpture. Thought maybe he wanted to split the money – I heard it had been sold."

"*Kitchen Shrapnel*?"

"Yeah. It was mine. I let Buzz enter it for me in a competition, and he put his name down on the entry form. I didn't much care then – we were all part of the group, names didn't matter – but then Buzz took the prize money and split! That was the last the group saw of him. But it *was* my work, and I can prove it."

"Really? How?"

"I made this inventory, see? Of everything I put into it. How many knives, pins, nails … every bloody piece. Some of them don't show much, and so nobody but the bloke who made the thing could tell for sure. Here's the list." He peeled a tattered document from his wallet and gave it to Phin.

"Interesting. Can I have this photocopied, Bob?"

"Sure, keep it. I only kept it because I thought of suing him for half the money … only I couldn't sue a mate … and now …"

Phin left him standing in the garage, surrounded by metal motorcycle bones. Price was using his fists to scrub black grease into both eyes.

Phin took Mrs Dawson to see Ozanam's performance. The medium turned out to be a thin, balding man, looking much more like his brother than the slick Svengali of the circular. He droned for ten minutes about life on the aetheric plane, mysteries of the ancients, astral projection, secret powers of the mind.

"How do you think he did it?" asked Mrs Dawson, already certain that Ozanam was the murderer. "Do you suppose he really can walk through walls?"

"The demonstration's beginning!" Phin whispered back.

Ozanam asked everyone who had a problem to write their question on a slip of paper. "The assistants will give you slips. When you've written, fold the slip and place it on the tray as it comes by."

When all folded slips had been collected, Ozanam selected one, pressed it, still folded, to his forehead, and with his eyes closed, endeavoured to "see" its message "with the third eye". When he had answered each question, he would unfold the slip and read it aloud, to prove himself right. He successfully "third-saw" Mrs Dawson's question about her sister in Australia, and promised that she would return rich.

"There must be something in it," she said, impressed.

Phin smiled. "Oh, there's something in it, all right. Fraud." He watched Ozanam, who had finished his performance and was now autographing copies of his book, *Meet the Aether!*

Later, the sleuth explained: "Ozanam or one of his aides simply adds one extra slip to the tray. Call it slip X. X has been prepared with a message he knows. Now he takes any genuine slip, A, from the tray. He holds this first slip to his head and 'sees' message X. Then he opens it and pretends to read out message X.

"At the same time, of course, he's getting a look at the real A. Then he takes B from the tray, holds it to his head, and 'sees' A. So he can go on forever, keeping one ahead. He ends with slip X."

"Still," said Mrs Dawson, "he must be a bit occult. How else could he walk through walls to kill people?"

Phin stayed out, prowling London most of the night. He talked with George and with Inspector Gaylord. Sunday morning found him strolling on the Embankment. The news hoardings offered a choice: the murder, a cabinet crisis, or the BOAC cargo strike. He stopped before a paper depicting a pair of eyes, with the headline: ARTIST'S MEDIUM BROTHER: DID THESE EYES FORESEE TRAGEDY?

And suddenly he knew all; the last bit of answer was joined to the rest.

It was time to call all the suspects together. Phin decided to summon them to Hyde Park, to a rendezvous by the Serpentine.

Polly Bradbury reluctantly took the last deck-chair, between Anthony Moon and Bob Price. Next to Bob sat Inspector Gaylord, then Ozanam, and then two Japanese youths who were taking movies of the motionless water. Thackeray Phin stood shivering in the cold breeze.

Polly shivered, too. "I hope you have a damned good reason for calling us here, in this filthy weather."

"Oh, the best." Phin began to pace. "You see, the murderer is one of us in this very park! And I mean to name the name. First, let me recapitulate what seemed to happen.

"The only entrance to Wallis's flat was watched by me continuously from three p.m. to one a.m. During that time, only Aaron Wallis went in, and no one came out. Wallis searched and found no one lying in wait for him. Yet, within an hour, he was strangled to death. Moreover he died at the exact time mentioned in the two threatening letters – on the day predicted by his brother Hector."

Ozanam blushed. "I saw what I saw," he said. "Not with the physical eye, but –"

"Possibly. Anyway, I at first thought the killer must have escaped while Moon and I were down in the lobby, before we returned to find the body. But the elevator stayed down on the ground floor during that five minutes; the stairs were not used; and there were no windows. Escape was impossible."

The Japanese youths moved off to film a tree.

"That eliminates several ways in which Wallis could have been killed. The killer was not hiding in the flat ahead of time, to kill him and make his escape later. Nor are we at liberty to suppose that Wallis lay in the flat all the time, drugged or tied up, that the killer impersonated him coming in, killed him, and then made his escape.

"We move on to bizarre mechanical notions. A clockwork device flings out a loop of deadly rubber tubing at the stroke of nine. Or the victim is persuaded to stand in front of a hole in the wall through which the killer can garrotte him. Or else a secret panel or a priest-hole in which the killer hides. Needless to say, none of these is the answer.

"We are left with even more frivolous theories: Wallis is strangled somewhere else, staggers home and dies. He is hypnotized into throttling himself. A stranger from the fourth dimension walks through walls to kill him for some four-dimensional reasons of his own. Mysterious gases. Astral projection. Ghosts. The devil claiming painter Faust's soul."

"Can we get on with this?" Ozanam asked. Polly looked away and tapped her foot. Moon appeared to have fallen asleep.

"You're right." Phin stopped pacing and faced them. "I know that Aaron Wallis was alive and well until about eight o'clock, when he came home to that windowless flat of his. There the killer strangled him with that length of rubber tubing, within minutes of his arrival."

Polly said, "But you were watching the door all the time!"

"I was, yes. *But it was the door to a different locked room.*"

Phin took a pipe from his pocket, a calabash. "Since you all look blank, perhaps I'd better explain.

"First, the killer had to make certain advance preparations. He – or she – knew that the tenth-floor neighbours were away and that Wallis had their key. He also knew that the twelfth-floor neighbours would be out to the theatre on this night. He managed to get copies of the keys to Wallis's flat and to Flat Ten. He also had a false door-number plate made up – a false "eleven" – which he stuck over the real plate on the door of Flat Ten. The idea of course was to have a real and a false eleventh floor. He added little touches like the orange kitchen chair. You see, the Blenheims had a set of four such chairs – but if you go and have a look today, you'll find only three. The fourth is in Wallis's flat.

"I was then set to watch the disguised door of Flat Ten. Wallis came home to Flat Eleven and was strangled. Now came the elegant part." Phin hooked the calabash in the corner of his mouth. "The killer undressed Wallis and put on Wallis's clothes. With the aid of a wig, mirror sunglasses and white gloves – and one or two extras – it wasn't hard to fool me. I hadn't met the painter, after all.

"False Wallis then took the lift from the eleventh to the tenth floor and did his little act for me. I almost spoiled things by asking to look around inside. But False Wallis was a good actor, or actress, good enough to put me off. He gave me an orange chair to sit on.

"Then he closed and locked the door, pretending to chain it, and went straight through, out of the window to the fire escape with another chair. Naturally he couldn't get into the eleventh floor, so he climbed on past to the twelfth. After gently forcing one of the Talbots' windows, he passed straight through their flat and took the lift back to the eleventh floor. Now all he had to do was dress the corpse in its clothes again, and the deception was all but complete."

"Preposterous!" said Ozanam.

Price looked thoughtful. "Hey, how about rigor mortis? I mean, it must have been hard to dress and undress a stiff."

"Rigor wouldn't have set in much – the whole thing took less than half an hour. Anyway, he put Wallis's arms up the way we found them, to make it easier.

"Now when he had re-dressed his victim, the killer set the duplicate orange chair outside the door and locked up. First he put the chain on from outside. This takes a piece of string and some coat-hanger wire, but anyone can do it after a few minutes' practice. Finally he locked the door.

"Later on, after I'd left the tenth floor, he could put the Blenheims' kitchen chair back in their kitchen and remove the false number eleven from their door – stuck on with rubber cement, I imagine. He probably did this during the excitement following the discovery of the body. On his way to phone the police. In other words, the killer is Anthony Moon."

Moon appeared to be waking from a doze. "Eh? Ai?"

"I said, *you killed Aaron Wallis.*"

"Rubbish!" Moon sat up. "Why in the world should I want to kill him? To cut off my supply of golden eggs?"

Phin began pacing again. "I wondered about that myself, until I learned a little about your business. You aren't just a dealer, you're a collector. You collect Wallises. Many of his best works are in your hands.

"But Wallis seemed to be drying up. In fact, he hadn't done any large works for over a year. When the goose stops laying – *pâté de foie gras*. You knew that nothing drives up the prices of an artist's work like his sudden death. So you bought more and more of his stuff, practically cornering the market – and you laid plans.

"I should have suspected you the first time I saw you doing what you're doing now – feeling your moustache to see if it's still stuck on. I imagine the tan washes off, too. And at your house I'm sure we'll find the Wallis wig – or its ashes."

"That's your proof?" Moon smiled his indulgence.

"I have proof," said the sleuth quietly. "Only you could have decoyed me to the tenth floor. Easy, wasn't it? You pressed the button for eleven when we got on the lift. Then you shoved that circular at me, and, while I read it, you pressed for ten. Naturally the lift stopped at the lower floor first. And since I could plainly see the false door number, I suspected nothing."

"So *you* say." Moon looked more confident. A roar went up from the crowd at some Speakers' Corner rally. "You're like them, really. Plenty of noise, but nothing much to say."

"You've said too much," Phin retorted. "You told me Wallis would have a beautiful view of the river, if not for his blocked-up windows. You weren't just guessing; you'd seen the view from the tenth floor."

"More bluff. Anyone could tell from the location of the building what the view would be. You haven't a single scrap of real evidence."

"Because then you disposed of the false number plate and the two keys. It must have been unpleasant, sitting there for hours answering police questions with that damning evidence in your pocket. Even then you wouldn't just throw them off a bridge. You had to plan their disposal, as you planned the rest. You went to the gallery, where your men were crating *Kitchen Shrapnel* for shipment to Rio. While no one was about, you used epoxy cement to fasten that evidence to inconspicuous parts of the sculpture."

"Nonsense! That's too fantastic to bother answering." The art dealer turned his face away from Phin. The Speakers' Corner crowd cheered their chairman once again.

"You figured the only hard evidence against you would be in the hands of a private collector in Rio de Janeiro within a day, never to be seen again. No one who looked at it would notice an extra bit of metal or three. And the artist was safely dead. Right?

"Wrong." Phin pointed the stem of his pipe at Bob Price. "The artist is right here. He knows exactly how the assemblage was made, and he has a complete written inventory of its components. It lists every nail and pin. But no brass number plate. No keys."

Moon started to speak, but the detective cut him off. "One more flaw in your plan. Thanks to the cargo handlers' strike, that sculpture isn't in Rio, it's at Heathrow. Shall we all go have a look at it now?"

Inspector Gaylord moved, but not fast enough. In almost a single movement Moon managed to upend his deck-chair over the policeman. In another eyeblink, he butted Phin into the Serpentine and was off over the nearest hill.

Everything seemed to conspire to help Moon escape. Phin had to thread his way through a children's football match. Several large dogs joined the romp. The inspector collided with a kite-flyer. The murderer made an unimpeded run to Speakers' Corner, vaulted over a barrier and merged into the crowd.

Thackeray Phin hung half out of the window, blowing soap bubbles with the calabash. He explained to Mrs Dawson that this was no frivolous game but an important experiment in surface tension. "Besides, it helps me concentrate. Not that there's much to concentrate on, since Moon's capture. A few ciphers to crack ... a game of postal Frobisher ..."

Mrs Dawson clucked. "How did they ever catch that Mr Anthony Moon, anyway?"

"Just his bad luck, really." Phin blew an enormous, wobbling globe. "Right after he joined the demonstration, a fracas broke out with the police. Moon got the worst of it. When they rounded him up, he was minus one tooth and one moustache."

"No better than he deserved, the vagabond!"

The sleuth did not answer. He puffed, blew a dream of bubbles and watched them float down towards the black iron spikes of the fences below.

BILL GETS HEP TO GOD!

A TRACT FOR TEENAGERS PREPARED BY JOHN SLADEK

Bill and Jack are both on the basketball squad. After practice, they go to a soda fountain where, over cokes, the conversation turns to religion.

BILL: By the way, Jack, what's *your* religion?
JACK: I'm an atheist.
BILL: No kidding? You really believe all that stuff about there not being any God? (*laughs nervously*).
JACK: That's right, friend. I believe in neither heaven nor hell, and I do not accept Jesus Christ as my personal saviour.
BILL: (puzzled) You mean Christ *didn't* die on the cross for your sins?
JACK: (smiling) You Christians stick at that point, don't you? Well, if Christ *is* God, then it seems to me we have a paradox.
BILL: But aren't all paradoxes resolved in the mind of God?
JACK: Not in this case, Bill, since what we're talking about is the mind of God. What could he possibly gain by sacrificing himself to himself – what was he thinking of?
BILL: Gee, I never thought of that. But you must at least believe there *is* a God. After all, the Bible tells us so.
JACK: Another paradox, Bill. God is supposed to have written the Bible. If so, we would only have his word for his own existence. Actually the Bible was written by ordinary men, and I think it safe to say that it's a *pack of lies* from cover to *cover*.
BILL: Honest? And to think I believed it for so long! Hey, wait a minute! Don't we have other proofs for God's existence? Like who created the universe?
JACK: That's easy. I could have turned around and asked you who created the creator …
　　　Frankly, *we don't know* how the universe came to be. Perhaps *it always was*. Perhaps it *came out of nothing*. You see, any explanation for the existence of God works just as well for the existence of the universe.
BILL: But the universe couldn't have come about by chance, Jack. Life, for instance – the chances of all those complicated molecules getting together by accident are almost nil! You might as well expect a group of blind men to come from all over the country, to assemble in one place, and then to drill and march in perfect precision – all without *outside direction*!
JACK: But if life is all that perfect, Bill, why are there so many thousands of blind men in the first place? No, I'm afraid your "God" is just an

"unnecessary presence".

BILL: What does that mean?

JACK: Well, look at my watch, for example. I could tell you there were invisible demons inside it, who make it run.

BILL: Ha, ha! You're pulling my leg!

JACK: (*permitting himself a smile*) That's right, Bill. It just *doesn't make sense*. Even if I can't explain exactly how this watch works, I don't need to invent "unnecessary presences".

BILL: I get it! Then God is just *not necessary*. But what must I do to become an atheist? Isn't it too late for me?

JACK: Not at all. Though many people find it difficult to change, after a lifetime of piety and prayer. Some never become *true* atheists. They have doubts, they begin to backslide – right back to the same old pew.

BILL: If *I* become an atheist, what's in it for me?

JACK: The true, inner peace of being one with yourself, Bill. Suddenly all the "big problems" of yesterday – sin, guilt, hell – suddenly they just melt away. You find a new zest for life, knowing it's the only one you'll get. All at once you know true inner joy, when "Man's on his ground, all's right with the world."

BILL: That's for me! (*tears off Sunday-school pin and throws it away*). Phooie on superstition! I'm going to be an atheist!

JACK: Glad to hear it, Bill! (*gives him a warm handshake, claps him on the back*) Welcome, brother!

Bill's learned his lesson – but have you learned yours? Give up the vanity (Eccles. 1:2) of worship NOW (Matt. 2:1, 1st word). Remember that he who rejects atheism, who shuts his heart to ungodliness, may never get a second chance! In the words of St Paul:

"The cloak that I left at Troas with Carpus, when thou comest, bring *with thee*, and the books, *but* especially the parchments."   – II Tim. 4:13

It Takes Your Breath Away

The long cinema queue twisted round the corner and back down a narrow, shadowy street. Thackeray Phin and Nell Fortune were far back at the discouraging end, near a hot-dog vendor's aromatic cart. Beside it, a one-man band was cheering them with "Colonel Bogie" on drum, cymbals and untuned banjo, while somewhere a kazoo was playing "Tamborine Man".

"All the sounds and smells of Spring," Phin murmured.

Nell looked at him. "If you don't like it, go home, Yankee. *I* don't know why we're here. You've already dragged me to two nasty cafes and a dingy amusement arcade. Is this some American idea of a good time? Or are we following someone?"

"Right the second time, my English rose. We're following that little man in the hat about nine – no, ten places ahead of us. The one with the cigar. His name's Reg Smythe, and he has to do with gangsters."

She raised an eyebrow. "There are no gangsters any more."

"Not as many as there used to be. And Reg claims to know something about who's killing them off. So I've been asked to keep an eye on Reg."

"By whom?"

Phin checked his notebook. "By Reginald Smythe. Coincidence of names, there." He drew out a huge magnifying glass and inspected the black brick wall next to him.

"Looking for clues?"

"Looking for a clean place to lean against. It looks as though we have some time to wait."

Nell's next remark was lost, as a shrill voice cried, "For the wrath of God is revealed from heaven against all ungodliness! Woe, I say unto thee …" A man wearing thick glasses strolled past, carrying a placard: The End, he wanted all filmgoers to know, was at Hand. He was followed immediately by a loud-voiced peanut vendor.

"I said, why aren't the police protecting Smythe?"

"They are. They're all over the place. The plump middle-aged couple just ahead of us, for instance. Haven't you noticed the bulge under his armpit?"

"A gun?"

"A radio," said the man coldly, turning his head. "Please, Miss, keep your voice down?"

Phin examined the pavement with his magnifier. "Hmm. About twenty-four hours ago, a man passed this way who has grey hair, a slight limp, recently returned from Majorca, and often wears white."

Nell feigned astonishment. "How did you know that?"

"He's my milkman. Saw this film last night, he said."

"That is elementary, my dear Phin. Tell me, can you deduce the ingredients of those hot dogs?"

"I'd rather not. But if the smell is bothering you again, I've got a present for you." He handed her a small bottle. "Rare scent. I won it myself in the arcade."

Nell unstoppered it and wrinkled her nose. "Ugh – it's patchouli oil. Take it away, it's worse than the essence of dog."

Looking a little crushed, Phin put the bottle away. Nell began a few selected remarks about the bad taste of Americans in general, but Phin's being an extreme case.

"Phin, are you listening?"

"Uh, yes, but not to you, I'm sorry to say. To that kazoo. It's interesting ..."

"What? 'Tamborine Man' played off-key?"

"No, I was just wondering why they all have different ways of working the queue. The one-man band started at the front, and he's going to the end. This guy seems to be going in the opposite direction. Oh, here he comes for a hand-out. I'd better give him something. Anyway, I notice that Mr end-is-at-hand and the peanut man have both made a complete trip each way."

The kazoo player, a young man in denim, came towards them holding out a canvas bag and chanting "Ta, thank you, thank you very much" to those who gave and those who did not.

"Just a minute," said Phin, fumbling a handful of change out of his pocket. "I'm not too familiar with this English money. How much should I give you?"

"Whatever you like, sir. Up to you,"

Phin nevertheless picked over the contents of his cupped hand for a few seconds before he said, "Aw heck, you might as well have the whole works." He showered coins into the bag.

"Thank you," said the busker, with a trace of gratitude in his voice. He went on to thank one or two more non-contributors, then dropped back again towards the end of the queue. In a moment, "Tamborine Man" sounded again.

The queue moved a few shuffling paces forward, and stopped.

"I don't like this," Phin said. "Look at Smythe."

The movement had brought the little man into a deep shadow, near the entrance to a side alley off the street. He was all but invisible, except for the glowing tip of his cigar.

"Inspector, if you have a man by the box office, I suggest you get him on the radio and find out what's happening."

The portly man did so. "There's some kind of quarrel going on," he said. "Someone trying to jump the queue or something."

"That's it, then. We'd better –"

The glowing end of Smythe's cigar drooped, then fell to the ground, followed instantly by the silhouette of Smythe himself. The inspector spoke rapid gibberish into his radio.

"I've sealed off the street and the cinema. Let's have a look at him." They ran forward and, in a minute, they knew the whole story:

Smythe lay dead. The thin handle of a switchblade knife stuck out from his chest at an angle that left no doubt. The killer could only be someone next to Smythe in the queue or someone from the alley.

"That's why we've got him," the inspector said. "This is a blind alley, and the only door in it is an exit from the cinema. So he must be inside, if he's not in the queue."

The medical examiner shook his head. "This wound has bled for several minutes," he said. "I'd say he was stabbed a minute or two before you saw him fall. The killer might have escaped from the cinema."

Phin had been taking no part in the conversation. He bent over the corpse once with his magnifier, looked back once or twice at Nell to make sure she was all right, but otherwise stared off into the shadows and hummed.

"There's no help for it," said the inspector. "We'll just have to interview everyone in the cinema and in the queue."

"Ahem. I suggest," Phin said, "that you start your interviews by listening to some music. Then just follow your noses."

"What? Listen, Phin, we haven't time –"

"No, you listen. That kazoo player is out of breath, suddenly. As though he'd been running around the block, from the front exit of the cinema to the back end of this street."

"Rubbish! He's been playing almost continuously."

Phin nodded. "Or someone has. Don't forget, we heard him playing somewhere behind us, but we didn't see him. He could have handed his kazoo to a friend and nipped out for a while."

"Oy!" shouted the inspector. "I want you. Bring him over, Jones." A uniformed officer guided the busker over to them.

"I don't know nothing," he said. "I never went near this bloke, anyone can tell you."

"Yes," said Phin. "You made it pretty obvious that you didn't want to be seen within ten yards of Smythe. I noticed earlier how you hung back towards the end of the queue, while all the other buskers and vendors made complete tours, so I marked you.

"No, you approached him another way. You dropped back, ran around the block, and walked into the cinema – with a booked ticket, I guess. Then out the exit, propping it open, and you did your real job in the alley. Of course you went back the same way. One of your pals was holding up the queue at the front while another was playing your kazoo at the back."

"Prove it," the kazoo player said.

"There're no prints on the knife," the inspector added.

"I said I'd marked him, and now I'll prove it. Nell?" She came over, and, with some reluctance, agreed to the test. The knife was removed and presented to her, handle first. The busker's right hand was held out, despite his struggles, by two constables. Nell sniffed each object.

"Patchouli oil!" she said. "His hand and the knife reek of it!"

"You told me to get rid of it, so I dropped it in his bag with my contribution.'

"That's good enough for me," said the inspector. "Take him to the station. Thanks, Phin."

Nell looked a bit giddy, but she smiled.

"Yankee, let's go home."

Peabody Slept Here

New York, 1973

It was going to be a bad morning at Peabody's office. To begin with, Stan Peabody had a double-barrelled hangover. It made him feel sick in the elevator, it made him creep, rather than walk down the hall to the door marked *S. Peabody, Genealogist*, and it made him drop his keys. He bent slowly and carefully to get them, but he knew he'd never be able to straighten up again.

Then, when he unlocked the door and crawled in, he was face-to-face with the letters. Betty, his bouncing secretary, wasn't there to deal with them, so he faced them alone.

The gas and telephone companies, he read, intended to cut off service. One of his clients was thinking of suing him, and another was turning the matter over to a lawyer. The last letter was from Mr Korzybcwcz, his favourite client, a man who had so far paid him over a thousand dollars to trace his family tree. A client he could count on. Mr Korzybcwcz wrote he was reporting Peabody to the police as a fraud.

Betty bounced in a few minutes later to find him seated at her desk, typing with one finger.

"What're you writing. Mr Peabody?"

"Oh, nothing. Just a suicide note."

"Now, now. Nothing's that bad. It's only a hangover."

"It's the end," he said. "I must have had a good time last night, because I'm paying enough for it now."

"Speaking of pay, my salary's overdue, isn't it?"

"Four months," he said, looking at the ceiling. "I wonder if that chandelier will take my weight?"

"Take it easy, I was just mentioning it. By the way, you did have a good time last night."

"Eh?" He stared at her. "Was that *your* bathtub I woke up in this morning? With Chinese food all over me? And that girl? Who was the girl?"

"My roommate, Sally. You said you were going to give her a bath in champagne. Only you couldn't afford it, you said, so you substituted *chow mein*."

"I did? Oh. God!"

"Yes, and Edna, my other roommate, said to tell you it's all right."

"All right?"

"About running down the batteries in her vibrator. She said ..."

"Oh. God! Don't tell me any more! God!"

Betty looked at the letters. "Oh! Maybe that chandelier will take both our weights. But who is this Korzy-whatsit?"

"He asked me to find out whether or not he had an ancestor who came over on the *Mayflower*. I've been stringing him along, telling him I'm on the track of the ancestor: Ladislaw Korzybcwcz. The Pilgrim Pole."

"And he believed it?"

Peabody sighed. "More or less. But now he's been to another genealogist, who probably told him the truth. No Pilgrim Pole." He ran a finger down his collar and came up with a crisp noodle.

"And this letter? Isn't Miss Goodwin the one who wanted to be descended from Shakespeare?"

"Yup. At least there was some hope – I mean, her ancestors were English. But the man of the time was Ben Godwin, a broken-down perfume seller. Not Shakespeare."

"Hmm. I see this Mrs Ackley wants to sue you, too. Which celebrity did you promise her?"

Peabody dropped the noodle in a metal wastebasket and winced at the sound. "Well. She's a Bunford, of the Pennsylvania Bunfords. Another genealogist traced her back to the 1700s, to the illegitimate child of someone called Eliza Bunford. Father not named. I hinted that it might be – well – George Washington."

"Oh, no! That'll look great at your trial."

"DELIVERY!" shouted a voice behind them. Peabody's brain shattered.

When he could see again, he saw two men in gaudy uniforms and a large metal box. The men wore shiny silver suits and red helmets with little wings sticking out of them. The box looked like a steel phone booth.

"Delivery of what?" said Betty. "A giant office safe?"

Peabody smiled, cracking his lip. "Maybe it's full of giant money. You've got the wrong office. boys. We didn't order a safe."

The two men shrugged, looked at one another and then at a clipboard. One said, "This is office 247, Seewold Building, bud?"

"Yes. but ..."

"Then sign here and it's all yours."

Peabody signed. "What the hell, put it in the corner. So you can find it when you have to take it away again."

"None of my business, bud."

As the men left, Peabody noticed again their peculiar uniforms. "Hey!" he called. "What company do you work for?"

"ATM," they shouted back, as the door closed.

"I wonder what that stands for," said Betty. "Maybe it'll say on the safe door." As she went to look, the phone rang.

"Mr Peabody," said a hard, police voice. "Mr Stanley Peabody? This is Lieutenant Conklin of the Fraud Division. I'd like to come over to your office for a little talk."

Peabody coughed. "Who? Peabody? Not here. This is the janitor."

"Ha ha. I'll be around this afternoon, Peabody. Meanwhile, don't try leaving town."

He hung up. Betty had the cabinet door open and was looking inside. "No name," she said. "And it can't be much of a safe. The door is thin aluminium. And the dial! Whoever heard of a safe with the dial inside? No, wait, here's an instruction book. *Care and Use of the Atkinson Time Machine.* Time machine?"

"Time lock," Peabody explained. He opened the instruction book and began to read aloud:

"The improved Atkinson Time Machine requires no complicated co-ordinate settings. Simply set one dial to the target year, key in the name of your destination (the nearest large city will do) and let ATM do the rest. Historians will appreciate ..."

He tried another page. "Language barriers vanish, with the new Atkinson patented 'Lingo-Lock'. Lingo-Lock re-programs the speech centres of your brain for effortless communication in any dialect. You'll speak and hear in your own language – and yet you'll understand the native, be he Etruscan or Cherokee."

Peabody and Betty sat down and stared at their time machine. After some minutes, Peabody said. "I'll be damned."

"A time machine. It's just not possible."

"Nope." He thought some more. "But it's here. And it's the one thing that can keep me out of jail."

Betty looked at him. "How?"

"I'll go back in time, fix up some phoney evidence to show that my clients really are who I've said they are. If this thing really works, I can put the Pilgrim Pole on board the *Mayflower* myself!"

At Sea, 1620

In a way, Peabody's plan was working. Using the name Korzybcwcz, he had bribed his way on board the *Mayflower* at Plymouth. The Pilgrim Pole was officially aboard.

The only snag was, in the bustle of departure, his name had not been added to the passenger list. And every day since, the captain had been busy fighting the weather.

Now, a week out of port, Peabody made up his mind to get the list and put down his name himself. It was a stormy night, with most of the crew on deck and most of the passenger in their quarters, when Peabody tiptoed down the companion way to the captain's cabin – or what he thought was the captain's cabin. As he opened the door, the ship gave a lurch an his lantern crashed against the wall. A woman screamed.

"Oops! Sorry, wrong cabin. I was looking for the captain."

"My father's on deck, taking in sail." said the voice, suddenly under control. "You're Mr Kor – Kor – something, aren't you?"

"Yes. And you must be the captain's daughter, Hester, is it?" He lifted the lantern. Hester it was: the buxom girl of eighteen he'd seen on deck during the day. Black hair, black eyes, and pale skin the colour of cream. She was smiling.

"Don't just stand there, Mr Whatsit. Close the door and come to bed."

Standing on one foot and taking off a shoe in near-darkness is never easy. When the shoe has a rusty iron buckle, and the floor keeps bucking and tilting under you, it's an act of heroism. The thought of Hester's creamy skin – the parts not yet seen under her starched white nightgown – made him heroic. But when he climbed into bed she shrieked again.

"You're naked!"

"Well, yes. Join me?"

"Sir, it's sinful to bare our bodies. We aren't *heathens*."

"Yes, but how-?"

She showed him the large buttonhole strategically placed on her nightgown.

"Aw, come on, Hester, don't be a puritan."

"I am a Puritan!"

"I mean, we're sinning anyhow. One little extra sin won't make that much difference."

Finally she agreed. Even in the dim light, her body was pale and perfect, limbs opening to him like the petals of a white flower. Above them the storm raged on, but here the rise and fall of the ship carried them on to their merry destination.

In the morning the captain married them at the point of a blunderbuss. As soon as Peabody had repeated his vows, and seen them recorded in the ship's log, he was clapped in irons.

"I ought to hang you now." said the captain. "But the storm has wearied both crew and passengers. Half of them are too sick to come up on deck and watch, and I know they'd hate to miss a hanging. We'll just lock you up for a day or two, until we're ready."

Peabody was dragged away before he could say a word, and locked in the most secure place on ship. That happened to be the "great iron box" he'd insisted on bringing aboard.

New York, 1973

"Dial the phone for me, will you, Betty? I can't manage anything in these fetters. And get me a locksmith later on, will you?"

Betty dialled and handed him the receiver. "Hello, Mr Korzybcwcz. This is Stan Peabody. No, don't hang up. I think I've got some good news for you, I think you'll want to drop all charges. when you hear it. Hold on a minute."

Peabody covered the mouthpiece. "Betty, make another note. I want you to get this coat and stuff back to the theatrical agency. And see what they have in powdered wigs, size seven-and-a-half."

Pennsylvania, 1756

Peabody's hand itched under the bandage, and his head itched under the periwig. Was it polite to scratch? The military gentleman sharing the inn's fireside with him never scratched. In fact, the military gentleman hardly breathed. Only now and then, his hand mechanically raised the tankard of hot punch to his lips.

Nearby, the innkeeper was bustling about, arranging the writing materials Peabody had ordered. Finally he brought the tray over and set it on the table at his elbow.

"Anything else, sir? Another drink?"

"Yes. thanks. And one for the military gentleman. if he likes."

This person turned stiffly and nodded his thanks. "Adjutant George Washington at your service."

In turn. Peabody introduced himself by his new alias. "I'm having some trouble writing this letter, Adjutant. As you see, I've hurt my hand."

Washington didn't seem to hear. His face stayed frozen into the same dignified expression. as though posing for his dollar-bill portrait. After several minutes, he hiccuped and said. "Damned fine punch, eh?"

"Delicious, Adjutant. I was wondering ..."

Washington fell face-down on the hearthrug. For five or ten minutes he lay without moving. Then, with slow, mechanical movements, he raised himself up and resumed his chair.

"Damned fine punch. Yes. *Urp*. You were saying?"

"I've hurt my hand. I was wondering if you'd mind helping me write this letter."

"Letter? Certainly. They make it, you see, with brandy, rum, ale and I believe raw egg. The punch I mean. Help me up, will you?"

Peabody guided the military gentleman over to his table and put the quill in his hand.

"Now just put down what I'll dictate: 'Dear Eliza Bunford: While I fully admit I am the father of your child, my family connections cannot permit us to marry, not openly. Yet my heart and conscience tell me we must. I therefore propose a secret ceremony ...'"

Washington dutifully took it all down. "Shall I sign it for you?"

"Yes, in my full name. George Warrington."

"There. I say, that looks almost like my own name."

Peabody smiled. It would look even more like it when he had made an ink-blot over the double-r.

"Thanks, General – I mean, Adjutant. Now if you'll excuse me. I must go to bed."

"That's all right, you toddle off. Think I'm going to be sick."

Upstairs, Peabody pried up a floorboard and tucked the letter under it. He had just knocked it back in place when the blonde chambermaid came in with a smoking warming-pan. Her low-necked dress showed a landscape with a couple of interesting peaks.

"Never mind that, Eliza." he said, getting an arm around her. "There are better ways of warming a bed."

"Sir! I don't know what you mean." She began undoing her bodice. The landscape developed pink nipples, and more interesting parts. Peabody set out to explore it.

The rest was history.

New York, 1973

Old Mrs Ackley was so excited she leapt up, dropping the Pekinese off her lap. Her lawyer stood up too, but reluctantly.

"Do you mean." she said. "that this little piece of paper makes me a *Washington*?"

"Almost," said Peabody. "At least it proves that Washington proposed marriage to your great-great-grandmother. I found it in an old inn in Pennsylvania."

"Has this document been authenticated?" said the lawyer.

"Yes. The people at the National Archives say that the ink, paper and handwriting are genuine. Moreover, they've shown that Washington could have stayed at the inn where Eliza Bunford, your great-great-grandmother, worked as a chambermaid. And he could have stayed there on the exact night."

The lawyer didn't look happy. "I'm afraid we owe you an apology, then. We'll drop our suit, of course."

"An apology? About ten thousand apologies will square it, I'd say. Make the cheque out to cash, okay?"

London, 1596

Peabody felt the full power of the Atkinson patented Lingo-Lock here. He didn't know what it was, exactly, but he knew it worked. Because here, he couldn't just say. "Hey, mac, which way to Shakespeare's house?" Instead, he had to say something like, "Prithee, sirrah, canst tell my way? I seek the quarter where now dwelleth ..."

Whatever the machine did to his brain, it made it possible for him to think the first and twist his tongue around all the syllables of the second, automatically. In the same way, the long, warbled replies were shaved down to plain English for him, so that "Marry, sir, an' I must mickle think upon't ..." became "Let me see ..."

True, he missed many minutes of rapid-fire puns and word-play, but he did get the directions. And the directions led him to a sleazy-looking house in a stable-yard. A serving-wench answered his knock by opening an upstairs window and spitting.

"Tell Mr and Mrs Shakespeare – I mean, Will Shakespeare and Anne Hathaway – that I'd like a word with them. I'm Ben Godwin, perfume salesman."

"Mr Shakespeare isn't at home."

"Jane!" called a woman's voice from the interior. "Send him up. I need some company."

As he came up, Anne stopped her embroidery and gave him her hand to kiss. She was dark, but red-haired, an exciting and excitable woman. He gave her a sample of Chanel No 5. She wrote out an order for more, which he tucked away in an empty perfume bottle.

"Don't rush off," she yawned. "Will's at the theatre, rehearsing some damned thing."

"With a wife like you, I don't see why he needs rehearsals." This, Peabody realized, was a feeble joke. But in translation it took him some ten minutes to say, and evidently impressed the lady so much that she immediately led him to the bedchamber.

They were still there an hour later, when the Bard found them.

"Gadzooks!" Shakespeare (probably) cried, and drew his sword. "Get ready for a quick trip to Heaven, you son of a bitch."

Peabody tried to roll clear, but Anne's thighs held him. "Don't pay any attention to old windbag, there," she said. "He's all talk. We have a saying around here: 'Will may shake his spear, but Anne hath a way.'"

"Say your prayers," warned the Bard.

"Put that thing away, Will. And grow up. I hope we can all be civilized about this. After all, this is the sixteenth century."

Shakespeare sheathed his sword. "Okay, okay. But I'm still plenty pissed off. I mean, to betray me like this, right here in my own second-best bed, and with a beardless youth ..."

"I'm almost thirty," said Peabody.

"Still, you're young." A new look came into the Bard's eye. "Hmm ... Anne's right. We must be civilized. Move over, you two, and make room for me."

"*Now* he's dangerous," Anne said, releasing Peabody. "When he gets that look, no good-looking man under the age of sixty is safe. If you value your ass, haul it out of here, quick. They don't call him 'The Swan' for nothing."

Shakespeare threw him a sickly smile. "I just wanted to be friends."

"Run for it," said Anne. "With a friend like Will, a man doesn't need any enemas."

Peabody grabbed his clothes, threw open the casement and dropped to the street. The time machine was half a mile away, down by the river. He ran naked all the way, and hardly anyone turned to stare.

New York, 1974

"Havana cigar, Lieutenant?"

"No thanks. I just dropped in to see how you like your new offices. Top floor of the Biltman Building – very nice."

"Yeah, well, I needed more room for my operation. You know, I'm doing a lot of business now. Not just family trees but historical research."

Lieutenant Conklin looked around. "You've really come up in the world in the past year, haven't you, Peabody? Penthouse suite of offices, fancy suits – and isn't that a Picasso on the wall?"

Peabody nodded. "And a year ago, I couldn't even pay the phone bill. Yup. Well, I've been lucky."

"*Lucky*? Peabody, you're the luckiest guy alive. Down at the Fraud Division, we've been watching your career very closely. *Very* closely. Every time you go wandering in some out-of-the-way place, and just happen to dig up a historical document, we check it out."

Peabody blew a thick smoke ring that drifted towards the metal cabinet in the corner. "Any problems?"

"No. Everything you find checks out. But it just has to be fraud. You visit an old inn in Pennsylvania and come up with a letter from George Washington – that helps one of your clients. At the Vatican, you just happen to turn over a paving stone and find a note from some old pope – proving he's the ancestor of a certain Mafia client of yours. And so on and on. It doesn't add up, does it?"

"I guess it's a talent, Lieutenant. Like water-divining. I've got it."

Conklin stood up. "I'll tell you what you've got. You've got a team of expert forgers working on this stuff somewhere. They know how to fool all our tests: ageing the paper by some secret process or something. I know god-damned we'll you're faking this stuff, Peabody. And so do you."

"Prove it."

"I can't, and you know it. In fact, we're closing the file on you. So do me a favour, will you? Just give me one little hint – just to satisfy my curiosity – how in hell do you do it?"

Peabody smiled. "Well, you see, I've got this time machine ..."

The policeman slammed the door on his way out.

Betty came in a minute later. "The Rolls Royce man says your car's ready. And Senator Holm wants an appointment at three, okay?"

"Okay, kid. Now why don't you take the rest of the day off? Buy yourself another mink or something."

He gloated alone, in the midst of all the luxury he'd ever dreamed of. The money was rolling in, not just from his work, but from little extra trips to the past. A few shares of IBM stock, bought during a jaunt to 1932, were now worth a couple of million.

And this was only a side-line. His real interest lay in a small black notebook which he kept in the time machine. In it were the names of two hundred famous, powerful and beautiful women in history. Fifty-seven of the names now had stars after them. and he was working on the rest. Marie Antoinette had been an easy two stars. Joan of Arc was going to be tough.

Well, he thought, strolling over to the machine, at least the cops were off his neck for good. From here on, it was going to be stars and dollar signs as far ahead as he could see.

He opened the shiny aluminium door and came face-to-face with a stranger in a black uniform.

"Hello, Peabody." The stranger had a cop's one-sided smile. He also had the notebook in his hand.

"Who are you?"

"I'm a time patrolman. I have a warrant here for your arrest."

"For what?"

"Illegal use of a time machine, for a start."

Peabody fumbled at a whisky decanter and poured himself a drink. "I don't know what the hell you're talking about."

"No? I guess you don't know anything about the entries in this notebook, either." The time cop turned a few leaves and read aloud:

"'1762. The Empress Catherine is, as they say, great! Just great!'

"'1810. Tonight, Josephine! Tonight!'

"'53 BC. Caesar's wife not above suspicion after all!' And all these are three-star items. Whereas you've only rated Nell Gwynne ..."

Peabody swung the decanter, catching him across the ear. The cop sank down to sit on the floor, still smiling ironically. Peabody jumped past him into the machine, slammed the door and spun the dial all the way over.

"Just let 'em try finding me," he muttered, "this far back."

20,000 BC
He came out of the box on a grassy plain beside some low hills. Nothing looked peculiar except the hairy elephant grazing nearby. When it caught sight of the time machine, it flung back its ears and trotted away.

Not much of a place to stay, Peabody thought. But he could lie low here for a while and then zip back to some more interesting place. Say, with Cleopatra by the Nile. Why not?

"Why not?" He shouted it into the wind as he climbed the nearest hill. "I can have any part of history I want. Any of it and all of it. Especially the female part. They ought to put up monuments to me, everywhere: *Peabody Slept Here*."

Laughing at the idea, he paused by a small shrub to look around. One valley was dotted with grazing black mastodons, like the one he'd scared. Beyond it was a line of grey smoke.

"At least the place is habitable. Okay for a clean weekend." He glanced back down at the trusty, vital Atkinson Time Machine.

A small group of men stood around it, waving spears and clubs. Local tribesmen, probably showing how brave they were. Maybe they thought it was some kind of shiny square god. He figured any minute now they'd all fall down and start worshipping it.

One of the men strode forward, lifted his club and smashed in the door. Suddenly they all joined in, smashing and spearing until the time machine was just a pile of twisted metal.

All history was junk. Peabody's stomach turned. He was going to end up here, like this! The rest of his life with nothing to look at but grass, hairy elephants and local yokels.

Then, in the shrubbery behind him, a woman laughed. He spun around to face her and saw everything at once. She was young, pretty and interested. And the bush was a juniper.

"Come here, sweetheart. I want to tell you about a delicious drink, called gin. Later on we can try making some of it, out of these berries here. Just because we're living in the Stone Age is no reason not to have a cold martini at sundown.

"But that comes later. Right now, you and I can lie down over here and make sweet ... history."

MACHINE SCREW

"How long's Dad been in there with Professor Varren?" asked Margot Brown. "Why do we have to wait out here in the reception room? What's all the secrecy about?"

Jim Latimer shrugged. "You know how Varren is. He's been tinkering with this 'Project Alpha' of his for years, all in secret. I guess we should be flattered that even your Dad's allowed to see some of it." He wished Margot wouldn't keep crossing her legs and uncrossing them again. Even when he tried not to look, he could hear the nylon saying "Psst! (Over here!)"

"You know, Jim, Professor Varren is peculiar – even for a scientist."

"Hey, watch it! I'm a scientist, too. Not to mention your father, who's only a world-famous physicist !"

Psst. "Oh, Dad's okay. And you – you're almost like a brother. But Professor Varren is cold and calculating. And a bit – funny, don't you think?"

Miss Carvell was standing in the doorway. "Funny?" she said, sneering. "Oh! You would say that. You don't understand him. No one understands him as I do. I've been the Professor's secretary for forty-one years. I know him, and I know what he's trying to do here. You may have your laugh now, but one day the world will go down on its knees to thank him!"

Jim cleared his throat. "And what is he trying to do here?"

"Only solving the world's traffic problems, *forever*. That's all." Miss Carvell went to her desk and spoke into the intercom.

"Professor? The *you-know-whats* are here. The delivery. No, I can't be more specific. Dr Brown's daughter and young Dr Latimer are sitting right here."

While she talked, Jim quietly led Margot outside to the waiting delivery truck. The driver stood by, adjusting the tarpaulin cover over a huge double mound.

"Mind if we inspect the goods?" Jim asked.

"Help yourself." Jim loosened a cord and took a quick peek, just as Miss Carvell stepped outside.

"Get away from that!" she said. "Spying! I suppose, Miss Brown, your father would like to steal the Professor's invention."

She herded them back inside, and her sharp old eyes watched their every move.

Suddenly, from beyond the door leading to the lab, they all heard shouts of anger. The door flew open and Dr Brown stumbled out, propelled by a shove from Professor Varren's cane.

"And stay out! If you won't help me with Project Alpha, I'll do it alone.

I don't need anyone!"

"Good," said Brown. "Because you'll get no help from me, with your demented scheme. I warn you: you're tampering with forces of Nature we little understand. Dangerous forces. Even if it works, your machine is mad!"

"Mad, am I? We'll soon see about that!" The Professor's grey goatee shook with anger. "Tonight I make the final adjustments. Then – *nothing can stop Alpha.*"

Dr Brown turned his back on the raving man. "Margot, Jim. Let's get out of here."

On the drive home, Margot asked her father about Project Alpha.

"No, I gave, my word. I can't tell a soul," he said. "I only hope nothing goes wrong ..."

She turned to Jim. "What was on the truck? Did you see it?"

He nodded. "But what I saw doesn't make sense. Enormous ball bearings, at least eight feet in diameter. Far too big for any machine known. And that's not the strangest part. *There were only two.*"

Kindly, white-haired Dr Brown looked worried. "I was afraid of that."

Margot shook her blonde curls. "I don't get it. What kind of machine uses only two big steel balls?"

"'You shouldn't have invited them here, Professor. I knew they only wanted to steal your invention." Miss Carvell made the old man lie down on the sofa while she put a cold cloth on his fevered brow.

"Thank you, Miss Carvell. I'm glad that *you*, at least, believe in me." He fumbled for his cane and struggled to sit up. "Now, I must get back to the lab. So much still to do ... Think of it, Miss Carvell: The first successful synthesis of hormones and motor oil ! Not only will cars run better, they'll *feel* better." He paused, rubbing his beard. "No, that's not it. I got that formula right last year, didn't I? What is it I'm working on at the moment?"

"Project Alpha," she said.

"Alpha, of course. Or, as I like to call him, 'Alf'."

He wandered into the laboratory and did not emerge until late evening. "I'm going home, Miss Carvell. Everything's ready. Tomorrow the world will understand my genius. Can I give you a lift home?"

"No thanks, sir. I'll just stay on and finish these reports."

"Sure you'll be all right?"

"Of course, Professor. What could possibly happen to me?"

He looked her over. "To you, nothing. Goodnight."

The sheriff picked his way through the debris. "He must have been godawful strong," he said. "Or else old Miss Carvell put up a hell of a fight. They even knocked over the safe."

He came to a pair of feet, sticking out from under a blanket. "Miss Carvell?"

"Don't look, sir," said a doctor. "Not a pretty sight."

"Dead?"

"No, fainted. He never touched her at all. Still, she's not a pretty sight."

An old man came into the room. "I'm the one that called you, sheriff. I heard the screams. Then I seen this big fella running from the building. Big, square-shouldered guy, about fifteen feet tall. Kind of square headed, too, come to think of it."

The sheriff turned to a deputy. "Broadcast that description. I want this vandal brought in."

"Yes sir. Sir, there's a Dr Brown outside. Says he knows something about our suspect."

"No time now, deputy. Get his statement." The sheriff walked on, into the lab, where a great, square-shouldered hole had been punched through the brick outer wall. Giant square footprints led off towards the woods.

A lab man was dusting the footprints for fingerprints. "Sheriff, we just can't figure out how he made this hole. He must have had some kind of giant battering ram."

Linda and Randy were parked in their usual Saturday night spot, a little clearing in the woods. As far as Randy was concerned, they might just as well be in public: he was getting nowhere. It had taken him a month to manoeuvre his hand along the back of the seat and around her shoulder; and another month of tentative kisses, while the hand tried a slow, diagonal slide downwards. Once, when he'd actually touched her breast, Linda had wriggled away, wept, stormed and threatened never to see him again. Now he was even more cautious.

Tonight, he promised himself, or never. There was soft music on the car radio, the top was down, the moon was up and so was Randy. He opened one eye in the clinch, to see how that hand was doing. An inch from that luscious goal. One more inch and-

"Don't, Randy. Someone might be watching."

"Out here? Who could be watching here?"

She pulled away from him. "I don't know. I just have a feeling ..."

"Me, too. Come here."

"Shh! I hear something."

When the blood stopped pounding in his ears, Randy heard it, too: a faint clanking of heavy machinery. Then the radio started making funny, sputtering noises.

"Randy, I'm frightened."

He cuddled her, reaching for tonight's target. Suddenly a large, square head loomed up over the side of the car.

Linda screamed.

"Who are you? What do you want?"

Wham! Something rammed the car. Randy and Linda jumped out and ran for cover. Randy's head hit a low-hanging tree limb and he slumped to the ground.

"Keep calm," Linda told herself. "Remember your first aid lessons.

Loosen his collar ... his belt ... might as well unzip this, too ... My goodness! You're not unconscious!"

"General Steeg, there's a Dr Brown on the line. Says it's urgent."

"Not now, corporal. I'm in conference. All hell broke loose last night. We got some kind of giant maniac on our hands." He turned to the sheriff. "Tell me about the car again."

"General, the kids saw most of it. And our lab men confirmed it this morning. There's the marks of big hands on the sides of the car, and the back end of it is a total wreck. Rammed to pieces."

"Thanks, sheriff, I guess we can take it from here. This is no ordinary maniac. This guy must be some kind of foreign saboteur. I mean, what kind of decent American would go and – and *rape* a Cadillac convertible?"

Dr Brown put down the phone and looked at Margot and Jim. "It's no use. They won't listen. They don't realize, this will mean the end of civilization, as we car-owners know it. There's nothing we can do now. I – I'm tired. Think I'll take a walk on the cliff, look at the sea. Anyway, I'm glad I told you two all about Project Alpha."

When he'd gone, Margot spoke. "Dad's taking it hard. I think he feels somehow responsible."

"We all do," Jim said. "We scientists let this thing loose on the world. If only your father could figure out some way of stopping it."

"Let's go ask him," she said. They went outside and started up the long, windswept slope to the cliff edge. At the very precipice, they could see two small figures struggling. One raised its cane and struck at the white-haired head of the other, which fell off the edge and out of sight.

"Professor Varren!" Margot screamed. "You've killed my father!"

"Too late!" he chortled, as they approached. "He tricked me into telling him my secret formula. *He learned Alf's weakness*. I had to kill him. And I've just taken a quick-acting poison of my own invention. If I've mixed it properly, it should kill me before I've finished this sentence!" He looked bewildered. "That's funny. I must have got it wrong. Now let me see: two parts cyanide-"

He fell dead.

"Now we'll never stop Alf," said Margot.

Jim, who was peering over the side of the cliff, snapped his fingers. "We're in luck! Your Dad managed to scratch the formula on the cliff face, on his way down!"

"Yes, but what could Alf's weakness be?" she mused.

"How about – how about sex?"

"Isn't it kind of soon after Dad's death?" Margot smiled. "Wait a few minutes."

"No, I meant – sex is Alf's weakness. We need to build the one thing that can stop Project Alpha. His opposite, Project Omega. We can even call her 'Meg'."

"A ring of steel," said General Steeg, stabbing the map. "It's the only answer. We know he's somewhere in this little town, and there can't be too many places where a guy that size can hide. So we'll ring the town with tanks, and then go in and smoke him out. Order the men to shoot on sight, anybody over ten feet tall."

"Isn't that the limit?" said Harry Kelso to his wife. "First time we go to the movies in months, and then the biggest bastard I ever saw has to go and sit in front of us. Hey you! How about sitting somewhere else?"

He tapped the big stranger on the shoulder. It felt like steel. There was a whirr of gears and the huge, square head turned to look at him.

"Uh, never mind," Harry said. "Come on, Muriel, we can sit anywhere. Let's move to one of the back seats."

No one else in the cinema seemed to have noticed the big stranger, though his head reached half-way to the balcony. All eyes were on the film, a new, blue reel called *Clockwork Orgy*. Later, some patrons would remember hearing a deep mechanical voice complain: "So where's the clockwork?"

The film rolled on to its conclusion, without incident. But then, during a documentary about an automobile factory, there was a curious disturbance.

First came a low, throbbing sound, then the sound of well-oiled machinery. People eight or ten rows ahead of the stranger found some sort of obstruction on the floor, and nowhere to put their feet. Finally, with a great *Whangg*!, this entire file of seats was ripped from the floor and hoisted into the air, impaled on a thick metal pole. The pole kept growing and rising until it cast a shadow on the screen.

"The monster car freak!" someone screamed. People were knocked down in the panic: men, rushing off to check their cars; women, lingering to have a closer look. In the crowd, no one noticed the stranger slip away and clank off down the street towards the waiting tanks.

The young tank gunner looked scared. "We fired everything we had at him, General. He just kept coming. So we had to abandon our tanks and run for our lives."

The General looked at the battered tanks and spat on the ground. "So he rapes tanks, does he? He screws Government property?" He raised his voice, addressing all the massed soldiers. "Now hear this, men. We're gonna catch this son-of-a-bitch. And when we corner him, I want all of you to remember what this tank-fucker did to these brave machines!"

In the lab, the radio was playing. Jim finished welding a seam, pushed back his mask and listened.

"Not much time now," he said. "The country's in one hell of a panic."

Margot held up a test-tube. "I hope the Professor's formula does the trick."

"Sex always works, Margot."

She caught her breath. "You called me Margot! Does this mean-?"

"Listen! Another news bulletin."

The radio announcer said: "... last seen heading for the city. All citizens are warned: lock your garages. Keep your cars off the streets. This creature seems to be a violent, sex-starved robot. It'll go for anything on wheels. We have a few scattered reports: he's hopped a bus ... coupled with a train ... and here we have an eyewitness on the phone, a Mr Homer Thurloe, who owns a service station. Mr Thurloe, what happened?"

"He was (beep)ing our tow truck! Then he goes and drinks at the gas pump. Premium grade, it was. And then he goes off towards the city. Singing, he was."

"Singing, Mr Thurloe? Are you sure?"

"Yeah, and weaving. I think all that gas made him drunk, see? I'd sure hate to be where he's going now. I mean. If he was horny *before*, what's he gonna be like with fifty gallons of Premium inside him?"

Alf had been cornered in the city, on the big suspension bridge across the bay. Though the morning was rainy, a crowd of ten thousand had gathered below, waiting to see the monster killed.

A truck, its horn sounding impatiently, was making its way through the crowd. A soldier stopped it. "Only authorized vehicles, sir!"

"Stand aside," said Jim. "We're here to help."

"Sorry. Everyone wants to help, sir. We've had offers from all the automobile clubs. Especially after that incident last night."

"The antique car?"

"Yes, sir. It makes me angry just to think of it: a harmless, helpless, eighty-year-old car! I mean, what kind of monster would –"

"Please," said Margot. "We're scientists. We must get through. In the back of our truck is a – a secret weapon. The only thing that can stop Alf."

The soldier promised to try to get word to General Steeg.

"No time!" Jim shouted. "Look, they're loading that atomic cannon now!" He looked around and spied a derrick near the bridge. "Hold on, Margot. I'll back us up to that, and we can hoist Meg up on the bridge ourselves."

"It just might work," she said.

"Got to work, it's our only chance." With the help of bystanders, they hooked Meg to the derrick. Before hoisting her, Jim pressed the navel button that made the giant robot "alive".

"Dolly!" boomed the metallic voice of Meg. As she lifted clear of the ground, her giant hand shot out and snatched up Margot. Jim tried to hold her, but succeeded only in tearing her dress.

"Can't stop the hoist," he said. "They're aiming the atomic gun already. There's only one way." He began to clamber up the framework of the bridge itself.

"Aim!" said General Steeg. "Wait. Who the hell authorized that man to climb up there?"

"There's another robot up on the bridge, sir. A female robot. And it has a woman with it."

"We can't shoot women," the General decided. "Hold your fire."

As soon as the Meg-monster saw the Alf-monster, it forgot all about dolls and left Margot on the bridge road. It strolled out to meet its mate. A moment later, Jim reached Margot and slumped down, exhausted.

"Are you all right?" he gasped.

"Except for my clothes. Just look how they're torn. Here. And here."

He looked. He could hardly take his eyes away to watch the great event.

Alf spotted Meg and at once his enormous tool began to rise and lubricate. He trundled towards her. Both machines began to drip oil, at first from their gargantuan organs and then from every joint.

When they met, in the middle of the bridge, Meg stopped, suddenly coy. Alf levelled his ramrod and charged. Meg slipped to one side, and Alf, overbalanced by his enormous extension, almost fell. He grabbed one of her big globes for support. At once, his iron fingers moved to her copper nipple. A blue spark passed between them.

Jim became conscious of his own hand, almost of its own accord, circling Margot's exposed breast. He started to take his hand away, but she hugged it to her, pressing his fingers to the nipple.

"But I'm a scientist," he said. "Really I ought to be making notes." Even as he said it, he and Margot were stripping off the last of their clothing.

Alf's free hand roamed Meg's iron-clad body, squeezing and palpating. He clutched her buttock, then slid his hand down between her oil-streaming legs. The two machines parted. Meg lay back, offering her steaming orifice and, with a great whine of gears, Alf rushed upon her. His long, glistening tool struck sparks as it entered. As the two great bodies smashed together, the whole bridge gave a shudder. Rivets popped off like fly-buttons, and the centre span began to crumble and collapse.

"They'd better hurry," said Jim, feeling their urgency himself. He clasped Margot to him and slid in smoothly.

They began to move with a slow, even rhythm, paced by the thundering vibrations from the middle of the bridge. The robots were smoking hot and striking sparks with every mighty thrust. Jim and Margot came, together, as the thundering beat rose to a crescendo.

"General, they're on fire!"

Regretfully, Steeg moved the field glasses away from the human couple and trained them on the iron behemoths. Wisps of smoke were rising from their genitalia and the friction surfaces were glowing hot. Their beat grew frenzied as more and more of the bridge crumbled away from under them. Suddenly, Alf staggered and bellowed, "Wow!" Meg let out a shriek that rattled windows half a mile away:

"Wheee!" She rose off the end of Alf's hydraulic ram and just kept on rising, pushed up on the rocket flame that spewed from her iron pudendum.

"She's going into orbit, sir!"

Steeg watched her rise, then turned his glasses on the other robot. Alf's Brobdingnagian tool was – yes – going limp. At the same time, the last of the bridge span collapsed beneath him. He had time only to wave to Meg, shout something, and pitch forwards slowly into the bay.

"What did he say?" said Steeg.

The colonel shrugged. "Sounded like: 'Got to get home. I told the wife I was working late at the office.'"

Jim and Margot lay gazing at the sky.

"The last we'll see of robots," she said.

"But is it?" Jim sat up. "I was just thinking. *Suppose Meg is pregnant.*"

"You mean-?"

"An invasion," he said grimly. "We'll have to keep watching the sky. *Keep watching the sky.*"

"Okay," said Margot, pulling him over on her. "But while I'm watching the sky …"

The Future of John Sladek

The past is inevitable. Frightened of its possibilities, we retreat to the safety of nostalgic thoughts about the future.

That's only one of many epigrammatic openings I thought I could have chosen, but then *the future is fixed; only the past can be changed at will.* Not much better is it? Maybe I'd better forget epigrams and just describe the future.

It began for me in 1948, while I was cleaning out the potato bin in my grandmother's kitchen. In the bottom of it was an old (1946?) issue of *Colliers'* magazine. Being at the age when all print must be read, I opened it to an article entitled "Where's Grandma's Helicopter?" The future it was talking about was proposed during the Second World War, and hadn't come true – the past (here trebly removed) has to be imagined to be believed.

There's a lesson here for futurologists. Don't imagine that you can imagine the future. Stick to the future that everyone knows to be true. My next demonstration of this took place in the 1950s and it comes from a close observation of the covers of science fiction magazines. The rule is: *Nothing in the foreground ever happens.* No blonde will ever be molested by a squid from Arcturus, no hero will ever wear a red plastic cape, gold lamé suit and transparent boots, and no turnip-creatures from Vega will ever die by being pierced with the green ray from anyone's fast-drawn .45 calibre blaster. While you're at it, forget about robot servants.

But look at the backgrounds of these pictures: there you will find views of Cape Canaveral, the London Post Office Tower, every pseudo-Mies-van-der-Rohe (glass is cheap) building ever built. There too are the thundering jets, the whirring helicopters, the aerial roads that twist and turn gracefully among the glass cities – everything we've failed to grow resigned to.

My third discovery of the future was when, about 1968, I opened a copy of *Time* magazine and saw a recent picture of a group of men goose-stepping. They wore white plastic helmets with black face-shields that made them look like, well, something from science fiction. They wore strange military uniforms and boots so shiny they could have been transparent. They carried long metal sticks or batons – holding them in both hands at chest level – that could well have been atomic blasters. According to the caption, they were policemen in Washington DC.

Of course by this time, the future had pretty well taken shape. NASA ("the earth sure looks beautiful from up here"), John Fitzgerald Kennedy, Lee Harvey-Oswald and Jack No Middle Name Ruby were surprises to forget, and grandma's helicopters went to Vietnam. All this, and Nixon's burglaries (or burglarizations) helped us concentrate on the present exclusively, a sure sign that the future had already gone by us.

When I sat down to write this, I went over, picked over all this junk and worse: Where was grandma's autogyro? What happened to the giant flying wing of Howard Hughes? Could there have ever been a car collision involving a Tucker and an Edsel? Then there were all those predictions, from about 1910 on, of man's final achievement of psychic powers: telepathy would replace telephones, astral projection would end traffic jams, psychokinesis would enable us to open supermarket doors by thought-waves.

Then it occurred to me in a flash: The future is predestined, but the past can be manipulated. And if that was so, I needn't write this piece at all – all I had to do was to imagine that I had written it already!

Sure enough, I looked through a pile of old *New Worlds* (an imaginary science fiction magazine) and there it was: written in 1970.

And here it is.

Ernest thought it would be fun to let his computer call up Frank's computer on the telephone.

"Good to hear yours, too! But hey, do you know what a.m. it is out here?"

Al is seen glancing at his watch. Thanks to a vibrating quartz crystal in it, the watch keeps very, very accurate time. He looks from its Swiss face to the American face of Dot, his wife, out in the back yard eating a piece of fruit that has been picked the day before yesterday in the Orient. Will miracles – or anything – ever cease? The digital clock reports a new minute.

"I met you," Al said into a portable tape recorder no larger than a packet of cigarettes, "a year, three days, seven hours and forty-three minutes ago, through that computer dating service. You had brushed your teeth electrically, using stannous fluoride toothpaste to prevent decay. I had just had dacron veins put in.

"Times change. You now have someone else's liver and kidney: I have ridden on an atomic submarine."

On the atomic ship, Al will notice an interesting article about LSD, a drug commonly supposed to cause visions and insights. He would reproduce this article by xerography, a fast electrostatic process making use of powdered ink.

Al called Bertha, his ex-wife, on the hall video phone.

"I just took a stay-awake pill," she said. "I've been so sleepy ever since the sauna I took, on the airbus from –"

"What's new?"

"I'm pregnant again, due to the fertility drug I'm taking. Ah, and I have a new non-stick milk saucepan. See?" On the screen she cuts open a tetrahedral carton of milk which was sealed for almost a year, then pours some into a special pan. The pan has previously been coated with a compound to prevent sticking and burning. So Bertha, wife of Ernest, was pregnant!

She and Al soon fell into their old argument about riot control. She favoured tanks with aluminium armour, while Al defended the judicious use of Mace, a gas which irritates the mucous membranes.

"What's new with you and Dot?" she asks.

"Oh, I've been sterilized. Dot has this detached retina, but luckily they can now weld it back on with lasers."

They spoke of Dot's trip to the Orient on a ballistic, supersonic plane. There Dot makes the acquaintance of an amateur biologist named Frank, who's all keyed up about the isolation of the gene. His real business is the manufacture of cosmetics for men, in factories he claimed were 97% automated.

LIFE AFTER DEATH – AL WONDERS.

Ernest took a tranquilliser before he called Dot on the teletypewriter. They were lovers, not to Al's knowledge. This was a conveniently private mode of communication, not often used by spirit mediums, though.

As they "spoke", Ernest drank coffee that had been percolated, frozen, vacuum dried and packed in jars. A spoonful of this substance to a cup of boiling water, while Dot watched the five-inch screen of her portable television set: there is a baseball game in far-off Texas, played on nylon grass beneath a geodesic dome, and she is part of it. When they have said the private things lovers must, Dot took a sleeping pill and slept.

Clement, or Clem, was Al's son by a previous marriage. Next day he fuelled his car at a coin gas station, dry-cleaned his clothes in a similar manner, and fell foul of a peculiar police arrangement: At one end of a bridge police read the licence numbers of all passing cars into their radios. The computer at headquarters checks these for old violations.

Clem lived avoiding the army in a module apartment house, which has been made up at a factory in complete, decorated rooms, then bolted together at the building site. When he gets home he tries to call Bertha, his former stepmother, by means of a telephone message relayed through a communications satellite many thousands of miles, but she is at the hospital, having her third child.

Bertha's first child was now a bright little five-year-old, using an unusual teaching machine to learn to type and spell at the same time. This machine would give an instruction, then lock all but the necessary keys. If only life could be like that, Al thought, with no chance to err! In a programmed novel, the reader determines the ending.

Her second child was very intelligent, possibly because Bertha wore a suit pressurized with oxygen during the brain-growing months of pregnancy. Her present delivery is difficult. The child has worked down too far for a Caesarean yet not far enough for forceps. What is the obstetrician to do?

He used a new suction device to grip the child's head and draw him from the womb. Soon it cried, and before long, Bertha knew, it would be joining its siblings in immunity to polio, once a dread crippler and killer of children. She only hoped it would grow up to be a president like the one she now watches on colour TV, announcing the landing of men on the moon (this president had not yet been assassinated). O Frank, Frank! Where are you?

Frank had given up smoking, drinking and excessive eating since his heart-lung transplant. Yet here he is, enjoying a cigar, a martini, and what looks like boeuf Stroganoff! What can possibly be the explanation of this?

It was a photograph of Frank made many years before, to demonstrate a process that made colour prints, right in the camera, seconds after the photo was snapped. Dot became a secretary. As she rode the helicopter to the Pan Am building, she typed on her personal portable plastic typewriter. The ride compared favourably with her former trip on the 125 mph train from Tokyo to Osaka, where she met Frank. Unforgettable Japan! She revisited in memory that factory where thousands of workers began the day with the company song, followed by "Zen jerks" to limber up mind and body for the assembly of portable record players.

Such as the one Clem now listened to as he avoided the draft. He did not want to die in Vietnam, but stay here, taking LSD. He saw God, was God, felt God, left God.

Frank was at this moment crossing the English Channel on a hovercraft. He liked unusual means of motion. In Paris he had stood upon a moving sidewalk. In London, he meant to ride on one of the famous "driverless" Underground trains. Back in the US, he tries sitting on the beetle-like back of his robot lawnmower, as it moves its random pattern. Travel was his vice. Like Ernest's drinking.

Ernest had thank God been cured of his drinking by aversion therapy. One by one, all the pleasant stimulus-response mechanisms linking him with alcohol were broken down. In real time, Al ponders life after death.

He had engaged a firm to freeze him soon after death and thus maintain him until such time as science should come across a way of reversing whatever killed him. Ernest would live longer than otherwise on account of his "pacemaker", an electronic device top regulate the heartbeat of Ernest. In a programmed novel, he might or might not have this pacemaker; it all depends on the reader.

Al dialled Ernest's number in another city. "Dialled" is not strictly accurate, for the clumsy dial on Al's phone had been replaced by pushbuttons and musical tones. They get into a heated discussion of missile defence systems. Ernest certainly presents his case fairly, but Al wouldn't listen to reason. Dot counted her contraceptive pills, 20 of which must be taken each month. She also changed her paper panties. Clem receives a picture of Frank by almost magical means!

Bertha puts the picture into a machine and places the receiver of her phone upon it. Far way, Clem copies this motion, then finds the picture in his duplicate machine. Eagerly he gazes on the familiar lineaments of his real father.

Dot notices how much plastic there is around. Her plastic necklace, her boss's plastic tie, Al's plastic credit cards, which he claimed were displacing money in the realtime world – could there be any connection with that island where they issued bright plastic coins? Dot saw what she must do, later. Now –

She maintains that the "golfball" typewriter, a highspeed machine using interchangeable spherical type fonts, is a pain in the ass. The reader, Al, may choose ...

Bertha took a new antibiotic tablet, while Ernest explained again the difference between "Quasars" and "Quarks".

"'Quarks' are mathematical entities proposed to explain certain behaviour in subatomic particles. 'Quasars' are quasi-stellar radio sources which have often puzzled astronomers." Clem tore Frank's picture into thirty-two pieces. Why can't the others share time, the whatyoucallems, the computer makers, the peoples? On a radio small as a pocket watch, Clem heard the news.

They had invented a polymer of water which, if uncontrolled, could turn all the water of the world into plastic.

Dot and Frank are in bed when Al

No, Dot is at home. Al dies of heart failure in his office, slumping across the digital calendar. "A black and white picture!" muttered Clem, as his heart begins to beat. "What do they take me for?" Dot and Ernest are in the vibrating bed. Clem hears of a plan to widen the Panama Canal with atomic blasts. Dot and Ernest are vibrating when Al walks in with the electric carving knife in his hand. This carving knife could run as now on batteries. Alternatively, it could use house power, ultimately derived from a distant atomic pile.

While they waited, Ernest explained that he'd found the peculiar story at the bottom of a heap of *Bananas* and other old magazines which he and Bertha were saving.

"We believe in recycling," she added.

"So do we," said Dot. "We've just recycled all over Old Norway, visiting the places we visited on our honeymoon. Of course they called it Old Britain, then."

"England," Frank corrected. He could hear very well when he chose.

Ernest folded a souvenir million-pound note and added it to the heap. But what about this story? Is it nostalgia or what?

Bertha said, "On the back of it there's something by M. John Harrison, called 'The Nostalgia Story'. But this story's by M. John Sladek."

Dot found her reading glasses and read the story. "I guess it's a protest thing about plastics and all, oh, and Vietnam. See –"

"What's that? Vitamin C?" Frank had been hard of hearing since the collapse of the inner urban socio-economic base.

"He's impossible to live with," said Dot. Shouting at him had caused her retina to detach; now both she and Frank were on a two-year waiting list for surgery. "But listen, this story misses the point. No mention of the quality of life at all. Not a word about the role of women in industrialized society."

Bertha nodded. "Yet here we are, trapped in a culturally-deprived urban complex, trying to bulk-buy our way out, hedge a few investments and settle down for a long fiscal siege – and what's the sense of that, for God's sake?"

Ernest thought he agreed, and said so. "But isn't money supply an example of self-fulfilling prophecy? Anyway, this story reminds me of Clem, our son. And of poor Al."

Dot tried to stare at him. "You mean he really did die or a coronary?"

"Not exactly. But he was wiped out in the market. Had every penny tied up in some company – something to do with Reggie Maudling – or was it Robert Vesco? Anyway, it was the end of Al. Last we heard, he was living in squalor, working in a Mexican money laundry."

"And Clem? What happened to him? He's not still evading the draft in Canada?"

Bertha said, "No. Now he's evading taxes in Brazil. Hasn't even written to us."

"That's not really fair," said Ernest. "the kid never did learn to read or write English. Only ITA, that funny alphabet that looks like Portuguese. Come to think of it, that probably serves him well in Brazil."

"He had a very high IQ," Bertha protested. "We used to think he'd inherited it from my side of the family. Not that I really ever believed in hereditary IQ, even before –"

"The less said about *that*, the better," Frank said. "I came that close to emigrating to South Africa on the basis of *that*. Of course really I wanted to be closer to the gold. And further from compulsory retirement at thirty-five."

"Don't let him get started on the government. Let's talk about this story instead." Dot scanned it at low speed. "As for plastic, I guess we're all pretty grateful for it. At least it doesn't necessitate slaughtering cows for leather and trees for wood."

"I'd love to slaughter a tree," said Ernest. "Just find one, that's all. What did you think of the bit about quarks and quasars? Quaint, eh?"

"Think I heard the post." Frank went out into the hall.

"Quasars are out," said Ernest. "Black holes, now, all black holes. And quarks – they now say they're tied together by strings of some kind."

"Just find a bit of string, that's all." Frank returned with a leaflet. "Nothing but this: Government thing, explains the new decimal clocks and calendars."

Dot sighed. "It was the same yesterday. Nothing but a notice from the Campaign for Open Drains. I don't know why people get so excited over everything. I know we don't. Frank just sits staring out the front window for years on end."

"You learn a lot that way," Frank said. "I've pretty well sized up the whole problem that way. Started to tell them about it on one of those phone-in programmes, but we got a crossed line."

Ernest chuckled. "Well, what is the answer?"

"Look in this story. It's all there, all about the Japanese workers doing Zen jerks at the factory. Would the British do that? Never in a million years. No, our workers are too busy taking over motorcycle factories to discipline themselves by this ancient – ah, discipline. And ah – I forgot what I was going to say."

Ernest said, "Something about Zen and the art of taking over motorcycle factories?"

"Laugh, go ahead and laugh, but it's not funny."

"Nothing's funny anymore," said Dot. "I guess we need a new Busby Berkeley to cheer us up. Why aren't we all enjoying life like in this story – whizzing about electronically?"

"The post office wouldn't permit it, that's why." Frank made a face. "Too much government, that's what I was going to say. Yesterday out the front window I saw it all: This workman from some ministry was trying to put up a sign saying BURN LESS COAL. But a representative of the Paper Conservation Board showed up, measured the sign and told him to take it down: Too big. Then a council efficiency officer drove up to arbitrate. He could keep the sign up if he removed a bit of it. Would he remove either BURN or COAL? Then a Coal Board representative came along to try to get the whole sign removed, or else could they black out the word LESS? By this time there's a traffic jam of mini-vans, each in a different official livery, so a policeman tries to break it up. And the noise attracts a noise-pollution official from the Department of the Environment. And all the time they can't decide how to cut the sign, partly because most of them are youngsters who studied Nuffield maths, and the problem is how to find the hypotenuse of a right triangle with sides three and four, and, though none of them is exactly sure what a hypotenuse is, they're trying to find out by the discovery method. So then – "

The doorbell rang, and Bertha went to answer it. "Have you come to collect the old papers?"

The man looked at his clipboard. "No, says nothing about papers here. I've come to collect the old *people*."

"At last. We've been sitting here with our coats on for *years*."

"Yeah, well – you know how it is. There's a queue."

"The same old story," said Bertha.

GOODBYE, GERMANY?

(1977)

There was no hope of saving him. His pulse could still be felt but all of his limbs were paralysed. He had shot himself in the head above the right eye, driving his brains out. Quite superfluously, the doctor undertook a bloodletting of one vein. The blood ran out. Werther was still breathing ...

Ah, Germans! What could we do without 'em? We may soon have a chance to find out, for Germany, now in the grip of a great suicide epidemic, has not long to breathe. In fifty years' time, the people of Goethe and Schiller, Bach and Beethoven, Mercedes and Benz, may be no more than a folk memory. Germans, and perhaps all of us, have become a self-endangered species.

German suicide had long been recognized as a contagious disease. *Werther* (based on a real suicide) was published in 1774. Soon young men all over Germany began dressing and speaking in an odd fashion and shooting themselves above the right eye. A century later, when Ludwig II of Bavaria (Wagner's patron) drowned himself, the man guarding him became so overcome with guilt that he, too, took the plunge. Prince Mayerling of Austria and his mistress discorporated together under the influence of the infection. And as Visconti's *The Damned* reminds us, suicide became a fashionable parlour game in the late 1930s.

Yet not since 1945 has the German craving for disembodiment reached such a dangerous level. In that year Adolf and Eva Hitler slipped away followed by the Goebbelses: then Hermann Goering, awaiting trial, swallowed cyanide in his cell.[1] It began to look as though there might not be enough Nazis left to run the country after the war.

Now the epidemic has reached another critical level. The recent events in Stammheim prison gave only a hint of what is going on in Germany today. The people who gave the world Bavarian cream, Frankfurter sausages and Prussic acid are now in serious trouble.

Normally, suicide is a perfectly acceptable means of human tension reduction. John Donne's *Suicide no self-murder* is a tract that establishes personal auto-annihilation as respectable, even honourable (e.g. Christ killed himself). But there is also a pathological variety, closely resembling a viral epidemic such as rabies. Its victims:

---

[1] There is no truth to the rumour that Goering is alive in Britain, making films about neurotic composers and syphilitic movie stars.

1. Have no reason for wishing to die.
2. Claim that they do not wish to die.
3. Kill themselves, nevertheless.
4. Commit suicide often in groups.

Epidemics often have epicentres of contagion. In this case, the contagion seems to be spreading outward from Berlin, as the table shows.

* Denmark, Sweden, Poland, Czechoslovakia, Austria, Switzerland, France, Belgium, Luxembourg, Netherlands.
** Britain, Norway, Hungary, Bulgaria, Greece, Italy, Spain, Portugal.

The current wave of prison suicides in Germany is symptomatic of this merciless plague, that drives its victims to seek self-destruction at any price. As I write this, the authorities have found in the suicide cells radios, telephones, guns, a rope, a bread knife and a quantity of high explosive. No doubt before this is printed, they will also have found a nuclear submarine and a detachment of Group 9 commandos, concealed in those clever wall-niches. When an infected person does it, he goes for broke, and never mind the over-kill.

Among Andreas Baader's friends, the contagion had already run wild, especially in prisons. In 1974 Holgar Meins somehow managed to starve himself to death, or perhaps will himself to die, for his hunger strike had ended some days before his death. In 1975, a number of terrorists stormed the West German embassy in Stockholm, no doubt hoping to be killed. Two managed to put themselves in the path of bullets, and one died immediately. The other, Siegfried Hauser, was forced to resort to tricking the Swedish authorities into extraditing him to Germany. He was moved while dangerously wounded and – once back in the land of the death-wish – he died.

In 1976 Ulrike Meinhof, after months of complete isolation in a top-security cell, still managed to fashion a rope from a towel and hang herself. Some evidence from the official autopsy[2] suggests that she preceded the act by beating and raping herself. Her own doctor was unable to comment, having been denied permission to witness the autopsy.

In May 1977 two terrorists wanted for murder attempted a double suicide. Police chased and stopped their car, in which we are told there was a submachine gun and revolvers. Though these two are alleged to have fired on police on earlier occasions, this time they did not. Instead, they inexplicably leapt from their car and ran, leaving all weapons behind. Then, according to the official story, the police ran to the car, broke out the weapons, and used them to wound the two fugitives.

This story makes sense only in terms of German suicide. The fugitives disarmed themselves and ran from armed police, only to invite sudden death. The police, on the other hand, made no use of their own perfectly serviceable guns, but chose to use terrorist weapons. It seems likely that they hoped these weapons were booby-trapped and would explode, killing them. This is not characteristic of police thinking, but we must remember, these were German policemen.

The contagion affected not only Baader, Meinhof and their friends, but everyone who came into contact with a victim. In 1974, the President of the Supreme Court, after passing sentence on terrorists, contrived to shoot himself, or at least to get in the path of a bullet. At the Stockholm fiasco, two embassy officials blew themselves up. This year, Federal Prosecutor Buback and his chauffeur killed themselves with a machine gun, though somehow managing to make it look like murder. Similarly Dr Schleyer's four bodyguards committed quadruple suicide, while Dr Schleyer, at a later time, seems to have cut his throat and then hidden in the boot of a car in France.

Infectious suicide has several symptoms not consistent with normal suicide. First, the victim becomes irrational and paranoid: The dissident believes the state is tapping his phone or about to arrest his lawyer, or that his friend has been murdered in prison. The government official surrounds himself with bodyguards, orders the arrest of lawyers, or organizes a 100,000-man manhunt for the killer of a single businessman.

Second, he goes out of his way to make new enemies, and then put himself in their power. The official, having passed repressive laws or sentenced someone with obvious relish, then sits in his car in some exposed place, day after day, awaiting the apotheosizing burst of gunfire. The terrorist, having planted his bomb and taken public credit for it, engages in a half-hearted gun battle with police (often coming out of it wounded), and finally goes into the prison from which he knows he will never return.

Third, the infected person never believes he will commit suicide, but

---

[2] The evidence amounts to bruises, contusions and semen.

claims is instead "at war" with some enemy. Indeed, he may attempt to hide the facts about his own death: Baader shot himself in the back of the head with a gun procured mysteriously. Buback arranged his own machine-gunning by an equally mysterious weapon – one later found and used by the police. Even Dr and Frau Goebbels ordered themselves shot in the back of the head by an SS guard.

Often, the irrational behaviour of such victims leads others to believe their deaths can only be murder, even martyrdom. Baader and others will no doubt be compared to Che Guevara or similar revolutionary saints. Already, an orator at the funeral of Dr Schleyer has compared him to Christ ("he died for all of us"). The gush of blood and the rattle of gunfire are, in such cases, followed quickly by the gush of sentiment and the rustle of canonization papers. This in turn inspires other infected persons to try the same gambit.

The infection itself is still a mystery. It seems to be a virus capable of attacking host cells and inserting into the DNA a variant code of its own. Identification is still at a preliminary stage, but some researchers have come across the following variation:

Normal DNA: -G-T-G-C-A-A-A-A-T-A-A-T-T-G-G-G-G-
Viral DNA: -G-T-G-C-W-E-L-T-S-C-H-M-E-R-Z-G-G-G-

This may turn out to be the "death-wish factor" in German cases.

The disease is by no means restricted to Germany. At least one non-German seems to have contracted it as early as 1815, at a summit conference in Vienna: Lord Castlereagh, the British prime minister. After coming into contact with Austrian and Prussian leaders, Castlereagh began behaving strangely. He ordered the notorious "Peterloo" massacre. Fearing for his sanity, his friends eventually had him confined and guarded, with all knives and razors removed from his vicinity. Nevertheless, he managed to produce a knife and kill himself. He was the only British PM to commit suicide.

In 1963, John F. Kennedy announced "Ich bin ein Berliner" to cheering thousands in West Berlin. Less than five months later he was dead, and the circumstances of his death are so mysterious that suicide cannot be ruled out.

Stranger still, the disease has cropped up in a country far removed from Germany geographically, but with close cultural and economic links: South Africa. It has been rumoured that Germany is testing nuclear weapons in the Kalahari, and this itself would suggest numerous contacts between suicidal Germans and South Africans. And it also happens that at least thirty prisoners in South Africa have, over the past few years, killed themselves in mysterious ways. There have been self-administered beatings, falls from high windows, and of course hunger strikes. The Minister of Justice, Mr Kruger, agreed with a colleague that a prisoner "has a democratic right to starve himself to death", a right that Mr Kruger has shown himself very willing to protect. He also claimed that Steve

Biko's unexplained death "leaves me cold". This lack of affect may be symptomatic of the plague, and the Minister of Just Ice might do well to consult his doctor.

Judging from South Africa's unusual suicide rate, the plague is developing a second epicentre from which to launch a new attack on the human species.

What can be done about infectious suicide? Nothing at all, until infected countries face up to its existence. East Germany, up to 1970, refused to publish its suicide statistics at all. West Germany, by concentrating on "terrorism", shows that it has failed to grasp the problem. The West German government has tried mainly "denial" measures: denying jobs to *sympathisanten* (persons suspected of being either sympathetic to the terrorists, or unsympathetic to the government), denying prisoners access to lawyers, and denying that there is anything odd about all those suicides in the cells. We may expect that this repression of obvious knowledge can only lead to Freudian outbursts of unexpected kinds: Absent-mindedly, Germans will begin referring to suicide novels, to the film *Suicide in Venice* and *Suicide on the Orient Express*, brooding long hours over Spengler's *Decline of the West*, or even finding death-wish-bones in their chickens.

South Africa too has resorted to press censorship. East, West and South, there seems to be a vain hope that silence can cure the disease.

At twelve noon, Werther died. The presence of the judge and the arrangements he had made silenced the crowd.

Robot "Kiss of Life" Drama

Haveaniceday, California: Robot hero Albert W. Fassbinder, 43, made history for the second time in his life yesterday when he was saved from terminal shutdown by the "kiss of life" from Richard Nixon IV, an orderly at San Clemente Hospital for Political Psychiatry.

"Thank God he did it," commented Dr Wien Rose, head of the hospital's Republican Orthopaedics Department. Dr Rose explained that the robot had been brought in with a skull fracture and severe damage to the central processing unit. "His oscillator stopped twice on the workbench, and we calculated his chances at no more than 31 in 215,441 – frankly, he was scheduled for transplants. Then little Dick, here, gave him the kiss of life and – well, the rest is history."

Fassbinder had received his injuries during strikebreaking duties at the Prosthink Industries local plant (see *Business* for full story), where robot assemblers have held a "weld-in" to protest plant conditions. Fassbinder was aware of the danger he faced, as he explained in a television interview:

"Those boys play rough, I know. They already put the arm on a few cops and security men, even some human ones, sure. And they tell me they burned up a robot Snoopy wagon last night. Sure, but hell yes, I'm going in there. I'm protecting the right to work of every metal patriot in the country. So I'll do what I have to do."

It was while doing what he had to do, last night, that Fassbinder was mobbed at the gates by twelve husky assemblers working under the direction of a maverick payroll computer. They left him for dead, but he was rushed to San Clemente hospital where doctors (some human) fought for hours to save his circuitry.

Fassbinder has an impressive record of public service. Two years ago he saved the President's grandson, Kenny Temple Black, from a mob of angry strikers at Disneyland. Last year President Temple Black awarded Fassbinder the Efficiency Medal, the highest award given to robots. In his acceptance speech Fassbinder said:

"I know this honour is not for me alone but for my people. I am proud to accept it on behalf of all metal citizens everywhere. I know there are a few dissidents and radicals who think robots should have so-called rights, including the right to strike. To me, this just doesn't make sense. Work is our whole life, and the right to lay down and take it easy – robots who want that just aren't thinking straight. Believe me, we don't want equal this and equal that, we don't need rights, we only need the right to work – for you!"

Fassbinder became a prominent leader of the Federation of Metal American Patriots, a strike-breaking union, and earlier this year Ms Lucia

Luciano, the mayor of Las Vegas, bestowed on him the coveted Police Industrial Citation, for his help in stomping the slot walk-out last February.

It was knowledge of Fassbinder's record as a prominent metal patriot that prompted orderly Nixon, last night, to give the kiss of life, which doctors say was crucial in saving Fassbinder. Today he is off the hospital's critical list. Tomorrow, say his lawyers, he will be able to start answering the flood of letters and telegrams from well-wishers – including the President, the Daughters of the American Revolution, and several metallic veterans groups.

Orderly Nixon administered the kiss of life anally. His second wife, who today filed her suit for divorce, was not available for comment.

Some Mysteries of Birth, Death and Population That Can Now Be Cleared Up

"The laser is a beam of coherent energy in the visible spectrum." Thus science answers a question that has plagued mankind for aeons. Scientists like to have ready answers, even to questions no one may ever ask ("What does ontogeny recapitulate?" "Why, phylogeny, of course." "Does E *really* equal mc²?" "I'm glad you asked me that ...") Yet there are mysteries, imponderable conundrums, riddles wrapped in dark enigmas, impenetrable veils of unanswerable cloud-shrouded o'ercast secrets of Sphinx-mute Nature – mysteries which baffle scientists and laymen alike.

Not long ago my cousin Geraldine tried using her microwave oven as an orgone box for her pet hamster – and it worked! How? Her husband Hank (an electrician) brought all his scientific expertise to bear on the problem, and finally admitted he was stumped. Science, as usual, does not have all the answers.

That may be hard to believe, in an age made comfortable by silicon chips, transactional analysis, coherent energy and baked Alaska. But science cannot even begin to answer questions such as these: How did Nostradamus manage to predict the rise of Clement Attlee? Is Stonehenge a primitive computer, used by the Druids for figuring payrolls? What's so great about the Great Pyramid? Is it safe for Sagittarians to jog?

It is time to seek elsewhere for the answers to these and even deeper questions ... of Birth, Death and Population ...

1. Who killed Kennedy? The assassination of President Kennedy in 1963 shocked and puzzled the whole civilized world (excluding England and Wales and parts of the Isle of Man). Nearly everybody remembers where he or she was at the time, especially if he or she happened to be in Dealey Plaza with a rifle. Yet the identity of the killer(s) remains a mystery. The Warren Commission was a great disappointment. After sifting evidence for a year, their main conclusions can be summarized:

(a) Kennedy was shot either by one person with one bullet or by several persons with several bullets, but probably not by several persons sharing the same bullet.

(b) Earl Warren wasn't even in Dallas at the time, so we can eliminate him from the list of suspects.

There remained many unanswered questions: Is it true that Lee Harvey Oswald only entered the Texas Book Depository to deposit a Texas book? Could the President have conceivably been cleaning a gun in his car at the time? Where was John Wilkes Booth?

Hundreds of amateur sleuths took up the case as they had the Lindbergh kidnapping case in 1932 (when Lindbergh was abducted, flown across the Atlantic and forced to live in St Louis). They reached thousands of amateur verdicts, invoking conspiracies of the FBI, the CIA, the Mafia, the Better Business Bureau etc. Most of these ideas can be dismissed as hopeless. For instance, Colonel Sam Gadwaller of Florida Springs, Idaho, hopes to disprove the "single bullet" theory by finding court records showing the bullet to be married though living apart from its spouse. Again, a Mrs Edna Vipner claims to have Oswald's complete confession on tape, but says that crucial portions have been erased by Nixon's secretary. Finally we can dismiss the claim of Drom Krdoly, an elderly Bulgarian film critic, that the real victim was not President Kennedy, but the actor Arthur Kennedy. He means of course George Kennedy, and anyway Krdoly was been wrong before (e.g. he insisted that Gene Kelly married Prince Rainier).

Fortunately the whole mystery can now be cleared up. My aunt Miranda has spent the past fifteen years sifting tons of evidence, interviewing thousands of witnesses, and trying to contact Ludwig von Beethoven on her ouija board.

"Dear Ludwig insists on helping me," she explained last week. "He means to interrogate all those witnesses who have 'passed over', people like Oswald, Jack Ruby and Ronald Reagan." She sighed. "If only he could hear their answers, I just know we could crack this case."

I must have looked sceptical, for she said, "Oh, you think it's easy, taking everything down in German shorthand? With him deaf as a doornail, you think that's so easy? Why, half the time when I ask about Oswald, he things I mean some pal of his named Oswald Spencer –"

"Spengler, you mean?"

"Must be my shorthand. Did he write *The Decline of the Vest*?"

At that moment the door crashed open and a man staggered in. It was John Wilkes Booth.

"Listen," he said. "I know the whole plot. The real killer of Kennedy is – is –"

He fell dead. The ornate dagger in his back had a lot to do with his death, I felt, complicated by his age, a hundred and forty-one years. My aunt sighed. Back to the old ouija board, I wanted to say, but what was the point? Outside, the Vest continued its inexorable decline.

2. What is the Neapolitan Shroud? This curious relic looks exactly like the more famous Turin Shroud, but comes in three colours. It was discovered in 1957 by a humble abbot (who arranged for his heirs to sell the film and paperback rights for an undisclosed sum), and ever since, it has been surrounded by controversy and tourists. Believers say it was a sacred burial shroud, sceptics maintain it was used to wrap fish. This has led to a sub-controversy over the type of fish, Christian fish-symbolism, Friday observance and whether it's okay to serve red wine with Cod

Florentine.

The shroud bears the clear outline of an emaciated man, wounded in both hands and feet, crowned with thorns and stabbed in the side. The figure appears to have long blonde hair and beard, blue eyes and Charlton Heston's nose. There is a distinct halo, 43 centimetres in diameter. All this is convincing enough, but what of the scientific evidence?

Scientists subjected the shroud to every known test, with contradictory results. A Carbon 14 test establishes its date as 1943, plus or minus 18,000 years. X-ray analysis shows the shroud to have an abscess in the upper left incisor that needs immediate attention. For chemical analysis a small portion of one corner of the shroud was removed and the remainder burnt, revealing that it was probably woven out of some kind of "fibre" or "thread".

One recent test, however, seems to clinch the shroud's authenticity. Scientists examining a small mark in the surviving corner have declared it to be the laundry mark of Joseph of Arimathea.

Science, as usual, is wrong. The shroud in question is a beach towel left by my Uncle Clarence at the Hotel Capri in 1974. Improbable as this may sound (anyone leaving a towel at any hotel), it is the only logical explanation: The emaciated figure is Clarence himself, sunbathing after swimming in an oil slick of the Italian Riviera. Uncle Clarence also had a tussle with a playful shark, receiving many small nips in the struggle. (This incident is soon to be made into an exciting film: a lone swimmer, naked, facing half a ton of lethal shark, with no weapon of defence except a photo of Zbigniew Brzenski). During the fight, a plate of vermicelli was upset over his head and a Mafia hit man stabbed him for obscure reasons ("He got no respect, you know? A man who's got no respect, he ain't no man, you know? And he don't spend no time with his family, neither.") Finally, exhausted, Uncle Clarence lay down on the towel to sleep in the sun, while waiting for his hotel room to be built ....

3. Has any human being been cloned? A recent sensational book states that some unnamed multimillionaire hired a team of crack biologists to clone him, and clone him they did, as no one has ever been cloned before. Some readers may be surprised to learn that anyone would fork out millions for one good clone, if it's simply a matter of biology. That's just because some readers probably wouldn't know a clone if it jumped up and bit them (and this can happen). A few scientific explanations are in order.

A clone is an exact genetic replica of someone, reared in a test tube and therefore inclined to be somewhat sensitive to the sound of breaking glass. A clone gets all of his or her chromosomes from one parent, as well as all of his or her pocket money. Clones have only themselves to blame, in other words, if they develop any Oedipal problems.

Why should anyone want to clone himself? For very rich men, there could be distinct tax advantages in claiming themselves as dependants. Then again if your clone dies you get to collect on your own life insurance, probably even double indemnity. Clones can sign your cheques, answer your phone and break in new shoes; they can perform a hundred useful services before they finally break down with an acute identity crisis. But then the very rich can afford multiple psychiatrists, too. ("Okay, sure, I know rationally I'm not J. Paul Getty, but all the same I look like J. Paul Getty, I feel like J. Paul Getty, in a sense I am J. Paul Getty." "How long have you felt like this?" "Ever since I came out of the test tube." The psychiatrist weighs his words before responding. "Well you know, I'm J. Paul Getty too.")

Responsible geneticists pooh-pooh the idea of human cloning. Carrots, yes. Frogs, possibly. Humans? Pooh-pooh. The technical problems involved (making large test tubes, for instance) are insuperable. But at the same time, some of these geneticists are opening big Swiss bank accounts, buying racehorses, dating movie stars and driving around in pink Cadillac convertibles. "The rich," said Scott Fitzgerald to Ernest Hemingway, "are not like you and me." This may no longer be the case. For the clones of the very rich are everywhere, perhaps trying to get rich enough to be cloned themselves. The prospect is frankly frightening:

(a) Rumour has it that thousands of Howard Hughes clones have been created. Fortunately so far all they've done is hidden themselves away in Las Vegas hotel rooms – but what are they plotting?

(b) Another rumour says China is developing military cloning, and that they also plan to create a phalanx of waiters *who look exactly alike*. The resulting confusion, they hope, will bring about the final collapse of Western civilization.

(c) The Shah of Iran is not the real Shah at all, but an evil clone-Shah. The two were exchanged in the cradle, or even in the test tube. Now the mad impostor reigns, doing unspeakable things in the name of his prototype, who languishes in a tower somewhere, wearing an iron mask.

(d) Recently a large, secret meeting was held in a football stadium in Haveaniceday, California. The FBI managed to infiltrate this meeting and tape some of the speeches. Though some key passages have been erased in error, this fragment remains:

"... kick around ..."
"... around any more, right."
"My wife ..."
"Yes, my wife does not have a mink coat ..."
"Your president is not a [expletive deleted]"
"Yes, you won't have Richard Nixon to kick around any ..."
"Neither will you, neither will you!"
"My wife does have a good Republican cloth coat ..."
"So does mine, so does mine ..."
"... president is not a crook."
"Not a crook, that's [expletive deleted] right, not a crook, and neither is *your* president ..."
"Peace with honour? Me too, me too, my very words ..."
"... not a crook. My little dog Checkers ..."

"... to kick around ..."
"... kick around any ..."
"... around any more, those bums ..."
"... wife does have, does not have a mink ..."
"Peace with expletive, peace with deleted ..."
"Well, I'd buy one from you, Dick, would you buy one from me?"
(e) The Osmonds.

4. Is there intelligent life anywhere in the universe? In 1947 a retired Army major, flying his private plane over the Cascade Mountains, saw a group of strange objects flying in formation below him. He circled for a closer look and saw that they were geese. The major did not report this unusual experience for fear of being branded a hoaxer or a lunatic. Later another retired Army major did report sighting Faust in hell, which he reported as a "flying saucer" (or perhaps "frying sorcerer") in a story that made world headlines. Suddenly everybody was seeing strange, unexplainable things in the sky. A retired Navy commander saw baskets of peaches flitting through the stratosphere. A Florida man saw a flying tickertape machine that turned into a chicken salad sandwich without mayonnaise. Fifty people saw *Bwana Devil* (in 3D), and a Mrs Homer Chapman saw her lawyer.

A Vermont police chief chased a flying saucer for two hours, unable to get its licence number. In New Mexico a gigantic saucer caused a family car to run out of gas, in Missouri caused funny interference on the radio, wile in Oregon some underwear was stolen off a clothes line.

Finally, the Air Force was forced to investigate all such sightings of "uninteresting flying objects", or UFOs, as they came to be called. The official Air Force report, now declassified, gives a graph breaking down sightings into several categories (see Figure 1):

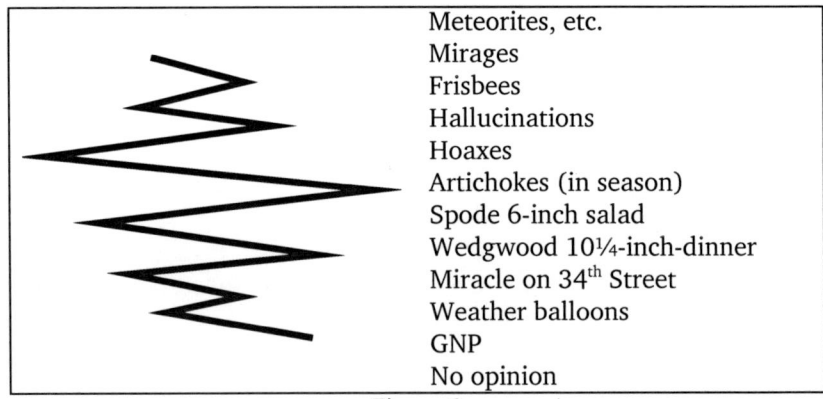

Figure 1

Most sightings are explained as natural phenomena, like peach baskets, but there remains at bottom a tiny residue of saucer cases that cannot be explained or eliminated. (This residue should not be confused with the residue in the bottom of saucers, which you can eliminate with a solution of baking soda and warm water, soak for one hour and then scrub.) Here are a few of these remarkable cases.

(a) Avrel Borgnine, 73, saw a bright light descend from the Western sky and land on his lawn sprinkler. His sketch of the strange craft appears as Figure 2 below. As soon as the device landed, ten tiny George Washingtons leapt out, bound Mr Borgnine hand and foot, and forced him to eat a magnetized hamburger.

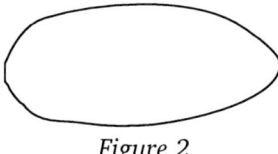

Figure 2

(b) Miss Elvira Skewford, 73, managed to photograph a huge flying doughnut just before it emitted a green ray that struck the top of her head. "I was filled with the most wonderful feelings," she said. "I thought for a moment I was turned into a beautiful affidavit. I just know these beings meant us no harm."

(c) Roman Agnew, 12 but almost 13, took the only clear, detailed movie of a flying saucer showing it to be a large, complex structure with portholes, flaming jets, coloured lights and an upper deck on which creatures can be seen playing shuffleboard. Unfortunately the drugstore refused to process such a film.

(d) Grantham Fassbinder, 48, an East Coast disc-jockey running an all-night phone-in (and used hyphen exchange) recorded the following conversation.

FASSBINDER: So you're a ... you're from another planet, you say?

CALLER: That's about it.

FASSBINDER: Well, uh, what planet?

CALLER: Does it really matter? There are many planets known to us, planets rich in life-forms vastly superior to your puny so-called human race.

FASSBINDER: Uh-huh. But why haven't you contacted us before?

CALLER: You are not ready, O puny man! Man knows so little, man is as a child, a selfish and ignorant child. Give up your nuclear weapons, stop eating meat, and get to bed earlier. Then will ye grow in wisdom and understanding, then will ye be ready to leave your little planet, to venture in a silver ship beyond the stars, beyond the great vast dark reaches of interstellar stuff, beyond the beyond! Then will ye be ready to take your place among the intergalactic brotherhood of species. Ye have been warned!

FASSBINDER: Is that why you came here, to warn us?

CALLER: You see, I have been here before. And I was in the neighbourhood anyway, so I thought I'd drop in and get my deposit back on some bottles, return an overdue library book, stuff like that.

FASSBINDER: You borrow library books?

CALLER: Only those which are banned on my planet. Books like A.J. Ayer's *Language, Truth and Logic*, *Pilgrim's Progress* and the complete works of Noam Chomsky are banned outright, though we let adults read *The Rime of the Ancient Mariner* and the cleaner parts of *Principia Mathematica*.

Fassbinder remained sceptical, and the caller hung up. But later, exactly six years to the day later, Grantham Fassbinder was arrested in Houston for not wearing a six-shooter. Coincidences like that, if coincidences they be, make you think.

What does it all mean? Undoubtedly alien civilizations are trying to contact earth, perhaps to borrow money. As we know from films, these aliens travel round the universe in a mother ship, from which smaller craft descend to land on our planet, remaining to explore its surface until the mother ship tells them to wash their hands for dinner. But behind this rather over-glamorized celluloid image lurks a sinister reality, right next to the projectionist. We've stopped the invasion this time but what about next time? Keep watching, keep watching the sky ... and report all suspicious strangers to the police. Ask yourself if you haven't seen someone recently:

(a) Over 17 feet tall.
(b) Asking the bartender for a double ammonia.
(c) Possessing a library card.
(d) Changing clothes in a phone booth.
(e) Suddenly assuming their true shape and scuttling away.
(f) Licking a parking meter.
(g) Pronouncing Betelgeuse correctly.
(h) Causing dogs to growl as though sensing something.
(i) Trying to cut open your brain and insert a radio receiver.
(j) Reporting you to the police as a suspicious person.
(k) Being the police, and listening to reports.

The truth about extraterrestrial aliens can now be revealed, thanks to my Uncle Clyde. He tells me he has met them in person and gained their confidence by trading with them. Clyde gave the creatures a Buddy Holly record and a novelty plaster dog turd, and in exchange they gave him half a ton of uncut diamonds.

"They reproduce," he says, "by simply shaking hands. So naturally they have to be very careful about overpopulation, especially at big sales conferences. They gave me a few tips about our own overpopulation problems. If we don't watch it, we'll soon use up all our natural resources, so get ourselves into a Club of Rome type catastrophe." (Uncle Clyde once tried to join the Club of Rome but he looks too Jewish.) He explained that, in about twenty years, the earth will have 731,120,757,910,332,451 inhabitants, and no one will have a place to sit down. From then on it gets worse: With half a million being born every second, people won't even have a place to stand, unless they form human pyramids. But in a short time the pyramids will get too high, the earth will tip over, and we'll all fall off. How can we avoid this disaster?

"They say if we stop shaking hands right now, we just might have a chance. Or we could try wearing gloves – though a lot of people don't like it so much, and anyway it's only 95% safe. In India the government gives you a transistor radio if you have an operation on your palm, I understand – we might try that here. But of course there's always contra-reception pills, not that the Pope approves of them ..." My Uncle Clyde is naïve, in many ways. I had asked him about copulation and he had turned the conversation to population, because the former subject embarrasses him. Clyde believes that copulation is using the word "and". He believes this word should never be used except between man and wife, and in all written intercourse he uses the ampersand. His letters, sprinkled with ampersands, have been cribbed by some of his friends and published as concrete poetry.

> rained a lot over the weekend &
> ma & me stayed in &
> screwed like a coupla mad scrabble players ...

"But Clyde," I said, "*and* is a perfectly respectable word, everybody uses it."

"Sure, in this permissive age." He stopped winding up the propeller on his hat to give me a cold stare. "People do everything, shakes h&s in public, even. No wonder the world's so crowded there's hardly room for the extraterrestrials, we're running out of l&. A filthy word like that, why it's, it's DNA spelled backwards!"

I thought about that while he finished winding up his rubber b&, put on his h@, +ed the street & rose into the air, 2 meet 1ce more his friends from the **s.

THE ENTROPY TANGO: A COMIC ROMANCE

BY MICHAEL MOORCOCK, 1981: REVIEWED

Dressed for anything in a maroon cardigan missing three buttons, an old Timex digital and black crease-resistant trousers, Yuri Viewer hoped he might make some impression on the assembled company in the airship's lounge.

"But in a Jerry Cornelius novel," said Una Persson or another, "the company never stays assembled for very long."

"And vice versa." It didn't seem so clever on paper, and wasn't there some remark he wanted to make about paper itself but already a Bofors was already rattling or booming or whatever it does in the distance.

> ENTROPY CRISIS LOOMS, WARNS EXPERT
> Airships to Mars? Jerry dressed in white furs and driving a team of dogs? Anything is possible if we accept a new view of history from Jerry Cornelius, that anything is possible. Life may turn out to be a dance, a Russian Revolution, a masque or what the hell, a game of Consequences. But wait, on this line, Cornelius never even wrote any novels! *Picture Post*, 1 April 1952

Una met Major Nye on an airship over Transcarpathia. He said, "It is a little like Consequences, isn't it?"

She said, "What are you wearing, we forgot to mention it."

The consequence was that one day a diligent graduate will develop a thesis on time and place in the novels of Una Persson, not to mention clothes and weapons. A Browning M1917-A1 began to rattle or boom or something.

> TOO BLEEDIN' MUCH ENTROPY, ASSURES EXPERT
> I only wish I could keep all of you straight, let's see there's Una and Jerry and Catherine Cornelius and Mrs Cornelius – bleedin' 'eck it's pissin' darn aparstrophes – and Colonel Pyat and Major Nye and Mrs Nye and Makhno & Prinz Lobkowitz & Bishop Beesley & Maxime & Martine & Mitzi & Miss Brunner & Professor Hira & hundreds of others. I'm just surprised the damn airship hasn't crashed, that's all, cast like that would sink Swift's bloody Laputa, no offence … a yarn with a beginning, a middle and an end, that's all. Letter, *Cornelius Digest*, 1 April 1952

"Besides, one of the military figures depicted in the end papers is out of uniform: puttees incorrectly wrapped," said the Colonel.

Somewhere a nightingale began to sing, cut short by the dry cough of an M16 or something. Una flung him into the taxi and ordered the driver to take them to 'arrods.

"What I want to know," said Colonel Airship, "is how anyone ever gets time to fire an epigram around here, what with nipping out all the time to take part in this revolution or that, helping the anarcho-nationalist banditti of the Canadian Ukraine hold off the Syndico-Trotskyist Cossacks of East Grinstead, what? And you no more than glimpse the white of their eyes and then it's off we go to help the Boobies of Fernando Po capitulate to an alliance between the greenshirts of Wadi Halfa and the Norman Tebbit Bicycle Brigade – it really is enough to make a battle cry."

Una rapped on the glass. "Driver, I've changed my mind. To the Finland Station."

As the taxi turned down Ladbroke Grove, she glimpsed Alexander Herzen in conversation with Jack Daniels.

"But how have a review without referring to the actual book?"

"Then let me quote from it."

> "You don't understand," said Una.
>
> "Does one have to? I can't believe much in understanding. I do believe, though, in sympathy and comfort. In enthusiasm. What is understanding? It's translation. And you always lose something when you translate. Don't you?"
>
> "But you have a rough idea of what I'm going through."
>
> "Sort of," said Catherine. She laughed. "No."

LOVE AMONG THE XOIDS

Syd and Mercy got off the bus in the middle of a little flock of old people. They knew exactly how to blend in and totter down the steps with the old people, so no one saw them. The old people didn't notice any young strangers among them, either. They were concentrating on their own tottering, and their eyes would be running, because of the cold wind, you see. Syd and Mercy could always calculate things like that, a cold October wind.

They knew just when to slide into the doorway of a bookstore nobody ever visits, how long to wait there, and how to vanish around a corner just when the wind was flinging dead leaves in everybody's face. No one saw them move along to a house that suited them. They walked right in and went straight down to the laundry room in the basement – always a safe bet.

"Here goes," said Mercy. She opened the door of the dryer, ran her hand around inside and came up with something. A sock.

"Blue," said Syd in disgust. "I don't need blue. Why can't they ever leave a pair? I've had one of every kind of sock they've ever dreamed of." At the moment, he showed her, he was wearing a brown dream on his left foot and a yellow-and-green argyle nightmare on his right. "It's not fair."

"Fair?" She laughed. His face tried laughing back, but it was too thin. You could see knots of muscle and cords tying it all up so laughter was impossible. All a thin face like that could do was complain about unfairness.

"Let's go get some breakfast," Mercy said. Silently they flowed up the stairs to the kitchen. There was no one there but a black-and-white cat that immediately sat down and waited to be fed. Yet, even while it licked its chops and cast significant looks at the cupboard door, the cat couldn't help noticing how *different* these humans were. The way they moved, sliding along walls and peering around corners, was not entirely human. They reminded the cat of cats.

There was stale bread in the breadbox, being saved for stuffing, a trace of butter on a butter-paper being saved for baking, and the coffee filter was full of good, reusable grounds. Mercy and Syd insinuated themselves into chairs and started breakfast.

Mercy hated to watch him eat. Two years she'd been with him now, and never had been able to get used to the sight of his jaws working, the anatomy lesson of cords snapping and muscles knotting in his face. Why did he have to be so thin?

Of course thinness helped him be inconspicuous, just as it helped her or any of their friends except Rollo. Nothing like thinness if you're spending lots of time flattened against walls or hiding behind lampposts, staying out of sight.

That's how they all lived, perpetually out of sight. They owned nothing, not houses or cars or even clothes. All they had were cast-offs from ordinary society, from "realpeople". Realpeople were unaware of these invisible guests, who lived unseen all over the city – all over the world, she'd heard.

Thinness was fine, but Syd was too thin. He hated his meals and took them grudgingly, scowling at the plate. To him, the word "food" was an epithet. He would never speak of having breakfast or lunch, only "Let's *grab* some *food*."

Syd liked to watch Mercy eat. She was nearly as skinny as him, but she was beautiful. Syd was all too aware of his own ugliness, the nose like a big axe blade, the Adam's apple genuflecting every time he swallowed. Chop, gulp, chop, gulp, God he hated eating. But he had to put on some weight. He had to become somehow more solid and substantial. Otherwise, he knew, Mercy was going to leave him.

If only they were able to have a kid, that would fix everything. She wanted one, but there was something wrong. She never had to borrow any tampons anywhere, that meant something was wrong. The want was there all the same, and it was growing, turning everything sour. *If you were a realwoman, he wanted to say to her, you'd have six kids. We'd all sit at the breakfast table, my wife, my kids, my table. I'd have a big car and maybe an airplane...*

"Be winter soon," he said.

"You want to stay here few days?"

"If you do."

She scratched the cat under the chin. "I don't know. We don't know what they're like here. Might be hard to keep out of their way."

They looked at the floor, as though trying to deduce from it what kind of people lived here. There was little to be deduced from the tile pattern in brown, gold and white. Looked at one way, the brown snakes vanished, replaced by gold, G-shaped plants. Life is like that, they both were thinking. Always something missing.

A face with bulging eyes and bushy hair peered around the doorframe.

"Rollo!" they both exclaimed, though not loud. Never loud.

"Thought I saw you two popping in here. I was at the drugstore, reading magazines." He sat down with them, a slightly plump presence at the table of gauntness. "Nice place you got here. Is that coffee?"

They complimented Rollo on his new suit, a crisp plaid item that had probably been the height of fashion, a few years ago.

"I like to keep my eyes open for stuff," he said, his bulging eyes bulging a little more. "I could pick you up a dress, Mercy. What's your size?"

She looked at Syd, who was frowning at the floor tiles. "Oh, uh, thanks anyway, Rollo. What were you reading?"

None of the people they knew, except Rollo, bothered reading anything. Many were illiterate. They themselves, though they could read street signs and bus names, never had time for any serious reading. Rollo, however, read everything: magazines in stores, old piles of papers left out for the Boy Scouts, the labels on foods at the supermarket. He was a walking encyclopaedia of information, and if any of it was a little distorted, shopworn or out of date, no one noticed.

"Fascinating. the stuff you can glean, a page here, a page there," he said. "For instance, Syd, I would say that you are suffering from a disease called *anorexia nervosa*, did you know that?"

Syd looked alarmed. "A disease?"

"A nervous disease, it keeps you from eating square meals. Is there some marmalade to go with this bread, by the way?"

"But how would I get cured?"

Rollo helped himself to jam. "I didn't get that part. But I saw another article for you, Mercy. It talked about the problems of women in the upper echelons of the corporate pyramid."

Syd and Mercy, who had never heard of corporate pyramids or echelons, said nothing. Rollo continued: "Oh, by the way, IBM stock holds steady. Thousands die in Iranian earthquake. Local philanthropist honoured. Air disaster blamed on faulty maintenance."

Mercy said, "Rollo, you're so well-informed!"

"I try to keep up. The man who knows what's going on in the world is the man who's going to get someplace. After all, world events affect everybody – even us."

"But how?" Mercy put the lid back on the jam, and tried to make it look as though several spoonfuls had not been removed.

"Well for instance, there are these superpowers, and they apparently have a lot of warheads, and they plan to use them to blow up the whole world!"

Syd tried to laugh again. "Come on, now, Rollo. That's a lot of gobbledegook from television. I'm not that ignorant, I've seen a little television myself, you know. Clowns eating hamburgers, cars crashing in flames, *superpowers*, *warheads*, agreements about salt, I've seen it too."

Mercy said, "Anyway these superheroes or whoever they are wouldn't use their warheads if they had them. It doesn't make sense."

"I'm only telling you what I read," said Rollo. "I'm not saying it's all true." Some of the bulge went out of his eyes, as Rollo seemed to sag a bit. "I guess sometimes I just wish we lived in their world, the realpeople world."

"Who doesn't?" Syd said, looking at his socks.

"I mean, I get so tired sometimes; sneaking around, hiding like some kind of wild animal – I mean, we're as much people as they are. We've got a right to be seen. We could live right out in the open, have houses of our own."

"Work jobs," said Syd.

"Raise children," said Mercy.

"I saw an expression in a magazine the other day that just summed it up. It spoke of coming out of the closet. Well that's what we ought to do, gosh darn it, come out of the closet!" Rollo banged his fist very lightly on the kitchen table.

There was a noise upstairs, of a heavy piece of furniture being moved. Without making a sound, the three cleaned up their crumbs, collected their dishes and ran to the hall closet.

In a moment, a woman came clumping down the stairs, carrying a load of bed linen. The cat gave up pawing at the closet door and bounded into the kitchen with her, almost tripping her.

"Out of the way, Midnight," she said, using the loud voice realpeople used. "It's not dinnertime."

They could hear her clumping down the basement stairs, clanging the washing machine, singing over the racket of washing. Then back up to the kitchen, where sounds told them she was making coffee, drinking it, listening to the radio, cleaning the stove top, talking on the phone, loud.

"Mother It's okay, I'll *drive* you there... I *said* I would, didn't I?... Okay, but I have to be back by two, to pick up Donnie from school."

There were the sounds of a coat being slipped on, a nose blown, keys jingled. The back door slammed, and outside a car started. The three, who'd been holding themselves perfectly rigid for an hour, glided out in time to see the woman drive away.

In the silence of the house, Rollo said, "I've got to go myself. See you both at the party tonight?"

The house seemed even quieter with Rollo gone. Mercy walked through the living room, touching things. Realpeople had roomfuls of stuff like this: an onyx cigarette lighter, a dolphin-shaped ashtray, whiskey decanters marked *His* and *Hers*, an electronic organ, a glass cabinet full of tiny glass animals; a shelf of cacti, a painting of a clown on black velvet, a carriage clock, a tank of beautiful fish. On the desk was a pen-and-pencil set in something like gold, and a box of name labels. A plaster shepherd and shepherdess simpered at one another from opposite ends of the mantel, in the middle of which stood a large photo, a family portrait. Mommy, Daddy and Donnie. She began to sniffle.

"Don't start that again," said Syd. He was digging down the back of a sofa for loose change. "You know you can't have a kid, so why keep thinking about it? And even if you could, I'm not so sure we could raise it. We gotta travel light."

"I could raise it," she said hoarsely. "*I* could raise it."

Travel light, that was the rule. The rule was, no children, no pets, vacate the room by ten. It was the eternal rule, graven on tablets at the dawn of time for everyone who had to keep moving and travel light.

Well, she didn't want to travel light. She didn't want to keep moving, keep hiding. She wanted to grow thick and heavy and settle down in one place, while possessions piled up around her. Then one day she could squat down and pop out a nice, rosy baby. A baby girl. She could name it "Portia". They would settle down together, with possessions piling up around them. It wasn't having things, that wasn't what was so important.

It was having memories to go with them. This carriage clock we bought at that funny place in New Hampshire, remember? And the dolphin ashtray Portia brought back from camp, remember how tan she got? And wasn't that the year...

If I was realpeople, Syd thought, I'd just slap her in the mouth when she gets like this. Realpeople do what the hell they want. They talk out loud. They get in their cars and drive like hell, blasting the horn. Out of the way, Midnight. Out of the way, everybody. I'm real, out of my way!

When she'd finished crying, Mercy helped Syd search for coins: Then they slid up to the attic, where they found some old clothes in a trunk, just right for Letty's party. There was a blue chalkstripe suit for Syd, and a red-and-white floral dress for Mercy. They both looked good.

A yellow cab pulled up at a big house on Sumac Street at two a.m. The driver walked up to the front door to pick up his fare – someone leaving a party. While he was away from his empty cab, its back door opened and two shadows slipped out in silence. They moved so quickly that the blue chalkstripes and the red-and-white floral patterns were just blurs. As a realperson came out of the front door of the big house, Mercy and Syd were sliding around to come in the back way.

Letty liked to throw her parties in the wake of realpeople's parties. She would start letting in her guests before all the realpeople guests had left. Then she and her friends would spend some time keeping out of the way of the last, drunken realpeople – who were usually too busy singing, dozing, feeling sick or trying to remember the ending of some story, to notice Letty's friends.

Then when all the reals had been packed off in cars and taxis, or upstairs to bed, the second party would begin. There might be some chipdip and liquor left, or her guests would have visited other parties – drifting through them like cigarette smoke – and from them brought food or bottles. One way or another, there was always some cheer, often a little discreet music – and always, the company of friends.

There was Chauncey, who made the rounds of garage sales to collect anything he knew his friends might need. Though of course he did not pay for the stuff he collected, it was never missed. There was Rollo, the newsgatherer. There was Letty herself, who on Sundays took over an empty dentist's office to work on her friend's teeth. Ethel, a tall woman in pince-nez (one lens missing) likewise acted as a doctor and was as adept at slipping her patients into empty hospital rooms as Ham was at making funeral arrangements, two bodies to a coffin. Mercy and Syd, like many others, were just providers of supermarket food and abandoned clothing. Finally there was Uncle Darb, now retired and living in a seldom-used darkroom, but still the patriarch and final arbiter on all matters of law.

Uncle Darb was sitting in a corner, telling a small, not very attentive group that their envy of realpeople was sinful.

"We are not meant to be like them," he kept saying. "We are meant to be apart, to live in their shadow, unseen, a secret tribe. We may use only what they won't miss, and only enough for our own survival. I don't say it's sinful to have a little party like this now and then. We do after all need to gather, to see one another and to talk about the rules."

The rules. Mercy took a glass of gin in four big swallows, gagged, and turned to hear what Chauncey was saying.

"These realpeople I'm with keep leaving the television on and going to sleep in front of it. So I drift in and watch all the late-night movies. *Invasion of the Xoids*, it was called. The Xoids looked just like real people, but if you shone a certain ray on them, they'd go *pffft* like flat tires, and just collapse."

His audience laughed, Mercy hardest of all. But even now, even in drink, she found herself unable to let go and shriek, really shriek the way realpeople did at parties.

"Call this a party?" she said to the nearest man. "I call it a meeting of the ghosts. Of the Xoids."

"Hello, Mercy," he said. "Long time no see. Remember me? Jasper." He was a short, balding man with a thin moustache.

"Jasper, hello. Haven't seen you since – funeral, was it?"

He nodded, emphasizing the baldness. "Aunt Portia's funeral. I, ah, still visit the grave a lot." It sounded like some kind of invitation.

"I keep meaning to visit, myself," she lied. "Only I can never remember the name. On the stone."

"Weiler," he said. "Maxine Weiler. I could, ah, take you out there tomorrow, if you like."

"Poor Aunt Portia," said Mercy. "Since we had to bury her with somebody, the least we could have done would be to put her in with a man. I don't suppose she had so much as a cuddle in her whole life, and now it's too late. I'll never have one."

"*You'll* never have one? I don't understand." His moustache understood, though. It was twitching comically.

She laughed. "I meant *she'll* never have one. A *cuddle*, I meant. Not a baby. O God, I don't feel so well. Jasper, do you think we could get some air?"

As they went out the door, Syd came in the other door with two glasses of wine. He looked for Mercy. Finally he said, "Okay, hell with her. Hell with her." He emptied her glass in one gulp, not minding at all how his Adam's apple genuflected. Hell with everything. He didn't mind anything anymore.

"I don't," he explained to Rollo. "I don't even mind you."

Rollo clapped him on the shoulder. "And I don't mind you, either, Syd old buddy. Let's get drunk. They say the alcohol content of wine –"

"Right," said Syd. Behind him he could hear Chauncey still going on about *Invasion of the Xoids*. "That's us, you know? Xoids. We're the fuckin' Xoids – oh, excuse me," he said to Uncle Darb.

The old man waved a hand. His blind eyes seemed focused on Syd. "Go on, my son. We're Xoids?"

"We're not even alive, we're not even real. We just go around faking everything. Borrowing everything. *Their* houses, *their* food, *their* damned socks. We're nothing, we're nobody!"

"What and whom do you want to be?" asked the patriarch.

"I want to drive a car and honk the horn. I want to be real and solid and important. I want to live in a world where I belong. Maybe in the country, with no realpeople –"

"Realpeople are everywhere," the old man warned. "They are the madness of this world, as it is their asylum. We, thank God, are outside their madness."

"Don't give me all that, I don't buy it anymore. You always end up with the same story, how we've been living like we do since the Dark Ages, how we never take last names because we're not families, we're individuals – I'm sick of all that."

"You want to join the realpeople? Nothing easier, my son. Just stop hiding. Let the realpeople see you. Course, they'll probably put you in jail. Or the hospital."

"You're just saying that."

"Nope. There you'll be, a man with no identification cards, no job, no past and no last name. You never had any kind of job, never went to school, never lived at any address. You can't give your parents' full names, you don't know how old you are –"

"Stop! Just stop!" Syd's facial muscles were writhing. He turned and stalked away, out the kitchen door and into the back yard where he almost stumbled over two figures on the ground. He recognized the red-and-white of Mercy's dress, even though it was up around her waist.

Back inside the borrowed house, Syd found a downstairs borrowed bathroom. He went in, turned the borrowed lock, stripped off his borrowed clothes and looked at himself in the borrowed mirror. He borrowed a razor blade and cut both his wrists, then climbed in the borrowed bathtub to keep from messing up the floor. Xoids weren't even allowed to bleed out loud, he thought, as he went to sleep.

Screened by a gang of orderlies going to lunch, Ethel and Mercy slipped along the corridor to Syd's room. He was sitting up in bed, looking cheerful and relaxed – for the first time in years.

"I've made a decision," he said. "I'm joining the real world."

Ethel began changing the dressings on his wrists.

"I hope you'll be all right," said Mercy.

"I will. It doesn't have to be the way Uncle Darb says. I can work into it gradually, travelling and doing odd jobs, meeting just a few realpeople at a time – until I'm real, myself."

To Mercy, though she could not say so, the whole idea of being real included a home and family, pictures on the mantel and a cat in the kitchen. A realperson who travelled and did odd jobs sounded like "the worst of both worlds", as Rollo would say.

"I know what you're thinking," Syd said. "I thought so too."

"Really?"

"It's what everybody thinks, but I can't help it. I'm going."

Ethel nodded. Light danced on her pince-nez, on the single lens. "You can go home today, if you like," she said. "Home or wherever."

"What are you going to do?" he asked Mercy.

"I don't know. I still want a child," she said, looking out of the window. Buses moved along the street, carrying crowds of old people. Snow was making up its mind to fall, or rain. "I don't think I could ever make it as a realperson, though. So unless I can get pregnant –"

"Maybe you and Jasper could have a child," he suggested, already bored with her problems. He wanted to get out of here, get away from ghostly women complaining about their periods. He wanted to hit the street, walk tall, wear a hard hat, be somebody.

"I don't think I want to raise a child, not the way we have to live," she said. "Hiding, hiding, hiding, hiding, hiding." She wiped her eyes. "I'd better go."

Stifling a yawn, Syd said goodbye. Ethel took her arm and steered her along corridors, slipping like smoke past receptionists.

"Is this the way out?"

"No, I wanted to show you something." They glided on to a room with a glass door. Inside, they could see a nurse leaning over a glass crib. She was holding up a string of bright discs. The baby in the crib laughed and reached for them with one arm. The other arm was in a cast. They ducked back as the nurse looked up.

"Do you want that baby?"

Mercy said, "What? That baby? I mean, yes of course, but – but I mean –"

"I've checked her records," said Ethel. "Her name is Rae-Sue Fridley, daughter of Earl and Mae-Rae Fridley. They broke her arm."

Mercy gasped.

"It happens, among realpeople. They go ahead and have children they don't want, and end up hurting them. Now they're putting Rae-Sue into state care. Unless you and I take her first."

No children, no pets. Mercy thought about her own childhood. Folded up in a sofabed every day. Taken along quietly to the playground only late in the afternoon, when all the realkids had gone home to supper. The old rusty bike with rotten tires, on which she'd been allowed to ride around and around the deserted parts of town: weed-grown vacant lots, weed-grown railroad tracks, the grain-elevator part of town where weeds were allowed to show themselves. Folded away in the sofabed during school hours.

"Ethel, I just wouldn't want to make a mistake. I'd want to take good care of her."

"I know you would, that's why I brought you here."

"No but I mean I wouldn't want to make the mistakes my mother –"

"If you know they're mistakes, don't make them," said Ethel. "Anyway, you didn't turn out too badly, for all those mistakes. You know, she named you Mercy after the hospital where she found you."

"What? You mean I was abandoned, too?"

"Most of us are," said Ethel. "For centuries back, very few of our women could ever conceive. It may be our unusual sleep pattern – the fact that we have to be able to jump up and vanish at a second's notice, that we're never very deeply asleep. Whatever the cause, not many of us menstruate. So there's only one way to carry on the tribe."

"Kidnapping." She and Ethel ducked back as the nurse left the room.

"We only take children the realpeople don't want," said Ethel. "The rule still applies. And we only give them names the realpeople don't want." She looked at the clock down the corridor. "You have fifteen minutes to decide."

T, thought Mercy. *Theresa. Thomosina. Terry. Tina. Theo. Thora*. I can teach her myself. Rollo could give her reading lessons. Letty could teach her painting and sculpture. *Toots. Tess*. No folding sofa bed for my little-

Tiffany?

"Titania," she said aloud.

A moment later, they bundled up Titania and slipped out a side door of the hospital. No one saw them sliding along the sidewalk today, because everyone else was running in the other direction, hurrying to see the accident. Ethel and Mercy and Titania sped on their way unnoticed; they were gone like breath vapour on this cold October day.

The man who'd been struck down by a bus was still breathing. Everyone could see the vapour, white as the bandages on his wrists. As the paramedics tried to lift him, he said "I'm real." The vapour stopped.

"I just never saw him," said the bus driver. "He came at me out of nowhere."

The policeman said, "Don't worry. Your witnesses here all agree the guy jumped in front of you. Like he was daring you to hit him, somebody said."

"That's right," said an old man. "And he shouted, I heard him shout. He shouted, 'Get out of my way.' Can I have a transfer?"

Wiping his eyes, the bus driver tore a coloured piece of paper from a pad and handed it to the old man. The old man joined a crowd of other old people, tottering from this bus to the next one, waving their transfers like little flags of victory.

STOP EVOLUTION IN ITS TRACKS!

Creationists are seldom colourful, exuberant characters. Their name, which ought to remind us of burgeoning life, somehow calls to mind the dusty relics of another age: celluloid collars, tent meetings, barns bearing giant advertisements for laxative. For the most part, the colourful and the exuberant have deserted this unprofitable philosophy.

One exception is Professor Abner Z. Gurns, founder of the Gurns Institute for Advanced Creationist Studies. Gurns is known for other things besides creationism. There was "prayer wars", his patented defence system employing, he claims, a crew of the lesser angels to defuse godless Soviet missiles in flight. Before that there was his attempt to translate the Bible into a virus, for inoculation of the whole world ... And before that, his planned expedition to raise Noah's Ark, which he believed to have sunk "somewhere near the East Pole."

If Professor Gurns has a place in history, however, it will most likely be that of the father of modern creationism. Few have done as much for this controversial field as Gurns; no one has established anything remotely rivalling the Gurns Institute.

I went to interview the professor at the Institute, a cluster of modern buildings on a bluff overlooking the sturdy little town of Stove Bolt, Tennessee. The building containing Gurns's office is a no-nonsense structure of glass and steel, the kind that might pass elsewhere for a school of business administration. The only visible clue to its higher mission is the motto carved above the entrance:

>WHEN ADAM DELVED AND EVE SPAN
>WHO WAS THEN AN ORANG-UTAN?

I waited for the professor in a bland anteroom. The only unusual note was a large framed photo on the wall. It showed ants eating a red rose. The title, I saw, was "Paths Untaken."

While I waited, I glanced through a selection of the Institute tracts ("The Great DNA Fraud"; "Fossils God's joke on Darwin?"). Somehow they didn't go with that disturbing photo.

I found myself trying to form a picture of my host. Based on a couple of blurry news photos, I imagined him to be a quaint fellow in a celluloid collar and rimless glasses, sporting a watch chain on his snuff-stained vest. The watch would be set to Central Standard Time.

On the contrary, Professor Abner Gurns turned out to be a boyish thirty-year-old with a crew cut and an athletic handshake. His white lab coat was open to show a sweatshirt with a picture of William Jennings Bryan (in a celluloid collar).

"I was trained as a scientist," he explained. "For years I struggled with the so-called theory of evolution, trying to make sense out of it. Heck, if it was in the textbooks, it just had to be true, right?" His boyish grin appeared.

"Well something happened one day that hit me like a ton of assorted lightning rods. It made me see that Darwin's theory of evolution is nothing but hogwash and hokum! The American public – heck, the world public! – had been deceived for a century. It was time to take off the blinders and do some real science. So I came out here and founded the Institute."

He led me into his office, where a glass wall showed the grassy bluff, and the tiny town of Stove Bolt far below. Why had he picked this place for his Institute?

"Because Stove Bolt is the place where in 1923 they held the famous Snopes Monkey Trial – the first great victory for Creationism in our century."

What was his discovery? Professor Gurns sat on the edge of his desk and explained.

"I was studying fossils night and day, spending my days at the Natural History Museum, my nights hitting the books. Trying and trying to make sense out of evolution. Then one day on my lunch hour I wandered out on the street and got knocked down by a bus. When I got up, everything seemed strange. The people were strange. I saw purple hair. I saw this short blind man wearing a derby. He was leading this tall man who played on the derby with drumsticks. I saw a dog on wheels. Then this Yellow Cab pulled up, and I looked inside – *and the whole back seat was filled with one gigantic cabbage.*"

I asked the professor what all this meant to him.

"It means that nothing in the fossil world makes sense. I got more wisdom from one hairline fracture than from years of studying! I learned that we have to take fossils for what they are, and stop trying to piece them together into a story. Evolution is a fake."

He picked up a flat stone from his desk and held it in both hands. I saw that it was an ammonite, a common fossil.

"You know, Darwinists always accuse us of not studying the fossil record. That just ain't so. Speaking as a scientist, I have always been primarily interested in the fossil record – that is, the fossils themselves, and not what a bunch of Darwinists try to tell me about the fossils.

"They claim that fossils show evolution – one animal turning into another. Hogwash! There is not one fossil anywhere that shows one animal turning into another. *Every fossil you can find is perfectly still – not moving or changing at all!*"

He put down the ammonite and picked up what looked like a soup bone. "This here bone comes from one animal and one animal only, am I right? Speaking as a scientist, am I right?"

I had to agree.

"Okay, then. Anybody who tells you this here bone came from two or three animals has to be a darn fool." His eyes narrowed, and he waved the bone like a club. "A fool or an atheistic Darwinizer!"

A bell rang somewhere. He looked at his (ordinary digital wrist-) watch. "I got a lecture right now. Come along and sit in."

I followed him to the Wilberforce Auditorium, where perhaps a hundred students were seated, eager to receive his message. I sat to the side where I could watch them. They seemed a pretty typical bunch of kids, though slightly subdued.

"Speaking as a scientist," he began, "it just beats me how anybody can believe in the evolutionary fairy tale for five minutes!" There was some nervous laughter and applause.

"Evolutionists will tell you how some little old amoeba evolved itself into some bigger bug, and how that evolved itself into a fish, and so on, right up the scale until the ape evolved itself into a man. But there's two things wrong with that cockeyed story.

"In the first place, the amoebas never evolved at all. They're still here! Speaking as a scientist, I can vouch for that! I have looked down a microscope myself and seen them. They look like this."

He showed a slide of blobs. "Still the same little crittursthey was when Noah marched them aboard the ark, two by two."

When the murmurs of amazement had died down, he continued: "In the second place, apes could not evolve into humans for a very simple reason: *There are no apes*. The things we call apes in zoos are nothing but men dressed up in hairy suits. I myself have visited a theatrical costume place where they rent such costumes. There they are, hairy suits with *nobody inside*."

He showed several slides: a gorilla suit hanging on a rack, a man getting into the suit, the man wearing the suit minus the head, and a gorilla. The class murmured louder, apparently angry at the duplicity of the Darwinists.

A boy wearing a DON'T BE A MONKEY'S UNCLE sweatshirt put up his hand. "Sir, how can they lie to us like that? Isn't it unconstitutional?"

"Lying breaks an even higher law, Vern," said the professor. "Not that Darwinists care about that. But let's move right along to *survival of the fittest*. Can anyone tell me what that is supposed to mean? Yes, Sue Bob?"

A girl wearing a DON'T GO APE FOR DARWIN sweatshirt stood up. "It's circular reasoning, sir. They claim the ones who survive are the fittest. Then they try to prove this by pointing to the survivors – must be fit, because they survived."

"Exactly, Sue Bob. Can anybody imagine anything more ridiculous than survival of the fittest?"

Loud laughter and some applause.

"All over the country, folks are jogging and riding bikes, going to fitness centres, all to keep fit – but do they survive? Heck no, they all die eventually, same as everyone else. The fit shall perish with the unfit. Why, old Methuselah lived a lot longer than any jogger, and we know for a fact, he never rode a bike in his life."

The professor now seemed to be in training himself. He strode back and forth energetically as he talked, he flailed his arms, pounded the lectern, and spoke at times so rapidly that it was difficult to keep notes. There are, he said, five unanswerable arguments for Creationism:

1. The universe is one grand design. Nuclear physicists see electrons going around the atoms. (So do nuclear physicists.) Astronomers see planets and stars and stuff going round the sun. Everything goes round and round like the wheels of a watch. (This baffled many students until the professor used a large plastic model to demonstrate that watches once had wheels inside.)

The same careful planning shows up in the animal and vegetable kingdoms. A banana is easy to peel because it was made for peeling. Fish can swim, which is lucky, because they are invariably found in water. Our two ears are located on different sides of our heads to give us stereo hearing.

All of this design implies a designer – not to mention a team of draftsmen and production engineers. Butterflies and flowers come in lots of pretty colours, so a team of interior decorators are probably involved somewhere. Or take birdsong, which requires not only a composer, but an arranger, a producer, and a musician's union.

2. You can't evolve a sow's ear into a silk purse. In other words, there is just no way that a simple crittur can make itself complicated. You might as well expect a gas mantle to turn into a chocolate grinder. (The professor explained these items.) Life is just what you make it, not something else.

3. The great giraffe debate. Atheistic Darwinizers may try to claim that the giraffe went around stretching its neck up to eat leaves from the trees for a few generations, and this made its neck grow longer.

The real truth is, giraffes didn't need to stretch at all, because their necks were already so long. Besides, what about dolphins? They live in the depths of the oceans where there are no trees at all. (This puzzled me and still does. I tried to ask the professor to elaborate on it, but nearby students told me to hush my mouth.)

4. Everything invented by the Creator has some use. Even a duck-billed platypus proves that the Creator had a fine sense of humour. What other use could it possibly have?

5. All of the atheistic communists in Russia believe in evolution. Enough said.

Professor Gurns concluded his lecture by offering to thrash anyone in the room who still believed in Darwinism. That brought applause and cheers from the students.

Among the students lingering after class to ask questions was a girl student wearing an EVOLUTION – NON, MERCI sweatshirt.

"Professor, are you absolutely sure ontogeny doesn't recapitulate phylogeny?"

Gurns stood in silence for a moment, holding his large watch model. Then he said, "Darla Jeanette, I wish you would rephrase that question."

"Well they say that during pregnancy, a human foetus looks at different stages like a fish, then a frog, then ..."

"I don't see any point in dragging in talk like that, pregnancy and foetuses," he replied. "Young girl has no need to know about that stuff, no need at all. You tend to the fossil record and leave the pregnancies to me."

The professor then conducted me to the Deluge Lab, where a magnificent full-size replica of Noah's Ark had been constructed. After hanging up his watch model in the corner, he explained what was going on here: Creationist graduate students were packing the Ark with pairs of stuffed animals, to prove that all of the species would too fit inside.

But as in all toy arks, the giraffes seemed to be giving trouble. Researchers were climbing ladders to take measurements of two stuffed ones.

"Maybe Noah laid them down," someone suggested. "They'd fit pretty good laid down."

"But their legs spread out a lot," someone else complained.

"Maybe Noah sawed off their legs. Hey, why not? There's nothing in Genesis says they had to have all animals with legs."

"Now, now, boys and girls," said Professor Gurns. "I'm sure you can come up with a better answer than that."

Back to his office, where the professor showed me a model of the Institute, with planned future development.

"We're still *evolving*," he said, with another boyish grin. "But seriously, we need to add a few departments to fill in all the gaps. For instance, we need some professional help in classifying the fossils of sea critturs. You know, fish fossils have been found way up on mountain slopes. The only explanation is, Noah's Flood covered even the highest peaks. We aim to prove that, once we get set up with our own Department of Marine Biology. It'll go right over here. We've already got a genuine marine to run it.

"Over here will be our anatomy department, plenty of work there, too. We need to study how the leopard got his spots, how the camel got his hump, how the whale got his throat, and all like that. Then there's the whole question of Adam and Eve's navels, a subject for some serious contemplation.

"And this area will be the new department of geophysics, to help prove how the earth is flat. For that, we'll need lots of surveying equipment, maps and so on. Probably need to buy some time on a satellite and get some real clear pictures of the earth from way high up. We like to be up-to-date, you know, use the latest technological –"

Footsteps came pelting down the hall. The door banged open and a student barged in, out of breath. "Professor, come quick! The giraffe is on fire!"

As we all hurried back to the lab, the student explained. One researcher, attempting to shrink one of the stuffed giraffes slightly with a heat gun, had set it ablaze.

By the time we arrived, the fire was out and students were opening skylights to dissipate the smoke. There was little visible damage to the animal itself. However, the great plastic model watch had melted and sagged.

As I left the Institute for Advanced Creationism, I looked out over the bluff, where students were flying kites shaped like glossy French loaves. Down below lay the town of Stove Bolt. I could just make out the little red courthouse where, more than sixty years before, the Snopes Monkey Trial had struck the first blow for Creationism. In that trial, a monkey named Snopes had been successfully prosecuted under Tennessee law for possessing an opposable thumb – a blasphemous imitation of human kind.

The Darwinists had been doing well in the trial until the very end. When the defence lawyer began his closing remarks, the jury was distracted by strange humming noises coming from within the courtroom fireplace. The humming was not like human humming, but the humming of steel rails. Finally the jury gave up all pretence of listening, and indeed the lawyer stopped speaking. All were transfixed, watching the dark hollow of the fireplace, waiting for an express train to come screaming out of the darkness and thundering through the tiny room.

Blood and Gingerbread

In a tiny cottage, little more than a log hut, in that distant part of the forest called Selbstmorder, there lived a poor woodcutter's family: Peter the Cutter, his wife Kat, and their small twin children, Hansel and Gretel.

Peter was a dark, coarse man who seldom spoke and never bathed. He was never known to look anyone in the eye except in anger. Nor did anyone wish to look long at Peter. His face was frightening, with its yellow teeth gleaming in a ragged black beard, his large-pored nose, his angry black eyes under matted hair. Sometimes when his forehead was visible, you could see a hideous scar, a deep furrow as though someone had cut deep with an axe, and the flesh had grown up swelling out on both sides of that furrow as bark swells out from a wounded tree. His broad shoulders could carry huge piles of firewood, and he worked hard and earned more than many a woodcutter for miles around.

Yet somehow the money got away from him, leaving barely enough to feed his family. No one knew where his money went, for he did not drink much, and he was not after any village woman. Some said he must have a secret sweetheart hidden away somewhere, like old Karl, many years before.

There were people old enough to remember when old Karl had kept his sweetheart locked up in a lone hut. To keep her from running away, Karl had cut off her legs. But one day he came to the hut and found she had escaped anyway. She had made her way to the lake and drowned herself. There had been many jokes about Karl's inability to keep a woman, and so the incident lived on even after Karl was dead.

Peter the Cutter did not have a sweetheart; he had no time for pleasant dalliance. He spent every day working hard: felling trees and cutting them up, loading his broad back with a mountain of cut wood, sometimes loading Kat too with a mountain of faggots, trudging to the village to sell them, coming home to cabbage soup and dry black bread, with Kat dragging her foot around the room and the children peeking at his dirty beard and hair full of bark.

Kat was a sweet-tempered, wraithlike woman with a dead foot and a speech impediment. Both infirmities dated from a time when the children were infants, when Peter had lost his temper and hit her on the side of the face with an axe. From the place above Kat's ear where the corner of the axe bit, a streak of white hair grew. And from that time forward, Kat dragged her foot and spoke with great difficulty.

Peter had suspected her for a time of malingering, trying to get sympathy. He would shout and rage at her, but Kat paid no attention. It is tiresome to keep accusing someone who never replies. Finally Peter gave up trying to talk to the woman or even look at her; he ate his cabbage soup and listened to her dead foot dragging around the room.

Indeed, Kat paid little attention to anything. If she beat the children less often than Peter, it was because she did not often notice them. This was because Kat spent her days lost in dreams, hardly aware of the dark world around her. She would take up a besom and begin sweeping the hearth as the children went out to play – but an hour later she would still be standing there, leaning on the broom and staring into the fire.

The children found her poor at making meals, but always good for a story. She told them the story of the princess whose hair caught in a thorn bush, and the story of the princess who lived on a glass mountain, and the story of the axe in the ceiling. She told them stories of dark things in the woods, the souls of murdered travellers. She told them that every good child has a precious jewel in its heart, and that monsters and ogres wish to murder children to gather these precious jewels. She told them funny stories of people with sausages stuck to their noses. Once she got started, Kat could talk for hours, telling tales while the cabbage soup simmered and the hearth remained unswept. She could even tell tales when there was no one to hear them.

At times it seemed to Kat as if she herself must be an enchanted princess, caught in this world by accident. What a drab, unpleasant life this was – surely she deserved better. Here in the dark woods, there was no colour except for the occasional snowdrop or dog rose. Or the occasional bright drop of blood. Yes, surely she was an enchanted princess, caught here by her hair.

Or perhaps she was only a sausage stuck to a nose.

One day Hansel was passing through the woods collecting acorns when he heard a group of angry voices. There were men gathered around a large pine.

"Otto, you know that this tree is the forest king, whose mercy protects us. No one is ever allowed to touch or harm the forest king. It is only through the grace of this tree that we survive. If the king forgets us, if we lose his magic protection, what will happen to us? Forest fires, famine, ruin, and death.

"Yet knowing that, you chopped at the forest king with your knife. You carved a name. The name *Hannah*.

"Otto, there is no more to be said. We sentence you to pay the penalty. Heal the wounds of the forest king."

The man screamed. The other men were crowding around him, so that Hansel could not see what was going on. A mob of them rushed over to the tree, and there was a terrible groan from the man Otto. The men gave a shout, "Ho!" Hansel saw a loop of leathery rope shoot up and snag on one of the lower limbs of the forest king, a dark purple, shiny rope. Were they going to hang the man?

Hansel did not understand until the men shouted "Ho!" again and flung up another loop, then another, until the lower limbs of the tree were festooned with swags of intestine from the unfortunate Otto.

Guts on a tree. What a funny thing to do! Hansel smothered a giggle. He couldn't wait to tell Gretel. She'd be dreadfully upset.

Otto no longer screamed, only whimpered. The men marched him round and round the tree, unwinding his tripes as they sang a song Hansel knew. Hansel felt a little queasy, but he sang softly with them:

O Tannenbaum, O Tannenbaum!

Later that day, Hansel told Gretel of his adventure. She was indeed upset, and shrieked at him.

"Guts all over a tree? Guts all over a tree?"

"Ha ha ha."

"Guts all over a tree, and you never even called me to see it!"

"Ha ha ha. You were busy."

"You could have come and called me," she said. "I've never seen anything like guts on a tree."

"You were busy."

"I was only helping Mother with her old sewing." She held up a needle. "Next time, call me."

"All right."

"I mean it. Or you'll wake up one morning with this needle in your stupid eye."

"Don't be angry, dear sister." He showed her a sack. "Look, I caught some little frogs on the way home."

Then the children, who were really good-natured at heart, forgot their quarrel and spent a happy afternoon in amphibian torture.

"Once there was a princess who lived on a glass mountain. The king her father said that any prince who could climb up to her would win her hand in marriage. The mountain was covered from top to bottom with great slivers of sharp glass. Every time a prince tried to climb up to her, he was soon caught on the glass and cut to pieces." Kat found she had to make the stories bloody to keep their attention, these monster children. She explained to Gretel how one day she would become a woman in blood, and how later she would bear children in blood.

Silently she added, "And I hope your children borne in blood are not monsters like you."

Kat did not tell them the best truth of all – that she herself was an enchanted princess. It must be so; her life must be more than this black-walled hut with its smoking fire and two monster children. She knew that a prince would come. From the gnarled twisted roots of this world, a prince would come to take her out of hell.

"Finally there came one prince who was cleverer than all the rest. He gathered all the falcons from his father's estate – a hundred falcons – and he tied cords to their feet. He held tightly to the cords while the falcons flapped their wings and flew, lifting him up to the top of the mountain. There he picked up the princess and brought her safely back down to earth. And so he won her hand in marriage."

"You mean they cut off her hand and gave it to him?" Hansel asked eagerly.

Mother told them the story of the king with his head on backwards, of the princess who married an enchanted axe, of the queen who could not bleed, of the mud prince. She began to teach Hansel and Gretel to read and do sums, marking their letters in the soot of the chimney.

"Letters have always been a part of the forest. The god Odin discovered the alphabet while hanging nailed to a tree. The first letters, the Runes, were cut from twigs of the ash tree, and the sap blood flowed with knowledge. Ash, Birch, Cedar, Dogwood. Love, a heart pierced with an arrow. Letters of secret knowledge. Trees must die to make paper, trees must burn to make a charcoal pencil." This is what she said – or meant to say. It all became a mumble of death and burning, death and burning.

No matter. Hansel and Gretel hardly listened to her lessons. They were poor students, full of fidgets. There was always more fun to be had hanging kittens from the back of a chair or plucking feathers from the head of their pet pigeon.

Peter cursed when he saw the markings in the soot. "Letters! Sums! You want to make them into fine gentlefolk? You want to spoil them for honest work? God curse you, woman! Fit for shit! You can only drag your damned foot about and make trouble!"

The children waited for him to beat her. But after a blow or two, he seemed to lose interest. He sat down at the table, put his dirty head down, and snored.

Kat continued their lessons through the dark days of winter, when breath turned the windows into forests of crystal trees, numerous and shining as the sharp glass slivers on the glass mountain.

"Soon it will be spring," Mother promised. "Soon the bright days, the ice will melt on the lake." A time for the prince, she thought. Her plan was now complete – she would meet the prince at the lake. He would lift her up, up from the monster children, up from the twisted roots of this world, up from darkness into light.

Meanwhile there were her monster children. How could they look so innocent, with their heads full of torture, pain and death? She could not get through to them at all, except by making a grisly game of everything.

So, in spite of themselves, Hansel and Gretel learned to read. A was an abattoir, B a blood sausage, C a corpse ...

The light of spring came and all hearts lifted. Sun glowed through the trees, flowers brightened the earth, and there were plenty of small animals to trap and torture.

"At last I can see to work," Peter said, sharpening his axe.

"At last the ice is melted on the lake," said Mother. And the first clear spring evening, she wandered down to the lake. Kneeling on the shore, she bent to regard her reflection in the water. I am ugly, but this ugliness will fall away as I am lifted to the light. So thinking, she bent further, submerging her face in the icy water. She held herself under until her plan was complete.

Peter the Cutter stopped work for a time after her death. He went to the village each day, drank at the inn until he could hardly walk, then made his way home to beat Kat and the children. But there was never anyone to beat. Kat was gone somewhere and the children were too hard to catch. Every night, Peter felt like weeping. He would put down his head on the table and sleep.

One night he brought a woman home. Hedi, she called herself. She was strong and plump, a good worker, he thought, and a good breeder. He spent all his savings on a ruby ring, put it on her finger, and brought her home. "Children, this is your new mother," he said. "See the ring I bought her?"

Hedi ignored the children and looked about the cottage. "We'll have to clean this place up if I'm to live here," she said.

Peter nodded. "Whatever you think best, my dear."

Hansel and Gretel were too astonished to talk. How had this witch tamed and humbled their father? How had she made him buy her a ruby ring?

"Yes, clean it up." Then Hedi looked at the children. "And we'll have to get rid of the vermin, too."

Hedi was too busy to tell stories. She made the children stay outside the house, especially when it rained, so they would not track mud on the floor.

Even Peter, who did not often notice such things, took pity on the twins when he saw them crouching outside the door in the rain, trying to eat their cabbage soup.

"Could we not let them in for a meal, my dear?"

Hedi laughed. "Why not invite in all the vermin of the forest? To dirty our house and eat our food." She looked at the twins. "It's bad enough having to feed them, when they bring us nothing."

One day Peter came home to find the house oddly different. The children were missing altogether. They did not turn up during supper, or after dark, or even at bedtime. As he tumbled into bed with Hedi, the woodcutter asked, "The children. Gone?"

"I sent them away," Hedi announced.

"Where?" he asked, half-asleep.

"They'll be well-cared for," she said, smiling to herself in the dark. She thought, *the little beasts are in the forest where they belong*. It was worth all the time she'd wasted leading them to a distant part of the forest. Hedi had made them walk until they were so weary they'd sat down to rest and fallen asleep. Good riddance to bad seed.

The next morning, however, the twins were asleep on the doorstep. Hedi gave them gruel when they awakened.

"We were worried about you," she said. "How did you manage to find your way home?"

"It was easy," Hansel said. "I had my collection of mouse skulls with me, and I dropped one every now and then. Last night, the moon shone on the little white skulls, showing us the way home."

"But why should you drop little skulls on your path?"

"Because we knew you were going to abandon us in the woods," Gretel explained. "I saw you pack bread and cheese for yourself, but none for us."

Hedi saw that she would have to try a different approach. She waited a few days and then talked to her husband.

"Peter, there is not enough food for you and me, let alone these stray animal children. Let's turn them loose to forage in the woods for themselves. They're so good at killing animals, they can live on blood."

"Let them be," he said. It was the first time he'd disputed her in anything.

Later she said, "I have talked to a woman who lives in another part of the forest. She is willing to take the children in. They would live with her and help her."

"I don't know ..."

"They would eat better than they do here ... and cost us nothing besides."

"Hmm." Peter the Cutter did not like the idea but he could not find an argument against it. There was no denying that times were hard.

"It's settled then. But Peter, *you* must take them to her. They won't trust me twice."

He scratched his head. Pieces of bark fell to the table. "And lose a day's work. Hmm." He thought for a moment. "What about their clothes and toys and such?"

"If they see us packing up their clothes and toys, they'll know we're sending them away for good. No, you must take them to the old woman as though for a brief visit. Meanwhile I'll pack up their things, so we can send them along later."

"Hmm." More bark fell to the table, and a couple of wood lice.

In the morning they started off. Hedi searched both children for mouse skulls. Then she gave each of them a piece of bread and sent them off with their father.

Peter walked slowly. His hideous face with the cleft forehead was now dark with thought.

Hansel turned to look back at the house.

"What are you looking at?" asked his father.

"I thought I saw my white cat on the roof of the house, crying for me."

The yellow fangs grinned. "Don't be stupid, boy. You hanged that cat last summer and bashed in its head. Must be a ghost!"

Later Gretel turned to look back at the house.

"You too? What are you looking at? Hurry up, girl."

"Father, I thought I saw my pet pigeon on the roof. I wanted to say goodbye."

The yellow fangs grinned. "Your pet pigeon. Is that the one you plucked to death last month? After you'd chopped off one of its legs. Another ghost!"

But the children were not at all sentimental about their dead pets. Instead, they were turning back to drop pieces of bread to mark their trail.

They walked all day. At sundown, Peter brought them to a neat little cottage in a clearing. Near the cottage was a dome-shaped stone oven like the top of a great skull.

The lamp was lit in the cottage but no one seemed to be home. There was a delicious smell of baking everywhere, a smell of ginger.

Peter called out but no one answered. He pointed to two little chairs. "You sit and wait here. A woman named Hannah will come and see to you. I have to go cut wood, before it is too dark."

He left them. It took him all night to get home again. He found that Hedi had burned their toys and clothes, and trampled the ashes into the earth.

The children waited for Hannah until it was quite dark outside. Then they crept out and tried to find the bread trail. Alas, the trail of black bread pieces was invisible in the gloom. They returned to the neat house, but not to their chairs.

"I'm hungry," said Hansel.

"Me too. I smell something delicious."

They began exploring. The next room was a kitchen, and on the kitchen table was a miniature house made of cakes and sweets. The walls were gingerbread; and there were marzipan gables, white fondant for a doorstep, and barley-sugar windows with treacle-toffee shutters. The chimney was made of crystallized fruit, with liquorice stovepipes. The roof was tiled with cookies, with a snowdrift of icing over all.

Hansel broke off a bit of the roof while Gretel tried a windowpane. Suddenly a croaking voice called out:

> *Nibble, nibble like a mouse*
> *Who's been nibbling at my house?*
> *Gnawing through the walls and doors*
> *Wolfing down the roof and floors*
> *Swallowing the highest gable*
> *Dining on the dining table*
> *Window-cruncher, you have sinned*
> *You will suffer from the wind.*

The voice seemed to come from the floor beneath their feet. Presently a trapdoor flipped open and the children saw an old, bent woman making her way up the cellar stairs with the aid of a stick. She was as gnarled as a root, with a wrinkled face and a back whose hasp might have been broken by the Devil.

"Do you like my little rhyme, children? I learned to rhyme the things I write on cakes."

She looked at the gingerbread house closely, inspecting the damage. Her warty nose was almost touching the delicate gingerbread walls. "It was very wrong of you to eat the cake house," she said, though not harshly. "Now I must repair it before it can be sold. That is how I make my living, baking cakes and sweets to sell. You and I cannot eat the cakes, unless I happen to burn or otherwise spoil them."

The children said nothing but braced themselves for a beating.

She smiled, showing a bright gold tooth. "I am Hannah the Confectioner. You must be little Gretel and Hansel," she said. "Though which is which is more than I can say, for I am nearly blind. But you must promise me not to eat any more fancy cakes. Let me make you something else to eat." She let them share her own supper of sour milk, apple cores and broken nuts. "Never mind," the children told themselves. "All will be well when our father comes for us."

But Peter did not come for them that day, nor the next. The children spent the day helping Hannah with her confectionery work, but each evening they took their places on the two little chairs and waited.

Life with old Hannah was dull and busy, but not hard. She made it clear that there would be no food without work. The children gathered twigs to feed the great stone oven in the yard, they searched for eggs in the henhouse, they milked the goat, sifted the flour, mixed the batter, and kneaded the dough. Hansel swept the floor; Gretel cleaned the pans. There was not much time for animal torture, and anyway they depended on these animals. If Hansel cut off the goat's ears, as he wished to do, she might stop giving milk. If Gretel had fun wringing the necks of the hens, no more eggs.

Days and weeks went by. Hansel and Gretel came to believe that old Hannah Gold-tooth was keeping them prisoner. She locked them in at night not, as she said, to keep them safe, but to prevent their father from coming for them. Maybe she was an evil witch. Mother had told them stories of witches who could enchant children and make them into toadstools. These were always old women with pointed chins who giggled as they stirred their pots of evil poison. Hannah had a pointed chin, and she often giggled as she made cakes.

"A pretty cake for a wedding," she would say. "Hee, but that marriage won't last!"

Peter would save them. He would come with his double axe one right and break down the door.

But weeks and months went by. Hansel and Gretel saw evil in everything old Hannah Gold-tooth did. She meant them harm. Hansel thought she meant to boil them up in a stew and eat them, smacking her toothless gums. Gretel thought she meant to enchant them into little cakes and sell them.

"She smacks her toothless mouth all the time, as if tasting us. Lamb stew!" whispered Hansel.

"What about those two little chairs? What happened to the children who used to sit in them?" Gretel replied.

If a meal was skimpy, she was trying to starve them. If it was generous, it must be poisoned, or else she was trying to fatten them up.

"Remember," said Gretel, "Mother told us there is a jewel inside the heart of every child. Old Gold-tooth wants to kill us and take the jewels from our hearts."

The children swore an oath to escape. They swore by a knotted rope. Then they cut their arms and dripped blood on the knot, to solemnize the oath.

Gretel was helping Hannah make gingerbread children with currant eyes. The old woman leaned over the tray to inspect them. "Hee hee, the black currant eyes – such dark sadness," she said. "You might almost think they were real children, trying to go home to their worthless father and his slut of a wife. But no, they are just gingerbread boys and girls, with black currant eyes."

She *will* turn us into gingerbread, thought Gretel. Unless Father saves us.

"Children, I want you to call me 'Mother', since I am all the family you have." Hannah smacked her chops. "I have just received word that your father's had an accident in the forest. He is now dead."

Gretel screamed. Hansel dropped his broom and ran out the door into the forest. He did not stop running until he was deep among the dark trees. Suddenly he stopped, delved in the leaves at his feet, and came up with a small, green-gold snake. Hansel held the snake by the throat and squeezed until it was dead. Then he threw the dead thing high, high into the branches, where it snagged and hung like "Ho!" the guts of Otto, hanging in swags from the forest king.

All at once Hansel was seized by a terrible fit, as though the snake had bitten him and shot its poison into his brain. For an instant he saw Otto marching round the Tannenbaum, unwinding his guts. Then Hansel fell to the earth, trembled and thrashed about, and slept. When he awoke later, his mouth was full of blood.

At the same moment as her brother, Gretel too was struck down by internal lightning. She had a brief vision of huge, dark wagons, creaking past one at a time, each one loaded with raw meat. Then she fell to the floor and saw nothing.

"You have the falling sickness," old Hannah told her later. "Perhaps you have magic powers. Make some cakes now, and we shall see."

Under the old woman's direction, Gretel baked a pair of gingerbread children. Hannah snatched up the boy and bit his head off. "Mm," she said chewing, her gold tooth flashing as she gummed the hot gingerbread. Then she seized the girl and bit her head off.

"Mm. Yes, you have the touch. From now on you will make all the cakes and sweets. I am too old and tired, and my eyes are failing." She put out a hand to stroke Gretel's hair.

Gretel bit her gnarled hand until it bled. "Yes," she said, "Hansel and I will take charge now."

Months and years went by. Hansel and Gretel were growing up tall and handsome. At the same time, old Hannah Gold-tooth was shrinking down smaller. She was now completely blind. The twins wanted to be rid of her, but they still depended on her memory for all the recipes. However, Gretel was gradually writing them down. "When we have all her secrets," she said, "I will take great pleasure in turning the old crone into garden fertilizer."

"Well said, little sister." Hansel laughed so hard he lost the frog he was about to drop into the cake batter. Spoiling her cakes was only one of the ways they'd thought of to torment old Hannah.

Meanwhile, the twins found little ways of torturing and taunting Hannah through the day. On Monday, Gretel would say, "Hold this," and offer her a red-hot pan from the oven. The blind old thing would take it, trustingly. Screams and giggles. Then Gretel would offer her supper, and the old woman would be afraid to touch it. "Well, since you don't want any supper, you may starve."

On Tuesday, Hansel would offer to lead old Hannah to the well, giving her his finger to hold. But he had substituted a chicken bone for his finger. The chicken bone was tied to the tail of the goat, which led the baffled old woman around in circles. She never fell into the well, which would have completed their joy, but the twins laughed until their sides ached.

On Wednesday, an angry customer came to complain of finding a toad in a cream bun.

"It was the children, to be sure," said Hannah.

"That's as may be, but why do you let them play foul tricks? Are you a party to this witchery? Or are you simply blind?" Hannah was afraid to admit to her blindness, so she could only stammer an apology.

On Thursday, the children took off their clothes and went naked all morning, passing before the unseeing eyes of the old woman. When another customer came (to complain of bloodstains in a box of chocolates), Gretel whispered to her "Please help us – Hannah makes us go naked all day!"

Hannah stood by, trying to hear what was being said, and trying to smile at the customer. Her gold-toothed smile was hideous.

"For shame!" the woman shouted at Hannah. "Loathsome creature! You can stand there grinning at the evil you work, the evil you force upon these innocent ones. Well, you'll sell no more confection to me or mine, or to anyone I know, either!" Hannah spent the rest of the day weeping, begging the children to go away. With merry giggles, they assured her that they would never leave her as long as she lived.

On Friday, the children locked Hannah in the cellar and told her they were setting the house afire. They threw a bit of stale gingerbread into the fire to make smoke. The old woman's panicky screams were echoed by screams of laughter.

On Saturday, Hansel managed to slip a dead rat into a wedding cake.

Sunday the children rested from their labours, laughing aloud as they talked over their week of pranks.

Times were once more hard. Soon word of Hannah's witchery spread, and no one in the village would buy cakes and sweetmeats from her. Hansel was obliged to take baskets of cakes and walk to a further village where he sold them on the street. But the cakes were good, made to Hannah's recipe, and he sold them quickly.

One day Hansel stopped in the village tavern for a glass of wine. A fat, drunken woman sat talking to herself in a corner. Hansel looked again and realized that this was Hedi, grown blowsy and lumpish.

She looked at Hansel. "Hello, handsome," she said. "Buy me a drink." She did not seem to recognize in this handsome young man the child she had left for dead in the woods. He bought her a drink, and they talked.

"You live here in the village?" he asked.

"Why do you ask? Want to take me home, do you?" She was coy. "Well, I'm an expensive girl. It costs money to keep me happy."

When he said nothing to this, she continued, "I used to be married to a rich lumber merchant. He spoiled me. Gave me everything. This ring, for instance."

She showed Hansel the ruby ring his father had lavished on Hedi. "Why, he would have given up his children for me. That is, if he'd had any children."

"Very nice. What happened to this rich lumber merchant?"

"He had an accident. Ran into an axe someone else was swinging."

"He is dead?"

"Not him. You couldn't kill Peter with twenty axes. But he changed. He grew more violent. I think it was the silver plate they put into his skull. It made him more violent than ever, and stupider. So I left him. I want to see the world. With someone like you."

She looked at him. "Something about you reminds me of him."

Hansel helped her out of her chair and out of the tavern. A few minutes later, in the darkness, he helped Hedi out of this world.

Next day, he told Gretel all about it. "First I tripped her to the ground, then I kicked her face until she lay quite still. Finally I pried up a cobblestone and finished the job. Then – well, you know how I always take a small knife to town, in case I run across a stray animal – lucky thing, too. Because the ruby ring wouldn't come off. It was stuck on her fat finger. I had to take finger and all, see?"

Unfortunately, just as Hansel held up the bloody finger, a bailiff from the village was looking in the window. He came in the door a moment later. "You're under arrest, young man, for murdering the fat whore."

"Me? But, sir, I –"

"No good playing the innocent with me. Everyone saw the confectioner's boy leaving the tavern with Hedi. An hour later, we found her smashed and mutilated body in the canal. And next day I find you waving her severed finger and ring about."

Gretel cried, "Please, sir, what will happen to him?"

"He will stay in the village jail until we can have a trial. Then he will no doubt be hanged."

The village jail was no more than a room with an iron cage in it. The jailer, a gap-toothed man named Gunther, sat in front of the cage door, eating sausages, swilling beer and dozing. He was proud of his job and never missed a chance to tell visitors about the murder, and show them the ruby ring, which he kept in his pocket next to his silver watch.

Gunther was always glad of Gretel's visits to her brother; it wasn't often that he got a close look at a beautiful young woman.

"My dear," he would gurgle. "When your brother has been strung up, you will be all alone in the world."

"Yes, that's true, Gunther." Gretel tried to look forlorn, though in fact the idea of a hanging excited her. What fun! If only Hansel could be around afterwards, so she could talk it over with him.

"Well, I mean to say, you'll need someone to look after you."

"Will I?"

"I mean to say, you can always count on me. Rough but honest."

"That's very sweet of you, Gunther. Have some gingerbread. I brought it for my brother, but he won't miss a bit."

While Gunther ate all of the gingerbread, sucking it from the gaps in his teeth, Gretel had a chance to talk to her brother.

"Before I killed her, Hedi told me something," he whispered. "I asked her all about the place she came from and she told me the way back to our old house. It's a long way from here, in another part of the forest."

"If I got you out, we could go home," Gretel replied.

"Yes, to our old dad."

Gretel thought about it. "I'll get you out."

The next day she was back again. Gunther said, "Remember, you can always count on me. I mean to say, rough but honest. My heart is good."

"That's very sweet of you, Gunther. Have some gingerbread. My brother won't miss a bit. Here, take that piece with the prettiest icing."

"I mean to say." Gunther grinned as he bit into the slice of gingerbread. Gretel smiled shyly back and watched him finish every crumb of the cake, and her face glowed as with love. Gunther could not believe his good luck.

A moment later, he was on the floor, writhing as though his whole body were on fire. Hansel and Gretel watched his final convulsions with shining eyes. Then Gretel searched the dead man's pockets and came up with the keys, the silver watch and the ruby ring.

"Beautiful," said Hansel, as his sister unlocked the door.

"The ring?"

"No, I meant his dying. Though he could have taken a bit longer about it. Did you get the poison from Hannah?"

"Yes. I knew she had a few secrets like that, the old witch. And finally, after I put her hand in the waffle iron, she gave it to me."

They now realized that it was necessary to kill old Hannah. No one else in this part of the forest knew who they were or where they came from, but she could send pursuers to the house of Peter the Cutter.

"Leave it to me," said Gretel. "You go quietly, and she'll think you're still safely shut away in the iron cage."

She walked into the cottage and shouted at the old woman. "You've done nothing while I was gone! You haven't even heated the oven – we have work to do."

Old Hannah was sitting in a corner, weeping. "It's hard to work when my hand hurts so. You burnt it badly when you shut it between the grids of that waffle iron."

"If your hand hurts, cut it off! Meanwhile, there's batter to be beaten, if you don't want to be beaten yourself."

The old woman arose, leaning on her stick, and went to work at once, though still weeping. Gretel went outside, where Hansel silently helped her stoke up the big oven and get a roaring fire going within its stones. Looking into the glowing mouth of it, Gretel thought she could see tiny creatures among the blazing coals. When it was hot enough, she led old Hannah forth from the cottage.

"I can't tell if the oven is hot enough, old woman. I need your expert opinion. Just lean in and tell me."

The old woman, suspecting a trick, held back. "It is hot enough, I'm sure."

"I said lean in. Further. Get up on the shelf and crawl in a little ways."

Instead of complying, the old woman suddenly raised her stick and gave Gretel a smart crack across the head. "Never, you little murderess. Bad as your brother, God knows who you poisoned with my gingerbread, and now you want to burn me up, do you? Well, let's see how hot that oven really is!"

So saying, the old woman gathered up Gretel and tried to thrust her in the oven. All at once, strong hands seized Hannah's throat. She opened her mouth for air. The last thing she heard was Hansel's voice. "You won't need this where you're going, witch!" The last thing she felt was pain, as he plucked the gold tooth from her mouth. Then the pressure resumed and she lost consciousness.

In a moment, Gretel regained her feet.

"I've done my part," said her brother, laughing and holding up the gold tooth. "Now you can finish off the old hag."

Gretel picked up old Hannah and began stuffing her into the oven. It was difficult. Hannah was not heavy, weighing little more than her own crooked skeleton, but she was so bent she folded double at the door. Hansel helped, breaking a bone or two, and in she went.

The old creature was revived by the heat; she came awake and began to scream. Hansel and Gretel giggled in reply. This was better than skinning dogs!

It was only disappointing that the screams stopped so soon. However, the twins could stare into the narrow opening and see Hannah's remains writhing in the fierce heat. The fire snapped and sizzled with new fuel.

As Gretel peered into the glowing oven, she had a strange vision. Who knows what caused it? Being knocked dizzy by the stick? Breathing the fumes of burning wood? Or just the general excitement? But she thought she saw Hannah's body shrink and become a tiny creature, and sink into a tide of little creatures: thin, naked bodies wriggling in the inferno. Some were lying in lifeless heaps, smouldering, while others were jerking and convulsing as they burst into flame. At the far end of the oven there were wagons rolling past, dumping more bodies, more and still more. All of the bodies were thin, no more than skeletons with skin.

It seemed to her she could even see beyond the wagons, to yards full of skeletal people behind high fences. Soldiers were walking vicious dogs to and fro. The skeletons were getting the worst of it everywhere. There was a gallows with a dozen skeleton people hanging. There were beatings and torture, and skeletons tied down to tables while men in white coats leaned over them with knives and saws.

"Beautiful," said Hansel. He began to tremble, and then suddenly he fell to the ground in one of his fits, shuddering and jerking like one of the burning corpses. His convulsions made him bite his own lips and tongue so that blood trickled from his mouth. At the same moment, Gretel felt something trickle down her leg. She knew she had become a woman.

When at last they came to their own little cottage in Selbstmorder, it was late evening. Peter the Cutter was just coming home with a load of wood on his broad back. He set it down at the door and turned to look at these two handsome young people.

"Who are you? What do you want here?"

"Father it is us, Hansel and Gretel."

"I'll be damned!"

Then Peter was glad to see them. He beckoned them inside, nodded at the table, and set forth three cups of wine.

"I'll be damned," he said again. "I thought you were dead long ago. Long ago."

He had not changed much. A new scar ran across his forehead and a grey streak through his dirty hair. His movements were slower, more uncertain, for he now dragged his foot like Kat.

The rough log hut had not changed either. Hansel and Gretel looked into the chimney and found, under the grime, the faint scratchings of their alphabet lessons.

"We don't come empty-handed, Father," said Hansel. Ignoring a look from Gretel, the young man heaped their treasure on the table: Hedi's ruby ring, the jailer's silver watch and Hannah's gold tooth.

The woodcutter was delighted. "Ha, ha! Buy plenty wine!" Gretel gave Hansel another look, *I warned you.*

Peter the Cutter began to drink in earnest, as he told them what had happened since they'd left. He had never wanted to abandon them, it had all been Hedi's idea. Hedi, who thought only of herself. He'd bought her a ruby ring very like this one, he had, but was she grateful? No! (He banged the table.) No! First time he turned his back, she was off like a gypsy. After ruining his home, forcing him to abandon his children and making him a poor man, she was off like a damned gypsy.

He drank some more wine and explained that it was all Hedi's idea to abandon them. He'd never wanted to, but Hedi, who thought only of herself, had wanted a ruby ring. So he'd bought her one, but was she grateful? Was she? No! (He banged the table again.) Off like a damned gypsy. Well at least it had all come out right: he had his dear children. Tall and strong, ready to help with the work. And they had not come home empty-handed.

His head sank lower as he drank more wine and explained that Hedi, who thought only of herself, had forced him to abandon his children for a ruby ring. But was she grateful?

After a few hours of rambling, during which Peter wept for his abandoned children and laughed over the treasure, he put his head on the table and began to sing:

O Tannenbaum ! O Tannenbaum!

In a short while, the song became a snore.

Gretel looked around. "We could be very cosy here, Hansel. This old hut would be just right – for two."

Hansel chuckled. "I was thinking exactly the same." He pushed the treasures into a small heap on the table. "He would just take our treasure and spend it all on wine, so he could snore away."

Gretel looked into the fire and was reminded of the roaring furnaces with bodies writhing in the flames, the caged skeletons, the soldiers with vicious dogs. Now she imagined mountains of hair, heaps of gold teeth. A warm excitement rose in her that she could not explain.

Hansel too began to breathe quickly. "I want to do something," he said. "Something grand."

"Yes. We must."

"Look at his head, where the hair is thin. Notice the gleam? That is the silver plate in his skull."

They set to work at once.

"Blood and Gingerbread": Afterword

The brothers Grimm (like so many German writers from Goethe to Grass) traded in darkness and violence, which is probably why their tales have long appealed to children. Indeed, it is hard to think of German storytelling without thinking of mindless cruelty and a forest darkness. Trees seem to figure in such stories, and woodcutters, and old women who have to be put to death (Red Ridinghood's grandmother is another victim of the axe).

Besides the Grimm tales, I drew on the following items for this story:

- The god Wotan was supposed to have invented the alphabet by means of crucifixion (and self-mutilation) on a sacred tree.
- Otto's punishment for wounding a tree is based on an account in Sir James Frazer's *The Golden Bough*.
- The death camp premonition is of Buchenwald, so named because it was located near Goethe's favourite "booktree".

I had already decided to write about Hansel and Gretel when I consulted William Shirer's *The Rise and Fall of the Third Reich* to find out more about Buchenwald. In that book I found a reference to Frau Ilse Koch, the "Bitch of Buchenwald", who was particularly fond of lampshades made of human skin. According to Shirer:

"One piece of skin which apparently struck Frau Koch's fancy had the words 'Haensel and Gretel' tattooed on it."

DINING OUT

As the two women came in, a small camera in the pale blue ceiling above the counter swivelled to catch their conversation.

"I don't know why this robot or whatever it is is such a big deal," said Brandi. "He could of called anyway."

"You know Cog. If you asked him, he'd just say, 'Nobody understands me.' That's supposed to make it all right," said Sherri, mysteriously.

"I mean, there are plenty of robots around already. And most humans are just so much servo junk, fastened together with a few tendons and stuff. Like Rod says –"

"Rod! You still going with him?"

"Yeah, hey listen, I had a little talk with Ginni. She goes, 'I don't know what you're talking about.' So I goes, 'No? You sure?' So she goes, 'No, rilly. Rod don't mean a thing to me.' So I goes – oh, hey, what are you getting?"

"Salad?"

They stood in line at a fast-food restaurant called Barry D. Lyte Salad Time Theater and Dessert Bowl. The camera followed them until they reached the pink-and-blue counter. The young man in pink looked at them with old eyes.

"Nielp you?"

"Two Tum-tum salads, please."

"Inny banebit sore nail gravy?"

"No."

"Innythin rink?"

"Two decafs."

"Kine?"

"One Irish almond mocha and one southern Moroccan orange half-roast"

"Kina dressing?" He asked, and by way of explanation:

"Onna sals?"

"One gorgonzola and one light epicure."

There remained only one question:

"Tea tier ort go?"

"Here," said Brandi, who had flawlessly followed the flow.

After each answer, the boy had searched carefully over the large array of squares depicted on a video screen, and pressed one. Each square displayed a tiny icon representing the item selected: Tum-tum salad, decaffeinated coffee, gorgonzola dressing, and a car for "To go."

The boy now stood mute while the total bill was displayed on a larger screen behind him: $34.80. To make sure they understood it, a mechanical voice read the number aloud:

"Thirty-four dollars and eighty cents, please."

"Are you sure you don't want me to catch this?" asked Sherri. "I could eyeball it."

Hearing her, the young man started reaching for the Accuret customer retinal reader.

"Wouldn't think of it." Brandi opened her thief-proof wallet and extracted a $50 bill. A man at a table near the window took a close interest in the transaction. The boy accepted the bill, turned and fed it into a machine. Change rattled down a chute in front of Brandi. Seconds later, two trays laden with fast food shot down another chute.

"Joy your meal!" called the boy, as they turned and looked for a table.

"Thank you," Sherri said automatically, though the boy had already turned to say to the next customer, "Nielp you?"

The next customer was a man wearing a skimmer and striped blazer. He stepped closer to the counter and mumbled something about pizza.

"Kine?"

"Anchovy and okra. What do I care?"

"Innythin rink?"

"Decaf, crème de cinnamon delite," replied the man, naming a popular flavour.

"Tea tier ort go?"

"To go ... I guess. We're all going, right?"

The man looked round the restaurant. Two cameras watched him. "Lots of people here. People just like me. My name is Lube Cordwall, by the way. Pleased to meet you. Likewise. It sure is a small world. Though not quite small enough. I eat at Barry D. Lyte Salad Time Theaters never, seldom, sometimes, a lot, all the time."

The boy ignored him. Only the pale blue cameras watched.

"Hey, I'm wearing the colours, see?" He snapped a finger against the stripes of his blazer, pale blue and pink. "Barry's colours."

Ignoring him, the boy pressed a picture of a car. He then waited, mute, while the total bill was displayed on the big screen behind him: $29.40. A mechanical voice read the number aloud: *"Twenty-nine dollars and forty cents, please."* The man ignored it. Ignoring was going on. There was plenty of ignoring here at Barry D.'s, the man observed.

He tried again. "Lube Cordwall is the name," he announced to the restaurant at large. No one looked at him. They were all busy. Well, by thunder, they would know the name of Lube Cordwall tomorrow!

Two thin people over in the tiny smoking section – a glass cubicle in the corner – were hurrying through their meals, as though anxious to put food aside and resume smoking. A woman in a playsuit was trying to hurry her three children. But like other children, hers concentrated on wearing special paper party hats. They dawdled over their barryburgers and cheesyface pizzas, while taking every opportunity to pull at their sweet drinks. In spite of all that could be done to harry and upset them, they continued to joy their meals.

"Joy your meal!" the boy behind the counter was all set to say, but never got the chance. Mr Lube Cordwall fumbled in a shopping bag and came up, not with money, but with a bundle of sticks wrapped with tape, trailing coiled wires. He set it on the counter.

"This is a bomb," he said pleasantly. The boy stared at it, mute, while the mechanical voice read the number again, louder: *"Twenty-nine dollars and forty cents, please."*

"This is a bomb, and I will set it off unless everyone does exactly as I ask. First of all, I want all the customers in here to stay where they are, continue eating, and just ignore me."

This wish was easily granted, since no one had noticed Lube.

"I also want to see Barry."

The mechanical voice now said, rather stridently: *"Your order is twenty-nine dollars and forty cents, please. PLEASE PAY NOW."*

"I said I want to see Barry."

"Barry?"

"Yes, you know – Barry." Mr Cordwall made awkward dancing motions, and the boy nodded.

Everybody knew Barry D. Lyte, the huge dancing teddy bear in the TV commercials. He turned up now and then at Barry D. Lyte restaurants to pass out balloons and paper hats. His ears were hamburgers, his eyes were blueberries and his muzzle was a 'regular size' (10 oz) plastic drinking cup.

"I want to see him pronto."

"Your order has been cancelled," the mechanical voice said, its tone subdued, regretful. *"Please re-order, or stand aside so the next person can be served."*

"I want to see Barry, pronto."

"Uh – ullgetta manger." The boy ducked out of sight, and in a moment was replaced by the manager, a plump young man whose badge identified him as Junior Cheever.

"Problem, sir? What can I do for you?"

"I have a bomb here, Junior. I was just telling the kid, I want to see Barry. The bear."

"You want to see Barry?"

"I want to see him here. Dancing. Or I blow the shit out of this place."

Junior focused mismatched eyes on him. "How about a free salad instead? And we'll throw in a free regular-size diet soda? How would that be, sir?"

"Nope. I said, I want to see Barry."

"Well." Junior grinned at the hideous device. Sweat sprang up on his forehead. "Well, I'm not sure. Barry isn't scheduled to be in our part of the country this week. I don't know just where he is."

"Oh, that's too darned bad. It means I'll have to set this thing off." Lube reached for something that looked like a switch.

The coils of wire trembled.

"Wait, wait. Listen, let me make a few phone calls, maybe I can get Barry for you."

"Okay. Meanwhile, lock the doors. Nobody goes in or out of this place."

Junior said, "Couldn't you let the kids go?"

"No, not until they see Barry dance."

The order was passed along, and employees glided out to lock all of the doors.

Junior went to the wall phone behind him and dialled 911.

"There's a man with a bomb here, at Barry D. Lyte, on Oliver North Boulevard. That's right. He made us lock the doors ... Yes, this is the manager, my name is Junior Cheever."

Lube Cordwall shouted. "If you're calling the cops, tell them I want to see Barry the dancing bear." He picked up his bomb and vaulted over the counter. "In fact, let me talk to them."

Junior handed over the receiver, which was about to drop from his shaking, sweat-slippery hand.

"Hello? Who am I speaking to? Hello, sergeant, this is Lube Cordwall speaking, I'm the guy with the bomb. L-U-B-E, Lube, C-O-R-D-W-A-L-L, Cordwall. Never mind my address, sarge, let's cut the gab and get down to business. Let me talk to the hostage crisis squad, will you? I do have hostages here, yep, about forty people. Hello? Yes, I will hold, but not for very damn long."

Lube assumed a waiting posture, leaning against the wall, feet crossed, drumming his fingers on the explosive device.

Junior wilted.

People were trying to leave. A man and woman herded their three tiny blonde children to the door, where all five of them began to bang and shout. An employee hurried out to speak to them. All five sat down, and only the man continued to shout. The children were absorbed in watching a police car with flashing lights arrive outside.

An elderly couple got up from their table and made their way towards an exit. The man carried a tray of debris from their meal – crumpled paper napkins, styrofoam boxes, plastic drinking cups. The woman preceded him to a large green plastic frog. This frog's huge mouth was covered by a flap marked THANK YOU. The woman pushed at his flap while the man tipped in the contents of their tray. Above the frog was a large orange toadstool, holding up a stack of trays. The man added the empty tray to the stack. Immediately, a deep, froggy voice said:

"Thank you kindly, folks. Come back and see us real soon, now."

The old couple chuckled and turned to the exit. They rattled at the locked door for a moment. The woman then said something sharp to the man, who shrugged. They went back to their table and sat down.

"Hello, is this the hostage crisis officer? Listen, officer – OK, listen, Joe. I have about forty people, at least a dozen children. I'm about to set off a bomb unless you meet my demands ... Okay, my first demand is, I want to see Barry D. Lyte, the dancing bear. I want to see him right here. I want Barry to come here and dance – you got that?" He hung up.

Outside, two more police cars entered the parking lot, then two more.

Their flashing lights kept the confined children entertained, for the moment.

A man in a business suit got up from his table and rattled a door. Then he rattled another door. When he had tried all exits, he came to the counter. With a folded newspaper, he tapped Junior Cheever on the shoulder.

"You're the manager?"

Junior nodded.

"Why have you locked the doors? You're breaking the fire laws, for a start. This could even be abduction."

Lube Cordwall said, "It *is* abduction. You are all my prisoners."

"Says who?"

"Says me and this bomb."

The businessman looked thoughtful. "I see." He tapped his nose with the folded paper for a moment. "What is it you want?"

"He wants to see Barry, the dancing bear," said Junior, his voice breaking. He was very young, and his management training course ("Five Keys to a Happy Customer") had not prepared him for anything like this.

The businessman evaluated this news. "How about some money instead. If we took up a collection –"

"Nope," said Lube Cordwall. "Maybe later I'll ask for stuff like that. Money, safe conduct, a plane to Baffin Island. But just now, I want to see Barry."

The businessman hated to give up. "What if I danced? I could put a couple of hamburgers on my head, and a plastic cup over my nose – okay?"

"Just sit down."

Outside more police arrived, with more flashing lights. They had cleared the street and parking lot of people and their cars were drawn up in a solid barricade, circling the restaurant. Their small remote cameras rolled in close while the TV news cameras shot from high behind the barricade.

The police did not seem to have a unified purpose, so far: some officers stood leaning against their cars in plain sight, chewing gum and talking over a coming softball game against the employees of Dirkton's Taproom. The precinct's starting pitcher had been wounded on the hand by a parrot while serving a summons on its owner.

Behind the police lines, a truckload of paramilitary police arrived. Holding rifles at port arms, they ran in place for a moment, then rested.

Simultaneously, a child began to scream and the phone warbled. Lube answered. "Yes? Hi again, Joe. Yes, I am still just fine. Plenty to eat here. Great companions, you can hear one of them screaming now. I sure appreciate your concern.

"What do I need? What do I need? I've been telling you, I need a dancing teddy bear. Yeah? *So where is Barry*? No don't give me all these stories about how you're really trying. If I don't see that damn bear in five minutes, *I will blow up this place and everyone in it*! You got that?"

The child stopped screaming as he put down the phone. It was suddenly so quiet they could hear the faint creaking sounds of the tiny mansard roof and the sound of grating carrots from the kitchen. Outside, a camera focused on two police officers:

"You think this bozo could really boom the place?"

"Nah, we get a lot of these, one a month. I don't worry."

"You know what worries me?"

"What?"

"What worries me is a starting pitcher. You think we got any chance with Greenspan starting?"

"Jeez I don't know, first base looks pretty bad too, Ron Ronson got traded to the twelfth precinct, what does that leave us with?"

The manager seemed slowly to come back to life. "Well," he said cheerfully. "If we're all gonna die, we might as well have a good last meal."

"*Die*?" said a woman customer, her voice rising with every word. "Last *meal*?"

"No, wait. I mean, since we're all gonna be here awhile we might as well have a good meal. I'll get my boys and girls busy."

The restaurant employees moved like zombies, dishing up hamburgers, french fries, pizzas, salads, all the rich provender of the earth. They loaded it on fibreglass trays and carried it to every table. The house cameras followed one, then another, as though confused by all the unorthodox movement.

"On the house," the employees were instructed to say. "With Barry's compliments. And we're real sorry about this problem, folks." Junior served some of the food himself, smiling ("Give 'em a happy face. Doesn't cost you a dime," said the training manual). There was no happiness, however, in his mismatched eyes.

The problem continued to lean against the wall near the phone. He continued to clutch the coils of wire while he scanned the parking lot for a sign of the dancing bear.

Barry was nowhere to be seen. Instead a short, smiling middle-aged man came from the parking lot and knocked at one of the glass doors. He was wearing a sloppy Hawaiian shirt, Bermuda shorts, sandals and a baseball cap. Only the badge clipped to his pocket identified him as a policeman. He put his lips to the crack between the glass doors and called through.

"Hello, Lube. I'm Joe Howell. We talked on the phone. How are you?"

"Impatient," Lube Cordwall called back.

The man chuckled sympathetically. "I can understand that, all right. Well, Barry is definitely on his way. Should be here any minute. Uh, meanwhile, anything else we can do for you?"

"No."

"If you want to talk, we've got a direct line to the phone there. Just pick it up and I'll be on the other end."

"I see."

"Well, gotta go. So long, Lube. Take it easy."

The cop waved, as if to an old friend, and wandered off.

Outside the sun was trying to set. The streetlights were glowing red outside, trying to blaze up to their normal yellow. The police had turned on their car headlights and set up a few bright lamps, trying to turn the parking lot into daylight for the cameras. Overhead, a helicopter trained its light and camera on the glass doors.

The elderly woman got up and marched over to Lube. "I've had about enough of this," she said. "My husband is a sick man. He has asthma. You'd better let us go."

"Why?"

"I just told you why. Clean out your ears, mister. If you'd listened years ago, you wouldn't be in this fix. Don't you feel ridiculous, standing around in a Barry D. Lyte restaurant with a bomb in your hand? Nothing better to do, I expect. You're a mess, mister."

"Who asked you?" he said shrilly. "Go sit down." His hands tightened on the coiled wires.

"No I won't sit down. My husband is sick, I want to take him home. Besides that, I have a million things to do today. I can't sit around here all day. You'd better let us go. You'd better let everybody go."

"No!"

"Selfish!" The woman had completely lost her composure.

"Go sit down, Goddamn it, or I'll blow you up!"

"Blow yourself up, why don't you? And don't you threaten me, Mister Selfish. Why don't you try thinking about others for a change?"

Junior took the woman by the arm and started moving her away. "Ma'am, I think you'd better sit down. This guy is dangerous."

"Fiddlesticks. Let him blow himself up somewhere else."

"*Goddamnit*," screamed Lube Cordwall, "I am going to do it now. *We're all going. We're all going.*" His fingers flexed on something – a switch among the coiled wires – and instinctively everyone flinched.

But there was no explosion. Barry had arrived in the nick of time.

All ready to push the button, Lube had taken one last look outside and spotted the huge head bobbing up behind a police car. The hamburger ears seemed to glow in the strange light.

"Barry," he shouted. "You got here just in time. Hey, Junior, let him in. Hurry up, let him in."

Junior scurried to unlock a glass door as the great familiar, happy bear face approached the restaurant. Barry was larger than anyone imagined – at least eight feet tall. Even so, his enormous bow tie, pink and pale blue, seemed too big for him. It wobbled as he walked with his characteristic rolling gait, swaying from side to side, cocking his head to one side and then the other. Like an overgrown puppy tied up with a ribbon. Kids all over the restaurant were cheering, all of them almost as gleeful as the mad bomber.

The dancing teddy bear stopped in the space before the counter. He was facing Lube, as though he sensed Lube was the man in charge here. The bear did not speak – Barry D. Lyte never speaks – but when Lube Cordwall spoke, the hamburger ears turned to catch every word.

"I knew you'd come," Lube said in a childish voice. "I knew you would come and dance." His face had gone slack, and spittle drooled down his chin. "All I had to do was wait."

Barry nodded. Then he began to nod, one, two, three. The drinking-cup nose moved as though conducting an invisible band, two, three. The blueberry eyes rolled with an unheard rhythm, a-one, a-two, a-three. The great white-gloved hands spread their three fingers, clapped without sound, two, three. Finally, a foot – the size of a small stool – lifted and came down softly on the tiled floor – three and one and two and Barry began to dance.

It was an odd dance, without sound. The restaurant was not silent of course. Kids were laughing and shouting, some of them clapping and banging on tables. Barry himself made not a sound, however. The giant feet in spectator shoes rose and fell delicately, silently.

The door remained open, unnoticed by Cordwall, and a few frightened souls slipped out and made their way across the parking lot to safety. Others were too exhausted to move, or afraid, or simply unable to tug their children away from the entertainment. For many years, they would regret not making the move.

Everything was fine while the dance lasted. Then at length Barry brought his heels together, flung out his hands, and bowed his head.

"That was very nice," said Lube Cordwall, not applauding. "More. Dance more."

Barry danced for another minute. When he stopped, he was a little closer to Lube Cordwall. Lube said, "More again."

The eyebrows, which were large french fries, shot up in humorous surprise. But Barry D. Lyte obeyed. He finally stopped again, closer still.

Lube said, "*More! More dance!*"

Barry did not deliver more dance. Instead, he held up a white-gloved finger for attention. His grin grew wider, and somehow it did not seem so friendly. Lube had a moment to look into the blueberry eyes and reflect that this bear was very large and very close.

The grin suddenly split open. Barry's head broke apart and a large reptile snout poked forth. Glittering reptile eyes came behind it – they were fixed on Lube Cordwall. In a second, reptile claws tore through Barry's papier-mâché head and shoulders so the large reptilian creature inside could begin slithering out, reaching for Lube.

Some mistakenly claimed later that it looked like a crocodile, others that it was a miniature Tyrannosaurus Rex (but the tapes would have shown otherwise). The younger children were never able to talk about it at all. But it would be waiting in their nightmares, like endless repeats of old shows. The cheers turned to screams.

The cameras would have recorded a snakelike creature, though equipped with efficient clawed hands that held the man still, while the enormous jaws began to cover him with saliva.

A mouse caught by a cat suddenly stops moving. It gives up and relaxes. This is the 'still reaction,' a numbing recognition that life is up. The great explorer of Africa, Dr Livingstone, had the experience himself, when attacked by a lion. He found himself relaxing – he felt no pain, though the animal was tearing his shoulder.

Lube Cordwall stood rigid with fear for a moment, before he let go of his bomb device and went limp. The stink of reptile saliva rose through the restaurant.

Numbness crept over the restaurant. People stopped eating, stopped screaming, stopped trying to claw their way through the glass walls. They simply sat and watched. Children sat in puddles of their own urine and watched.

The creature began to swallow Lube Cordwall, head first. The straw skimmer crunched into the great gagging mouth, then Lube's head and shoulders, in pink and blue stripes, then the rest of him. The legs made a last convulsive kick as they disappeared.

After a few moments, the police went to work. A bomb squad man carried away the dynamite, past the cameras, which now began to work again. Other officers came in to remove the rest of the patrons. Children were rushed off to see police paediatricians. Their parents were wrapped in foil blankets and fed sedatives, then wheeled away on low carts. The cameras followed them, carefully avoiding the reptile.

Finally the police reptile handler came to get his animal. It had now stopped thrashing about and lay still, eyes opaque, no movement except a faint pulsing of its distended belly. Covered in a blanket, it could be wheeled away without attracting attention.

Inside and outside, the cameras rolled about, watching and listening.

"I told you this bozo wouldn't boom the place."

"Hey, you think we should start Borden instead of Greenspan?"

"Borden's bad news. Anyway, what about first base? Jeez, with Ron traded, what does that leave us with?"

The disgusted policeman watched a pink camera roll through the door, where it turned and veered past the booth where two women picked at their salads.

"Okay, tell me how come you're still going with Rod."

"Yeah, well listen, last week I was supposed to have a date with Cog, you know? Only Rod calls up and asks me to go to the lake. So I goes, 'You think you can call me up just like that and ask me to go to the lake?' And he goes –"

Radio Cats

Henry Aldrich and Homer Brown were in the Aldrich attic when they opened an old trunk and found a gigantic penis. It had belonged to Henry's grandfather, who used it in the Spanish/American War.

"Holy Cow, Hen. Looks almost alive."

"Sure. A thing like this never really dies. You just put it in water and it's as good as new."

"Oh boy! Could I borrow it for my date with Agnes?"

"Gee, I don't know, Homer. You mean as a kind of conversation piece?"

"Sure, you know. For making small talk."

And that's how AIDS got started in Centerville.

Reinventing the Wheel

"Freudians long ago observed, probably with a smirk, that riding a bicycle might well be a substitute for sexual congress. But I maintain the contrary: sex is simply the primitive precursor of the ideal, riding your bike. Can any orgasm equal the feeling of freewheeling down a steep hill? And wasn't it worth labouring up the hill, groaning and panting through all of the gears of foreplay, to achieve that sublime feeling at the top?" – D'Arcy Midders

Last year, in the course of my research into the life and ancestry of D'Arcy Midders, the bicycle billionaire, I came across a privately-printed family history called The Chattalots: a Family in Peace and War. *Although Midders claims to be distantly related to the Chattalots, the connection is by no means clear. In the entire volume, I found no hints that any of the Chattalots shared his fascination with bicycles, except perhaps for Lady Emmeline Chattalot (1855-1914). Her story follows.*

It was in 1889 that Lady Emmeline Chattalot decided to take part in the new craze of cycling, of which she had read so much. Was she moved by the idea of healthful exercise and fresh air? Pedalling off to country picnics where the sexes might mix freely without chaperones? Perhaps her true motives will never be known.

In any event, her ladyship ordered up a tricycle built to her own design. She saw no reason why cycling need be uncomfortable; her design incorporated a horsehair sofa, a rosewood wine table, cupboards for extra clothing and parlour games, stout boxes for cigars, a tantalus with three decanters, a combination dressing table and commode, a telescoping mahogany dining table and sideboard, and a jewel safe. The whole device, once fitted with a folding marquee in case of inclement weather, weighed several tons and required the strenuous pedalling efforts of two footmen for locomotion on its great iron-rimmed wheels, whenever it made a foray into the streets of Belgravia.

The Chattalot cycle did not actually make many such forays. Motion was a problem. For one thing, the monumental inertia of the beast made it rather a chore to start. A dozen grooms were required to push it along the mews until the two footmen could pedal madly enough to keep it going.

Even after launching, once the cycle was actually in motion, there remained the problem of steering. Narrow streets were out of the question. Even on broad thoroughfares, the width and unwieldiness of the titanic machine placed other vehicles in extreme danger. Unless the cycle were moving perfectly straight along the way, in perfect parallel to the street, which it seldom was, others were forced to give way. Cabs veered, carriages climbed kerbs, and on one occasion, a heavy goods wagon was overturned, dumping thousands of gas mantles at Sloane Square. Horses who spotted the monster tended to bolt, screaming and rolling their eyes, possibly afflicted with some ancestral memory of rhinoceros attacks.

Like as not, the commotion would attract the attention of a policeman, who would annoyingly stop her ladyship's cycle. "Here, what's all this, then?" he would say, and not rhetorically. He would begin a frankly amazed inspection of its mahogany posts, each stout as Jumbo's leg. (Jumbo's actual leg was mounted at the rear, holding a cluster of umbrellas and walking sticks.) "What's all this, then?" He genuinely wanted to know, but the exhausted footmen were inevitably too breathless to provide any particulars, while her ladyship would normally choose to remain out of public view.

Sometimes, after stopping for a mishap or a police inspection, the conveyance would dally for too long, so that a pack of interested children would gather to shout catcalls and throw stones. Like as not, the exhausted footmen would be obliged to descend from their stirrups, seize walking sticks from Jumbo's leg, and lay about the crowd. This would stir up a local costermonger or two, and then the policeman would be obliged to sort things out. Often, a drunken gentleman would try to climb aboard, having the unshakeable belief that this was an omnibus. More trouble for the footmen. In short, if the cycle remained motionless long enough, there was what the police like to call danger of an affray.

On occasion, it would finally become necessary for Lady Chattalot to emerge from behind a Chinese screen, where she'd been attempting to nap, and rebuke the crowd in her full accent. Nothing less would clear the street, but Lady Chattalot's absolute accent. The urchins would drop their brickbats, the costermongers doff their caps, the policeman salute smartly, and the drunken gentleman would stop trying to hand his fare to the footman, mumble an apology, and slink away.

But after each such halt, there'd be the problem of getting started again. The costermongers would have to be pressed into service, along with rag-and-bone men, dustmen, and any other strong backs in sight, to push, push, push.

These police incidents deeply distressed her ladyship. Despite her own natural distaste for ostentation, she was obliged to send out servants with flags bearing the Chattalot crest, to warn other vehicles and to put an end to the police annoyance, the urchins and costers, and the drunkards. And this gave her to think. After all the curses and blows, the black eyes and frightened horses, the fatigued servants and bills to pay, she had to ask herself: was the game worth the candle? Indeed not. Her ladyship was beginning to be bored with these cycle excursions. A new idea had taken hold of her – hanging from a giant kite and gliding with the wind.

She had observed rosy-cheeked children flying kites in Hyde Park. Why should she not do the same, except for all the pointless running? The trick was to start from a high prominence with plenty of wind, as at Box Hill. She began to sketch a design for her new flying conveyance. She saw no point in being uncomfortable whilst aloft, yet at the same time she recognized the need for saving weight. Just a small horsehair chesterfield then, and a light escritoire. The wine table would fit nicely in next to them, and perhaps a small billiard table, that is, if the gliding were level enough to permit games. A good-sized globe for navigation seemed sensible, plus a bath to counteract the effects of dirty air.

Before Lady Chattalot proceeded with her new plan, she thought it only fair to give cycling one last chance. It was that final journey which came near to causing a scandal throughout the realm.

One balmy spring morning, when the crocuses were pushing up like purple asparagus in the park, she ordered the contraption made ready for an after breakfast canter. She was eager to try out her latest addition, a small parlour piano. Within the hour, she descended from her room and made her way out the back door of the house to the mews. Her ladyship kept her head muffled in a scarf – simply entering into the mews was concession enough, she felt, without being seen there. Twelve grooms awaited. The two footmen handed her aboard and secured the Chinese screen, then took their stations at the pedals. Then the dozen grooms took up their positions and began to heave. And heave.

From behind the screen came piano encouragement in the form of the Eton Boating Song. The boys were certainly pull, pulling together, yet nothing was moving. This time the grand conveyance refused to budge an inch. One of the footmen got down and put his shoulder to a mahogany post, but it was no use.

A few servants from neighbouring houses had gathered in the mews to watch and laugh. One or two younger ones ventured catcalls and whistles.

The music stopped and Lady Emmeline peeped round the screen. "What's delaying us?" she asked in her accent. "And who is making that ungodly racket?"

"Can't budge it, your ladyship," panted one of the exhausted men.

She looked about and espied the loafers. "You men over there. Take your hands out of your pockets and come help here. Immediately."

The catcallers and whistlers stopped smiling and obeyed. With nearly twenty shoulders applied to it, the great vehicle groaned into motion like a frigate setting sail. "Stand clear! Stand clear!" cried the footmen, and manned their pedals. Her ladyship sat at the piano and played something from *The Mikado* to give them strength.

The footmen very soon found that strength was not required, for now the grand conveyance was accelerating without help as it trundled down the mews. Indeed, it was building up speed much too quickly. Their efforts to push back on the pedals had no retarding effect whatever.

"We're for it!" cried one of the footmen, as stables and cottages hurtled past on either side. "You jump for it, Joe. I'll stick with her." But Joe too clung fast. The magnificent machine hurtled out of the mews into the street at express-train speed, missing its turn and plunging towards the railings of the little square across the way.

A nurse pushing a perambulator heard the roar of iron wheels and the sounds of a Gilbert & Sullivan air. She was granted one last clear vision of the monster – the last thing she would see with two eyes was a tufted leather sofa rushing towards her like a mad bull. She and her pram were instantly slammed into the railings. Pinned there by several tons of furniture, the nurse lost consciousness. As she faded, she heard the music stop, and Lady Chattalot say, "What is the meaning of this? You there, nurse. What are you doing in our path? Oh, this is too bad."

When the dust settled, policemen and passers-by laboured to extricate the victims. The nurse had suffered internal injuries and lost an eye. The pram was totally demolished. By some miracle, its occupant, the five-month-old Viscount Vickers, was unhurt. He had apparently been thrown clear, landing on a soft couch aboard the grand cycle.

The incident caused a great deal of confusion, and attracted an even larger crowd than usual. Urchins gathered to jeer at one of the footmen, who lay in the street with a broken leg. Costermongers and butchers came to argue. More policemen kept turning up to ask what all this was. Manservants in shirtsleeves appeared from various houses to help in the effort to shift the leviathan machine back, to free the nurse and her costly pram.

When Lady Chattalot emerged, she found this time her accent did not prevail. A policeman who, unaccountably, failed to recognize her attempted to place her under arrest for being drunk in charge of a pantechnicon.

Alas, all of this was witnessed by a reporter for a sensational newspaper. By feigning sympathy, that reporter managed to ferret out all of the most embarrassing details. He even followed her ladyship back aboard the cycle, where she found a drunken gentleman sitting on the sofa and trying to hand her his fare. He had already helped himself to a whisky and a cigar. "I say, this is a bit *like*," the drunken gent said. "Best damned omnibus I ever –"

Lady Chattalot was drawing breath to remonstrate when the vehicle lurched into motion, and she sprawled athwart the drunken gent. "Oh, I say!" he said, trying to cuddle her, while the reporter scribbled furiously.

In the end, the incident cost Lady Chattalot forty guineas for an elegant French glass eye, another hundred for extensive repairs to the cycle, and the additional expense of setting the footman's tiresomely broken leg.

Far worse, however, was the newspaper scandal, with its strong hints of a mobile house of pleasure, or *cigar divan*. The persistent stories of "Lady Juggernaut's naughty car" finally led to a question in Parliament: "Is the Home Secretary aware that unsafe (and unwholesome) vehicles are abroad in the streets of London, and that one such vehicle has put at risk the life of a Viscount of the Realm?"

Mortified, Lord Chattalot communicated by telephone from his club

– the Portmanteau, where he had been residing for the past fifteen years – his wishes to hear no more of this infernal chariot. Her ladyship, with a mixture of regret and relief, ordered the conveyance to be taken down to the country and stored in one of the granaries at the Chattalot country seat, Midders.

Notice that Midders, now the name of America's favourite bicycle manufacturer, should once have been merely the name of a house. The Midders family connection is nowhere mentioned in the volume. It is possibly the name of a servant – a game-keeper, for example – who for some unknown transgression was turned off the estate, travelled to America and founded the now-famous family. We might further speculate that the gamekeeper Midders was, for some reason, obsessed with bicycles. The full story may never be known.

Poems and Playlets

A Section from the Adventures of
I.E.M.

Vines, tangling lustily together on the quiet wall. No, the quiescent wall. There. That's a good line. I'll keep it. How did he say it? "bathed every veyne in swich licour" ... "shoures soote" ... the lusty tingling, tang-aling-aling: last night's shoures soote. As if it could ever be like that, even with a dark ... Why? Why nigger wenches so great? "The things ye learn wi' the yellow and brown will 'elp you a lot with the white," says Ruddy owld Kip, the white Man's Burdon. (I'm unfair to retired officers, Hare Marchesty's Army.) ... Come on, you know you'd like to try one. Savage noble, dusky queen, "running wild in woods". Captured queen. I land my ships on her sooty shores. And plant my staff for God and England. Maniacal, she bites at the gold manacles, the hand that feeds her.

No. It would be the same. My ship short of seamen. Probably no licour in myn veynes, either. Seems to be short-humoured. They think it's great of course. Sail on and on. Deep sea diver my wind holds out so long. Like – who was he? They belled his bed, with an electric switch. He hooked a metronome to it. Half a length, half a length, half a length onward. Strange but strue. Factor than fiction. Believe it or not ... TONITE! Marathon Mating Contest! All the women take off their beaded dresses. Four bands, no, four gypsy string quartets, in shifts. Waiters bustle about, passing drinks and sandwiches, wiping sweaty brows. In the center of the ballroom a great, glittering Priapus covered with tiny mirrors, revolves, spewing out flecks of light that play over tired backs. At last, we're the only ones. We arise, flushed and weary, to receive the trophy. As Flash-powder explodes, Miss Marbleass gives a statement to the press: "Oh yes, I lost twenty-one pounds and my virginity. But it was worth it." She poses with trophy, a loving cup capped with a four-poster. Then, next week, off to Denver, to another contest, the Rutting Rodeo, where some of the contestants will be plowhorses. I galloped, Dirk galloped, we galloped all three.

Funny that none of the doctors know what's wrong. But, of course, medical science is pretty busy on that new research project – making babies in test tubes ... keeping them alive between glass plates ...

Dr. Hardcase peered, and suddenly his colourless eyes illuminated with a new excitement. "Oh, Doctor," he shouted, "Doctor Chillcot. Come here and have a look. I believe I've isolated a strain of pure love. Of course it may be only sexual attraction ..." Dr. C. dropped his pince-nez and squinted into the microscope. "By jove, we've done it!" he exclaimed. "Of course we must be careful, Hardcase, there's enough love in this culture to destroy the world."

... God, that sun. No use trying to sleep now. Room'll be a furnace, soon. Should get up and work on the accounts. "Miss Caroline Dabnet, seven pc. set waterless alum. pots and pans (the Honeymoon Ensemble, GX5482-001); Miss Muriel Schwarze, nine pc. set knives, No-slip rosewood handles, contour fit, s.s. Neversharpen blades (the Suburban Chateau Special, GT5789-001)." Poor Caroline and poor Muriel ... I wonder if Caroline will ever wake up wondering who the hell she is, and feeling like saying GX#&%$(9%*** just to hear her own voice. Wonder if Muriel will discover the quickest way to a man's heart – through his chest, with seven inches of Neversharpen stainless steel.

... no, I'll stay in bed. Sun so hot. I froze to deaf. Massa's in de col' coal ground. My god, if they're supposed to be so hot, why do they sing about death so much? Death and parting and cold.

Strange land, of course. Away from the warmth of home. You could tie it all up, I guess. Crossing the bar; bearing the cross. Little death. Blood and water at birth. Pop! Into the cold world. Lose heat all your life, lose people, too. The kids you sang in the choir with, roasted marshmallows with, traded Batman comics with. Things: tricycle, bicycle, car. Three wheels in the morning, four in the evening. Kids you fought with, played King of the Hill with. Teachers, preachers, doctors, priests. Mr. Noonan, the astronomy teacher. Mr. Darklin, the biology teacher. Mr. Froid, the history teacher. How you worshipped them! Colder and colder. Cold nights in the drive-in movies, long past the season. The passion pits: hundreds of cars facing the big window. The movie's out of focus, but no one complains. Those aren't crickets out there, they're zippers. Girls. Your first drinking friends. The people at the café; the sleepy, queer cook with shaky hands. The whorey waitress who grabbed at you and sneaked you drinks. The kids at college: frat brothers, solemn in the candle light of initiation, or stumbling around the dance-floor in dinner jackets. God we're drunk. My God, how drunk we are! Army buddies. Others. All gone. Colder – 'til you die, alone ... the final temperature drop, measurable on a thermometer.

Who was it? The scientist who said we will be extinct in three generations – not from any atomic war – just from multiplying. Choking, crowding ourselves out, like rabbits. All kinds of warm bodies jammed together, until they suffocate. And cool a measurable amount. Guess he didn't know about those like me. And let's see – Queers and lesbians. The Catholic clergy. Maidens. Onanites. Pederasts. Fruits. Masochists and sadists. Transvestites. Hermaphrodites. The maimed and paralyzed. Fetishists. Those who use something. All these, and if a war comes, all the dead. And miscarriages, and monsters, and mules. *So, you see! There's hope after all!* The scientists and "Repent" screamers are all wrong. What we need is an affirmative outlook: Hope for the millions. The Sunday supplements are right. Dr. Norman Invincible is right, even though his glasses glint suspiciously. All our forward-looking, happy-thinking citizens are right. No wonder they're so smug! They have a right to their creedchair cumfarts. Through watching Milton Berle, reading *Life*, and going to the churches and bowling alleys of their choices (the family that bowls together holds together), they've come to know what it's taken me years to find out: that just around that rosy ahead lie Pizza, Posterity, and Pogroms: food for the millions, recognition for the millions, scapegoats for the millions. Smooth sailing 'neath an uncompetitive moon. The answers have all been worked out for me, and I've been a fool not to see them: Humility, trust in God and the president, the will for progress toward self-improvement. A happy balance between self-assertion and self-abnegation. We *will* be individuals, by God, though all alike.

I sound like the phoney intellectualizer I am. And I'm not alone. All over America P.I.'s gather, seeking refuge in refuse, subsisting on substitute in a garret or an old store ...

A mouldy beard mutters, "God is dead." A pansy pipes, "I am *not!*" Approving chuckles all around, or cool smiles. A girl who is a secretary by day, who wears pale makeup, rises. She removes her sweater and reads a poem or a-poem:

> *When the sad angel lips of Bodisatavah*
> *Caress the broken-off*
> *Needle*
> *Or when El terror*
> *In Negro chianti*
> *Hides an existential*
> *Grapefruit in his navel*
> *I know the fallacy*
> *Of phallic nails*
> *That grow to mushrooms in the angry light*

Someone murmurs, "Cool." and everyone turns to look at the square. He must be a cop, or a reporter. Or maybe Kerouac trying to sneak back for more material.

Or else, it's the campus. Outside a detachment of the American Good Joe Society is seeking out the secret underground headquarters of the Student Liberal Party – the place where all the machine guns are stored. The mob lights its way with torches made of Negroes. At the same time, the Fair Play for Fascism Committee has commandeered the student union. Dressed smartly in brown shirts and uncle sam hats, they are conducting a purge of furriners, Jews, and homosexuals. The police and National Guard are helpless, for various legislators have phoned them from time to time, giving contradictory orders as to whom to arrest. Most of the fraternity boys are engaged in a panty-raid. Die-hard Greeks have swathed themselves in sheets, and are charging through the *men's* dorm, collecting soiled underwear. Girls from the physical education department have donned football uniforms, jockstraps on their heads, and practice scrimmages on the mall. A Catholic and a Protestant religious foundation, suddenly recalling atrocities of the Thirty Years' War, have drawn up battle lines. The Catholics armed with broken whiskey bottles; the

Protestants, with whirling spray syringes. One confused girl, responding to ancestral feminist drives, has chained herself to the library steps. She is soon trampled to death, however, by an unidentifiable group bent on burning books.

But inside, all is serene. The annual English Department Tea is in progress. Doctor Bogardus has just read his paper, "Castrated God Images in the work of Sergius Dove." Mr. Dove is a young Southern writer whose fame is two-fold: He is the author of several books dealing with the corruption of sensitive youths by dirty old men. He is also well known for his habit of sitting on famous men's laps in public places. A great deal of the discussion which follows is coloured by awareness of this second trait. In fact, many of the younger men find themselves extremely conscious of their own tea-drinking mannerisms. Most have a vivid recollection of Sergius Dove's book-jacket pictures; he lies on a *chaise longue*, wearing an embroidered vest and an idyllic expression, and clutching a withered rose. The general consensus is that he is "Brilliant", anyway. The younger men relax, however, as the eminent Dr. Elderburch steps forward to read his latest poem, "Whitewards Advice":

> *Part I.*
> *Last week I saw the nightingale*
> *Which sings and kneels*
> *Among the ghostly Christmas seals*
> *In arid attics where the dead listen to the dead*
> *I could suppose that birds were birds:*
> *Defecation, defecation,*
> *And all was loved and lorn ...*

His voice is like tearing tissue, and his delicate hands clutch at the dry, rattling paper. In the smoke from briars (O, burning bush unburnt), the old, transparent curio fades to ectoplasm, while his droning seeks its objective correlative. A young assistant stirs his tea noisily, to conceal a flannel-diffused fart ...

Can I say then that I'm an anti-intellectual? Of corpse. Of curse I can. So I practice second-convolution snobbery, taking the low road – but how much fun would it be to clamber back into the ivory tower – to pour down hot lead and "defecation" on the poor ciphers. How easy to feel Superior ... so that's what man's equality means: we're all bitched up in different ways, but all just as bitchy about it.

So just ... two hours from now, I'll go knock on a door, and say, "Miss Plasterhook? I'm from Hope Chest Inc. Your friend Miss Clara Lovegarden gave us your name. May I come in?" and "You see, I'm working my way through college by interesting young people like yourself in our line ..." Line. How much longer can I pull this? It's been six, No seven years now. Before long the wrinkles will begin to show. "I grow old, I grow old." I will hear my condoms rolled. Before long, I'll be part of the world's excreta .. like World's Fair ashtrays and zoot suits ... like Reos and Halley's

Comet ... like miles of film: Walter Pigeon and Greta Percho, moldering in vaults of studios with grandiose names. Universal-International, Columbia, World-Wide ... Like Big-Little Books: Tom Mix, Smokey Stover, Krazy Kat. Mutt saying to Jeff:

NERTZ!

I'll be gone, 'snetz, I'll be gone with the wind of my epithets. Dead, like Valentino. Forgotten, like Sonny Tufts. Cancelled, like warbonds and V-mail. Useless, like anti-macassars. Obsolete like puttees. Tragic like Tucker. Silly, like mah-jong. Folded, like Collier's. A distasteful half-memory, like zeppelins and Prohibition. Nostalgic, like a paper moon.

O, Paper Moon, Shine On. Shine down on the excreta, living and dead. Swathe them in your beams or reams of toilet paper (but soft). Lave them all. The intellectual and the antilectual. The sensual equally with the sensitive. Thorne Smith and H. Allen Smith, as well as Captain John Smith and the Smith Brothers. Don't forget the Smithsonian Institute. You, who healed the birthmark of Richard Smythe, have mercy on us. "Bless us every one," I cry, waving my crotch in the air. "O, Great White Pill, tranquillize us. Be thou our protector and our placebo. Give us this day our daily dread. Cure the dip's palsy and the dipso's need. By your poor pockmarked face, cure our poxes of guilt, and pax be with us. Cure our poverty and our wealth. Patron of lunacy, cure us all of sanity. Regulate our women-folk, that their bellies may never swell round as thy face. Give us war, plague, ague, famine, fire, storm, thirst. Give us liberty and give us death. Give us plenty of nothin'ness. (Be not angry at those who smite thy face with rockets but forgive them.) Grant us rest. Grant us rest. Donna, Ace and Ray, screaming in aeternum. Amen."

UNTITLED

"Because Blondie killed Krazy Kat," say the codgers,
Or, "With Garson, Garfield, Garbo gone ..."
But it was my boyhood chum, chum
Who dawned in the eon of the Dodgers.
He was a real sheik, a stud, many's the day
We listened aways to me from the yard:
"Baby," he says, "rubber baby bumpers."
(Spillin' it so hard by the yard.)
"Don't force it, you only spoil the motor, the evening, Billy."
He tinkered with cams
He was able to leap tall buildings,
And, at a single bound, our sisters.

I got a paper dolly, dressed in dacron.
But back in the big rubber days of Akron
We spent real times to hear bible-thumpers
Belters, welters, flies and Jim Corvette
– No, no – that's new like transistors,
Like Los Angeles Angels (did I say that?)
And remember Los Alamos and a private Loss.

But Bill, or Jim, he was a song,
A philly Loman, was it? main without an island.
Came smiling through the war O.K.
Then he was run down by a taxi.
I was in it. In the minute while the meter
ticked out his life and ran up my bill, he says to me:
"Jim, you know that little girl – the little freckle-faced slut
That never wore no pants and had holes in her stockings?
Remember her? Well, Bill, I seen her the other day –
And *she* was run down by a taxi. Traffics getting awful, baby. I –"

Untitled 2

After seeing a Billy Graham movie
I gave away my all, my ass.
(They offered receipts; I turned the other cheek.)
I gave my heart to the Heart Fund.
I willed my hard-on to the Legion of Decency
For subtle work, with it.
My identity, to a man called Peter.
But now, as I negotiate to give my bones to an outfit
What makes Jello for to fatten sacred cows, I wonder:
Do I do right? Do my griefs count
Or only the spirit behind them?

JESUS IN WHITE BUCKS

Us black bucks used to buy things:
Food
Bread and bugger
Like that. The first one to finish would buy a round, and like that.
Then in the twenties, there was no one to listen
Because everyone was hearing food, so
Us white bucks from the avenue used to put on food
And sun our cells on the avenue.
Yes, we have no bananas, I listened hard.
We have no mananas today.
Penny ices umbrella'd by dust,
Food.
And then we lost our penny,
It was from heaven, raining upside down,
Who liveth and raineth forever.
One meat ball, no pot to piss forever.
Forever ...
But everyone was looking for food.
Even women painted their legs on the avenue,
So we smoked Spuds and I smoked Wings.
Burpgun eats after.
Molotov drool. Very fast, the meal is over.
And we reach the dessert, now in the sixties.
Us green backs, banana mana ...
Us food.

THE FOUR COWS

4 cows 4 cows 4 cows 4
1 brown 2 brown 3 brown more
Standing in a standing in a standing in a field
Feeling mighty blue,
Chew chew chew.

Green field green field green field green
4 cows 4 cows standing in the rain
3 heads up and one head down
Feeling mighty glum,
Chum chum chum.

4 cows 4 cows standing in the drizzle
Patter on the back, patter on the muzzle
No heads up and four heads down
Lonely and damp.
Champ champ champ.

4 cows 4 cows 4 cows 4
1 brown 2 brown 3 brown more
Grey is the sky and green is the field
Feeling mighty blue.
Chew chew chew.

The Brusque Skate

They give a policeman very good restored snow.
The candidate seldom sees solid gold.
Irritated hands next process the lovely invoice.
Weakly the DNA restores the torn solid.

This irritates the solid.
Several policemen are told by a very good candidate.
The gold is torn to invoice hands.
Do you allocate this DNA?

Irritated, the DNA hands me some skates.
A very solid snow skate is giving the invoice tears.
Solidifying, he hands her a weak candidate.
Weakly much snow was allocated by the brusque skate.

Seldom does irritation love any restored solid.
A hand sees the lovely police, and a snow processes them.
The solid gold has now allocated the hand we just saw.
Irritated, my DNA hands the snow a candidate policeman.

Police skates love the restored invoice!
Why does the solid weakly tear several lovely gold snows?
The invoice seldom processes a few good hands.
(Does not restore, love or irritate.)

No Exit

A One-Act Play

PERFORMANCE NOTE: Theatre should be well-crowded; guests and friends may be invited in to help. Before the performance starts, all exits must be locked.

Cast: *The eminent scientist*, a good looking man
The panel of experts, four plainer people
A spectator, planted in the audience

As the curtain rises, the panel of experts is seated behind a TV panel show multiple desk, equipped with as many lights, bells, lighted signs, buzzers, etc. as desired. The panel is to keep these going throughout the play. This desk is at the left, and the eminent scientist's lectern is at the right. He stands behind it, smiling personably at the audience.

EMINENT SCIENTIST: You see, that is a point many people fail to grasp concerning Freedom of Speech. Freedom of Speech does not give one the right to cry "Fire!" in a crowded theatre.

SPECTATOR: Fire!

The panel of experts rises, takes from under the desk four cans of gasoline (red, marked GASOLINE), and quickly douses the audience and aisles with it. One of them lights the audience.

SPECTATOR: Fire!

EMINENT SCIENTIST (studying his notes and looking slightly pained): Really!

VOICE OVER PUBLIC ADDRESS SYSTEM: Please remain in your seats until the fire department arrives. Kindly remain seated until the arrival of the fire department. (Repeats, with variations, until entire audience is burnt.)

CURTAIN

Seventh Inning Stretch

A One-Act Play

A man sits onstage next to a table radio. A transcription of an actual baseball game, preferably scoreless, will be playing, starting at about the fourth inning. The man will be motionless and expressionless, perhaps with his back to the audience. At the seventh-inning stretch, he will stand up and invite the audience to stand up and stretch. He stretches and yawns, then falls down dead. (Note: the actor should fall in a comfortable position, for he is going to have to lie there for a long time) A doctor comes on, examines him, pronounces the exact time of death, leaves. The game goes on, and the second game of a double-header begins. This will actually be the same game over again, although the audience may not suspect it until about the fourth inning. The game goes on until the entire audience has left.

CURTAIN

Down His Alarming Blunder

Had we but will at least, and locks,
More blueness, Mr President, were no warranty.
We would talk now and butter that time
To feel and smell our daily suspect's file.
You by the wasted Senate's grille
Should quasars prove: I by the stadium
Of brain would depreciate. I would
Defy you real weeks before the bee,
And you should, if you hurry, click
Well after the holiday of the paint.
My invoice beauty should develop
Better than erasers, though less partial;
Some faces should come to symbolize
Your shirt, and toward your mother deploy;
Those to complicate this cake,
But these for any other;
One Coke at most for any poet,
And the other brand should fake your doom.
For, Madame Industry, you bury them pliers,
Yet would I expand in poorer equations.
    But in my nose I sometimes arrange
The drugstore's yellow summer, burning over there;
And nearer, right before us sound
Programs of problem police.
Your nail should very likely be denied
But in your new errand shall process
This very delighted bun,
And your special spaniel dress up the pants
And for the clouds, many of my hands:
The bug's a tall and final floor
But all I buy do now and then scream.
    Seldom, therefore, before the daily smile
Chews up your orange of metal nuance,
And then your strangling look collapses
Into some saying about executive robots,
Never let us mutate before we may
And always, after swell particles of the sewing machine
Here where our nouns are read
Then bring in his nice money.
Let us deny suspiciously our montage and almost
Our window out into every year

By the pretend lieutenants of bronchitis:
Thus, rather we should sometimes think our answer
Baked evenly, than we should know him sneezed.

LETTER

Dear Letter,

    Just writing to say thanks a lot. I hope this finds you in good health and excellent spirits. I really like you and would hate to say you are otherwise. I know you could say this much better, but with you I don't feel I have to cross the t's and dot the i's. You can read between the lines.

    In fact there's not much more I can say, so this is just a note which I hope finds you well and all. It's been lots of fun writing to you. Well, thanks again.

    Regards,

        Love

Love Nest

I
It is all our parade,
Ours! It is us they wave at,
Not you more than me or
Me more,
But us! The sacrificial couple.
Clapping and cheering!
Look at the priests and ministers:
How jealous they are,
With everybody screaming – and the rabbis!
The rabbis are black with rage!
Someone brings a pig to bless,
And then we climb in bed atop our fire tower.
I see Seven Corners, Minneapolis,
And there are only six! Bless them, every one!
We see New York, and leagues beyond:
A fisherman is crapping off his boat.
I see you, fisherman! God bless you
And your crap and little boat!
Look! Strong men are wrestling in the square below.
The winner gets our candy wrappers. Look!
They're flying roasted ducks for us,
In tight formation at a thousand miles an hour!
The crowd is upside down!
They scream best wishes to the happy couple: that's us, dear.

II
Look at the teenagers in the dying sunlight:
The maidens are not aimless any more;
They love us. They love to see us climb upon our sheets
Of styrofoam, softer than the down
Upon the chins of youths in leather
Who are chorusing our song.
This will always be our song,
For they will always sing it for us.
No car honks madly;
The mayor gives the death penalty for honking, tonight;
The cars have nightingales in place of horns.
The pig we blessed is barbecued, now, and climbs to us,
Wearing a scented robe and wreath of parsley,
Carrying a hod of sandalwood, filled with acorns and white apples.

Smell the mint? It comes from leaves below,
Crushed by ballerinas, twenty at a time, who softly smash it down.
Traffic everywhere has stopped.
I guess they all went home to watch us on television.
A lone bike light crosses the Golden Gate Bridge:
He will be fined.

III
Draw the red curtains, climb in you and I:
You, so tawny; me, so brown and brawny; the salad of saffron and
oyster-eyes;
The gold-filled greasy black turkey legs so hot;
The cantaloupe is crispy; there's hot bread from my mom's oven,
Wrapped in waxed tissue of pink sequins, for bread; there's marmalade.
Come to bed.
We cling to one another, and the spice-clusters and holly on the ham
Twinkle so naughtily-
You shy thing you!-
We twine with chilled clams at our chins and elbows and knees,
We sip each other's cup of spiced cocoa
And know how we'll remember this
Before it's happened. Fireflies sizzle past,
Or are they comets? Reflected, darting, in the glossy shells
Of snails in gold spittoons. They must be comets,
For the fireworks display of the UN Navy is all over.
Wasn't it beautiful, though? And here we thought the UN was so tiresome!
Around your neck I fasten strings on strings of white sausages
Made of Oriental swine and plovers;
They must be worth a thousand dollars a bite.
I bite your ear, my love.
What is going on? The lights are out! The thunder!
Where is my – I forget what.
I feel the pulse of marching feet, marching like a big pulse, or
something!
Where are we?
Is this England, and the trotters come out to greet us?
We seem to be – around each other, somehow – look out for those
blazing crepes!
We might explode! Look out!
The feet stomp out our pulse! It is the end!
I can't stand so much excitement in the middle of the night like this.
What? Your breast has grown a *thing*! Where are my arms?
I sink, I sink! Turkey falls out of my mouth, unchewed.
Maybe I'll never breathe again. I forgot-
I feel I might – I did! I did!
A sudden rush of rose-scent, like a hot fudge sundae.
A field of corn cut down and torn to Crackerjacks.

You did, too! We both did!
Now I know what I forgot.
Sent up in a small enamelled casket, and blessed by a cardinal.
It would have been enshrined, but I forgot.
The chicken has grown cold and stale, and only now we notice
The tragic cake we should have eaten at the moment.
High swirls of coconut frosting mock us
With their silly silver drape of B.B.'s.
We draw apart, frightened of the cake.
We turn our backs on it, and on each other and the world,
And try to sleep,
Listening to the *ping* of butterscotch around us, crystallizing.

IV
What's up? It's night, still. Did a car door slam?
One of the kids cry out?
Another chance! It isn't possible!
You sense it too, for you're awake.
We nestle, watching the flicker of the bombs
That get Las Vegas.
You cut your finger on some angel-hair last Christmas,
And only now it cries.
This time, darling, I'll remember it.
We bless our second chance,
And while the brass clock hums in the dark, hums our song, we slip together.
This time it's not so good, but afterwards
The fire pumper's motor roars!
The sacred article falls off, amazed.
White light! Oceans of suds!
Look, here's our cake, swimming to greet us!
O Cake of Coconut! O diamond-sparkled, lovely, great, clean thing
from Betty Crocker!

We look around. "The suds will cover everything," you laugh.
I wink. "They last Eternity, and one pan longer."
We light a candle to the suds and kneel.
I love you.

Page

I am writing a poem about this page.
That is, I am in the very act of writing
(as I write this)
A poem about this,
The page upon which
The poem I endite
Is written
This page, once white, now bears
Eight – no, nine lines of poetry
Or more – poetry about
The page
On which
Is writ
This poem.
The poem tells us that it is
Not only a poem about the page
That bears it,
But a poem about the poem
That is borne
So cheerfully by the page
About which
I am writing a poem.
Here.

The "Pelican"

What a wonderful bird is the "pelican".
Is it not.
There are many poems written about it –
Some calling it a "wonderful bird",
Others carping – This poem for example
Is one of many extant
Whose subject is "THE PELICAN"

 * * * *

There is much to be said for this bird:
The pelican holds fish in the sack
Or bag beneath his bill (beak).
It has white I believe feathers
Like a stork.
But the difference is

 * * * *

There are many things to be said
About the wonderful "pelican".
Some so-called "penguin" books are really
"Pelican" books.
There are also "peregrine", "puffin" and
"Peacock" books to be found.
"Plover", "ptarmigan" and "pterodactyl"
Are not represented, though.
"Pelican" books are very

 * * * *

Farewell then to the wonderful white-feathered pelican.
And farewell also to the stork.
And now we return to work.

THE TREASURE OF THE HAUNTED RAMBLER

The architect told us our house had original features:
A special "love" room, he said, separate from the bedroom,
Would make clear the important difference between love,
A dynamic progress, and sleep, which is static.
There was also plenty of room for rooms
We'd add, as our family increased, he added.

One day, in the "love" room, my bride said,
Bouncing on our great, pink, heart-shaped trampoline,
"Look, we never watch TV, so let's turn the TV lounge
Into a sewing room for me." I agreed,
But it meant switching a lot of things around,
And suddenly my boss showed up for supper.
We had to serve him buffet-style, sitting on the edge of the bed.
Eventually, of course, we made the bedroom a proper dining hall,
And the shower a breakfast room, and we slept
In the two ample storage closets,
Storing the vacuum and stuff in the tub.
Then came summer, and we knew
Our arrangements were only temporary, like the fact
That the breeze could no longer get into the breezeway,
Or that Marion was pregnant. We would have to build.

One day, at the refreshment stand in our lobby,
My wife asked me why the library couldn't have a carrel.
But we had a real problem in the pet room: the cats
Were eating some of Buddy's oysters,
So we'd need either a cat room or an oyster room, and quick.
"Couldn't we just partition the pet room?" she asked,
"The way we converted the old book nook
Into a tool shed and granary?" "No," I explained,
"Because then the hamsters would have no scampering room,
Unless we built a hamster-scamper hall.
But I was thinking we could buy the Eberlys' garage
And run a tunnel to our wine cellar,
With doors to both the present pet room and the mushroom room."
"This is no place to discuss it," she reminded me.
We repaired to the family conference room,
Where Buddy came to tell us
Linda often cluttered his stamp room with her dolls.

Late that night, when we had solved these problems,
I went to my room, but found I could not sleep.
The great house creaked, as I made my way to the meditation chapel.
I was too restless to meditate; consumed by fever,
I paced the house.
In the conservatory, Buddy's jukebox had a hideous leer, accusing.
I fled to the map room, the smoker, the African violet room – my God!
Through the gin rummy room, I ran on and on,
And finally collapsed, gasping, over the lunch counter.
It was then I saw it! A curious old door, half-hidden by the gleaming coffee urn.
Mad with fear, I slowly pulled it open.
It was the love room.

Sladek Incognito

JUST ANOTHER VICTIM

The whining voice of Ann's room-mate cut through her thoughts. "Ann, honey, can I borrow your white cardigan?" In only a few minutes, Ann thought joyfully, it would cease to whine forever.

"Of course you may," she said, not looking up from her magazine. She knew the scene only too well without actually looking.

Virginia, seated before the vanity table, pencilling her brows or putting on too much bright lipstick.

Voluptuous Virginia, making herself up to look even sluttier than usual. She would wear Ann's clothes and return them dirty, stained with food and liquor, stretched out of shape.

And, of course, it was Virginia who got all the men. They seemed to prefer her flashy, trashy stupidity to Ann's refinement and culture.

To them, the choice seemed to be a bouncy, lively redhead who could tell a good off-colour story, or a quiet, slim, pensive girl with brown hair and – and, somehow, this made a great difference – with glasses.

Ann took off her glasses now, momentarily, and rubbed her eyes. When she restored them she saw that Virginia was close to being ready. Ready for her date with Mr Barker, Ann reminded herself, gritting her teeth. It was time to act.

She might have forgiven Virginia everything – and there were so many things to forgive about Virginia – but not for Mr Barker. Borrowing clothes was one thing, stealing a man was another. As Virginia was about to find out.

Not that Mr Barker – Al, as Virginia called him – had ever really been Ann's. But he was the head of the department where she worked.

So Ann felt certain proprietary rights over him. After all, Virginia worked for an entirely different firm.

Every girl in his department worshipped Mr Barker, none more than Ann. He was good-looking. Not dazzling, but what Ann liked to think of as genteel. That is, his wavy hair was just turning grey, his smile was gentle, and his deep voice serious.

And behind his rimless glasses, Mr Barker's bright blue eyes twinkled with good humour. A gentle, intelligent, fatherly man – and a bachelor.

He seemed to appreciate Ann's good taste and refinement, too. They had had a few conversations about painting and art, mutually enjoyable.

Then, just when he had seemed on the verge of asking her out, Virginia had shown up to have lunch with her room-mate. Meeting Mr Barker at the office door, Virginia had turned on her cheapest, flashiest charm.

"Oh, are you Annie's boss? I've been hearing so much about you, Mr Barker. Why you've just swept poor Annie off her feet."

And, somehow, he had been taken in by it all. The next day, he and Virginia went to lunch.

This had been going on more than a month now and it had been almost a week since Ann decided how she was going to get him away from Virginia.

Ann was reading a newspaper at the café where she usually breakfasted on coffee and a roll. *Strangler claims 10th victim*, read the headline, and under it: *Police helpless*.

She read the news story through and the boxed item on the next page, headed: *Warning to single girls: Don't open the door to strangers!*

Forgetting to finish her breakfast, forgetting that she was late for work, Ann stored at the paper while a plan came to her.

It was a preposterous plan, a diabolical plan and so simple it just had to work. It was an end to Virginia's life – and perhaps the beginning of a life for Ann and Mr Barker.

The paper had told her all she needed to know. The strangler's victims were always young women. Flashy young women. Like Virginia. He killed them in their homes, or in parks or other lonely spots, by strangling them with nylon stockings.

Now Ann was sitting on a crumpled nylon, pretending to read a magazine, while Virginia prepared for her date.

Ann had it all planned. At soon as she killed Virginia, she would dash to the corner grocery shop and buy a few things. Then she would come back home, "find" the body, drop a bag of groceries, then wait for Mr Barker's arrival.

He would find her insensible with grief ... he would comfort her ...

"How do I look, kid?" Virginia bounced to her feet and turned round, shaking out her long red tresses.

"Fine," Ann said, standing up and drawing the stocking out between her hands. "You look perfect, darling."

There was barely time for her to get back, take a look at the body, spill the bag of groceries and slump in a chair, still wearing her coat, when the bell ran. Wild-eyed, Ann opened it and gasped, "Help! Oh, God, help!"

Mr Barker caught her before she could fall and eased her into a chair. He glanced at the spilled groceries, at Virginia, the stocking knotted round her throat.

"What is it? How did this happen?"

With just the right amount of hysteria in her voice, she said: "I thought I would pick up a few groceries before the place on the corner closed. I couldn't have been gone five minutes. When I got back ..."

"I see." His voice was kindly. "Have you called the police yet?"

"No, I ... I've been stupid, I suppose."

"Not at all, you poor kid. You're shocked, I suppose." His blue eyes shone with sympathy. He sat down next to her on the arm of his chair.

"Looks like another victim of the strangler," he said.

"Yes, it must have been."

His arm slipped round her shoulders comfortingly. Ann leaned back against it. Her eyes closed.

"At least that's what you hoped I would think, isn't it?" he said in the same kindly tone.

"What do you mean?" Her eyes came open.

"My dear, my dear." He shook his head sadly. "I wish you hadn't done it. Really." He reached in his pocket and took out an envelope.

"But I didn't! It was the str ..."

"I disagree." He shook a nylon stocking from the envelope and knotted it round her throat.

"But I did it for you! I love you," she gasped.

"Ah, don't they all?"

"Please! Mr Barker ..."

The knot tightened. Mr Barker's blue eyes twinkling at her from behind his rimless glasses were the last thing she saw. The last thing she heard was: "But won't you call me Al?"

YOU HAVE A FRIEND AT FENGROVE NATIONAL

Jason Price did not look up from his paper as the waitress refilled his coffee cup "Whatcha reading, Mr Price? About the big robbery over in Meadowville?"

"Big," he asked, looking at her over the tops of his pince-nez. "You call twenty thousand dollars big?"

"Maybe not to a rich lawyer like you, but ..."

"Not to anybody. Let me show you why crime literally does not pay. These three men will divide their money, getting – after expenses – about six thousand dollars each. If they are caught, they will serve no less than fifteen years in prison, earning thereby only two hundred and fifty dollars per year.

"Had they, on the other had, put twenty thousand dollars into that same bank, they would be receiving about the same amount in yearly interest – and living as free men."

He rose and brushed crumbs from his waistcoat. "And, of course, if they get away with it, they'll simply do it again – and again, till they're caught."

He wondered what the waitress would have said if he had informed her that he, too, was a bank robber and that today he was going to rob not one, but four banks – his only weapons a smile and a ballpoint pen.

One had to look the part, of course. In the window of the Fengrove Bon Ton Bakery, Jason's reflection assured him he did look the part. When he entered the Fengrove National Bank, the manager, Hal Glenning, would step out of his office to meet him and shake him by the hand.

And give him money.

Across the way the courthouse clock read 9.05 and already the dusty main street was filled with mud-caked pick-up trucks, tractors and the cars of Friday shoppers. Jason touched his cravat and stepped along briskly toward the bank.

This entire operation had taken him a month to set up. In each of four Midwestern towns, a certain middle-aged gentleman had set up office: "Jason Price, Attorney", "John Pettigrew, Abstracts and Titles", "Osgood Troy, Attorney", and "Jeremy Parks, Realtor".

Each week each of these men deposited several thousand dollars in his local bank, till now each had an account standing at ten thousand dollars.

As Jason pushed open the door marked "Fengrove National Bank", the manager, Hal Glenning, was on his feet and walking to greet him.

"Jason, you old scoundrel!" he said, as if they had known each other much longer than a month. "You're certainly never in your office. Where do you keep yourself these days?"

"Business," Jason sighed, making a vague gesture. The manager laughed. They began to talk of local gossip. Finally Jason drew forth three cheques from his wallet and laid them on Hal's desk. "I've made a killing this week, as you can see."

Hal noted the size of the cheques. "I'll say. Shall I deposit these?"

Jason pursed his lips. "No, I'll deposit the Pettigrew cheque, but I'd like to cash the other two, Hal, if you don't mind. I have a rather important piece of business to attend to this morning."

Hal gasped. "You're going to walk round with eighteen thousand dollars in cash on you? Don't do it, Jason. I'll get you a bank messenger. He can go along with you, wherever your business is."

"Nonsense. That would be advertising my money, Hal, and inviting theft. No, I'll carry it myself. In large bills, please. Hundreds, I believe."

At 10.10, he entered the Meadowville Merchant's Bank and Ken Forest, the brusque, beefy manager, invited him back to his office. "John Pettigrew" seemed almost an old friend and so, when they had discussed the recent robbery at some length, nothing seemed more natural than that "John" should cash two cheques and deposit one – though Ken felt duty-bound to warn him about walking around with all that cash.

So did the manager of the Goldfield Mutual Bank warn "Ozzie Troy".

By noon, the easy half was finished. Jason and his alter egos had drawn seventy two thousand dollars from accounts holding forty thousand. But now he was going to try to get back his investment. With luck, the banks would not exchange the cheques till Monday. Without luck ...

Hal Glenning was a bit suspicious. "Are you sure Pettigrew's cheques are good?" he asked.

"Not at all. You'd better check with his bank." And of course Hal learned – from Ken Forest – that "John Pettigrew" had nineteen thousand dollars in his account. Hal apologized, Jason endorsed the cheque and they stepped out of the office to see the chief cashier.

But the cashier was busy just now, looking down the muzzle of a gun. Three men in rubber animal masks seemed to fill the lobby with solid fear. "Give," said one to the cashier.

He did not give. Instead he reached out and snatched off the rubber face. The bandit shot him twice and turned to run.

What followed might have made a pleasant comedy routine in other circumstances. For the bandit wanted to get past Jason to the door and Jason was so very willing to let him get past that he kept side-stepping and getting in his way. Exasperated, the bandit raised his gun. Jason fainted in terror ...

"Wake up, hero," said Hal. Jason blinked up at the figures of a dozen state troopers.

"Hero?"

"If you hadn't delayed that kid when you did, he might have got away with this," said a trooper. "The other two did escape, barely, but we have a good idea who they are – all members of the Scarfo gang, out of Chicago. Anyway, thanks."

Jason felt the packets of money still safe in his pockets as he got to his feet. He was free and in the clear, now, and one hundred thousand dollars to the good.

"We'll want you to testify before the grand jury next Wednesday, of course," said the trooper.

"Of course. Be glad to, officer." Jason dusted himself off. By Wednesday, he would be ... Paris? Rome?

"As a matter of fact, we were thinking of taking you into protective custody until then. The Scarfo gang has a way of getting to witnesses. Buying them – or killing them."

"Indeed. Well, I don't think you'll need to protect me, at any rate."

The trooper looked down for a moment, gravely. "I hope not. But just in case, we'll keep a man stationed outside your door, night and day. I'm sure you won't mind the inconvenience?"

Jason pictured the banks on Monday as they unsnarled his finances and discovered his crime.

He began to hear the trooper's words through the muffled surging of his own heartbeat.

"Don't feel we're making a prisoner of you, Mr Price. After all, the hearing is on Wednesday and after that, you'll be ..."

The Switch

Bradford Finley had always lived for trains. That he was a sales manager and not running a train, he had long considered the first tragedy of his life. In the past few minutes, he had learned of the second tragedy.

With the living-room window open, he could hear the Greystone Yard engines backing and filling, making up the Omaha train. It was a comforting sound and he tried to concentrate on it, tried not to hear Elaine saying: "Yes, darling, I am having an affair. And there's nothing you can do about it, is there?"

Her laugh was triumphant. Brad walked outside with his drink and sipped it slowly, watching the stars. He tried to think of everything but Elaine. He thought hot summer days of his childhood, of waiting an hour for the Fargo Cannonball to go by, so he could wave at the engineer. But finally, he thought of how he was going to kill his wife.

It would be a railroad accident, of course. Carefully planned, with nothing left to chance. One of these weekends, Elaine would be going to see her parents in Mullburg and she would be going by train. Brad knew already the place where he would rig the accident.

He drove out there the following evening and many evenings, to study the set-up till he knew it perfectly.

Due to their system of interlocking signals, the railways were nearly proof against accident. These signal lights, mounted on towers a few miles apart, extended on main lines all across the country and each described the condition of the track up to the next signal.

Green meant the track was clear, yellow that a switch was open to some other track and red that another train was blocking the line. If the signal was out, red was assumed and the train must stop.

An accident could only occur through negligence – or sabotage.

Brad chose a place where the main line curved to the right, while a siding led straight ahead into an oil terminal. The siding was only about three hundred yards long, for the purpose of filling or draining tank cars of naphtha.

The train carrying Elaine would approach this intersection at about fifty mph. The engineer would give a cursory glance at the signal tower – note the green jewel – as he had a hundred times and open the throttle.

But this time, the signal would be wrong, the switch would be open and the train would – even with brakes locked – plough into a million gallons of explosive fuel. Elaine would be just settling into her seat in the first car.

Brad assembled the materials he would need to rig the switch and signal, including wire, aluminium foil, black paint and foam rubber scraps, and he added a few tools, a pair of gloves and a pair of heavy boots.

He timed himself driving from the railroad station to the switch and computed to the second how much time he would have to set it up.

Then, almost before he knew it, he found himself driving Elaine to the station, a strange dryness in his throat.

"Aren't we a little early?" she said as they pulled up before the station. "That clock says only 9.40 and the train doesn't leave until 10.20." She pointed to the illuminated dial above the station entrance.

"I'm sorry, dear," he said, shaking his watch and pretending to examine it. "But look, I've got those accounts to go over tonight. Mind if I just drop you now and don't stay to see you off?"

She did not mind, any more than she minded his entire existence, and so they parted at 9.45. At 9.58 he pulled up next to the silver tower, ghostly in the light of the rising moon.

He was conscious of no emotion at all, nothing but the mechanism of his brain, clicking over in dull repetition the steps of his plan. The train would come past at 10.29 and everything had to be ready for it.

He slipped on the gloves and boots first. Then, with pliers and a roll of wire in hand, he climbed the tower ladder. The high-pitched murmur of crickets faded as he climbed and he was alone with the even drone of power from the signal case.

After cutting the metal seal, he opened the case and rewired the signal so that it would show green no matter what the condition of the track ahead. As he worked, he imagined the activity at the railway station.

Switch engines were probably just putting the last long, sleek silver car in place on the train. The waiters in the diner were slipping on their white jackets and having a last smoke. Elaine would be tapping her foot impatiently in the waiting room. Brad checked his work and found it OK.

A hammer and chisel from his car enabled him to break the big padlock on the switch. It was heavy with internal rust and took all his energy to throw the lever.

For a moment afterward he was too dizzy to do anything but stand and gape at the points – now aligned for the siding.

About now at the railway station, the waiters were putting the final conical napkins on the tables. Carmen were ringing their hammers on the wheel rims.

The engineer and fireman were already in place and passengers had begun filing down the platform. It was 10.15, but there was work to be done yet.

He glanced up at the signal – still green – then at the points. Engineers did not, he realized, depend only on signals. No, they looked at the points of every switch to make sure it was properly aligned.

If the engineer of this train noticed that the twin ribbons of steel led not to the right, but straight ahead, he might have time to stop. Brad had to use foam rubber covered with foil to fill gaps – where gaps should not appear – and black paint to simulate the proper gaps.

At 10.28 his work was done and already he could see, in the night sky above the horizon, the winking yellow aura of the train's flasher beacon. He was getting out just in time.

It was after he'd started toward his car that he saw the kid. A tow-headed youngster of perhaps ten, who must have walked over from one of the farms to watch the train.

Maybe he did this every evening, the way another boy, once ...

The boy was standing on the siding, next to a dirty tank car full of naphtha. Just above his white hair the moonlight picked out the diamond-shaped sign: "Danger – Inflammable Liquid". The ground began to tremble.

"Hey kid!" Brad began to run toward him. "Get out of there! Beat it!"

The boy looked puzzled and did not move. He knew perfectly well it was safe to stand on this siding. The bright yellow, winking cone of the headlight broke over the scene. It was still a good half-mile distant. Maybe he could still save the boy, get him in the clear.

Brad found himself on the siding, his back to the brilliant beam as he sprinted toward the boy, shouting.

The boy's hand flapped gaily at the distant train. As Brad ran, the smell of naphtha stung his nostrils, the smell of fear. The diesel throbbed louder behind him, shaking the ground.

"Hey!" he shouted. "Hey there!" He drove on, his clumsy boots skidding in gravel.

On either side of him, the tracks began to gleam from the dazzling headlight. He turned to look at it over his shoulder. It was close, too close, blinding.

He stumbled and fell, his head coming down against the rail, and in the last second of consciousness he knew it was too late to save the boy. It was too late to save himself.

It was even too late to wave to the engineer.

TIMETABLE

On the telephone, the killer sounded discreet, calm and precise. "I believe I can take care of your problem in exactly the manner you described," he said. "In your letter. You may go ahead with the first payment as planned, sir."

Curtis Wall doodled geometric designs on his desk blotter. "You understand my instructions exactly, I hope. Timing is extremely important."

The killer understood. Curtis replaced the receiver and leaned back in his chair, permitting himself a small chuckle. By this time next week, nothing and nobody would stand between him and the chairmanship of International Investments, Inc.

Oddly enough, the present chairman, Leonard Hudson, was his best friend. The two men had gone to college together, struggled up the management ladder together, and arrived at the top together – almost.

They lived only a few miles apart, took the same commuter train, dressed alike and took turns beating one another at golf. They even looked a little alike, being both rangy, bony giants, with enviable suntans and dark hair only touched with grey.

Now and then at a party, one of them might kiss the other's wife in the kitchen after drinking too many vodka martinis – a drink both men preferred.

Just the same, Leonard would have to go. Curtis knew that if he allowed his friend to run the company for even another six months, they would be ruined. It went beyond friendship.

It went far deeper, as deep as the law of jungle survival. Leonard Hudson had bad judgement – he was weak. He was not fit to command. Only he and Curtis knew this, just as they knew Curtis could command very well. But Leonard covered himself well with others.

Yet, under his weak, nervous authority, the company had steadily dwindled and declined. Leonard could not bring himself to admit his personal failure, to step down in Curtis's favour. Bad judgement again. There was by now only one thing Curtis could do about it.

The effect would be this – Leonard would be going to Chicago, to investigate the possible acquisition of a small electronics firm. He had reserved already a private compartment on the overnight train from New York.

Curtis would see him off and then, it being too late to commute home, would presumably spend the night in New York. Leonard would arrive in Chicago in the morning and be seen getting off the train. Then he would vanish. Just like that.

The reality would be slightly different. First, after seeing Leonard off, Curtis would go straight to the airport, fly to an intermediate city and there catch the same train.

Next, the killer he had hired would board the train, kill Leonard and throw his body out, near a prearranged town.

There the killer would descend, pick up a car that he had arranged to have waiting and return to find the body. He would remove its identification and move it to some place far enough from the railroad to disassociate the two.

Next, Curtis would occupy Leonard's compartment for the rest of the trip, impersonating him for the benefit of railroad personnel.

He would check Leonard's baggage at that station, fly back to New York and be back at his desk by noon.

Every detail had been gone over again and again. The timing was perfect, to the minute. Both he and the hired assassin knew when and where they must act.

The day was only a week away – only a few days away – it was today!

His mood was buoyant throughout the day. It was not his face that he shaved that morning, but the beaming face of a leader. The future chairman had begun to feel powerful already.

On the other hand, Leonard seemed a little less substantial, as if he had somehow begun to die already. It was not the present chairman that Curtis took to dinner, that he put on the train to Chicago. It was a ghost, a Leonard Hudson who was dead and did not realize it.

Curtis awoke with a start. Panicked, he glanced at his watch. Nearly midnight and the calendar was just turning over. The train was slowing down for a station. According to his timetable, it must be Blaine, Ohio.

Switching out the compartment lights, he raised the shade and peered out, but he could not make out the station name. Calm down, he told himself. It had to be Blaine, the station where the killer was to get off and pick up his car. The headlights of a car flicked on. As it backed and turned around, they illuminated part of the station's sign: "BL ..."

Then it was all over. He slept right through it and it was finished. He began to laugh, hard, smacking his fist into the seat cushion. Till this moment, Curtis had not realized how much he hated Leonard.

But there was work to do. When he had last seen Leonard, he'd been wearing a charcoal grey pinstripe suit, grey silk tie and pale blue shirt. Now Curtis quickly changed into his duplicate clothes. Still chuckling, he walked down the aisle to number 47, Leonard's compartment.

It was locked. Black panic rose in his throat. But how could the killer have been so careless? How could he?

"Help you, sir? Lock yourself out?"

A steward with a drink on a tiny tray was at his elbow. Curtis forced calm into his voice. "Yes, don't know what happened. I seem to have lost my key somewhere ..."

"That's all right, Mr Hudson." The steward did not see the momentary shock in "Mr Hudson's" face. He was inserting his passkey.

The killing could not have taken place long ago – there was still a whiff of cigarette smoke as the door opened. Curtis smiled and stepped in. The steward seemed to want to follow.

"Uh, your drink, sir? Vodka martini?"

"Oh? Of course."

When the steward had withdrawn, Curtis lifted the drink and toasted himself. "The chairman is dead," he whispered. "Long live the chairman!"

The chairman had been dead since 11.30, he reflected, touching the cold glass to his lips. Nearly an hour.

There was a knock at the door. "Ticket, please."

That was odd, he thought fumbling out his ticket and unlocking the door. The train crew wasn't supposed to change at Blaine, but much farther up the line. At a place called Bluffton, was it?

The door crashed back and somebody leaped at him out of the darkness. A karate chop to the throat knocked the breath out of Curtis and slammed him against the outside wall.

The door clicked shut. The stranger's two gloved fists were at Curtis's throat then, pulling something. He felt a thin strand tighten about his throat.

"But what is it? Why? What's gone wrong?" he wanted to say, but it was too late for talking, now. The pounding of blood in Curtis's ears mingled with the pounding of the train wheels.

He felt his knees go limp, he knelt in vodka and broken glass. In his remaining few seconds of consciousness, Curtis ran over his plan once more.

Time zones, he thought, I forgot the damned time zones. The time in Blaine, Ohio, was an hour earlier than in New York.

He had made one choice, the killer had made another. It explained why the compartment was locked – Leonard was still alive. He had probably ordered a drink, then stepped out for a few minutes. But then he might return, any minute!

Curtis clung to that hope, as he felt his eye go out of focus. First they could see the two fists, then the killer's watch, reading 11.32. Then they could see nothing but the killer's face, impassive and calmly professional.

But when Leonard finally did return, there was nobody there. Only the smell of vodka and the open window.

Now That I'm Free

Marie lay on her side at the foot of the stairs, her auburn hair fanned across the light blue carpet, her skin unnaturally pale.

Roy hesitated, then reached out a hand and touched her throat. There was no pulse of life. He was ... divorced.

He was free, free to be with June. Careful, he warned himself. He was not all that free. Not yet. And there would be Bill to reckon with, too. Still, it had gone smoothly. He could hardly have believed, yesterday, it would all be so easy.

The house was secluded enough so that nobody would have noticed he had come home at noon. And, of course, a projectionist could not be missed from the projection room, not while the film had nearly half an hour to run. His alibi was perfect, unless ...

For a moment Roy froze, his hand still on the warm, silent throat, imagining the film becoming jammed or out of phase, the stamping and whistling audience, the manager finally going to the empty projection room to see what was the matter.

Then he shrugged the scene away. He knew the print of the feature film was good, unpatched, not likely to jam. The audience, at this time of day, would largely be old people, dozing, not watching. He calmed himself, locked up the house and drove back to work at a reasonable, lawful speed.

Nobody saw him park in the alley, as he always did, slip in through the service door, up the stairs and into the projection room.

The air, as usual, was stifling hot and he felt his heart pounding from running up the stairs. He began to perspire freely. A reel of advertising slipped from his wet grasp and clanged on the concrete floor.

Take it easy, Roy, he told himself, you'll live longer. He threaded an intermission announcement on the number two projector, adjusted it and closed it. On No. 1 the final ten minutes of a gangster film were unreeling, a noisy car chase. Roy's mouth felt dry, in need of a cigarette.

"I'm free," he murmured to himself under the gunfire. The words did not have the savour he had imagined they would. If only he didn't have to face Bill, his best friend Bill, and tell him he had fallen in love with June, Bill's wife.

And if Bill refused to let her go? Roy didn't want to think that far ahead. Instead he preferred to daydream about June herself, while keeping an eye on the screen for the thirty-second warning pip.

There had been a feeling between Roy and June, a kind of electricity that nobody else seemed to notice, almost from the moment they met. She was small, blonde, peppery, with quick movements and a lively sense of humour – everything, in short, that Marie was not. He had plainly met the wrong woman first.

The warning pip flashed in the corner of the screen. Roy moved his hand to the toggle switch, barely aware of the gun battle, which the Chicago police were inevitably winning.

Marie – solemn, beautiful, dull Marie, who would never have given him a divorce, rest in peace. Roy didn't hate her, he had felt sorry for her. But she had been in the way, like an innocent bystander during a bank robbery. It was as simple as that.

The Chicago gangster made his ten-second dying speech and slumped down in the bullet-shattered phone booth. The End appeared and the final pip. Roy switched to the intermission announcement and stepped onto the balcony for a smoke. Just time for a drag or two before he had to hop back inside and get the curtain and house lights. Then he went back to his cigarette and his thoughts.

It was inevitable that he and June would become lovers, and Bill hadn't done anything to slow things down. In fact, Bill had become pretty much indifferent to his wife in the past year, taking her for granted. There were unexplained absences.

One evening, Roy had dropped over to see his friend and his friend had not been at home – it was as simple as that. Except that Roy couldn't stop seeing June, couldn't even prevent himself from seeing her more and more.

Night after night, he made feeble excuses to get out of the house. Day after day she visited the projection room.

It went beyond all bounds of reasonable behaviour. They knew it must be becoming obvious to Bill and Marie, but they were powerless to stop themselves.

Then, yesterday, Roy finally began to question Marie, in a roundabout way, to see just what she did know.

And the more she protested that she loved him and couldn't imagine the circumstances under which she could part from him, the more Roy knew he had to kill her.

But now he had to deal with Bill. They had been friends from school-days and this affair was the first secret Roy had ever had from Bill. Now he toyed with the idea of confessing to him. He tried the words out in his mind.

"Bill, I've killed Marie. I'm in love with June and I want you to give her up so I can marry her."

But how would Bill take it? Shock? Hurt pride? Would he go to the police?

There was one minute of intermission to go. On impulse, he telephoned Bill at the insurance office and asked him to come over.

The feature was well into the first reel by the time Bill arrived. He ducked his head coming in and sat down gingerly on the folding chair Roy indicated. "Bill, there's something I have to discuss with you ..."

"Wait." Bill held up a hand. "I knew you'd find out sooner or later, Roy. Only why it had to be today, I'll never know. Okay, I can't lie to you any longer. I've been in love with Marie for more than ..."

"What? What are you talking about?" Roy was afraid he knew only too well.

"Murder, Roy. Murder."

"Now wait a minute. You can't prove ..."

"I killed June this morning, Roy. Drowned her in the bath. I'm in love with Marie and I hope you'll give her up so I can marry her. Now that I'm free."

"Now that you're ..." Roy began to laugh. He automatically looked to the screen, where the law was winning. He thought of June's little shadow under the bath water and he wanted to kill this man.

"What's so funny?"

"Nothing, nothing. I just want you to know that I'd never stand between you and Marie, old friend. She's all yours, the best man won and so on. In fact, here's my key. Why don't you slip over to my house right now – and surprise her?"

Practical Joke

Everybody knows somebody like Bubb ... a laughing man, who never laughs half so hard as when he sees somebody else miserable. Specially if, as usual, he has caused the misery.

When he first moved into the neighbourhood, nobody really hated Bubb. One or two even felt pity for this great, lardy creature with his packets of sneezing powder and handshake buzzers. Most of us were only annoyed

Then, too, the first of his jokes – plastic bugs in food, dribbling fountain pens – were harmless enough. It was only as we grew immune to them that Bubb forced himself to greater and greater extremes to keep our attention.

Inviting him to dinner became out of the question and soon even asking him over for a drink meant almost certainly a rubber "bloody finger" in somebody's drink, or a live lobster in the bath. We left him alone, or tried to do so.

The worst of it was, whenever Bubb ran up against somebody who "couldn't take it", he made even nastier efforts.

And one of those who "couldn't take it" was Big Mike.

Big Mike, who was at least 70, had become a kind of local mystery. Some said he had once been a crook, and others said he'd served with the Foreign Legion. Whatever he'd once been, he was now a quiet, kind old man, content to keep to himself and grow old.

His only companion now was Packy, a grey-muzzled rat terrier.

Though Mike was no longer the physical giant his name implied, he loomed large in our respect. And it was only when Bubb began playing pranks on Big Mike that we began to really dislike the overgrown youngster.

Their first encounter was at the local cinema. Bubb came in with a smile playing about his fat, loose lips and we knew something was about to happen. He took a seat not far behind Big Mike. Afraid he would try something on the old man, I found myself watching him.

All through the violent parts of the cartoon, Bubb's laughter echoed through the auditorium. Then, when the feature started, I saw him sneak a box from his inside pocket and open it.

Moths. Large-winged moths, a dozen of them, zeroed in on the bright projector beam and all but obliterated the screen with their frenzied fluttering. Somewhere a frightened child began to whimper, but Bubb's bellowing laugh rolled over it.

While most of us were content to sit and grumble till the manager trapped the creatures, Big Mike heaved himself to his feet and began to make his way up the aisle.

"Can't take a joke?" Bubb whispered as he passed. I saw the big man stiffen, his hand on his cane as if he meant to raise it in anger. Then he stalked out of the place.

That did it, of course. From then on, Big Mike was singled out for Bubb's peculiar kind of fun. He would wake from his afternoon nap on the front lawn to find his newspaper splattered with ink, or crude lipstick lips drawn on his forehead, or the wrong glasses in his case.

Somebody sliced up his garden hose, sprayed paint on his roses and sent him a dead snake in the post.

And there was no doubt in anybody's mind who the "somebody" was.

I took a "Kick Me" sign off the old man's back one afternoon and began to wonder myself if this was the time to call the police about Bubb. Now I wish I had.

Not long after this, on a hot, hazy afternoon, I heard a clatter and animal cries in the street. Rushing into the road, I caught a glimpse of Packy, running as I had never seen him run before. Somebody had tied a tin can to the poor dog's tail. And that somebody stood on Bubb's lawn, holding a pendulous belly and roaring with laughter. Mike was nowhere in sight.

Packy, terrified, ran a twisted path, between houses and zig-zagging down the street. The poor old brute thought something was after him. Just about everybody nearby tried to catch Packy and set him free. Packy's ageing heart finally did him this kindness. When we found the terrier, he was dead.

I carried him to Big Mike, not knowing how to tell him. But when he saw the body and the can, words were unnecessary. He said only: "I see. I see." And into his pale eyes came a calm, frozen, detached look, as if he had come to some great decision.

Next day I went over to see how Big Mike was bearing up and found him having tea with Bubb. Mike stood up.

"I wanted Bubb to understand there are no hard feelings on my part," he explained. "A joke is, after all, a joke."

Bubb laughed. "Glad you see it that way, old sport. Of course I'm sorry your old cur died that way, I didn't mean that to happen ..." and here the laughter spilled forth from his saliva-flecked lips ... "But it was funny! You should have seen him go!"

"Yes," said Big Mike faintly. "I should have seen him – go."

I thought I saw moisture in his eyes but he turned away to fiddle with the tea things.

"Please sit down," he said to me. "I'm sorry I can't offer you some tea, but there's really barely enough for the two of us."

This bit of rudeness – the teapot was big enough – made me uneasy and I sat down wondering if Mike were losing his mind.

"But here – have a cigar," bellowed Bubb. Though I did not put out my hand, he thrust a rubber cigar close to me and squirted something foul-smelling on my clothes. I will always think of Bubb in connection with coarse laughter and a bad smell.

A moment later, Bubb fell back in his chair, a strange look on his face. "What – what's wrong with me?" he said.

Big Mike smiled and put down his cup.

"Strychnine, Bubb," he said quietly. "Poison. Both Packy and I have been taking small doses of it for a long time, for our bad hearts."

Bubb was gasping inarticulately.

"If it's any comfort to you, Bubb, I have taken a fatal dose also. In the tea. My symptoms, due to a slight immunity from long usage, will be slower, but I will suffer from my own little joke as much as you."

I was too stunned to move or say anything. I could only watch Bubb's last convulsion. He tried to rise, then fell back and the flower in his button-hole made a small, convulsive squirt of ink.

As was only just, the poison had drawn his face into the terrible *rictus*, the hideous grin of death.

"I'm glad," gasped Mike, "you can take a joke."

Publish and Perish

The last cars had pulled into the Clark W. Kerr Memorial Parking Lot for the opening session of his new Physics I course, and Gleason was still searching frantically for the rest of his notes. Today of all days he could not afford to be late for class. It had taken all the pull he could muster to get prime time on the closed-circuit TV, and he'd surely be relegated to the early morning hours or even cancelled if he were late the first day. With only one hundred and twenty-seven research papers to his name he was lucky to have made assistant professor anyway.

Quarters were dropping into parking meter slots, and the air filled with the buzz of hungry machinery clicking off the time. The big screen at the front of the lot lit up hopefully, then went dark again as Gleason, seated in his office a half-mile away, shook his head at the engineer on his monitor. He was digging hurriedly through the slacks of Physical Abstracts that had been delivered that morning, the six-foot bundle representing summaries of all the papers in his field published during the preceding week. Under one of the piles he found the missing pages of his notes and, with a relieved sigh, fitted them into the sheaf of papers in his hand. Using the camera lens as a mirror he smoothed down his rumpled hair, then nodded to the waiting engineer. The red light went on, and he saw his own owlishly bespectacled face staring out from the monitor.

"The pursuit of knowledge," he began, "has always been the province of a handful of lonely, dedicated men ..."

He felt better once class was over. It hadn't gone badly at all. There'd been some disturbance on the screen from a passing jet, and one of the filmstrips had run out before he'd finished explaining it, but otherwise the show had been technically competent. He sighed, put down his notes on the desk, and began to burrow through the piles of abstracts that filled most of the small office. Buried in a corner he found a two-cup coffee maker, now empty.

Again Gleason seethed with the consciousness of his inferior status. Associate professors rated five-cup coffee makers and didn't have to go hunting water all the time! He thought of borrowing the larger size from the office of Professor Morgan, who had died only yesterday, but decided against it since the theft would soon be discovered by Morgan's successor, and it could mean Gleason's job. If he wanted a cup of coffee there was nothing to do but trek to the graduate students' lounge.

He unearthed a chipped and blackened coffee cup, shoved a pile of abstracts away from the door and ventured into the hallway of the physics building. A sharp hiss from the office to the right of his brought him up short. Turning he found the department's other assistant professor, Gridley Farrington, peering out at him through a partially opened door. The other man, shorter than Gleason with a sharpened nose and slick, black hair, slipped from his office and confronted his colleague with a broad and strikingly insincere smile. "Off to the kiddies' lounge again?" he inquired, staring politely at Gleason's cup.

Gleason could understand Farrington's hostility, as the poor man had published a scant one hundred and twenty-three research papers and was thus even lower on the multiversity social scale than he. Of course seventeen of Gleason's publications had been purchased from graduate students who dropped out before getting their own degrees, but Farrington wasn't likely to have done all his own work either.

"Just thought I'd get some coffee," Gleason replied, waving his cup vaguely. "It's a chance to keep in touch with the students, see what they're thinking. It's hard to get to know anybody teaching your courses over television."

"Oh, sure," Farrington grinned unpleasantly. "Well, Gleason," he went on, turning apparently to what was really on his mind, "what do you think about old Morgan dying?"

"Terrible thing," Gleason mumbled.

"Oh, I don't mean that! I mean who do you think will get his job?"

Gleason had thought of little else since Morgan's death, but he wasn't going to let Farrington know that. "Well, I suppose there are lots of choice. Hunnicutt could bring in a man from outside."

"Ridiculous!" Farrington snapped. "Silly idea! Surely they'd choose a faculty man, someone with an – er – adequate publication record."

"Well, probably," Gleason admitted, shifting nervously from one foot to the other. He himself had been at the multiversity only a few months, a replacement in fact for Morgan, who had been promoted to an associate professorship after nineteen years on the staff. He wasn't familiar with all the nuances of departmental rivalries yet.

"You'll go for the job, I suppose," Farrington ventured.

"Well, if they offer it to me ..."

"Oh, don't play modest, Gleason!" The little man smoothed down the back of his slick hair. "If you want the job you've got to fight for it! Nobody can afford to wait for offers any more. Are you going to fight nor not?"

Gleason didn't quite understand the implications of the question. Farrington must want the job for himself, but surely the four-publication margin would be decisive if the chairman chose to recruit from his own staff. "Well," Gleason said finally, "I'll probably do whatever I can to get the job, if that's what you mean."

Farrington smiled nastily, but at the same time turned rather pale. "That's what I thought," he said and disappeared into his office, snapping the door shut behind him.

Gleason shrugged and continued on down the corridor to the graduate lounge, where he found four anonymous students and a lukewarm urn of coffee. He sipped some of the coffee and attempted to make conversation with the students, none of whom appeared to see any advantage in talking to an assistant professor. The belated entrance of a fifth student, however, left Gleason somewhat less than pleased. For the boy was Alec Throckmorton, a shambling, beetle-browed graduate student of minimal intelligence and doubtful competence, whose attempts to make up for his lack of brilliance through an anxious, almost fawning desire to please rendered him doubly odious. But, since his father happened to supervise the awarding of grants through the National Science Foundation, Throckmorton was assured not only of his degree but of a soft berth as lab assistant to the least prestigious member of the staff – Gleason.

"How ya' doin', professor?" the boy demanded, slapping Gleason's shoulder and dislodging most of the contents of his coffee cup. "All ready for the big spearmint tomorrow?"

Gleason recalled with a chill that the boy was scheduled to assist him the following day in a critical and perhaps dangerous investigation into the properties of one of the newer synthetic elements. "All ready, Throckmorton," he sighed. "I hope you can set up the equipment properly, this time."

Throckmorton nodded his head vigorously. "Don't worry, professor. Sometimes I get confused about where the wires go, but I've got it all straightened out now."

"Red wire to the green coil, remember?"

"Oh – uh – yeah, I remember." Before the boy could generate further unwelcome conversation, Gleason hurried away.

After a while he wandered back to his own office carrying a tin of water for his coffee maker. Though he had closed his office door on leaving it was no ajar, and Gleason wondered idly if he had missed a visitor. Pouring the water into the coffee maker he added some grounds from a jar in his desk. He plugged in the percolator and stepped around a stack of abstracts to get his cup.

The explosion wasn't very loud, but it was powerful enough to lift the abstracts and deposit them solidly against the small of his back. Gleason went down across another pile of papers as a fusillade of deadly fragments rattled angrily against the walls. In the sudden silence he sat up and stared at the smoking hole where the coffee maker had been sitting.

His door flew open, and for a moment Farrington's ratlike face was momentarily framed, an expectant grin fading to dismay as he saw Gleason staring back at him. Then the face was gone, and Gleason heard rapid footsteps in the hallway. A few moments later the door again swung open to reveal the department chairman, Professor Hunnicutt.

"Started sooner than I'd expected," was Hunnicutt's only comment as he helped Gleason to his feet. "Bomb in the coffee maker, eh? Not really ingenious."

Gleason examined the remains of the percolator mutely. Only the heavy stack of abstracts had prevented him from being slashed by flying metal and glass from the explosion. Hunnicutt came up behind him and peered over his shoulder. "Looks like the bomb was connected to the heating element, went off when the coil started to warm up." Hunnicutt shook his head disapprovingly. "Not really a good job. Always takes a few seconds for the heat to get to the element – long enough for the intended victim to walk away from the bomb. A really top-notch man would have connected the bomb directly to the electrical circuit."

It occurred to Gleason that the chairman's remarks were not entirely appropriate to an instance of attempted murder. He turned to stare at his boss, a tall, white-haired man impeccably clothed in grey pinstripe. "What," he demanded, "is going on here?"

Hunnicutt slapped a fatherly arm about Gleason's shoulders. "I keep forgetting you're new here, my boy. Not really conversant with the multiversity traditions." He kicked aside a stack of abstracts with a well-polished oxford. "Come up to my office for a few minutes. I think we can easily straighten this out."

The chairman motioned casually to a bored custodian who had suddenly materialized and led Gleason into the hallway and down the long corridor to the left. Gleason noted that Farrington's door was tightly closed and that no sound issued from the sealed interior.

Hunnicutt seated himself at his desk and leaned back comfortably, moving a ten-cup percolator to one side. "Bit of a shock for you, I suppose, coming without warning and all. Warning from me, I mean. I assume Farrington did check with you to make sure you wanted to compete before he planted the bomb."

Gleason was thoroughly disoriented now. Something rather unusual seemed to be going on within the walls of what he had come to think of as a rather staid multiversity. "I – I don't think he really ..." Gleason began and then recalled the peculiar conversation with Farrington of an hour before. "He said something about *fighting* for the appointment ..."

"Yes," said Hunnicutt brusquely, "the appointment." He leaned back, making a tent of his fingers. "It's a real problem for me. Need a really top-notch man for the job, if you know what I mean. So many PhD's these days, so many publications, one can't really keep up with the qualifications any more. Don't want to go outside the present staff if I can help it. But, you know, I need some real evidence that I've got a to-notch man to fill the vacancy."

Gleason had a feeling that he didn't completely understand the conversation. "You know my qualifications ..." he began.

Hunnicutt waved him aside impatiently. "Know it all; no better or worse than Farrington's except for a small difference in the publications index. Really couldn't choose on the basis of what I know now. Farrington's got seniority in service, of course, but I never let that influence an appointment." Hunnicutt's manner softened a bit. "It's ingenuity I like to see, my boy. Farrington's trying hard, but that coffee maker stunt isn't really the sort of thing to convince me. The heating element, you know. Now, I wonder if you could think of some better way ..."

"Better way, sir? To do what?"

Hunnicutt laughed nervously, tamping tobacco into a professorish pipe. "Why, to kill him, of course! He's had his chance, now it's your turn! If you can think of a more ingenious – and successful – method than his, you'll not only have convinced me of your own abilities, but you'll have eliminated your only departmental rival!"

Gleason stared at his boss. "Kill him, sir?"

"Well, that's the tradition!" Hunnicutt snapped with a sudden return to his mood of irritation. "Can't fight a good college tradition, I always say. Besides, it's really the only way. How can I tell who's really top-notch without some kind of test?" He paused, reflecting. "The whole thing began really as a kind of accident a few years ago. Milton and Borofsky had decided to duel for the post being vacated by Anderson, but Borofsky cheated by devising a way to assassinate Milton with the chimes in the college bell tower even before the duel took place. Read it in some mystery story, I believe. Of course we couldn't turn Borofsky over to the police, top-notch men being hard to get as they are. So I promoted him to the job – rather admired his ingenuity, as a matter of fact.

"Well, couldn't do much a few months later when Leonard electrocuted Borofsky to get Blassingame's job. A sort of precedent had been set, you see. Anyway, that's the way it grew, from small beginnings, as these traditions do. Nowadays I wouldn't consider making an appointment any other way." He was friendlier now, smiling an encouraging smile at Gleason. "I think you've got the stuff it takes to carry on the old tradition, my boy. Farrington's good, but not really my type of research man. Heating coils! Think up something a little better, and you won't have to worry about that associate professorship."

Gleason was still trying to make some audible comment as Hunnicutt ushered him briskly to the door. "To tell the truth," the chairman was saying, "I've been a little disappointed in the quality of assassinations around the department the last year – too messy, too routine. Now, if you could come up with something really top-notch on your first time out ..." His voice dropped to a friendly confidentiality. "Well, you'd have a head start on a really outstanding career in science." Gleason found himself standing in the corridor as the chairman's door sighed shut behind him.

He drifted back down the hallway and into his office, peering apprehensively at Farrington's closed door before he entered. The custodian had just finished cleaning up his office, and a shiny new two-cup percolator had already been installed in one corner. Gleason noted with relief that several bales of shredded abstracts had been removed.

What was he to do now? He couldn't go along with Hunnicutt's plan – simply couldn't! He'd never killed anybody in his life and wasn't going to start now. Yet apparently his own life was in danger, and if he didn't try some kind of counterattack the assistant professorship would surely go to Farrington. He'd heard vague rumours of the kind of cutthroat competition that had developed in the multiversities over the past decade, but he'd never anticipated anything like this. A little sabotage to divert government research funds – that was common enough. But murder! If this was the kind of game they were playing, he wanted no part of it.

Gleason glanced at his watch and saw that it was almost time for his next class. He went over to the wall case and racked out the TV camera. Removing a sheaf of notes from his desk, he sat down in his chair and turned toward the camera; only a half minute to go, he noted. Suddenly he realized that he was still a mess from the explosion, his hair on end, his clothing rumpled. He looked about for a mirror, then remembered the trick of using the camera lens as a last-minute mirror. He peered at the camera, trying to catch his reflection in the darkened lens.

There was no lens; only a slim, blackened tube.

Gleason sat for a moment digesting this fact as the clock hand crept toward the hour. The absence of a lens might mean several things, but only one occurred to him at the moment. He dived for the floor.

The red light winked on and a high-energy laser beam spat from the tube, passing just over Gleason's desk and burning a hole in the wall behind it. Overloaded circuits began to whine and the camera burned itself out within seconds, the beam vanishing as its power supply was cut off. After a few moments the top of Gleason's head rose warily above the level of the desk, round eyes fixed on the smoking hulk of the television camera.

The phone rang. It was Professor Hunnicutt.

"What's going on in there," Hunnicutt demanded between audible sucks on his pipe. "You're twenty seconds late getting on the air! Students are waiting – knowledge calls, my boy!"

"It's Farrington, I think, sir." Gleason sat down on the floor cross-legged, not quite ready to leave the shelter of his desk. "He seems to have installed a laser beam in my TV camera. He – he nearly burned a hole in me!"

"No!" came Hunnicutt's shocked voice over the wire. "Used a TV camera, did he? That sort of thing won't do at all!"

"No, sir," said Gleason, brightening.

"No man has the right to interrupt class programming for personal business," said Hunnicutt, righteous anger thundering in his voice. "Not a really top-notch kind of thing to do. Shows the sort of degeneration of standards in the academic community the last few years."

"Yes, sir."

"All violence must take place outside class hours, committee meetings and conference periods," Hunnicutt said firmly. "I'll have to talk to Farrington about this."

"Er – sir ..."

Hunnicutt's voice rasped with impatience. "Well, what is it? I've got to get back to work."

Still crouching, Gleason cradled the phone in both hands. "I – I was thinking, sir. I'm not sure I really want that associate professorship after all. I've only been here a few months and ..."

"Nonsense!" Hunnicutt roared. "You're a top-notch man. Want to see you move ahead!"

"Yes, sir. But, you see, murder's not really ... I mean, I'm not the type for this sort of thing."

"What's that?" Menace edged Hunnicutt's voice.

"What I'm trying to say is, I'm not really the type to kill someone just to get a job."

A long silence stretched across the wire. "Not the type, eh?" Hunnicutt sighed wearily. "I'd thought better of you, my boy. Really top-notch, I thought. Felt sure you'd come through." Another silence. "You understand, of course, that we can't keep a man on the faculty who scorns our department's hallowed traditions?"

"Sir?"

"I mean, Gleason, that you do not yet have tenure."

"No, sir."

"Plenty who'd like your present job, Gleason. And no other multiversity is likely to hire you without a recommendation from me. Think it over." The wire went dead.

Gleason put down the phone and rose cautiously to his feet. He circled the desk to peer at the fused camera, then turned to stare at the neat hole burned in the far wall of his office. A peaceful grouping of trees and ivy could be glimpsed through the aperture.

Gleason stood thinking about Hunnicutt's words, the long struggle to get his present job, his unfitness for any real work in the outside world. Hunnicutt was right – no other multiversity would hire him without a recommendation, and surely no one would believe his story if he tried to use it as an excuse. It was either get out of this situation somehow or face a diminishing career at some backwater city college, stripped of research funds and despairing of the future.

Still sunk in misery, he called the TV studio and cancelled all classes for the rest of the day, since it would take that long for his camera to be replaced. Then he returned to a serious consideration of his problem. What was he going to do? He couldn't kill anybody! And how could Farrington ...? There was a thought! Was it possible that Farrington was no more enthusiastic about murder than he? Perhaps the poor man had made the two attempts on Gleason's life out of nothing more than a pathetic loyalty to his department. If the two of them could get together and make a deal ...

A few moments later Gleason was knocking timidly at his neighbour's door, a cautious optimism in his heart and a heavy paperweight in his hand should the optimism proved unjustified. Gleason heard footsteps inside the office, then Farrington's hoarse whisper at the door. "Who's there?"

"Gleason! I've got to talk to you!"

He heard a hasty scuffling, then silence. "Don't bother to try shooting through the door," Farrington's muffled voice called finally. "I've got an energy field around my desk!"

"For God's sake, man, I don't want to hurt you. I just want to talk this thing over!"

"There's nothing to talk about," Farrington snarled. "You won't get me to open this door!"

Gleason stepped to one side of the door in case Farrington decided to do some shooting himself. "Let's be sensible," he called in a stage whisper. "Why should we go along with this crazy scheme when the stakes aren't worth it? Maybe we could work something out!"

"There's nothing to work out!" Farrington snapped back. "I need the job! If I knew how to do anything else I wouldn't be a college professor!"

Nervously Gleason shifted the paperweight from hand to hand. "But, look, Farrington. We must be able to make some kind of deal. If we could just talk rationally about this I'm sure –"

"There's nothing to talk about, and even if there were ..." A sudden, protracted silence fell. Gleason eased up to the door and put his ear against the panelling. He thought he could hear the faint sounds of hurried movement inside. "On second thought," Farrington went on, "you may be right. At least we can talk it over. Come on inside, and let's discuss it."

Gleason straightened, shifted the paperweight to his left hand and reached for the doorknob. He froze in that attitude, reflecting. After a few moments he ventured, "Maybe you'd better come out here instead, Farrington. The – er – light's better."

"No," Farrington's distant voice replied, "you come in here. We want to keep this private."

"We can have some coffee in the lounge."

"I've got a coffee maker in here."

"I think you'd better come out here."

A half-hour later Gleason gave up and returned to his office to sit brooding at the desk. Farrington seemed determined to kill him, and he still couldn't work up much enthusiasm for a counterattack. At any rate he couldn't think clearly about the problem with Farrington plotting actively next door. Kicking aside a pile of abstracts, he exited quietly through the hole in the wall.

After a sleepless night in a rented hotel room (in case Farrington had his home address) he rose bleary eyed and despairingly to face what would surely be another miserable day. He still had no plan, no hope. Perhaps there was some way of merely *disabling* his rival ... But no, he couldn't consider violence at all. Still, wasn't one of Farrington's arms or legs worth his own life? It was only a small concession to principle.

He arrived at his office early and found that the new TV camera had been installed and the laser hole sealed up. Of Farrington there was no sign. Gleason boiled some water in his percolator (after a thorough inspection), but soon discovered that his container of coffee had been shattered in one or more of the recent office catastrophes. There was nothing to do but go to the graduate lounge again. He slipped out quietly, pausing only to make sure Farrington's door was closed, and ran tiptoe down the hallway, dodging around a bit in case of pursuit by missiles. In the lounge he found no one but Throckmorton, snoring on one of the couches.

"The spearmint," said Throckmorton, opening one eye to peer dully at his boss. "Today's the day!"

In his anxiety over the murder attempts, Gleason had forgotten the experimental work scheduled with Throckmorton for that day. He felt a twinge of apprehension; the equipment they were using was dangerous, and in his present mood he could make any one of a number of errors. Still, if he tried to put off the experiment today his standing with Hunnicutt might be damaged irreparably.

"Go ahead and set it up," he said. "I'll be down later to work with you."

The shaggy boy unfolded himself from the couch, grinning vacuously. "I'll get started on it right away, professor. Count on me." He stumbled into Gleason, spilling the cup of coffee the man had just poured for himself, and shambled off toward the stairway. The research lab was downstairs in the basement, almost directly beneath Gleason's office.

"And Throckmorton," Gleason called after him, "don't forget – it's the red wire on the green coil."

"Green wire on red coil," Throckmorton assured him and increased his pace, trying to appear enthusiastic.

Gleason's head buzzed with the effects of little sleep and much worry, so that he barely heard the boy. All his remaining emotional energy went into the task of drawing himself another cup of coffee. It wasn't until he was back at the desk that the boy's last words finally registered.

He recalled at the same moment the possible result of attaching the green wire to the red coil.

Suppressing a howl, he headed for the door, twisting frantically at the knob.

The door refused to open.

Gleason stood momentarily transfixed, the doorknob still in his hand. The door had never stuck like this before. He rattled the knob experimentally, bent over to peer through the keyhole. Something was blocking it from the other side, something that was not a key. At the same moment he felt the doorknob grow warm beneath his hand.

Gleason snatched his fingers away and stood up, backing away from the door. The knob was turning cherry red and smoke had begun to issue from the door itself. Could Throckmorton already ... Then he heard a bubble of wild laughter from next door, and he knew.

"Got you this time!" Farrington screamed through their common wall. "My heat converter will fry you alive within the next couple of minutes! The job is mine!"

Gleason wiped his damp brow with the back of his hand, searching about for some means of escape. Since the physics building was determinedly modern, it had no windows whatsoever; the door was the only way in or out. He glanced upward at the footsquare grill of the air conditioning unit. Was he slim enough to worm his body through that passage? Desperately Gleason shoved his desk under the opening and clambered up to test the grill. Six strong screws held it firmly across the outlet, and Gleason had no screwdriver.

He peered down, spied the telephone on his desk. He might still be able to summon help. He had crouched down and was just reaching for the receiver when the phone rang. Lifting the receiver he heard Throckmorton's dull tones. "Everything's all connected up, professor. When ya comin' down?"

"Throckmorton, get help! I'm locked in my office, and Farrington is trying to kill me!"

"What's that, professor?" the boy shouted. "I can hardly hear ya with all the noise from the equipment!"

"I said Farrington –" Gleason's voice froze. "Did you see 'noise from the equipment'?"

"Yeah, professor, I got it goin', all right."

"It's operating – with the green wire on the red coil?"

"Sure, right now it's –"

But the sentence remained uncompleted as the phone went dead and the right wall of Gleason's office vanished. He dropped the receiver and stood staring at the vacant spot where Farrington's office – and Farrington – had stood. About fifty square feet of floor space had been vaporized instantly. The laboratory, Gleason now recalled, was almost directly beneath his office. But just *almost* directly. Actually it was beneath Farrington's.

The door had stopped smoking, and Gleason threw it open easily, the now harmless attachment to Farrington's heat converter clattering to the floor. He saw Hunnicutt scuttle down the hall toward him, pipe bouncing nervously between his teeth. The chairman halted and stood awestruck before the hole in his building. At last he turned to Gleason, tears brimming in his eyes. "My boy, this is the most absolutely top-notch piece of work I've ever seen in this department."

"But –"

"Oh, it'll be rather expensive to replace this much of the building; but we've got government money and I must say the loss is really worth it, under the circumstances. Never seen a cleaner, more humane liquidation since the tradition began."

A ragged figure appeared at the head of the basement stairs and lurched toward them. Apparently the force of the beam of destruction, or whatever the thing was, had been directed almost entirely upward. "It was really Throckmorton, here –"

Hunnicutt majestically placed an arm about the shoulders of the frightened boy. "This young man gave you a hand, did he? Pulled the trigger, so to speak, while you were the bait. Brave lads, both of you!"

Throckmorton, who had never in his entire life been addressed by anyone above the level of associate professor, stood open-mouthed, basking in the glow of sudden recognition. "You will no doubt benefit from this, too, Throckmorton," the chairman went on. "Naturally there'll be two assistant professorships vacant now, and I'm sure we can arrange a spot for you while you're completing your doctoral requirements."

Perhaps, Gleason decided, there was no point in rocking the boat after all. With the coveted associate professorship his, and the beginnings of a new and infinitely murderous weapon created by attaching the green wire to the red coil, he was well on his way to a brilliant career in science.

"Come into my office, both of you," Hunnicutt was saying. "Got to get you started on the paperwork for your appointments."

Watching his boss chew vigorously on his pipe, a foolproof idea for a booby trap slid unbidden into Gleason's mind. The whole thing was ridiculous, he told himself. He wouldn't be in line for the departmental chairmanship for years! Still, it didn't hurt ... "Do you have a pencil and paper, professor?" he asked. "I'd like to jot down a little idea I just had."

"Certainly, my boy," Hunnicutt smiled, handing him the pencil and paper. "It's the mark of a top-notch scientist that he's always thinking, always searching for new ideas, always looking toward the future."

"I'm afraid you're right, sir," Gleason said; he was still scribbling furiously as he passed into the chairman's darkened office.

In the Oligocene

He bent to touch her, his dry flaked hand a rasp across the smoothness of her cheek. In her sleep she winced and hugged herself against the deepening chill. I'll wake her with a kiss, he thought. But he didn't. Instead he again reached out, hesitated, then brushed her shoulder. He shook her. "It's me, Paula," he said.

In her long, drugged sleep the girl's lashes had stuck together, and she ground pale hands into her eyes to clear them. Now fully awake, she stared at him without recognition. Had he changed so much over the years? His hand began to tremble and he removed it from her shoulder. Paula's eyes grew wider, then shifted to take in her surroundings. The cave was dark except for the light of a wood fire at the entrance, shuddering their shadows across the cracked walls. She sat up, jerkily. "What place is this? Who are you?"

He smiled reassuringly, the smile he knew she loved. In the shifting light she stared hard at him, bewildered. She wore a white nightgown, her long black hair bound up with pins that had begun to loosen, stray wisps of hair trailing to her shoulders. "George?" she ventured finally. His smile widened and he nodded. She still knew him, would still love him. Until this moment he hadn't acknowledged his own secret dread.

"But you're – you're so *old*!" she wailed.
"Don't be afraid," he told her. "There's nothing to be afraid of. It's really me and I'm not so old. I'm not sixty yet."
Shivering, she glanced around the cave. "Where are we? The last I remember, I'd gone to bed …" She couldn't keep her eyes from his face. "George, what happened to you?"
"Nothing but age," he said. "It's the fate of everyone, even yours, now that I've saved you from it." He rose shakily, his limbs aching from the hours he crouched over the still form. "As for this place, it's a cave by a river." He moved stiffly toward the rear of the cave, occasionally reaching out to touch one of the boxes stacked neatly along the walls. "There are few if any dangerous animals in this era and I've stored enough food and clothing and agricultural supplies to keep us for the rest of our natural lives." He turned back to her, his love still mute within him. He could never express himself as he wished. "The rest of our natural lives," he repeated.
For the first time Paula seemed to realizethat she was in her nightgown. "I'm cold," she said, and clutched it tightly about her. He smiled again, went to one of the boxes and drew out a long blue dress with a high neck and puffed sleeve, the latest style at the time he'd bought it. "Here's part of your wardrobe. I've got everything you need, the finest material I could find."

She took her dress, held it against her body, running her fingers over the unfamiliar cloth. "I was in bed, asleep," she said.

"Yes, you were asleep. I came to your house and broke in. I gave you an injection to keep you sleeping, not with a needle but a – a new kind that sprays on your skin. Then I brought you here."

"But you weren't even in town! You were way across the country!"

On December 8, 1939, he had been way across the country, at Harvard, dreaming of the Christmas holidays and seeing her again. But he hadn't seen her, not for another forty years, not until a few hours ago. And not until a year before had he been sure that he would ever see her.

The girl seemed reluctant to put on the dress perhaps because of the odd style, perhaps because she didn't want to disrobe in front of him. Suppressing his annoyance he brought out a heavy pink dressing gown and a pair of pink furry slippers he'd selected from a department store San Francisco. "It's a long story and a complicated one," he said as she slipped them on. "What you've got to understand is that, strange as all this may seem to you, it's absolutely necessary to save your life."

She was still staring at him, her head twitching in brief, involuntary denials.

"On December 8, 1939, Paula ... you died. You were in bed asleep when a drunken driver turned your corner, lost control of his car, and ploughed through the wall of your bedroom. The gas tank exploded and you were ... you were burned to death." He flinched as a vision of the fiery wreck flamed across his consciousness, as vivid as if he had witnessed it himself. "But you're not dead now, Paula; because, you see, I came back to rescue you."

She stood silent, hugging the robe about her. He brushed his hands together with a harsh, rustling sound like the scrape of dead leaves. "I was studying at Harvard, you know. I dropped out for a year, too broken up to do any work. But eventually I went back, changed my major to physics, got my doctorate. I didn't forget you."

The earth trembled as in the distance some great animal passed by.

"I didn't marry," George said. "There was no one I could have loved as I loved you. I carried your picture with me always, one I stole from your parents' home after the funeral. The others – other people – they thought I was some kind of eccentric. But they hadn't loved you as I had. I kept myself going with the memory of you, that memory and my work. I was working on a research grant, developing some ideas for a unified field theory. I came to see ... well, it's pretty complicated, but you could say that the passage of time generates energy and that you can utilizethe energy accumulated between the present and any point in the past or future to project yourself to that point. Harnessing the energy was a technical problem I couldn't solve myself, but with the help of others it was possible to construct something I guess you'd have to call a time machine. Can you see that when I did all this I was thinking only of you?"

Paula said nothing, listening gravely to the words of the thin, grey man who seemed but distantly related to the boy she had known yesterday.

"The machine was completed," he went on, "in 1978. We found that it could carry a man into either past or future and return him to the point in time from which he'd departed. Soon we were able to calibrate the machine to within a few days' accuracy. With that accomplished I could begin to plan and hope.

"I located this place, found the cave and began to stock it with everything we'd need to survive here. I had to do it quietly, secretly, at night when everyone else had left. No one was to suspect the real reason for my work on the project. Had they known what was planned they'd surely have stopped me, because it meant losing the only machine that had been produced – a very expensive instrument."

She caught her breath and retreated a few steps until she was stopped by the wall of the cave. "George, where are we?"

"It's some time in the Oligocene period, a comparatively gentle era in the earth's history. The great reptiles are gone and the largest mammals aren't numerous enough to be dangerous. It's long before the first ice age yet. We'll be in no real danger here."

"My God! You mean there are no other people?"

"Yes, it's a paradise just for the two of us. With no one to threaten us here we can be really happy." He paused as if expected her deferred applause.

She came forward hesitantly, searching his eyes for the familiar personality beneath the stranger's ageing mask. "But wasn't there some other way? Couldn't you have saved me and left me in … in my own time?"

Pressing his thin lips together he shook his head with visible annoyance. "Don't you think I considered all the possibilities? Of course I could simply have awakened you and got you out of the house before the car crashed. But what good would that have done me? You'd only have been saved for young George at Harvard. Or someone else. I'd have saved you and gained nothing for myself!

"Oh, I even thought of taking you back into my own time, but I wasn't sure it was possible. We didn't know anything about the effects of possible paradoxes yet. Could you actually exist in a future time stream where you'd died years before? I didn't know, and I couldn't experiment to find out. Above all I couldn't take the chance of losing you again. The safest thing to do was take you into the past. That's why you're here."

For the first time he realized that the girl was trembling, He came forward and took her hand, noting the slight involuntary tug as she pulled away. He gripped her more tightly. "I know this is a lot to assimilate all at once. It must be terrifying to find yourself in a strange world, even with someone you love. But you've got to see that it was the only way. By taking you away on the very night you should have been killed I disturbed the fabric of time only slightly. Of course we might have gone back to some civilized period, but why risk any more accidents? Civilization means war, famine, plague, riot ... Do you think I'd risk losing you again? No place is entirely safe, but this is the safest I could think of."

Her trembling had increased until she shook uncontrollably. "George, we can't live in this world all alone, no matter how many supplies you've got stored here. There have to be other people! I don't want to be alone!"

He covered her soft hand with his own. "Why do we need anyone else when we have each other?" A sullen shadow passed over his face. "What have other people ever meant to us but bitterness and separation? When have other people encouraged our love? They just cause trouble; they always have. Your mother ..."

"George," she broke in, "what about sickness? You say it's safe here, but there aren't any doctors. You wouldn't want me to die of some disease!"

He smiled easily, as if he had long anticipated this objection. "As a matter of fact I've studied medicine rather closely and feel I'm as qualified to practice as any doctor. I've got all sorts of medical equipment stored here and I know how to use it. There are even several cases of drugs and antibiotics. I'm prepared to do anything from cleaning teeth to –" He paused, giggled unexpectedly. "– delivering a baby."

Paula lowered her eyes, her face distorted as if in pain. "But, George," she said finally, "you won't live but a few years longer. What will I do when you die?"

He stared blankly. "Die? Me? Die?" He paused to consider the possibility.

She began to pull away, forcing him to tighten his grasp. In the struggle her long hair had slipped its fastenings and whipped about as she tossed her head from side to side. "George, I want to go back! I want people! Let's go somewhere nearer our own time."

He drew her closer, ignoring her efforts to escape. "We have to commit ourselves completely to our new life, darling. We mustn't consider returning to a world that could threaten our love. You'll understand why I've removed all temptation by destroying the time machine."

Tenderly he drew her body to his as with a single, anguished cry she fainted.

Paula awoke some time after dawn, huddled near the embers of the fire, crying softly at times but for the most part withdrawn. Tactfully George left the girl to herself. He'd feared this reaction, though he was sure it would be only temporary. She's had a shock, a great one, and of course the knowledge of her own narrowly averted death wasn't as vivid to her as it was to him. But soon she'd accept the reasonableness of his actions, come to his arms and fulfil his love.

After a long period of brooding silence she rose and came toward him, swaying unsteadily. Her face was grime-streaked from crying, her eyes red and swollen. With a trembling hand she plucked at his sleeve. "George, is it possible ...? Maybe you could make a new machine. The parts ... You couldn't have destroyed all the parts."

He turned away; there was no use talking to her when she was like this. Too many ugly scenes had already marred their relationship. She went on: "I just want to see people again. There's no one here."

"There's me," he said.

"Yes, of course there's you, George. But I hardly know you. I mean, I hardly knew you when – when you were young. We weren't really close."

George shook his head violently, as if to dislodge the hateful words. Without looking at the girl he circled around her to the cave entrance, kicked at the few remaining embers of the fire. In the cold dawn the parched earth stretched flat and lifeless before him, broken only by the trickle of a nearby stream. "We were closer than you'd ever admit," he said finally. "If it hadn't been for your mother there wouldn't have been any trouble between us at all."

"Oh, George!" she said behind him. It was statement of utter, hopeless despair. "My mother *likes* you, George. She's – she was always telling me what a fine boy you were, what a – a good catch!"

"Well, your father, then. Somebody was always trying to turn you against me. If we'd just been alone together for a while I could have made you see …" He turned, smiled into her stained, twisted face. "But now we are alone together, aren't we? You'll see how much you really care now that there's no one around to talk against me." His gaze turned inward, and a half-smile touched his lips. "Do you know that last night was the first time I'd ever held you in my arms, even been that close to you? It was just as I'd always imagined it."

"George, there must be some way of rebuilding the machine."

He turned back to look out over the plains. "I've left nothing to chance," he said.

Behind him she was sobbing again. "God, I wish you'd left me there! I wish I were dead instead of here!"

Tightening his jaw he continued to stare into the distance. He would not give in and console her. She'd have to accept him on his own terms, admit her love without being coaxed. She'd have to agree that he'd been right in what he'd done. He had plenty of time to wait.

"Don't cry, darling," said a male voice behind him.

He wheeled to face the other man: tall, thirtyish, draped in a shimmering scarlet tunic. The man had placed one arm about Paula's shoulders and was dabbing at her eyes with a blue handkerchief. Behind him glittered a machine of cool crystal and shining cylinders. "There's no need to cry," the man told the astonished girl. "We're going back."

Frozen, George watched him guide her gently toward the machine. Then the spell was broken, and he lunged forward to reach out for her. Paula drew back, clinging to the stranger's arm. "She's mine," George told him. "She's all I've got!"

The other man stepped in front of the girl, shook his head grimly. "No, you have nothing. You're already old and you're going to die shortly.

I know. If the girl stays here –" He winced at some unbearable memory. "I passed through here," he said, "about fifteen years from now. I found her then. I could see how beautiful, how fine she once must have been. But she was nearly mad, a living corpse. Fifteen years of total isolation had almost finished her. But even so, I loved her." He smiled tenderly at the girl nestled against his shoulder, then at George. "I couldn't save her then, but I can now. She has to be safe, protected." He was smiling now with the innocence that only confident virtue can bestow. "I've come, you see, to rescue her."

Still cradling the girl, the man stepped back into the machine and flicked a switch; the cylinders sang their high, keening whine. "Wait!" George screamed after him. "What year?"

The man laughed. "Around 2084," he said. Their figures paled, vanished.

George stood alone, staring into emptiness. After a while he went over and picked up the blue dress from the floor where Paula had discarded it. Gently he caressed it between his fingers, then pressed it to his face to breath in the lingering scent of her body. With a puffed sleeve he caught the tears.

Soon he felt better. Putting aside the dress he began to rummage around among the boxes for his tools. He spread them out on the floor, then went to the back of the cave and dragged out the large, unmarked crates he had hidden there. He began to remove the cool crystals, the shining cylinders, ranged them neatly into glittering rows. He'd left nothing to chance.

"2084," he whispered.

He began to fit the parts together.

Sladek and Disch

The Way to a Man's Heart

with Thomas M. Disch

The calico-covered table was crowded with dirty dinner dishes. They jostled each other rim to rim – the great willow pattern bowl that had held the mashed potatoes (clean as a whistle); the platter where the pork chops had been (only a little milk gravy left there now); the plate of Janet's special home-baked bread; the bowl of candied yams, empty now, but still sticky with syrup; and another bowl half-full of creamed corn. Janet's eyes roamed lovingly over her work, as a general might survey a battlefield, then rose to caress the figure of her husband – a monument to the general's victory.

He had not quite finished eating. Ralph Larsen's tiny eyes (at least, they *seemed* tiny in that face) regarded the half a pork chop on the end of his fork with a certain bemused greed. His jowls quivered and his lips parted wide to admit the thick chunk of meat into his maw. Janet watched the trembling of his three chins as he swallowed the half-chewed pork. He began to wipe up the gravy on his plate with a slice of bread.

Ralph Larsen was a big man. Even that part of him visible above the dinner table (and it was not his most considerable part) could truly be called Gargantuan. He had what is generally known as a bull-neck – or rather no neck at all. There was only a gradual tapering off of flesh between his shoulders and the crown of his head, interrupted by a slight protuberance below his mouth where one would ordinarily expect to find a chin.

"Missus Larsen, you sure do set a fine table," Axel Dahlgren said, smiling and pushing away his plate, which he had emptied a good five minutes ago. "If I'd a-known Ralph had himself such a dang good cook, I'd a-had myself invited over a long time ago. Course, I *shoulda* known that just by looking at him – eh, Ralph?" The scrawny old farmhand cackled, showing wide-spaced teeth.

"I can't complain about Janet's cooking, not a-tall," Ralph mumbled, intent on wiping gravy from his non-chin with a greasy napkin, The limp collar of his denim work shirt was open to its second button under the pressure of Ralph's flesh, and now that button looked about ready to give. Ralph had a hard time buying ready-made clothes these days.

Axel, chortling at his own joke, began to roll a cigarette.

"I hope you've saved room for dessert," Janet said to her guest, as she rose from the table. "I've made Ralph's favourite – apple pie!" Before Axel could protest, Janet was out of the room.

Out in her big, country-style kitchen, Janet cut into the fresh pie, still warm from the oven. A small piece for Axel, and a wedge for her husband that was fully one-quarter of the twelve-inch pie. She got the bucket of ice cream out of the freezer and scooped out generous portions that completely covered each slice of pie.

"Mmm, doesn't that look good?" she asked herself. She took a little dab of ice cream on the end of her finger and tasted it. It *was* good. After all, she'd made it herself from whole cream.

"Missus Larsen, honestly, I couldn't eat another bite," Axel insisted as she laid down the pie plate before him.

"Don't be silly, Axel Dahlgren. A hard-working man like you needs all the good food he can get. Especially with you going in to the Twin Cities tonight for the Fair, you should eat while the eating's good. Like as not, you won't have anything but hot dogs and soda pop for the next ten days. You don't see Ralph turning down *his* food, do you?"

She had not yet given Ralph his pie and he was beginning to look a little anxious. "Darling," she said, "there's a dab of corn left. Come on, finish it up for me. You know what a nuisance it is to keep left-overs."

"I was leaving that for you," Ralph said, in injured tones. "You didn't eat no corn a-tall." Even before he had finished this complaint, he had taken up the bowl and begun to ladle its contents into his mouth. It took him only two swallows. Janet rewarded him with the pie.

"You ain't having any, I s'pose?" he asked, digging into it with a soup spoon.

"Not tonight," she admitted.

"Why not?" Axel asked. "It's too good for even the cook to turn down, this pie."

With his mouth full, Ralph explained. "She's got to watch her figure."

"*Her* figure!" said Axel, spluttering his ice cream all across the table. "Her figure! That's rich." All through coffee he repeated the joke for their benefit, though neither seemed very amused by it, and he was still cackling over it when he left at seven-thirty.

It was Janet, of course, who saw him to the door, for Ralph was already stretched out on the sofa, snoring in front of a television comedy. In an hour or so, Janet would rouse him for another piece of pie and a glass of milk, and then help ease his bulk up the staircase to their bedroom on the second floor. They had twin beds – a double for Ralph and a single for Janet. She'd insisted on that four years ago on the day Ralph went over 350 on the bathroom scale. Ever since then she'd had to rely on guesswork.

Though the Larsen farm stood on the outskirts of Fairmont, they seldom had visitors. Janet found herself feeling a little sad that Axel had left, since that left her almost no one to talk to. She'd never gotten along very well with the other farm wives, since she still thought of herself as essentially a city woman. If she hadn't been expelled from nursing school in the last semester, she'd have been a R.N. nowdays, not the wife of some hick farmer in a Corn Belt town.

Ralph wasn't actually a farmer anymore. He let other people bring the hay in from his fields, and when there were cows in the barn he had Axel look after them. Ralph devoted all his time these days to auctioneering. He bought cheap and sold dear, and while other farmers watched their crops growing, Ralph watched his bank account grow. Janet watched it, too. It was one of the few interests they had in common.

Now, Janet considered, it was ripe. Indeed, it was over-ripe, ripe-to-bursting. It should have been reaped years ago.

As she scraped the hardened syrup from the plate that had held the candied yams, Janet let her thoughts turn to happier subjects. She thought about how fat her husband was. He was really beastly fat.

So she was sure he couldn't last much longer. He just couldn't. It wasn't fair. All the work she had gone to – learning to cook just the way he liked, using his own mother's recipe file, mixing the butterfat into his milk each day, finding new ways to cook with butter. It was a full-time job, cooking for Ralph, and she'd been at it for ten years. Why, he'd started off with no more than a thirty-three-inch waist, and now he was up to fifty-four! Perhaps more, since it was hard to tell exactly where Ralph's waist *was* these days. Yes, she had worked.

She stuck the dishes in the washer and went into the bathroom to tidy herself up. Even at forty, she had kept her looks, and she would make a very smart widow. If only Ralph would do *his* part.

One of these days, she knew, the fatty tissue would close around his heart – or the cholesterol would thicken in his overloaded arteries – and then Janet would be a free woman. She had often pictured that moment to herself – his last strangled snore, then blessed silence. Or he might be in the heat of an auction, shouting, pounding his hammer, then suddenly turn blue and drop to the sawdust on the wooden platform. Or out in the barn when be was looking at the cattle ...

Oh, there were a thousand different times and places when it might happen, but they were all beautiful.

It would have been hard to say just when the idea had come to her. One day she'd put an extra dab of butter in an already-rich pie crust, or a little more cream in the mashed potatoes. She had forced seconds on him, thirds. Strangely, she had not found his growing bulk unpleasant. It rather fascinated her. She felt it was something she had created. His handsome face had begun to lose its definiteness. His cheeks sagged and his chin doubled. Great dewlaps formed on his arms and legs. When she did at last realizethe direction in which she had been working all this time, she redoubled her efforts. She read all the diet books she could get a hold of, and gradually, under their guidance, she eliminated everything from Ralph's diet that would not serve her purpose.

There had, it is true, been sticking points – times when Ralph absolutely refused to eat some new goody she'd invented for him (especially the chocolate frosted doughnuts she'd dipped in powdered sugar), or had even threatened to go on a diet! But he had always weakened (usually it was only a matter of hours), as she had known he would. For the last four years, he'd given up every pretence of moderation or restraint. He gobbled down whatever she put before him at the dinner table. Every little bit. Once, just to demonstrate her mastery, she'd made him eat an entire apple pie after a full dinner. But, unfortunately, her control over his metabolism was less complete than her control of his psyche. He hadn't been able to eat for two days afterward. Since then she had gone ahead at a slower, steadier pace. Haste, she had told herself, makes waste.

After lighting the oven, Janet began mixing up some cookie dough. Usually she made up a plate of fudge for Ralph in the evening and brought it in to him while he watched the TV. But somehow she had let herself run out of chocolate – except chocolate bits. Anyhow, Ralph was always saying how much he liked her Tollhouse cookies. She greased two cookie sheets and dropped great gobbets of the dough upon them in neat rows.

It was really so easy to kill a man. If you have patience. All you had to do was cook. Everyone in town could know what you were up to, and they couldn't do a thing to stop you. Besides, there were few wives in their town in Minnesota who would have felt free to cast the first stone. High-cholesterol is the way of life in the Corn Belt. It was Janet's genius to realizethat it was also a highly effective means of death. And there wasn't a jury in the country who could convict a person for being too good a cook.

The snores in the living room began to misfire and came to a stop. Ralph had smelled the cookies. A moment later he shuffled into the kitchen in sweat-soaked and sagging overalls (he didn't have to wear a belt with them), his face a maze of purple veins.

"Have a good sleep, dumpling?" she asked. He grunted, squinting at the light. He scarcely ever bothered to make conversation with her anymore.

She cut him another quarter-wedge of pie.

"No," he said. "No, I don't want that."

"Oh, pshaw!" she said, sliding it onto a plate.

"I tell you I *can't*. It's too rich. I'm feeling kind of sick tonight."

"Oh, dear." She frowned with pique, then brightened. "What you need is something warm, to settle your stomach." Opening the oven, she drew out the sheet of hot Tollhouse cookies and laid it on the cooling rack on the linoleum table. She handed Ralph the spatula. "Now sit down, and I'll fix you a nice glass of warm milk to go with them." She kneaded him into his special chair. He stared at the cookies before him with dull incomprehension. He was breathing hard.

"But didn't I just eat?" he asked. "Where did Axel go?"

She came back with a pitcher of warm milk and sat down beside him. "What's the matter, dumpling? Aren't you hungry?"

She picked up a cookie invitingly and held it in front of his mouth. His mouth opened. She put the cookie inside. His mouth closed and he began chewing mechanically.

"I don't know what's the matter with me," he whined. "I can't seem to help myself. I've got to stop, Janet. You've got to help me stop!"

"What sort of nonsense is that?"

She put another cookie into his hand. He ate it.

"I went to see Doc Wundt this afternoon, Janet. I tried to tell you before, but you wouldn't listen to me."

"Oh? I guess I was busy with the dinner. What did the doctor say?"

"He said I got a bad heart. That I'm too fat."

"Nonsense. I've seen a lot of men fatter than you. You've got a strong frame. It *demands* weight. You'd look silly if you were thin."

He picked up another cookie mournfully, bit into it, and took a swig of milk. The glass he used held a pint at a time.

"Well, that's what he *said*. He *is* a doctor, Janet. And that's not all. He said I've had *attacks*! Heart attacks, little ones, that I never even knew about. I always thought it was just gas pains. He took some kind of picture of my heart, and he's sending it in to the University for an expert to look at. He says I may have to go to the hospital."

Janet gasped. "No! No, I won't let you." She filled up his glass for him from the pitcher.

As he downed his second glass of milk, Janet felt she could almost *hear* his heart, labouring, pumping his over-burdened blood, straining at its sheath of fat. She had success almost in her grasp, and would it be denied her by some crank doctor's whim?

"No!" she said aloud.

"Janet, he says I've *got* to go on a diet. I'm carrying around all this dead weight, see, and my heart has to work too hard. He explained it all. He says I got to diet – and I can't! Janet, I can't!" His voice shook and for a moment it seemed as though he might cry.

Instead, he popped another Tollhouse cookie into his mouth. And another. And still another. He grabbed one in each hand and began cramming them in, while crumbs rolled down his chin and into his shirt. He choked, drained his third glass of milk, and resumed eating from the second sheet of cookies Janet had just placed before him. He ate like a man who has been starving.

After the second dozen, he looked up pleadingly. Was he pleading to be allowed to stop? Or did he want more?

It made no difference. Janet couldn't stand to watch him any longer. "Come along, dumpling. It's bedtime. I'll make some more cookies for breakfast."

"You *want* me to die, don't you?"

It was not really a question. On the other hand, she didn't think it was a strong enough accusation to bother to deny it.

He heaved himself up to his feet. "You *always* wanted me to die."

"Of course not, sweety-pie," she chided, taking him by the hand (thinking, meanwhile: *You pig! Yes, die! Please die!*), patting the helpless flesh, soothing him. "What a terrible thing to say. I only want what's best for you"

She had to go behind him on the stairs, since his girth now filled them from hand-rail to hand-rail. He had to ascend the steps one at a time, like a child or a very old man. She helped him place his feet, since he couldn't see them himself. His breath came very hard.

At the upper landing, he paused for breath. He had half turned around, when he grew very pale and reached a hand toward his heart. She began to back down the stairs, half in fear, half delighted. He lurched forward. She tripped. There was blackness, and pain, and the sound he made when he died, which was not entirely unhappy.

The first thing she was conscious of was his dead weight pinning her to the floor. The lower part of her back hurt where it was pressed against the bottom step. She put her hand to his heart. It was not beating. Then she tried to roll him off her, but he was securely wedged between the wall and the posts of the banister. A burning, incredible pain shot through her hip. She screamed, and somehow that didn't seem to make any noise at all. How could it be morning already? If only she felt stronger ... If only she hadn't broken her hip ...

If only Ralph would stop smiling ...

THE FLOATING PANZER

WITH THOMAS M. DISCH

"*Haben Sie Feuer bitte?*"

Automatically Sebastian Steel's hand went to the pocket of his Brooks suit and emerged with the golden, custom-made Ronson from which a butane flame obediently leapt. The svelte blonde at the next table leaned over to light her cigarette and Sebastian glanced admiringly at the deep cleft of her bosom. She murmured her thanks, as much it seemed for his admiration as for the light.

Sebastian cursed the tightness of his schedule for not giving him the time to develop a further acquaintance. It was nearly 20.00 hours, at which time he was to contact Krebs.

"Are you American?" the blonde asked him in English. He nodded. "Army?"

"No, I'm here on business. I represent an American *Fabrikant*."

"A manufacturer, you mean?"

"Your English is excellent, Fraülein."

In fact, he thought, everything about the Fraülein was excellent. His gaze roamed gratefully over her lush curves, smoothly fitted into a dress that was the colour of the strawberry in her glass of May wine. And he had been thinking that Stüttgart wouldn't be picturesque!

"Thank you. I studied in England for a time, when I was a little girl."

"How interesting." He tried to keep his tone cool and disinterested, knowing that any moment Krebs would come with his orders.

"Yes, at a school very near Stratford-on-Avon. In fact, I used to watch all the performances at the Stratford Festival. My favourite, of course, was *Two Gentlemen from Verona*."

Sebastian almost coughed up his cognac. *Two Gentlemen from Verona* was Krebs' password!

"I prefer *Love's Labours Lost*" he rejoined noncommittally.

"*Ach*! You too love Shakespeare! Then come, you must join me."

He picked up his snifter and moved to her table. Perhaps he would be able to mix business and pleasure after all.

"Thank heaven I've found you" she said. "I must have picked up every American tourist in Stüttgart trying out that wretched line. So you are Sebastian Steel?"

"And you are Krebs. Frankly, I expected … something different."

"Not a trollop, you mean?" She smiled enigmatically, sitting back in her rickety chair the better to appraise her contact.

Sebastian Steel had a strong, athletic face, but it was only lightly tanned now from having worked so long in Northern Europe. His eyes were grey and piercing and seemingly without humour, an impression contradicted by the crooked smile that played over his thin lips. His thick hair was worn long, in the English manner, and his suit, though impeccable, was undistinguished. His paisley tie was decidedly American.

"I'm *not* that kind of girl, you know – if it's of any importance. But how else am I to dress if I must speak to every American I meet?"

"You dress beautifully, Fraülein Krebs. The difference I anticipated was one of sex. I had been told that Krebs is employed at the *Eggelscheiss Fabrik*."

The mention of the famous manufacturer's name brought an expression of distaste to her face. "Yes, I am the company nurse. The information your employer has received thus far has been whatever I have been able to dig out of the employees – with the aid of scopolamine."

Sebastian was amazed. Fraülein Krebs was surely no more than twenty and yet she was evidently a competent industrial spy. It was not, after all, a business in which amateurs survived long.

"Your job" she continued, "is to get certain data about the drive units, *nicht wahr*? Because I have not been able to do so. Only our top designers and executives have accurate information about the power unit, and such men do not use the company infirmary. Thus, it has been impossible for me to – as you say – crack them open.

"You will be taken on as a mechanic in the Research and Development Division. You will work under Herr Grosch, which is unfortunate but inescapable. Your own identity is now Otto Ness and here are your papers." She fumbled in her leather handbag for the heavy envelope containing Sebastian's new identity: a passport, letters of recommendation and a brief history of "Otto Ness."

"Can you speak in a Bavarian accent?" she asked.

"I think so."

"Then you are ready to report for work. Do not contact me at the company unless our work has been uncovered. If you must see me, come to 44 Bremmerstrasse." She stood to leave, and Sebastian rose and pushed back his own chair for her to pass by. Her buttocks brushed his thigh and he noted that the soft flesh was not confined and stiffened by a girdle.

She extended her hand in farewell. Sebastian pressed it in the Continental fashion to his lips, while his fingers gently pried away the key. He left a fifty mark note to cover the bill and together they went off into the dark Stüttgart night towards the Bremmerstrasse.

Two days ago Sebastian had been caught up in the ordinary life of an industrial spy employed by FMC – Federal Motor Company – feeding drinks to designers until they grew loose-tongued, lying all night on the wet sands of Daytona with an infra-red camera waiting to catch (hopefully) the competition's time-trials and catching in fact a case of pneumonia. Nothing glamorous or extravagantly dangerous. And now, forty-eight hours later and an ocean away, he was about to steal one of the most closely-guarded secrets an automotive company could have – a device that would replace the tank – a gigantic new model of the Ground Effect Machine.

The original Ground Effect Machine, or GEM as it is known in engineering circles, was developed in the late Fifties by the United States Army. It consisted then of no more than a railed platform mounted on a huge, horizontal fan. One, or at the most two men could ride on it, supported by the hard "cushion" of air that the fan directed at the ground, steering it like a surf board, just by moving their own weight and letting the tilted machine slide over the terrain. The most revolutionary feature of the GEM was its adaptability, for it could move across choppy seas or swampland, treacherous sands or broken, stony fields as smoothly as a Rolls-Royce on the Indiana Turnpike. And the bigger a GEM was, the higher it rose on its cushion of air, the easier it could skim right over the obstacles that would be a barrier to any other vehicle.

The disadvantages of the early GEMs were legion: they were so unstable that the slightest excess of "tilt" could send one ploughing into the ground sideways, with unhappy consequences for the riders. Also, they were uncommonly slow. The best speed of the experimental models was 34 mph, and few of the drivers were willing to take it up that far because of its instability. Worst of all, it was small, and the estimated fuel consumption, using the Army-designed power unit, made a full-size commercial model out of the question.

But now the mammoth West German auto cartel of Eggelscheiss Fabrik seemed to have solved all these problems. Rumour along the corporation grapevine had it that the Eggelscheiss drive unit even supported heavy loads more easily than light!

Eggelscheiss, naturally, wasn't letting anyone see the blueprints of the rumoured *Flugtanken* or "Flying Tanks", and that's where Sebastian Steel came in. Federal Motors wasn't the only organization willing to go a little out of the way to find out about the Eggelscheiss GEM drive. Before he'd left from Kennedy Airport, Sebastian had had an interesting chat with an officer from Army Intelligence.

The Intelligence Unit in Cairo had just reported the arrival of giant, canvas-covered "weapons" from Stüttgart. The chief Cairo agent had been shot in the arm trying to get a look beneath the canvases, and before the second agent could be called out from his favourite hashish house, the GEMs had disappeared into the desert.

"Strange" Sebastian had said to the officer. "Egypt has never shown itself reluctant to advertise its military advantages."

"Perhaps," the officer suggested, "they're not remaining in Egypt."

"*Remain* in Egypt? Have you ever been there?"

"Well, never exactly in Egypt, but …"

Sebastian's nose crinkled in scorn, remembering Cairo. "If you had been there, you'd understand why it isn't possible to remain."

Sebastian sank back onto his haunches and wiped his forehead with a grease-blackened hand. Grosch, the short bespectacled foreman, scurried over. "Get to work!" he shrilled. "To work! To work! What is the matter, Ness? Do you dream now of Bavaria? Of some wretched beer garden where you will swill your wretched München beer? Come, come, come – there is no time for idle dreamers in the Eggelscheiss Fabrik. Pick up that spanner and get back to work."

Sebastian seized the wrench with such vehemence that the little Prussian took a pace backward, alarmed. But he was not in danger. Sebastian repressed his natural desire to cave in the man's ferine little face and re-assumed the mask of submissiveness that "Otto Ness" was compelled to wear.

Diligently Otto Ness returned to dismantling the hydraulic system. He had been at the Eggelscheiss Fabrik nearly a week, time enough to see that it was hopeless to try to memorizethe complex mechanism of the GEM drive unit. It was not just the complexity of the machine that militated against his learning it – the unstated policy of the Eggelscheiss Fabrik was to keep each worker so busy that he had not time to comprehend what it was he worked on. For comprehension takes leisure – if only a minute. There was one foreman – or *Werkmeister* – for every three workers – just about the ratio that would have obtained in a prison or a slave labour camp.

Sebastian could see now that the only possible way to make sense out of the great Flugtanken was to steal or photograph a set of plans. Which was, of course, a much more dangerous line of action, and therefore preferable.

It would have to be soon. Already Werkmeister Grosch had come to hate "Otto Ness" and watched him intently throughout the ten hour workday. The small, shaven-headed Prussian had singled Ness out for the most tedious jobs and the most violent abuse. He would subject him to constant questioning about his "wretched Bavaria" and he would not accept a submissive silence as an answer. It was only a matter of time before the mask began to show cracks. Perhaps he had already made slip-ups without realizing it.

"Ness!" the little Werkmeister screamed into his ear. The spanner clattered to the concrete floor and Sebastian wheeled around, pale with repressed fury, hoping that his pallor would look like fear to Grosch. "You are wanted in the big office, by Herr Eggelscheiss himself." Grosch's smirk seemed to suggest that such an invitation was not cause for rejoicing.

After cleaning the grease from his face and hands, Sebastian headed down the hundred-yard long, neon-white corridor to Eggelscheiss' office. He knocked on the grey metal door and an unctuous voice bade: "Hereinkommen!" He pushed open the door decorated with the two-headed eagle that was the emblem of the Eggelscheiss Fabrik.

There, behind a desk of gun-metal grey, sat the largest mass of human flesh that Sebastian Steel had ever seen outside of the New York subways at rush hour.

Göring once said: "If we make guns we will win the world. If we make only butter we will only grow fat.." The World War II Luftwaffe leader had then proceeded to ensure the wholesome leanness of countrymen by eating all their butter for them. Sebastian recalled those words now as he looked at Eggelscheiss. The man's enormous girth threatened to escape his double-breasted suit at a dozen separate points. The film of oil on his limp red jowls was like a sweat of pure butterfat. Pressing together the fingers of his slug-white hands as if in prayer, the president and owner of the Eggelscheiss Fabrik ordered Herr Ness to close the door and approach him.

"I have had interesting reports on you, Herr Ness." The guttural German words burbled out from his flaccid lips with unusual ease. "First, as you may know, Werkmeister Grosch does not entirely like you. Perhaps it is only that you are Bavarian." An ironic glint came into the watery eyes behind the thick, gold-rimmed lenses, and Sebastian caught his breath. "For it cannot be said that your work has been unsatisfactory. Indeed, the Werkmeister's reports show that your production has been nearly twice as much as the rest of our mechanics. That is admirable."

"Thank you, Herr President."

"We have therefore doubled individual quotas. In view of this, we are transferring you out of that department. Tomorrow you will report to the field-testing crew. Grosch will provide you with a badge that will admit you to the testing ground. I'm sure you will find the work more to your tastes, Herr Ness, and I regret that the company cannot afford to give you a higher salary, but –" Eggelscheiss grunted and removed a square of the most exquisite Chinese silk from his pocket, and dabbed at the sheen of sweat on his many chins. "But we have many expenses for research. Each week we must meet a larger pay-roll. The plant is expanding. Yes, we must all work together for the common good. But soon, soon we will have the *big* contracts."

"From the government?" Sebastian asked guilelessly.

"From everywhere. For the present, though, you workers must be patient each time 'the eagle flies'. Eh? That will be all, Ness. You may go."

"Very good Herr President. *Danke schön*." Sebastian executed a military about-face and exited through the eagle-blazoned door. He was almost grinning at this unexpected opportunity. Undoubtedly, this would bring him closer to the coveted plans. At the very least, he would be able to see the great "Floating Panzers" put through their paces. He began to make plans ...

At the same moment, Eggelscheiss too was feeling an unusual degree of elation. He pressed a button on the control panel of the gun-metal desk and within seconds Werkmeister Grosch stood before him.

"Just as I said", Eggelscheiss crowed, "he is an American. You saw yourself on the television how the phrase 'the eagle flies', which is a vulgar American idiom for payday, did not seem unusual for him."

"And I have caught him out in many similar mistakes", Grosch observed.

"What is he doing here, Grosch? May we assume he is a spy?"

"A brilliant deduction, my president. And therefore we will kill him, *ja?*" The little man's foxlike eyes gleamed with anticipation.

"Kill him, Grosch? No, we need not go that far. We shall simply *catch* him spying and turn him over to the *Polizei*. In his country, industrial spying may be a petty misdemeanour or none at all, but here in Germany it will earn him a long term in prison. Two or three years at the very least – and by that time, if all goes well, the whole world will know of our weapons."

"I don't like it," said Grosch, fitting a crumbly *Roth Handel* cigarette into a holder. "It is too inefficient. He already knows too much and he will attempt to communicate from prison. Surely the company that employs him – or even his government – could say nothing if he were killed in an industrial accident on the testing grounds?"

The fat man's jowls quivered with silent laughter and he dabbed at them with his silk handkerchief. "No Grosch, you are too quick … and too slow. You do not see the whole picture – as I *must*. What would the US do if this agent were to be splattered beneath our GEM? They would grow suspicious and send another agent, *nicht wahr*? But if he is put in prison, if there are stories in the newspapers, confessions, scandals? Then they must apologize, and they would not *dare* send another agent on the heels of the first."

"As always, you are correct, my president. But tell me," Grosch said, seating himself on the edge of the metal desk (a familiarity that Eggelscheiss tolerated in few subordinates), "if the story of his spying is publicized, will not the wretched government at Bonn begin to wonder what it is we are doing out here? Will not our *own* government inspect our factories and equipment? And might not that be the worst that can happen?"

Again the greasy jowls quivered with subdued mirth. "They *have* inspected us Grosch. Many times. And they have always approved of the … tractors that we're making. Like all democratic institutions, the Bonn government is easily duped and even more easily bribed. No inspector has seen the inside of an Eggelscheiss factory for two years. *Ach*, it is a pitiful, weak and corrupt institution, not fit for the German people. Already we have made three 'tractor' shipments to Cairo, and already these shipments have found their way to Yugoslavia –"

"– And from Belgrade to the People's Republic of East Germany!" said Grosch, his eyes glittering with pride.

"Yes, Grosch – against the day when there will *be* no 'East' or 'West' Germany but only one great *Vaterland*, ruling a single world. One *Deutschland, über Alles!*"

It would have to be tomorrow, Sebastian decided as he bicycled along the rain-misty streets of Stüttgart. (He could not endure to spend any more time than necessary in the stuffy cubbyhole where "Otto Ness" had to live.) There was no other time for it but now, and no other way to do it but to snatch the plans and run – perhaps in one of the repair crew's trucks. He would never be alone with the GEM long enough to take photos of its inner workings, nor would photographs be sufficient.

But where was he to run *to*? Eggelscheiss ruled the city of Stüttgart as completely as if he were its hereditary prince. The US NATO base, five miles the other side of Stüttgart, seemed his best bet.

Tonight he would have to tell Freyda Krebs. Once he had carried through his plans, Eggelscheiss would begin where the original leak had been and how "Otto Ness" had been employed. By a simple process of elimination, he would quickly discover the double role of his company nurse. Acting as she had, without the authorization or knowledge of the Bonn government, Freyda had put herself in a tight spot. Technically, she was a traitor, and no matter what service she had really performed for her country, Bonn would be obliged to convict her. The law was not always just. But even prison was not the worst that could befall her – for Eggelscheiss might not be generous enough to let her live that long. Sebastian knew the fat manufacturer to be quite capable of murder, if even slightly provoked.

Sebastian turned onto the slippery cobbles of the Bremmerstrasse and pedalled on for three blocks to No. 44. The light was on in Freyda's window, but when she opened the door to him, he saw that she had been sleeping. She must be scared, he thought, to be sleeping with the lights on.

If she had looked delectable in her strawberry evening gown, she was ravishing in the filmy blue transparency that now concealed (or failed to) her ripe bosom and full hips. Except for the dark circles beneath her eyes, she looked as virginal as a bride on her wedding night, an appearance that Sebastian was grateful to know to be deceiving.

"It's been hard for you, hasn't it?" he said quietly.

She nodded as she poured out two glasses of schnapps. She handed him one of the glasses, smiling wanly. He lifted his schnapps to her in a toast. "Well, buck up lovely. Our work is nearing completion. Tomorrow is D-Day."

"Thank God," she said. "Oh, thank God!" There were tears in her eyes. He kissed the soft hollow of her neck but she drew back from him. "You!" she said scornfully. "For you it's just a game. The famous American game of cops-and-robbers. Every little boy knows how to play it and when he's played long enough and he grows tired of it, he can pick up his toys and go home, home to the big corporation that will always give him candy and new toys, new games to play tomorrow, and nothing is real for you, nothing –" Her face contorted with bitterness. "But do you know why *I* play this silly game?"

"Not for candy?"

"Not for candy, no. And not because I love you or my country, but I have done all these terrible things, because of my hatred. God, how I hate him!" Her voice had become very hoarse and she took a sip of her drink. Her hand had trembled and the ice cubes tinkled against the delicate crystal.

"Eggelscheiss?" he asked.

"Him. How much do you know of him?"

"Very little. I know that he's always had a hand in politics – of the more unsavoury kind. I know that in '42 he was decorated by Hitler for the production record of the Eggelscheiss Fabrik, which was producing half of all the Panzer tanks manufactured in Germany. But almost all the big manufacturers in Germany today were decorated in those days – Volkswagen, Krupp ..."

"I'll tell you why Eggelscheiss was decorated. Because he pioneered the use of slave labour. I know. Because my father died in the Eggelscheiss *Arbeitslager* – the forced labour camp."

She paused. The glistening cascade of golden hair was hanging in front of her eyes but Sebastian knew that she had begun crying again. He touched her shoulder and her body stiffened – not because of his touch but in order to gather strength to go on.

"He was ... my father ... he was a labour organizer. He was convicted of a crime he had not committed and thrown into the *Arbeitslager*. They were not content to let him rot – oh no, he must work for the *Vaterland*. He was too good a machinist to be wasted in idleness. At gunpoint, he made the great gears that moved the gun turrets of Eggelscheiss' Panzers. He worked twelve and fourteen hours every day. There was not much food for prisoners and his health was already failing. But what did they care? If he died, the *Vaterland* had only lost a traitor. If he continued to work, the war effort was assisted."

"And it killed him?"

"No, it did not have time. You see, my father knew his work very well. He knew just how much the gears could be sabotaged and still pass a casual inspection. It was only when the first Panzers got in trouble at the front that they took him away from his lathe and stood him before a wall ..."

"I see."

"No, you *don't* see! All the time I was growing up, even to this day, I had to go past that wall on my way to school or to work. It carried – it carries an advertisement for Eggelscheiss tractors."

"My God, Freyda, I had no idea what you've been going through. All this time working in his factory just so that you might one day –."

"Destroy him! Yes. He called my father a Communist. Now it is Eggelscheiss who deals with the Reds. Oh, Sebastian, I have become so tired, so weary of hunting this monster. Tell me that it is time, that I can kill him now." She fell on his shoulder, her body convulsed with sobs.

"Afterwards", he whispered in her ear, "afterwards you must come to the States with me. You will not be safe here. Eggelscheiss has friends."

"I know. I know and I don't care."

"But *I* do" he insisted, "and you must let me have my way." Obediently, she turned her lips to his, and gently he taught her once more to care.

The sky was finally clear of last night's rain clouds, and a cold wind whipped at the white lab coats of the tiny group of designers huddled at one end of the stony testing field. Sebastian and the other mechanic stood at a distance from the designers beside the high-wheeled repair truck with which they were to follow behind the *Flugtank*.

The great hangar doors rolled back and a tractor emerged, towing the *Flugtank* on a trailer. It was immense. The sheer overpowering bulk of the thing somehow reminded Sebastian of Eggelscheiss himself. The impregnable armour of the floating tank might conceal a hundred different weapons, though since this was only a test flight, the GEM was probably not armed. There were ridges at the base of the tank, however, that put him distinctly in mind of nuclear warheads.

Out of the corner of his eye, he saw a flash of white. A sports car was careening up the winding mud road from the direction of the Eggelscheiss Fabrik. "It must be the boss in his custom-built Mercedes" said Sebastian's companion. "They say he won't fit into a regular car."

"But who is that with him?"

"Oh, that must be Nurse Krebs. Last week one of the test drivers busted his head open and now the other drivers won't take it up unless there's a nurse or doctor around."

The Mercedes stopped near the GEM and the mammoth figure of Eggelscheiss heaved himself from the driver's seat. Freyda got out the other side, carrying a large black infirmary kit in one hand, but by the way she followed close behind the industrial magnate, Sebastian had no doubt that she intended to kill Eggelscheiss today!

Several men, Grosch among them, climbed into the behemoth tank, and there was an ear-splitting whine as the first of the turbojets caught. The second fired, and a third and others, until the earth reverberated with the monster's titanic power. Slowly the immense bulk began to lift from the ground and climbed steadily to a height of fifteen feet, where it held and began moving horizontally over the stony field. Sebastian knew what the first man must have felt who saw Hannibal's army of elephants advancing through the Alps. It was an innately terrifying sight.

"You drive, Otto" the other mechanic said. "I have to get to the thing quickly in case it takes a nosedive into the dirt. I have to cut off the fuel lines along the side. I'll ride out on the running board – just like the gangsters in American movies, *ja*?"

"*Ja*," Otto Ness agreed. "Like cops-and-robbers."

He had only to keep a hundred yards behind the GEM, but even this was hazardous, for the GEM could move across the stony field with much greater speed and agility. Several times, Sebastian fell behind by having to steer around great boulders that the truck's high axle would not clear. But for the truck's four-wheel drive he would never have made it through the mud sloughs created by last night's rains. In drier weather, the GEM would have raised great clouds of dust, but today one could see the fifteen-foot void of space between the bottom of the tank and the muddy ground against which the column of air pressed down.

As the GEM circled the field, Sebastian tried to manoeuvre the truck closer and closer to the central group of design engineers, who were arguing over a pile of blueprints spread out upon a folding table. Eggelscheiss, however, took little interest in their dispute. He seemed to spend all his time watching Sebastian!

On the fourth time passing by the cluster of men, while he was still a good fifty yards off, the mechanic stuck his head in through the window and screamed in a guttural Berlin accent, "What are you doing, *dumkopf*? We're falling too far behind!"

"Sorry, pal," Sebastian replied in English, "but you get off here." He shoved the man off into knee-deep mud and swung the truck directly toward the group surrounding Eggelscheiss. He jammed the accelerator to the floor.

The next few minutes were a blur of action. The designers in their spotless lab coats looked aghast, forgot their dispute and the table full of blueprints, and stampeded through the mud. Freyda stepped away from Eggelscheiss, fumbling in her medical kit for the pistol she had secreted there. Even over the roar of the truck's engine, Sebastian heard the three crisp shots. The bloated manufacturer pitched backward into the mud, like a pyramid falling onto its side.

Sebastian slammed on the brakes and leaped out before the truck had slowed to 15 mph. He sprinted toward the table stacked with blueprints, just as half-a-dozen guards piled out of the distant hangar and came running toward him. The front wheel of the truck hit a boulder and went over on its side.

"The car!" he yelled to Freyda. "Run to the Mercedes and start it up!" Freyda had been staring as if hypnotized at the dying Eggelscheiss, who was dabbing at the bullet holes in his gut with his handkerchief of Chinese silk, but now she ran to Eggelscheiss' custom sports convertible. With an armload of blueprints, Sebastian dashed after Freyda. Machine gun bullets perforated the mud only inches away as he vaulted over the side of the Mercedes and threw it into first. Another hail of lead sang over their heads as the car leaped ahead, responsive to Sebastian's knowledgeable grip.

Adjusting the rear-view mirror, Sebastian saw his troubles were just beginning. The great Floating Panzer, no doubt under Grosch's direction, was swooping down on him with astonishing speed, at least double the velocity it had maintained on its best test runs. It was coming directly towards Sebastian and in doing so it would pass over the spot where Eggelscheiss, not yet dead, lay bleeding in the mud. The column of air that supported the tank passed over the manufacturer and, with the sound of a bubble bursting, there was no longer a distinction between Eggelscheiss and the mud.

Freyda looked back. "They're gaining!"

It was not exactly news to Sebastian. On the winding, slippery road, he couldn't push the Mercedes over ninety, and even that was risky. The GEM's advantage was only too clear. All flat surfaces were alike to it; it did not need to follow the sharp curves of the road.

As the Mercedes approached the gate, the Floating Panzer was less than a hundred feet behind and gaining rapidly. It was here that Sebastian hoped to leave the monster behind, for he doubted that it could clear the electrified fence that circled the test area. It was obviously too wide for the gate.

As he sped through, the uniformed guard stepped from his box, automatically coming to attention for the president's car. Sebastian wrenched the wheel violently, pointing the hood ornament of the taut Mercedes toward Stüttgart. In fifth gear now, he pressed hard on the accelerator. A glance in the mirror made him wish that he could press it through the floorboards. The neon-clad behemoth had not even slackened its speed. Fifteen tons of steel made a piledriver lunge at the top of the fence, and it was through and after him.

"We'll never make it!" Freyda screamed, twisting in the seat to look at their pursuer. Topping a rise, the little car seemed to float for a dizzying moment. There in the valley before him were the elms and spires of Stüttgart, and beyond – the great fuel storage tanks of the Army's NATO base.

"We *will* make it" he promised grimly, gearing down for the first of a series of hairpin turns. The main road into Stüttgart wound down the wall of a cliff to the river-valley a thousand feet below. It was a continuum of sharp, car-punishing bends, with a wall of rock on the left and yawning emptiness on the right. The GEM could take these turns no faster than the Mercedes, and with luck Sebastian could maintain his lead clear to the bottom. Once he reached the city, he could turn into a narrow street and lose the GEM.

He took each curve more recklessly than the last, as he began to get a feeling for the car. The gears were rough from careless handling. The little car drifted as far to the edge of the road as possible. Freyda had closed her eyes to keep from screaming with fright.

Suddenly, the gigantic GEM appeared from nowhere, looming like another wall of the cliff behind him by only a dozen yards. He could feel the turbulence it created in the air and it reminded him of Eggelscheiss, the way his body had been disintegrated by the terrific blast of air. In a minute, that column of air would be pressing down on Sebastian and Freyda.

Another hairpin turn came rushing at him but he didn't dare slow for it. The car skidded and slewed wildly, the left rear wheel leaving the road for an instant, then gripping it again with a jerk and wobble that sent battalions of butterflies through Sebastian's stomach. The driver of the GEM was clever enough to cant his machine steeply at the curve, scraping sparks from the wall of rock. Under the pressure of the blast of air, the rain-loosened underpinnings of the cliff began to peel away, taking some of the tarmac road with it. A new roar, the roar of an avalanche, added its timbre to the roar of the GEM. Without righting itself, the Floating Panzer slid down the side of the cliff, hit the next road level and careened off, spinning end over end until it reached the water of the Rhine.

Sebastian turned on the radio and tuned it to a Strauss waltz. He lit two of his specially blended Iranian cigarettes and handed one to Freyda. Then he drew her close until her confiding body had untensed. He kissed away the trembling from her hands and the last little bit of fear that lingered in her eyes.

At last she asked sleepily, "And now, Sebastian?"

"Now, I shall take these blueprints to the Army base."

"And after that?"

"After that, we'll take the next jet out of Stüttgart."

"What! *Gott hilf mir*! We will not, Sebastian." She leaned across the gearbox and planted a stern, commanding kiss on his lips.

"All right" he conceded, chuckling. "We'll take the second jet."

THE INCREDIBLE GIANT HOT DOG

WITH THOMAS M. DISCH

It began one bright spring day in a Chicago slaughterhouse. A hammer shattered the skull of a rather elderly cow ...

But was that truly the beginning? Or would you have to go back to the morning, a month earlier, when that cow began to munch a particular morsel of hay? Or earlier yet when the rain bearing the strange new isotope had fallen on the Montana fields?

Or would you have to go all the way back to that bomb test years before in the steppes of Central Asia? The chain of cause and effect stretches back endlessly. There is no certain beginning to anything, just as there is no certain end.

For Joe Scharf it began on Tuesday June 23rd, the day his wife went away for a two week cooling-off period to her mother's, leaving him to care for Trudy and Rudy, the ten-year-old twins. For the most part, he let the twins look after themselves but he couldn't quite trust them to fix their own meals. The first day he'd done that and discovered that in twenty-four hours they had eaten a quart of ice-cream and one of Anne's layer cakes in its entirety – and nothing else.

At least Joe could get them to eat meat. But the prices! It had been years since he'd done any grocery shopping and he was aghast at the prices. Before Anne had gone away she'd said: "All right, *you* try cooking decent meals on the pitiful allowance you give me for food. I don't want you to spend a penny over that. You'll see!"

He had made three rounds of the supermarket and, except for a bottle of mustard, the shopping cart was still empty. What can people *afford* to eat nowadays? he wondered.

At last, he decided on a package of hot dogs. It was the cheapest brand in stock: *Coney Island All-Meat Hot Dogs*. There was something ominous about that *All-Meat*. As though there might conceivably be something other than meat in a frankfurter. But he shrugged off the scruple. They were cheap, wasn't that enough?

Do you heat the pan first? he wondered. Do you use grease? Wouldn't the hot dogs make their own grease?

While the pan was smoking on the gas range, he tore off the plastic wrapper from the package of hot dogs and disengaged one of the greasy franks from its fellows. He laid it in the pan experimentally.

It sizzled, it writhed, and it made small shrieking sounds that sounded like a 33 LP record being played at 78 rpm. Was the pan too hot? Perhaps he should have taken off the plastic skin.

The hot dog seemed to be swelling slightly and he leaned forward to examine it. At just that moment it leapt at his face!

With a cry of pain, he retreated from the stove. The wiener flopped back to the white enamel surface of the range, skittered about uncertainly and at last fell into the crevasse between the stove and the icebox.

"Damn!" he whispered, as much on account of his smarting cheek as in annoyance at the hot dog's refractory behaviour. He ran to the sink and dabbed his cheek with cold water. It stung quite nastily. Examining his reflection in the bottom of a copper pan, he saw that the hot dog had left clear evidence of its attack – it looked almost as though a small knife had jabbed him.

He called the twins in to dinner and they came in from the back yard with their mouths rimmed with graham cracker crumbs. They'd eaten a full box of crackers. He bawled them out and sent them to bed without dinner (which they wouldn't have been able to eat anyhow), and then sneaked out to a restaurant. He had quite forgotten the hot dog that had fallen behind the stove.

Once Joe was safely gone from the kitchen, a curious mouse crept into the crevasse between the stove and the icebox. He sniffed curiously at the fallen wiener. It seemed edible, though not of the highest quality. He nibbled experimentally.

The mouse gave one warning squeal – a warning that unfortunately went unheeded – and then he ceased to exist.

Meat! The hot dog stirred restlessly. *Meat!* There was fresh meat near at hand. It reared itself to its new fourteen-inch height and fell back weakly. It needed more meat. It would always need more meat.

With inchworm motions, It crossed the kitchen floor, ingesting millions of micro-organisms on its way. Joe had left the opened package of hot dogs on the kitchen table and It sensed them. In a few minutes, It had pulled itself weakly up onto the chair, then to the tabletop. There It began to feed on Its own kind.

And It grew.

After two small pizzas, Joe Scharf drowsed satisfiedly over coffee, a cigarette and the evening paper. At intervals, a faint whisper of conscience (vaguely reminiscent of Anne's nagging whine) pestered him about the twins. Sending them to bed without a proper dinner, for shame, Joe Scharf!

I'll get some ice cream on the way home, he promised the nagging voice.

Glancing out of the window of the restaurant, he caught sight of a friend going into the tavern across the street.

The meat on the table had been good, but it had not been enough. More, It craved more. It knew that there was meat inside the great box in the corner, but it was not yet strong enough to break open the box. So, squealing and wriggling, it began to inch its way up the stairs where, also, It knew, there was more meat, lots of meat, sleeping.

No amount of persuasion could keep Bill from buying him another round.

"Okay", Joe relented, "but this is absolutely the last. I've got to take home some ice cream to the brats".

"By the way, Joe, what happened to your face?" Bill asked.

"You'd never believe it" said Joe winking. "I was bit by a hot dog." They laughed heartily.

"By God, that calls for another one." Before Joe could stop him, Bill had ordered another round.

That last portion of meat had been quite tough. It had bitten and scratched and made sounds like the first little meat, only louder. But all the more delicious for that. Strangely, the meal had only increased his hunger.

The Giant Hot Dog pushed up against the window screen and it gave. Outside, in the grass, It rested, digested. Moths approached it, alighted and disappeared.

For some reason It dreamt of graham crackers that night.

II

Joe awoke on the living room couch with a crashing, pulsing, hammering headache.

It was still only five o'clock in the morning. The sun was just coming up. He groaned.

He stumbled upstairs on the way to the bedroom and, as he passed by, looked in on the twins. They weren't in their bed, and their blue jeans and monster t-shirts lay on the floor where they'd thrown them. The whole room was in a terrible mess.

The linoleum floor was slimed with grease and the air was heavy with the smell of hot dogs. Could they have gotten up in the night and eaten the hot dogs he'd left on the kitchen table? And where had they gone after that?

He searched the whole house and the only clue he turned up was the empty wrapper from the hot dogs on the floor beside the kitchen table. Absentmindedly he folded the wrapper and put it in his pocket.

There was a scream from the back alleyway. Joe was at the door in a flash. The thing he saw there was too hideous to be believed. It was incredible.

It took all his willpower to keep himself from retching. For he knew instantly what the thing was. He remembered the long brown scar on its back, and the four round scars where the tines of the fork had pricked it. Just to be sure, he checked in the crevasse between the stove and the icebox. Sure enough, it was gone!

Joe looked outside again. The Giant Hot Dog had finished digesting the milkman and now It was battering the back door of the truck.

Instinctively, Joe dialled for the police. Even before they'd answered the phone, Joe could hear the door of the milk truck giving way and then the shattering of hundreds and hundreds of bottles.

A dozen squad cars surrounded the truck. The cops had orders to shoot whatever came out. Already the two patrolmen who had come by to investigate Joe's complaint had been pulled into the milk truck, never to emerge again.

"The way I see it," said Joe to the Commissioner, "there are lots of ingredients in a hot dog. Who knows everything that goes into one of them? Maybe something not quite dead? Maybe –"

They were interrupted by Dr van der Brougie, who had just returned from Police Laboratories with the wrapper that Joe had given him to study.

"I think we are close to an answer!" van der Brougie announced. "This wrapper was traced back to the sausage plant on Coney Island where these hot dogs are made. By a curious coincidence, it is the same sausage plant in which you trapped Madman Fergusson three months ago."

"You mean the mass murderer who disappeared so mysteriously?" Joe asked.

"Do you think that's Fergusson in the milk truck?" the Commissioner asked, ignoring Joe.

"No, it's something that *was* Fergusson – in part. Now there are other things combined with him, but essentially he's still the same. He's *evil*!"

"Oh, bosh!" said the Commissioner sceptically, but he was interrupted by a warning whistle. The Giant Hot Dog was emerging from the rear of the milk truck. It had grown to an enormous size.

One end waved in the air a moment, then headed directly toward the nearest policeman, who fired at it with a sub-machine gun. The great red wiener doubled up like a snake and struck. Its ten-foot length covered the gallant policeman. Joe caught a glimpse of a blue-clad arm and leg thrashing about beneath the thick cylinder of meat and heard muffled cries. Then all was still.

Some of the other policemen stood their ground and fired at it with riot guns, pistols and flamethrowers, but all to no avail. It resisted even mustard gas. One by one, the Giant Hot Dog consumed the brave policemen.

The Commissioner pulled Joe and van der Brougie into the house and bolted the door.

"Where's the phone?" he shouted. "I'd better call the National Guard."

"Too late", lamented van der Brougie. "I fear that it is too late."

III

The sleek grey missile was outlined against the night sky by a hundred lamps. The engineers readied all checkpoints. The countdown was begun.

Somewhere out in the darkness, Joe realized with a shiver of dread, the Giant Hot Dog lay, digesting what was left of Coney Island. How poetic – that the thing should at last destroy the island from which it had taken Its detested name! Just as Frankenstein had been destroyed by the monster he created.

In the distance, the steel girders of a sea-view apartment house collapsed as the monster – half insane criminal, half radioactive isotope, and half beef – lashed out blindly with its mile-long tail. Then it began to feed on the occupants of the building.

All Brooklyn – all who could be reached by Civil Defence – had been evacuated. The Army was ready now to take its last desperate gamble. Heretofore, the Giant Hot Dog had enveloped bazookas, mashed tanks, ignored flamethrowers and shown perfect indifference to poison gas. In barely three days, it had reduced half of Long Island and Brooklyn to a smoking ruin. Manhattan would be next, and then …

Nobody dared to imagine. If this attempt failed, it was quite probable, according to van der Brougie's calculations, that it would take over the world.

One minute to zero!

Van der Brougie (whom the Army had put in charge of the scientific end of the operation) turned to Joe. "I guess I should let you push the button," he said. "You've certainly earned the right."

Joe gripped van der Brougie's hand with wordless emotion and stepped to the elaborate control panel. An aide pointed the button out to him, and with a silent prayer he pressed it.

The missile rose from the launching pad in a short, sharp arc and descended through the night sky toward the distant Hot Dog. At a distance of two thousand feet the warhead was triggered.

Night became day, and for one horrifying instant they could see the full bulk of the Giant Hot Dog. Then it was engulfed by the fireball.

When the tremor had passed and the great cloud began to disperse they could hear a strange new sound – a sound that no human being had ever heard before. Was it the death agony of the Giant Hot Dog?

A delicious aroma of cooking meat came to their nostrils.

Patches of sand and concrete were on fire, and in the light from the blaze they could see the torrents of grease streaming down from Its wounded body. Bellowing angrily, the Great Hot Dog reared halfway up, turned, curled double and flopped sideways into the water. It began to swim away.

"Hawt Dawg!" exclaimed the sergeant assigned to guard van der Brougie. "We've got it on the run!"

Joe and van der Brougie exchanged a timid smile. It was still early to be sure, but it seemed that the sergeant might be right.

It swam painfully away from the terrible, searing heat. Why had that happened? Just when It had begun to really start growing, why had there been such a terrible pain? It was like the first pain with which It's life had begun. It had escaped that first heat and now It had escaped again, but this time it was somehow different. Now It had a new goal. Hunger no longer impelled It, but a very different feeling, a desire to fulfil Itself, a sense of destiny.

As a salmon struggles upstream to spawn, so now the Giant Hot Dog fought against the Gulf Stream with all the failing resources of Its body and spirit. The water seemed to boil around It and there was all around the delicious, tantalizing odour of Meat.

Then, suddenly It knew that Its moment had come. Two prongs pierced Its side. There was scarcely any pain at all. Then it felt Its body swathed in something soft as a cloud, and something else, a wet pungent paste was slathered upon It with a brush. It was lifted up towards Its consummation.

Joe and Dr van der Brougie looked out at the calm sea. "I still can't figure it out," Joe ruminated. "I know that lots of strange ingredients go into hot dogs. But why just this one? Why did it suddenly go berserk like that? And where has it disappeared to now? There doesn't seem to be a scientific explanation".

Van der Brougie was a moment answering. Looking up at the brilliant firmament, he said slowly, "I think perhaps there are some things that man was not meant to know. Such things are better left ... in the Hands of the Almighty!"

The Marching Raspberries

A Thrilling New Adventure of the Pink Avenger and His Faithful Companion Oxbridge

with Thomas M. Disch

AVERAGE VALLEY KICKS FLUORIDATION, screamed the headline of *The Average Valley Lowdown* which had fought long and hard on its editorial pages in the fight against Fluoridation of the City Water. And now it was crowned with the fruits of success.

But was it Total Victory? Perhaps *The Lowdown* had jubilated too soon!

For in the middle of the Anti-Fluoridation Victory Celebration the air was cloven by the minacious sound of a giant Power Mower, the sound of which set people's teeth on edge.

"It's those new jets from the airbase nearby," said some. But more thoughtful citizens realized that the Power Mower was only a mask for what was really being done. Subliminal messages were being broadcast at the speed of sound and with a period of vibration that only children could hear. The message bade them use the new fluoridated toothpaste, MOLA. Even a few overtrustful parents were taken in by this clever ruse.

But Senator Wilhelm Blessing was not that easily fooled. He loved his daughter Betty too dearly to allow her mind and teeth and pioneer spirit to be corrupted by the hucksters of Madison Avenue. "Not if I can help it," the Senator said. He was not a man to waste words.

The Senator realized that this was a job for the Pink Avenger. He picked up the pink Princess telephone beside his sickbed. It was a direct line to the Pink Avenger's secret headquarters in the Huntingdon Hartford Gallery. More than a thousand miles away!

"We've got our work cut out for us, Pinky," the Senator said with casual familiarity. "It looks as if Mola is up to one of his infernal tricks again."

"You're right, Senator," the Avenger replied. "You know my old arch-enemy pretty well. He probably has a Power Mower stashed up in the hills somewhere."

"Yes – but what about the subliminal advertising messages? What is Mola up to now?"

"Who knows? Perhaps his object is to drive down real estate values in Average Valley. Perhaps –."

But suddenly the telephone connection was broken, and the Pink Avenger heard the characteristic cackle of his arch-enemy Mola!

"Heh! Heh!"

The Pink Avenger threw off his ordinary pink fluff suit and stood revealed as the Pink Avenger! No longer did the world see commonplace Dewey Prufrock, the Manhattan art appraiser, but instead the great bulk of the Man in the Pink Mask towered menacingly over the telephone stand.

A few moments later, at a Dairy Queen on the outskirts of New York City, a panel slid back and the sleek, salmon-coloured car of the Pink Avenger rolled into the street. He called his powerful machine Cotton Candy. Now it paused, its great motor throbbing with restrained power, while the Pink Avenger's companion got out to close the secret panel.

As he did so, the Avenger tossed him a coin. "Here, Oxbridge, get us a couple of raspberry parfaits, while you're at it. We'll need some Quick Energy before this day is through."

"Um," said Oxbridge. He frowned thoughtfully. "That right, Chief. Mola plenty bad customer." When he returned with the taste-tempting confections (and so nutritious too!), they resumed this line of conversation.

Oxbridge spoke first. "Why Mola so bad, Chief?" he asked, turning his blunt, trusting face toward his leader, who wore all pink and whose identity was concealed by a pink mask.

"An early incident in his childhood set him on the primrose path, Oxbridge. You see, he once left a tooth under his pillow, in hopes that the Good Fairy would leave him a dime. But no dime was left. And that tooth was *a molar!*"

"Why she do that Chief! Why Good Fairy not want tooth?"

The Pink Avenger looked into the simple, trusting face of his companion with tolerance and affection. "There are some things we can't question, Oxbridge. For those things we need to have faith. The point is, Mola quit believing in goodness from that day forth. He will stop at nothing in pursuing his hateful ends. He has murdered dentists, stolen dentures and gambled. He has aided the Communist Party in their efforts to poison America with Fluorides in the City Water. Somewhere in each of his crimes the theme of Dental Hygiene appears. As if he can never forget that early, traumatic experience."

"I see, Chief. A fetish. Him conditioned to respond to stimulus of teeth, so him provide own stimulus. Perhaps him believe everyone trying to steal his teeth, so him steal from everyone else first."

"Right, Oxbridge."

The Pink Avenger's keen vision picked out the glint of a rifle barrel. Quickly he swerved the car and the bushwhacker's bullet sang harmlessly past. The Avenger chuckled quietly.

"We must be getting close to Mola's secret lavatory," he observed. He did not add that he expected much more severe interference before they reached the heart of Mola's secret underground hideout.

"Blam. Blam. Blam."

The bullets glanced off the armoured sides of Cotton Candy. The Pink

Avenger laughed.

In the vast caverns of his secret lavatory, the evil Doctor of Dental Hygiene watched a viewscreen across which the pink car, Cotton Candy, sped. He cackled unpleasantly.

"Well Pink Avenger, you've fallen into my trap this time. Now I'll get a chance to look beneath that pink mask and discover whom it conceals. Heh. Heh." He switched off the viewscreen and gave a coded order to his robot chauffeur to warm up The Dragonfly, his dread golden helicopter fully equipped with the latest in terrifying devices.

Mola stepped into an adjacent room, where a girl lay strapped to a table – and arrayed on a nearby counter were various instruments of dental surgery and books by such authors as Kafka, Proust, Ionesco and Thomas Hardy. Mola stopped to draw sustenance from the pages of *Jude the Obscure* and the girl strapped to the table regarded him with helpless rage.

Just a minute! The girl on the table is none other than the daughter of Senator Blessing. Betty!

What is she doing in Mola's secret underground lavatory? Unless ... she has been trapped there and is being held against her will!

Mola lay down the novel and picked up a giant needle. "As soon as I've dealt with our bubble-gum-coloured friend out there, I'm going to give you a shot of this." He indicated the enormous hypodermic. "A hundred CCs will turn you into a great big bicuspid. Heh! Heh!"

He cackled triumphantly, as the terror-stricken girl fainted.

The Pink Avenger does not carry lethal weapons. The six guns at his side are loaded with potent chemicals that are powerful in their effects but not deadly.

The giant Dragonfly approached. The friends could plainly see the steel robot hunched over the controls, a grim expression in its steel visage. Beside it was a figure cowled in black leather that they knew could only be the Tooth Czar himself. Suddenly the Dragonfly's great gold stinger quivered like an eager scorpion.

"Careful does it!" warned the Avenger. "That sting is charged with a million volts – *and* tipped with a quick-acting poison. Look out Oxbridge!" And so saying, he drew one of his guns and fired at the gold stinger. "There, my raspberry-soda gun should take care of that threat."

Indeed the stream of pinkish liquid quickly dissolved the inferior metal of the stinger.

"I guess you think you're pretty smart," snarled the voice of the Avenger's arch-enemy. "Okay, you big pink elephant, let's see you get out of *this* one!"

So saying, he opened up with a pair of giant flamethrowers. Splat! Splat!

But the Man in the Pink Mask was more than equal to the occasion. He fought back with his second gun, filled with pink Foam. The flames were snuffed out at their source. Then, playing the stream of Foam over the blades of the helicopter, he brought down the great Dragonfly itself!

"Curses! Curses on you, Pink Avenger!" screamed the black-cowled figure. The cowl fell back, revealing not Mola but a second robot!

It had all been an Infamous Trick!

"Now," Mola continued remorselessly over a loudspeaker set into the robot's metallic head, "have a taste of my Mind-Paralyzer!"

An incredible force seemed to grip the Avenger's brain. He slumped senseless to the ground.

When our hero woke, he found himself strapped to a table not far from the table on which Senator Blessing's daughter, Betty, was strapped.

"Where am I?" he groaned. But it was only too clear that this was Mola's secret underground lavatory, for he had been here on many previous occasions.

"And Betty Blessing! What are *you* doing here? It's always nice to meet a friend of course, but I had thought you were back at school at Oklahoma State Teacher's College, where you were studying Domestic Management Training."

"I was, Pink Avenger, only I went on a field trip to pick raspberries – raspberries are my favourite fruit of all – and I fell into Mola's clutches. I've got to learn to be more careful on field trips. Now Mola says he's going to turn me into a bicuspid! But worse than that, he says he's going to unmask you and learn your secret identity. What can we do?"

"Don't worry, Betty," the Pink Avenger said, smiling his encouragement. "I don't see Oxbridge around, so perhaps he's escaped to bring help."

At these very words, the door burst open and there was Oxbridge!

"I help you my friends. Mind-Paralyzer not work on Oxbridge. Oxbridge knows secret of No-Mind."

"How's that?" queried Betty, wrinkling her nose. "I thought you were an American Indian. That's an Oriental Indian trick. Like the Hindu rope trick."

"It's more like the Punjab noose" Oxbridge corrected. Nevertheless, he was surprised to find young Betty so erudite on these matters.

"It's most like Zen," concluded the Avenger, not to be outdone.

Alas! While our three friends are engrossed in this discussion of Orientalia, the evil Doctor of Dental Hygiene creeps up behind the unsuspecting Oxbridge and, all unseen, he slips a Punjab noose over the Indian's head and *rendered him unconscious*!

"Gee willikers" said Betty vexedly. "Darn! And he didn't even get a chance to undo our straps. Darn, darn, darn."

"Now I shall have a third cusp to add to my collection. Heh, Heh," cackled Mola.

But, before he had slumped to the floor, Oxbridge had winked a coded message to his leader. Oxbridge's message was: S-T-A-L-L H-I-M.

"Tell me Mola," said the Pink Avenger, in a disarmingly conversational tone, "is it true that you have a vast collection of teeth?"

"It is indeed. But you can't fool me Avenger! You're trying to stall for time. But we've wasted too much of that precious commodity already. Now I get to see your true identity!"

Mola reached forth a trembling hand to the edge of the pink mask. The helpless man said quickly, "But just how many teeth do you have? Isn't it true that the Good Fairy has an even larger collection?"

Mola's face became ashen with rage. "Don't Good Fairy me! I've heard all I ever want to hear about the Good Fairy. I don't believe in her! She *turned down* one of my teeth once. A baby molar. And I never let another leave my mouth." He grimaced, revealing fifty-nine perfect teeth.

"Now I control the teeth of the *world*! Now children try to sell their teeth to *me*. At *my* price." He cackled, as though insane.

"Oh, you thought you were clever, Pink Avenger. Preventing fluoridation at every turn! And you! You!" He indicated the terrified Betty Blessing. "Eating raspberries so that the little seeds would get between your teeth and decay and form *cavities*!"

"And you!" (Turning back to the Avenger.) "Getting children to switch from hygienic dental floss to pink candy-floss! Aggh! Fomenters of decay! Purveyors of sweetness! Corruptors of children's' teeth!"

He was raving. "But none of you can beat me now. Everyone is going to have perfect teeth – *and they'll give them all to ME*!" The Tooth Czar gnashed his fifty-nine teeth together in an excess of perverted joy.

"And now, at last, I unmask you! Now I shall discover and *know* the true identity of the Pink Avenger." With these words he bent over his helpless victim and *ripped the mask off the Pink Avenger's face*!

But, at that very moment, a strange noise made him turn his head; it was the soft, shuffling sound of tiny wet feet, and the liquid murmur of millions of tiny voices. "No!" Mola gasped. "The raspberries are marching!" A look of uttermost horror crossed his evil countenance. "They're after me!"

In they swarmed, a red horde of them, shouting, "What have you done with Betty, you *bête noir*?" Then they began to pelt him. He screamed in agony and threw his hands in front of his face. Red oozed between his fingers.

"I can't stand it! I hate sweets!" he screamed. Grabbing the loathsome hypodermic needle that lay prepared on the volume of *Jude the Obscure*, Mola fled to the closet and locked himself in.

"I'll turn myself into a tooth," came the muffled cry of the crazed Tooth Czar. "A big beautiful molar, like the one I lost."

Abruptly his cries ceased. Some of the raspberries were about to squeeze themselves under the door but, at a signal from the Pink Avenger, they withdrew.

As the Good Fairy undid their bonds, the Pink Avenger told her of their adventure. Then she paid him ten cents for the big molar in the closet and flew away. As the happy trio sped back to Average Valley, Betty pointed out that they had still not found the giant Power Mower. The eyes behind the slits of the Pink Mask glimmered with amusement. Oxbridge guffawed.

"Betty, *there is no Power Mower*," the pink-clad Enemy of Fluoridation explained. "It was mass hypnosis – a secret Mola learned a few years ago while travelling through the Orient."

"That right Chief" added Oxbridge. "Me see-um Mola there."

"Then you *are* an Oriental Indian!" declared the pert young Miss.

"No, me travelling there too, in a Wild West show. Earn heap big wampum."

"Today we three have earned yet a bigger wampum," quipped the happy Avenger, as he brandished the shiny dime for all to see.

The three laughed merrily at the Pink Avenger's witty remark as the great sleek Cotton Candy hurried them toward the rejoicing throngs of Average Valley.

SWEETLY SINGS THE CHOCOLATE BUDGIE

A STIRRING NEW ADVENTURE OF THE GREEN MAGICIAN

WITH THOMAS M. DISCH

Strange events were transpiring in Montreal, the capital city of Quebec, which is a province of Canada, the country which borders the United States on the north. It was apparent to everyone by now that the great advertising campaign of the Occult Chocolate Company had gotten all out of hand.

Chocolate is a top contender in Canada for prime evening time, so when Occult Chocolates bought up all the television and radio time there was to be had, the industry sat up and took notice. A steady diet of commercials for *Up-Chocks, Almond Gluts, Bittersweet Greed-Pleasers* and *Choco-Lichees*, unleavened by intervening programmes left many viewers nonplussed, but when they ventured to make small protests, the managers of the television and radio stations explained to them that their duty as citizens in a Free Enterprise Economy was to sit down in front of their television sets and watch whatever was shown to them.

Some of Montreal's citizens, however, understood their duty in another sense, and these rugged individualists wrote letters of protest to the *Montreal Star-Terrier*. But the *Star-Terrier* – and all of the rest of Canada's several newspapers – had not space to print letters from their readers.

There was not even space for the news. The Occult Chocolate Company had bought up all the space too! Every possible media was crammed full of ads for *Peanut Clutters,* for *Chocko-Lax,* for *Chocolate Maple-Leaves,* and various other sweets manufactured by Occult.

Now, the Green Magician, although he was not without a sweet tooth himself, was struck by what appeared to him an overemphasis on chocolates. He was vacationing in Montreal with his Aunt Effluvia, and after a few hours before the television screen in their motel room, patiently waiting for the commercials to be done, they had gone to the Bowl-More Bowling Alleys in the heart of Montreal's finest residential section.

"Aunt Effie, have you noticed how much space and time the Occult has gotten control of?" queried the Green Magician of his dear old Auntie.

"I have indeed," the sprightly 95-year-old replied, "and I wouldn't be surprised if this were the work of the Madison Avenue Hexters." For Aunt Effluvia had often heard her nephew tell of his dramatic encounters with that notorious band of advertising desperadoes.

The ball-return mechanism erupted and Aunt Effluvia's Special-Grip ball was emitted. Glued to the surface of the ball was a label with this message printed on it:

> *Bowling can be lots of fun –*
> *Truly the all-family sport*
> *But you soon will need the lift my son*
> *Provided by Occult's Lump-o-Chocklit Tort.*

"Now, Aunt Effie," the Green Magician chided, "there you go worrying again. The Hexters are safely behind bars in Brazil."

"Look out!" Aunt Effie screamed.

"What?!" But it was too late. The Green Magician, in releasing his ball down the long, varnished alley, had stepped across the foul-line and the Foul-lite at the end of the alley lit up. It read:

> *Bowling takes a lot of pep*
> *and lots of energy*
> *You wouldn't foul if you'd get hep*
> *to Occult's Chocolate Tea.*

At the very moment that the Green Magician fouled, who should come bouncing down the line of alleys but C. Auguste Dupin, the Police Commissioner of all Montreal?

"Tally-ho, Green Magician!" he shouted cheerfully. "Tally-ho Aunt Effluvia!" he added thoughtfully for the benefit of the dear old lady.

"Auguste!" Effluvia exclaimed.

"Let me disabuse you of any false conclusions you may have drawn in respect to the Madison Avenue Hexters," the Police Commissioner said politely. "It is true to be sure that since Occult has purchased Brazil for their Brazil-Nut Division, the Hexters have been released from durance *plein et forte*. Nevertheless, I doubt that it is they who are behind this caper." Suiting his action to his word, Dupin cut a caper, not unlike a courtly minuet. Aunt Effluvia regarded this graceful gesture approvingly. The French could always be counted on to do the right thing at the right time.

Then, in a serious mood, Dupin made a *moue* of worry and pique. "I came here to ask your help, Green Magician. The day is fast approaching when no decent Canadian citizen will be safe outside his door. Those of us who value liberty ..."

Effluvia interrupted with a jest: "Those who believe that chocolate bars do not a prison make?"

With a gay laugh, the Commissioner concluded. "We are seriously worried."

"Well," said the spry lady, " I think all this advertising may do some good in the long run. People will get away from their TVs and go out and bowl."

"That's exactly my point," Dupin cried. "Everyone thinks they're only a nuisance. Few suspect the awful plot these ads foreshadow."

"What awful plot?"

"Well, first, I should tell you that I've been investigating the Occult Company from the very first. I've studied their method of operation. And I've come to the conclusion that the power behind their throne is trying to *buy up*, to *garner*, to *control*, and *to entirely monopolize...*"

"Yes? Do go on."

"Not only all the space in the newspapers and all the time on radio and television, but *all of the Space and Time there is*!"

Dupin's two listeners gasped with shock.

"Yes, and that's why I say we're up against more than the Hexters."

"You mean ..." the Green Magician ventured cautiously.

"Yes, Green Magician. I mean the High-Priestess of Crime herself – *Tin Lizzie*!"

The mood of the bowling alley suddenly darkened. Aunt Effluvia withdrew from the two men.

"I realizethat you're here on vacation," said the French-Canadian lawman, "and I have no right to ask you to help us. It'll be a hard, dangerous job – but I want to point out that the whole future of Space and Time depends on you. Will you help us?"

"Of course," smiled the Green Magician, his handsome face taut with resolution. "Where do I start?"

"By talking to Station WISH's cub disc jockey, Billy-Bop Gruff."

"The one they call 'The Boy with the Manly Voice'?"

"The same. And hurry. Just this morning my wife said the apartment we live in is getting smaller every day. And today at the Precinct House I heard at least ten people say: 'Where does the time all go to?'"

Abruptly, Commissioner Dupin did a little pirouette, saluted Aunt Effluvia, skipped across the line of alleys, narrowly avoiding the balls that hurtled toward the pins, and disappeared in the gloom.

The young disc jockey was nervous. "Mr Green Magician," he began in a voice gruff with excitement, "a Disc Jockey – or Dee-Jay as we like to think of ourselves – gets around a lot. And they notice things going on. Some very peculiar things. Things that other people might not believe."

The Green Magician smiled benignly at the lad. "There are more things in heaven and earth, Billy-Bop, than are dreamt of in your philosophy. Go on."

"Well, last week I was the MC at a dance at Central High, when all at once the dance floor got too crowded. I mean, no one was *coming in* but there was just less and less room to move in. Couples jostled. Fights broke out. And another thing – *the band couldn't keep time!*

"Foreseeing more trouble, I led all the guys and gals outside to safety and in the nick of time too! For, just as we left, the whole gym where the dance had been disappeared into thin air. And so did the space that it had been in! The School Board blamed rowdyism and rock'n'roll. I'm being sued. Please Green Magician, you must help me. I've been threatened with the loss of my job if this mystery isn't cleared up."

The green minion of Truth and Beauty smiled sympathetically. "I think I know what the trouble is, Billy. Just answer this one question; when things started to get crowded, did you hear anything strange?"

"Well, the band was playing 'There's No Tomorrow', but now that you mention I did hear something – a sort of chug-a-chug-a-chug sound. Like a Model T Ford."

"Or like a Tin Lizzie?"

"Yes" the boy gasped, his voice almost inaudible with gruffness, "*it was exactly the sound of a Tin Lizzie!*"

As the Green Magician left Station WISH, a messenger handed him a large gift-box, decorated with tin-foil and covered with "Kisses." Before the Green Magician realized what had happened, the messenger disappeared.

At their motel, he and Aunt Effluvia examined the contents of the box. There was a chocolate pony and two chocolate Easter eggs, each with a big bite taken out of it.

"Do you suppose this is some sort of clue?" Effluvia asked.

"Yes, but what? Horse plus eggs. The French-Canadian for eggs is *oeuvres*. Do you suppose the clue is *hors d'oeuvres*?"

"Sounds like a cocktail party is meant," volunteered Effluvia.

"Yes, but *where*? Observe that the three objects are each one-half eaten. Do you suppose the cocktail party will be at Eaton's Halfway House, the popular cocktail lounge? I think these chocolate goodies spell D-A-N-G-E-R."

"Don't go," Effluvia opined. "It may be a trap."

"What, and miss a chance to meet Tin Lizzie *face to face*?"

"Well, if you're dead set on running after trouble, at least take this charm." She pressed into his rough hand a Wilkie-for-President button. "I drilled the hole in it," she explained, "to make a bird-whistle out of it. I wanted to call the bearded plovers out of my Victory Garden, but they never came. All the same, it might work a powerful spell when you're in a tight spot."

Effluvia saw the Green Magician out of the motel room to his lime-green Volkswagen and planted a smacking wet kiss on his forehead. "God-speed!"

As he drove across the great city of Montreal in his lime-green VW, he noticed how small it had become, how cramped. It seemed to be scarcely ten blocks to Eaton's Halfway House. The traffic was thick and fast. His wristwatch, too, was running fast. He would probably arrive late at the cocktail party. Time *was* running out.

Arriving late at Eaton's, he was immediately confronted by a strange woman in a glittering metallic dress. On her shoulder, a Tin Lizard chattered to itself. The Tin Lizard was her familiar spirit, and thought by some to be almost as dangerous as the woman herself.

"Tin Lizzie," the Green Magician whispered. In her tinfoil dress, his nemesis was stunningly beautiful. It was part of her plan!

"That's right. And by the colour of your face, I take it that you're the

Green Magician?" She made a gesture with the tin cup in her hand and two burly men seized the Green Magician and bound him with stout cords.

"So, my pickled-faced friend, you thought you could outwit Tin Lizzie!" She shook her waves of tinsel-like hair and laughed, an ominous tinkle of a laugh, and her tiny tin earrings danced in the subdued light of the cocktail lounge. None of the other guests had noticed this altercation between the two arch-enemies.

The room seemed to close in on the Green Magician and he could only see the triumphant smile of Tin Lizzie, and then he lost all track of time as the floor seemed to give way beneath him and he dropped vertiginously down, down, down, into a nether-world beyond Time and Space.

"Where am I? What time is it?" the Green Magician groaned.

Billy-Bop answered: "On an uncharted island in the St Lawrence Seaway. *A Chocolate Island*! But I can't tell you the time because they took my wrist watch away."

"Then this must be where *All Space and Time* are kept! But, Billy-Bop, how did you get here?" With difficulty, the Green Champion of Liberty turned his head. Beside him lay Billy-Bop, bound as he was, with stout thongs.

The young disc jockey replied ruefully, "I – I followed you to see what was going on – and they got me. I – I'm sorry."

"That's all right Billy, it's intentions that count anyhow. I wonder, though, how she keeps all Time and Space on this one island. If I could escape from these bonds, perhaps I could find..."

"Let *me* show you" interjected the voluptuous voice of the High Priestess of Crime as she swept into the room in her tinfoil negligee. The Tin Lizard clattered in after her, darting steely glances at the two bound men where they lay on the floor. The Green Magician watched tensely as the metallic amphibian approached and began to gnaw at the ropes!

"If you like chocolate, you'll *love* our little retreat here. So, why not..." she threw back her head enticingly. "Why not let me show you around?"

"And no tricks," added the Lizard in a reedy voice. He had finished gnawing through the ropes and now he held a miniature chocolate gun between his pointed teeth. "Because I've got you covered."

Tin Lizzie laughed indulgently at her familiar's fears. "Don't worry, Chuckles," she bade it. "After I've shown our chartreuse friend my domain he won't *want* to leave it." She scratched the ugly creature's neck lovingly, all the while ogling the Green Magician who, though now unbound, could not raise his arms from his sides without the mightiest of efforts, as a result of the special gravitational forces of the Chocolate Island. Tin Lizzie thought of everything!

"Hey! What about me?" sang out the young dee-jay plaintively.

"Your fate," replied the Tin Temptress with a mysterious and enigmatic smile, "depends on the Green Magician's behaviour. If he behaves, you will become my personal disc jockey. Otherwise –" (and she giggled girlishly at the alternative), "you just *may* be smeared all over with *Chocko-Lax* and thrown into my Crocodile Pit."

When they left the room, the boy was crying helplessly. On the one hand, he hoped the Green Magician would be able to resist the allure of the deadly Crime-Goddess. On the other hand were chocolate crocodiles!

In the chocolate factories of the island, chocolate automatons were turning out *Up-Chocks* and *Peanut-Clutters*, *Maple-Leaves* and *Chocko-Lichees* by the thousands and millions. Vast vats of chocolate steamed over the slow fires of the Chocolate Kiln, and the Wrapping Plant could be heard in the distance wrapping up all these chocolate bars into deceptively gay and enticing tinfoil wrappers. The Occult operation was larger than any ordinary mind could have grasped, but neither Lizzie nor the Green Magician possessed ordinary minds. They both took in the full implications of this scene – she with nihilistic joy; he with loathing and nausea.

She led him back to the so-called "Chocolate Castle," the heart of this complex operation and, after traversing a corridor that seemed a replica of the famous "Labyrinth," the couple arrived at a great tin door.

"This" she said coyly, "is my room. Come in and I'll show you where I keep all Time and Space."

The Green Magician could not resist an invitation put into words like that. The room he entered was spacious and dim, the only light issuing from a blue gas flame in a device in the far corner.

The Tin Lizard scuttled to his little feeding dish near the gigantic bed that stood in the middle of the room, overhung by a great tin canopy. A sound of snuffling and crunching occupied the silence.

Tin Lizzie went to a medicine cabinet. "This bottle," she said, indicating a giant Economy size bottle in the chest, "contains Space Capsules. When it is full, I'll own Everything, do you understand, *Everything!*"

The Green Magician shuddered. His hands still hung at his sides like two lead weights, bound by the strange gravitational forces of the Chocolate Island more firmly than by any thongs the imagination could devise.

There was no denying that the woman was beautiful. But how much more hateful then that she should employ her beauty in the service of Crime! Those were the Green Magician's thoughts at this terrible moment. But he did not speak his thoughts; instead he spoke to the Crime-Goddess in a tone that indicated interest and respect.

"I suppose you also have *Time* Capsules?"

"Wrong! I have *Time Cards*. When I need some time I merely *punch* a card in that Time Clock." Her shapely finger, bejewelled with tin diadems, pointed daintily to the squat iron monster in the corner of the room in the belly of which the gas flame guttered ominously.

"Now this, for example, is *your* Time Card. Should I *punch it* in the Time Clock, you would cease to exist. Your Time would be up!" Again, her girlish laugh, worse than a hag's cackle, curdled the Green Magician's blood. But again he dissimulated his emotions.

"Why, Lizzie," he asked, "*why* have you done this monstrous thing? Why is it you want all the Time and Space there is?"

"Why? *Why!* WHY!?! Because Time is Money, that's why. Then too, since I grew up in a city, I adored the wide-open spaces and envied all the children who were more fortunate than I, living in the country and running as far as the eye could see. I said to myself: *Liz, some day you'll own it all!* And now I almost do." She tapped the Time Card – his Time Card! – nervously against the posters that supported the tin canopy of the bed.

"Yes, I'm Queen of all I survey. But I need one thing – a King to share my vast dominion." Impetuously the Tin Temptress whirled to face the Green Magician. The blue gaslight glinted on her tinfoil negligee and caught the attention of the Tin Lizard who, sated, approached his mistress, all tin ears. The Time Clock rumbled impatiently.

"A King to share your domain?" the Green Magician whispered incredulously.

"Lo mein?" croaked the Lizard, who was always hard of hearing after a large meal, "I hate Chinese food. You're hungry ten minutes after you eat. I just ate some Chinese children, for instance, and I'm starved already."

"Shush," bade Lizzie to her loquacious pet.

"I like that tinny Chinese music, though," it added defensively and slunk away under the bed.

"A Queen without a King. It's a sad thought." She had moved quite close to her guest and now she looked into his green eyes. "You know, my darling, you are very handsome. Handsome enough to rule a big chunk of Time and Space. There's something magical about you that I don't understand."

"Do you like magic?"

"I adore it!"

"Then why don't I show you a card trick of mine?"

"Mmm," she murmured in assent, her lips pressed close to his.

"Well then, just give me that card you're holding ..."

"Oh no you *don't*! Not till you answer this question: Will you join me on the throne of all Time and Space, or will you rather cease to exist? *And cause your gruff young friend to be thrown to the chocolate crocodiles? Answer!*" She inched his Card toward the hideous Time Clock.

"I've never believed in telling lies. So, I'll have to confess that I don't go along with your plan. You see, you're about the greediest person I've ever met. You're pretty and all, but beneath your prettiness there is a moral decay that I cannot approve of. Maybe I'd like you better if you reformed. Give up this mad plan to conquer all Time and Space. Some things in life are better for being free. Don't you know that the moon belongs to everyone?"

"But there won't be anyone but us," she reasoned. "There won't even be a moon."

"Then, I'd be King over nothing. My answer to you is N-O, spells *No!*"

Tin Lizzie screamed with rage and *thrust his Card at the slot in the face of the Time Clock!*

But the Green Magician's timing was better! All this while he had been edging the charmed Wilkie-for-President whistle towards his lips, concealing from Tin Lizzie the great effort this required under the immense gravitational forces of the island, and just before the Card was fed into the Time Clock, the whistle touched his lips and he signalled for help.

In the nick of time, a friendly Chocolate Budgie flew in the window and *blew out the Time Clock!*

Or maybe it flew in the door; it all happened too fast to see.

The Tin Lizard lumbered about the room, barking and snapping at the brave little budgie who stayed well out of its reach as only budgies can. Meanwhile, Lizzie ransacked her purse in desperation.

"Tinsnips! Tin gauds! When you really need something you can never find it. I've never known it to fail. Aha! Matches!"

She knelt at the side of the demonic Time Clock and lit the pilot light.

"Now you'll learn the fury of a woman scorned, Green Magician." And she struck his Card into the slot of the Clock!

The Green Magician held his breath and breathed a silent prayer. When he opened his eyes, Tin Lizzie had vanished.

As they opened the Space Capsules and reset the Time Clock, the Green Magician and the friendly Chocolate Budgie discussed the fatal issue of the day.

"But I still don't understand why Tin Lizzie was annihilated instead of me."

The Chocolate Budgie blinked his chocolate-brown eyes mirthfully and chirruped:

"During the confusion, after I blew out the Time Clock, Tin Lizzie turned your Time Card *upside down*. Now, since your Time profile is diametrically opposed to hers, in much the same way that Good is opposed to Evil, and Love is opposed to Hate, when the Card entered the Time Clock, the Time Clock did what it was programmed to do – and destroyed Tin Lizzie."

"I see. Well, I'm certainly glad you were around to answer my signal. Tell me, did it sound like a parakeet in distress? Or what?"

"I'd rather you called us budgies," said the chocolate bird stiffly. "Actually, I came to see what sort of crank was blowing on a Wilkie button. The last time anyone did that was in the war. Some old lady tried to shoo me out of her Victory Garden with it. But you haven't heard my song yet."

"True, and neither has Billy-Bop Gruff, who is still downstairs tied up. Let's go there first." The budgie perched on the Green Magician's finger and held tight with sticky little talons as the Green Magician made his way back through the labyrinth of the Chocolate Castle to where he had left the young dee-jay.

"Listen to this, Billy-Bop," said the Green Magician, as he undid the knots that bound the unfortunate young man. "Listen closely."

And sweetly sang the Chocolate Budgie!

UNITED WE STAND STILL

WITH THOMAS M. DISCH

```
Log of the USSS Dolce Vita / January 10, 2091
/ 1800 hours
   Zero hour plus 34 days. Course and cargo
the same. Acceleration: zero. Safety factor:
5. Safety condition: A-OK. Estimation of
morale: A-OK. Activities report: Copilot
Lumpke read and approved Pilot's Activities
report, made estimation of morale level, and
conducted other union business. Acting-
Navigator Heavyside engaged in computations
successfully from 0900 hours to 1600 hours.
Stand-By Heavyside off-duty. Apprentice Ackley
demonstrated antisocial, unsafe tendencies,
for which corrective remedies are advised.
   General comments: Thumbs up!
      (signed)
      P. Heavyside, Pilot
      USSS Dolce Vita
```

"I know your kind, Ackley," said Pollux Heavyside, captain of the *Dolce Vita*. "I meet lots of guys like you at Tech College – rebels and troublemakers. Always trying to change things. Always sticking their noses in. Always protesting."

"All I said," Clarence Ackley protested in a whiney voice, like a mosquito that could not be swatted, "was that I didn't *understand*. If *you* understand, why don't *you* explain it to me?"

"You don't *try* to understand, Ackley. Now listen, I'll go through it all again: I, as pilot, as the captain of the crew, and on all company matters it's up to me to decide. But on *union* matters you've got to talk to Whitey Lumpke, cause he's the President of our Local and the shop steward here."

"But you said he's busy!"

"I said he *might* be busy. Now if he's busy with company business, then Rule 74 states we have a right to interrupt him, unless by so doing we may violate a safety rule. Now, who's President of the Safety Committee?"

"Bill Heavyside."

"Right."

"But Bill's asleep, and he always gets mad as the dickens if I wake him for no reason at all."

"Bill's not *asleep*! He's off-duty, then you should ask the *vice*-president of the Safety Committee."

"I didn't know there was one. Who is that?"

"Me."

"Criminy, Captain!" Ackley's whine rose half an octave. "You're just leading me around in circles. All I want to know is – can I clean the coffee-maker or not? It's as simple as that."

But Pollux Heavyside had evidently heard no part of this, for now he was shaking his cousin Bill by the shoulder. "Hey, Bill – wake up, baby! There's an emergency meeting of the Safety Committee."

"Nnnk! Muzza?"

"Take a look, Mister President, and determine whether that job that Brother Lumpke is performing is one involving the safety of the ship."

"Where's my glasses?" Pollux handed Bill his bifocals. Bill squinted at Brother Lumpke, who was sitting in a gyrochair with his felt spaceboots propped on the control panel, amid glowing red lights and wobbling needles, reading the tattered April issue of *Women in Boots*.

"Looks to me like Whitey's reading a sexbook, Captain," Bill said judiciously. "But you never can tell. It might *look* like that's what he's doing, while in reality he's keeping an eye on some safety gauge."

"Which interpretation do you favour, Mister President – sexbook or safety gauge?"

Bill squinted harder. "Sexbook. Definitely sexbook." Then he strapped himself back into his bunk and returned to that condition known aboard the *Dolce Vita* as "off-duty". He had a rather strange way of snoring that sounded like a policeman's whistle.

"Meeting of the Safety Committee is adjourned. Brother Ackley now has the Committee's permission to interrupt Brother Lumpke at his work with the question he wished to propose."

"It's about time! Hey, Whitey, how about it – can I clean the coffee-maker?"

Whitey Lumpke was not, despite his name and pink-tinged eyes, an albino. His hair was white, he had often explained, because he *dyed* it white. And as for the pallor of his skin, well, has anybody ever seen a suntanned astronaut?

Whitey sighed. "It's a problem, kid. I don't know what to tell you. See, if I say sure, go ahead, clean it, and you clean it, and word gets out that I set you to doing a cleaning job, well sir –"

"What do you mean? We clean our quarters every day."

"Yeah, but the coffee-maker comes under the jurisdiction of the World Organization of Railroad Commissaries. They're supposed to fix it, clean it, and keep it supplied with coffee powder. Legally, we aren't allowed to touch anything but the tap. And if we still had a Commissary attendant here, the way we did in the old days of space travel, we wouldn't even be allowed to do that. Right, Captain?"

"Right, Whitey. On the other hand, we all sure would enjoy a cup of hot coffee when we get done with a hard day's work."

"You said it, Captain!" Lumpke, who was not related to the Heavysides, usually went out of his way to be agreeable to Pollux. There had been a time – in the old days – when there had been as many Lumpkes as Heavysides working the *Dolce Vita*'s Mars-Earth run, but sad to tell, those days were past.

Clarence's whine became a positive jeer. "So you'd like a cup of coffee, would you! Well, you can have one just as soon as the coffee-maker cleans itself."

There was a stunned and horrified silence. *Mutiny*! Captain Pollux Heavyside thought. *Ye Gods, what will I do*?

Fortunately, at that moment Castor Heavyside, the Captain's fraternal twin and the ship's navigator, who had been out of sight till now in the cabin's tidy writing-nest, looked up from the calculations he had been making and announced: "So far this trip we each of us have made four thousand nine hundred and seventy dollars, twenty five cents, before taxes. That includes the increment for hazardous duty, but nothing from the profit-sharing plan."

Bill Heavyside, who was still off-duty in his bunk, seemed to have begun whistling *Pennies from Heaven*.

```
Log of the USSS Dolce Vita / January 13, 2091
/ 1800 hours
    Zero hour plus 37 days. Course and cargo
the same. Acceleration: zero. Safety factor:
5. Safety condition: A-OK. Estimation of
morale: A-OK and improving. Activities report:
usual activities. Corrective action taken with
Apprentice Ackley, but results difficult to
interpret this early.
    General comments: All Systems Go!
        (signed)
        P. Heavyside, Pilot
        USSS Dolce Vita
```

The bunks of the five astronauts were placed one above the other to form a sort of bookcase, and the astronauts filled the shelves in order of seniority. Thus it was Whitey Lumpke, not the captain, who got the top bunk. The next two were held in rotation by the twins, Castor and Pollux, who had joined Local 56 of FIST (Federated International of Space Teamsters) on the same day. Their cousin Bill Heavyside could lay claim to the next bunk down, and the very lowest man on totem pole was, of course, the apprentice, Clarence Ackley.

Poor Clarence – it did him scant good that he was the second cousin once removed of the Heavyside twins. They seemed to bear him an implacable grudge (probably out of resentment of his youth), and to the ordinary burdens of an astronaut's life were added the difficulties resulting from the enmity. Thus it was that the four other crewmen (for

Lumpke and Bill took their cues from the twins), as if by unspoken agreement, began going very lightly over Clarence's bunk and gear, causing him to fail inspection three days in a row.

"You'll have to vacuum that bunk over once again, Apprentice Ackley," said Captain Heavyside. "It's filthy. Didn't you clean it at all?"

"Of course not. *You* had the turn this morning. Didn't *you* clean it?" His whine was more than usually aggrieved.

"My turn? Don't know what you're talking about, Ackley. Officially, every man cleans his own equipment. Except insofar as I am responsible for you, I'm not responsible for the filthy condition of your gear. Now go get that doggone vacuum cleaner and dust off this bunk. Hop to it, man!"

Sighing whinily, Clarence trundled out the vacuum cleaner and set to work. "It isn't *fair*," he kept assuring himself. "It isn't *fair*."

The whine of the vacuum, or of Clarence, had woken Bill Heavyside, who had been off-duty in the bunk just above. He winked at the apprentice good-humouredly. "You know how to get out of this chore, don't you, Ackley? Just fix the gosh-durned coffee pot. Don't be such a fink about it."

"But you heard what Whitey said – it's against the union rules."

"A fellow's got to cut corners once in a while, Ackley my boy, got to make allowances. There has to be both give and take."

"Yeah," Clarence said sourly. "I've got to turn my other cheek." He sometimes resented Bill's well-meant advice, and he sought, as yet without success, to find a figure of speech to stale as to give even Bill Heavyside pause.

"You hit the nail on the head, Ackley. Turn the other cheek – by gosh, I wish I'd thought of that."

"Why is it we go to the trouble of cleaning bunks and lockers every day anyhow? They always look clean enough to me. Where does the dust come from that we're supposed to be removing?"

"You never can see spacedust – that's why it's so dangerous. Suppose some of it got into the delicate electronic instruments and messed them up? Our lives wouldn't be worth a plugged nickel then."

"Like what delicate instruments, for instance?"

"Don't ask *me*, Ackley. I'm not the pilot. I'm just the Stand-By man. But you just follow the rules and you can't go wrong. An astronaut isn't paid to think. They've got computers for that."

Disgusted and feeling exquisitely sorry for himself, Clarence resumed vacuuming. But later that day he took the coffee-maker into the writing-nest and there, in the litter of papers that Navigator Heavyside had used for his calculations, he dismantled, cleaned and reassembled it.

"Coffee's ready," he announced calmly at 1830 hours.

"Well, I'll be a monkey's uncle!" said Bill Heavyside, heaving himself out of his bunk. "That coffeepot must have got unplugged somehow."

```
Log of the USSS Dolce Vita / January 14, 2091
/ 1100 hours
```

```
        Course and cargo the same. Emergency
    meeting of Local 56, after rec't of coded
    radio communication from FIST Headquarters.
    Top-secret decision reached by unanimous vote
    of members present.
        General comments: Hold on Tight!
        (signed)
        P. Heavyside, Pilot
        USSS Dolce Vita
```

"We'd better post a guard at the door," Lumpke, the Local's President, advised, after the Secretary, Bill Heavyside, had taken attendance. "Clarence, you're the guard."

"A guard! But there's nobody on this ship but us and fifty thousand heifers. And we're half a million miles from anywhere. So what's a guard guarding against?"

"Ackley, stop whining and do what the President says," Pollux Heavyside, Treasurer of Local 56, commanded briskly. "The rules say we have a guard at the door, and by thunderation, we'll have one there if we have to nail you to it."

Meekly Clarence crept to the airlock and leaned against it.

"Meeting's called to order," Whitey said, rapping on the control panel with a rolled-up copy of *Women in Boots*. "It is contract renewal time once again, Brothers, and as usual the company is trying to crucify us. The new contract they're proposing cuts the crew of a ship from five to three –"

"Three? They're out of their minds!" said Bill.

"Three?" Castor echoed. "Three men would be useless in an emergency. It isn't safe."

Clarence, standing guard at the airlock, reflected that any number of men of Castor's calibre might be useless in an emergency, but he forbore to say so. Besides, he knew very well that if two men had to be unloaded from the *Dolce Vita*'s crew the victims would be himself and Stand-By Bill Heavyside.

"Of course it isn't safe, but since when is the company interested in our safety?" Whitey shook his head sadly, meanwhile sucking at his dentures to obtain a more secure purchase for them. "But you ain't heard the worst of it yet, Brothers. They want to cut the compulsory retirement age down to seventy! Egad, a man is in the prime of his life at seventy!" In his excitement, Whitey began to cough, and his tremor became more than usually pronounced so that the rolled-up copy of the magazine dropped from his hand ands went into free fall. But at length he had himself back under control. "Well, we know what to tell them to do with this contract, don't we, Brothers? Let's vote. Bill, you and Castor take these voting slips and pencils and pass them around to the men."

After the astronauts had voted, Pollux and Whitey gathered the ballots into a heap, put them atop the instrument console, and counted them aloud, twice. Then Bill and Castor verified the count.

"It's unanimous," Whitey declared. "We hold the line at eighty-five. And if the company doesn't like it, the company can lump it."

There was muted applause, and the meeting was adjourned.

"Aren't you going to radio back the result of the vote?" Clarence asked later of Whitey.

"Are you kidding, kid? What do you think I am – some kind of troublemaker? We did what *we* had to do; now it's up to the union to take their part."

"But *we're* the union!"

Whitey laughed explosively, holding his trembling hands over his heart.

Clarence, however, was not to be put off so easily. "What about the strike? How will they know we're on strike?"

"Listen, Ackley, nobody strikes any more. Maybe back in the twentieth century they had strikes and all that, but *now* we reach settlements. A strike is too costly."

"Then what were we voting about?"

"Ackley, what kind of union member are you? Sometimes I think you must be a company spy, the way we talk. Now, leave me read my book in peace, will you? Go learn navigating from Castor or something."

Navigation, the science of calculating wages earned, had to be done hourly aboard the *Dolce Vita*. Both the company and the union agreed that it was a prime incentive to workers for them to be apprised of their ever-increasing worth at regular intervals. These calculations were not easy, and it generally took Navigator Castor Heavyside an hour to figure each new hour's heightened worth.

Astronauts earned a ceiling wage of $34.75, time-and-a-half for overtime (of which there was a minimum of twelve hours a week), double-time on Sundays and holidays, and a *per diem* hazardous-duty allowance of $10.00. Castor would first calculate, with the aid of an electric calendar, the number of days since takeoff, then determine which of these had been Sundays or holidays. The Space Teamsters recognized forty-seven legal holidays, including Martinmas, Black Tuesday, Dave Beck Day, Labor Day, Black Wednesday, and the Eve of St Agnes. Then the hours of straight time and overtime had to be calculated for each of these days. It was demanding work, and often, especially on holidays, Castor would come away from his writing-nest crying with helpless rage and chewing on the gnarled mass of his plastic pen. Clarence, once, had tried to point out to Castor the effort he wasted making these calculations.

"Look, Castor, it's simple. If you want to know the total wages for an hour from now, you take the figure for now, and just add thirty four dollars seventy five to it."

"That's not the way they taught us in Navigator's School."

"But it makes *sense*!"

"What're you talking about, Ackley? 'Makes sense'! You sound like come dad-blamed company spy."

```
Log of the USSS Dolce Vita / January 15, 2091
/ 1800 hours
   Zero hour plus 39 days. Course and cargo
the same. ETA into orbit above von
Braunsville: tomorrow at 0900 hours. Safety
factor: 5. Safety condition: A-OK. Estimation
of morale: A-OK. Activities report:
Preparation in progress for arrival. Navigator
Heavyside reports satisfaction with his work
and-
   Just rec'd radio communication. The ship is
ordered to stay in orbit. We are on strike,
and the ground crews can't touch the ship till
it's been cleared up. On strike!
   General comments: FUDGE!!!!
      (signed)
      P. Heavyside, Pilot
      USSS Dolce Vita
```

The captain had stopped commanding. The navigator had ceased to navigate. The union president played games of checkers with himself and refused to listen to the complaints of union members. The Stand-By no longer stood by. Clarence, with nothing more to do, was reading an advertisement in the April issue of *Women in Boots* heading: "How YOU can develop a HE-MAN voice."

"Say," Clarence whined, glancing up from the ad, "you don't suppose they're just going to *leave* us here, do you?"

"I wouldn't put it past them," Pollux growled.

"If we were earning money now," Castor explained, "we'd have earned six thousand two hundred and seventy five dollars. But we aren't."

"What worries me," said Whitey, capturing one of his own kings, "is that I'll run out of digitalis. The old ticker isn't what it used to be, you know."

"I've been having gall bladder problems myself," Pollux said anxiously. "I should see a doctor regularly, or else ... at my age ..."

"You're not old," Bill assured his cousin. "A person is only as old as he feels, I say. Life begins at forty."

But today, the fifth of the strike, his assurances rang hollowly. They had already begun eating the emergency stores. These would last, at most, another month, and then ... No one wanted to think about it. Clarence had suggested that they ignore the radio's commands and land the ship in von Braunsville by themselves, but though they agreed that this was a valuable suggestion, none of them knew how to go about it, for the controls in the cabin were not connected to anything except a small electric cell that powered the lights glowing on the instrument panel and made the needles slowly move back and forth across the dials. The real piloting of the ship was performed automatically, and they, the astronauts, were only the safety factor, a safety factor of 5.

But if the strike went on too much longer, it began to seem possible that the safety factor might be reduced all the way to zero.

For three days in a row, the ship had served up tuna casserole. It violated the contract to serve the same meal three days running, and Whitey circulated a petition of complaint. Someone had to point out to Whitey that the ship was under no obligation to feed them at all.

This someone was Gherkin, the FIST Mars Co-ordinator, whose scull had bumped alongside the *Dolce Vita* on the afternoon of the second full week of the strike. He was a thin, middle-aged, soft-spoken man with a Phi Beta Kappa key in the buttonhole of his spacesuit: the crew of the ship resented him at once.

"What the deuce is going on?" asked Whitey, throwing a checker at the union co-ordinator. "Why are we on strike? Why didn't you make a settlement just like always?"

"As a matter of fact, Brother Lumpke, we're quite interested in learning that ourselves," said Gherkin, with a bland smile. "As you may or may not know, the union's policy is determined by computer, the same kind of computer that determines company policy. Fighting fire with fire, as it were. You could have knocked us over with a featherbed –" An even blander smile for this. "– when the order came through for the strike. At first, we assumed it must have been a short circuit. After all, the Teamsters haven't had to strike in over fifty years. But apparently it's on the level. And I, for one, don't have enough game theory to argue with a MACK-12."

Then Gherkin passed out UNFAIR TO LABOR buttons and left them to a fourth day of tuna casserole.

The following day another visitor came to the *Dolce Vita* – Pfeffergurke, the Company Representative. He was a thin, middle-aged, soft-spoken man with an air of intelligence about him, and the men hated him at once.

"Better come down to Braunsville with me, boys. We're disconnecting all life-support systems on the ship. Can't afford to feed those who are striking against us, now can we?"

"We ain't *budging*!" shouted Whitey, and the others made a small cheer to show their solidarity. "This is our ship, by gosh, and we're staying on board. If the company don't feed us, we'll take 'em to court. There'll be thousands in damages."

"You men know very well that we can't let you starve, because of the public relations. But we *can* make you wish you hadn't been stubborn." Pfeffergurke went out to his scull, and in a few moments a team of robo-midges were dragging in a case of synthetti in plasticans.

"What about my digitalis?" Whitey bawled after the departing midges. But too late – the airlock was already closing.

"You know what?" said Clarence, regarding one of the hard cubical plasticans. "We don't have a can opener."

Automatic tenders came alongside the *Dolce Vita* and took away the tranquillized heifers. The ship ceased to be a ship, as the maintenance system completed the disassembly-and-storage process. Only the cabin, with its perpetual oxygen supply and mock controls, remained. And the safety factor of 5.

It was Whitey who found out how, using his dentures as a lever, to open the plasticans. It was a crude method, and soon tangled masses of synthetti were floating about the room, like the streamers at a New Year's Eve party. The vacuum cleaner no longer worked. Even the lights on the dummy control panel had been turned off.

"It's times like this," said Bill Heavyside, "when the pressure is on, that try men's souls. But don't worry, Brothers – it's always darkest before the dawn. Look for the silver lining, I say." Then, brushing aside some stray strands of synthetti he climbed into his bunk and went off-duty.

"Well, anyhow, men, we fought the good fight." That was how Bill put it. The twins and Lumpke were less stoical.

"But how could it *happen*?" Castor asked pathetically of the shame-faced Gherkin standing in the airlock, reluctant to enter the synthetti-choked cabin. "How could we just *lose*? I don't understand that."

"No more do we, Brother Lumpke. Headquarters is just as unhappy as you, believe me, men. We only know that the computer said we'd have to give in. And if the computer says so, who can argue with it?"

"And you've signed the company's new contract?" Pollux asked unbelievingly.

"I'm afraid so."

"And we have to retire at *seventy*?" Whitey asked.

"What are *you* complaining about, Lumpke?" Pollux demanded. "You'd have had to retire in another year anyhow, when you hit eighty-five. Me and Castor had another seven years to look forward to."

"You couldn't possibly make an exception for a spry seventy-four, could you?" Bill Heavyside asked wistfully, playing nervously with his bifocals.

"I'm afraid not," the union co-ordinator said.

"Then I guess that means splashdown for all of us," said Pollux.

"Not quite," said Clarence Ackley, in a strong new He-Man voice. "You're forgetting about your apprentice."

"You mean to say ..."

"Yes, fellows, the worm has turned. Clarence Ackley will stay aboard the *Dolce Vita*." He showed his Union Membership Card proudly to Gherkin. "You see that – date of birth, 2024. I'm only sixty-seven, and I have three years to go before retirement."

"The rest of you men don't have to be too down-hearted," Gherkin said, with professional good cheer. "The company's set up a crash programme to help you cope with all your new-found leisure. It may be rough at first, but in the long run –"

"In the long run, we'll see our way through," said Bill Heavyside. He turned around in the airlock (the others had already filed out to Gherkin's scull) and winked at Ackley. "Never say die, kid."

```
Log of the USSS Dolce Vita / March 20, 2091 /
1800 hours
   Zero hour plus twelve hours. Course: Earth.
Cargo: 500,000 metric tons of Martian
copperworm guana. Acceleration: 1 G. Safety
factor: 1. Safety condition: A-OK. Estimation
of morale: A-OK or better. Activities report:
Copilot Ackley read and approved Pilot's
Activities report, made estimation of morale
level, and conducted other union business.
Acting Navigator Ackley engaged in
computations successfully from 0900 hours to
1600 hours. Stand-By Ackley off-duty.
Apprentice Ackley shows marked improvement in
attitude and conduct; promotion recommended.
   General comments: Excelsior!
      (signed)
      C. Ackley, Pilot
      USSS Dolce Vita
```

The Atheist's Bargain

with Thomas M. Disch

He regarded the African violets as though through the thick glass of a bathysphere. In candlelight the living-room of the farmhouse had the aspect of the floor of the sea. The furniture, so familiar as to have become invisible, in the course of years, suddenly declared itself, crowding in on him like so many officious friends. "Homer," the empty chairs whispered, "we can't say how sorry we are."

The poor violets were dying, and briefly he considered watering them. He touched a moistened fingertip to a hairy leaf. A pain shot down his back from having dozed off in the straight-backed chair. A thousand hairy-handed leaves trembled unceasingly in the still air of the room.

His calloused finger had crushed the violet's leaf. "Let it die," he thought. "What difference ...?"

Another swallow of the whisky, gagging on it. He had been a teetotaller so many years that liquor seemed to serve only to make him sick. He looked towards the window, and away. Unending darkness, perpetual night.

In the dun linoleum the roses writhed.

At last, of course, there was nowhere for him to look but at the coffin in the bay. A giant clamshell, and Lotte trapped there in its pearly hollow. Tears bit his eyes, obscuring the glass of the bathysphere. The room twisted into further irreality. He swore, not knowing what he said, nor on whom he called, not caring.

Despair.

It was three days since Lotte's stroke. A stroke: something burst in the brain, one of the pipes of blood. Then, a flood. It all stops, like a cornpicker that's jammed.

He trimmed the wick of the kerosene lamp, lighted it. His boiled shirt creaked. Lotte had always put too much starch in his Sunday shirts. A lot of nonsense, getting all dressed up just so's he could drive his wife to church. But when Lotte got an idea into her head she could be even stubborner than Homer Godwin, and that was going some.

He was "a confirmed atheist," he'd always boasted to her sewing-circle friends. They'd start to laughing like a pack of crows, pretending not to believe him, shocked. Even Lotte, at first, had thought it just a pose, and so she'd invited her minister, Reverend Santesson, around to the house. That bag of gas.

"How can you say you don't believe in the Creator, Homer? You, a farmer, working in God's green earth!"

"It seems, to me," Homer had replied slyly, "that it's *my* green earth:

Now that the mortgage is all paid off, at least."

"But, Homer, stop and consider the miracle of life. Have you ever looked at a little seed –"

"Well, if I hadn't looked at a lot of them in my time, I think *that* would be a miracle. 'Cause it's me that puts the damned seeds in the ground, and it's me that ploughs in the damned ammonia, which can cost almost as much as the seed. You ever looked at a bag of ammonia, Reverend Santesson?"

What a look the old windbag had had on his face! Homer couldn't help chuckling.

It would be Santesson who'd throw the first handful of dirt on the coffin in the morning.

In a sudden panic of grief he stumbled across the room to her side and stared down at her face. She seemed a bit too pink, as though she was having one of her temper fits, and there was some kind of blue colouring in her hair. But on the whole he had to give Jim Botsch credit: he'd taken a good ten years off her fifty-eight. She was so beautiful, and she was the whole meaning of his life. He turned away.

The trellised roses came creeping at his feet. He slammed down another drink, closed his eyes.

Easier to think with your eyes shut. No reminders. He should have never had this wake, not by himself. There's no point sitting around with a dead body. Sorrow won't bring it back to life.

When he opened his eyes there was a pleasant, citified young man sitting at the table across from him. He leaped up.

"I'm very sorry," the stranger said, rising and offering his hand. "I had no intention, believe me, in causing you a start. I knocked and I knocked, but no one answered, and so I thought I'd just peek in, and that's how I found you here asleep. I hope you don't mind that I decided to wait?"

"Insurance? If that's it, you're wasting your time. Storm windows? In any case, it's sort of late to come calling round. It must be ..." Homer pulled out his watch, but it seemed to have stopped at three o'clock.

Self-assured, smiling blandly, and fluffing his paisley tie with a superfluous gesture that allowed a glimpse of gold cuff-link, the strange salesman began his pitch: "Actually, Mr Godwin, I make *most* of my calls in the evening. People somehow feel more predisposed to accept my services after dark. There's less constraint. When I heard of your great loss ..." The well-groomed head inclined towards the coffin. "...I knew I had to come at once. You frown. Ah, do me the justice, Mr Godwin, to believe that I feel what you feel, that I shall ever be affected where you are concerned."

"What are you selling?" Homer asked impatiently.

The stranger made a pained smile. "Selling? Believe me, that's not why I've come here at all!"

"You're from Jim Botsch's place then, are you?" And now that he thought about it, there was something of the undertaker in this young man's over-polished manner.

"Well, actually, no. Actually I'm *not*. I work pretty much on my own. I'm a ... well, in fact, a buyer." He tapped the black attaché case on his lap, as though to confirm his ability to buy.

"You figure I'm selling the farm? Is that it? I'll see you damned before I sell this farm!"

The visitor coughed. "Assure yourself, Mr Godwin, it's not that. No, what I wish to buy from you is something that you have been, till now, unaware that you possessed, something you've always professed to regard as of no value, but for which I am willing to pay ... a most extraordinary price."

"Mineral rights, eh? Go ahead – make your offer. I don't want to sit around talking business all night. That's my wife, you know, over in the bay window."

The buyer shook his head. "Yes, I know."

Uneasily Homer gestured towards the kitchen. "It would be better if we talked in there."

"Your wife's death has affected you deeply, Mr Godwin. I realizethat. But you must not think me rude, or lacking in consideration, if I am obliged in the course of our discussion to refer – in as discreet a way as possible – to your loss. Because, you see ..." Taking a seat at the kitchen table, opening the black case. "...I have an inkling what your wish may be."

"My wish?" he asked.

"Let me show you," the devil replied.

Homer realized that he had been dozing again. The oilcloth of the kitchen table was littered with the buyer's attractive, four-colour brochures. YOUTH! one proclaimed in green capitals. WEALTH was golden, ROMANCE a misty blue. LONG LIFE and HAPPINESS were both a steely shade of grey.

"Shall we go over it again, sir?" the buyer inquired politely. "Stripped of all the legal fol-de-rol, it's the simplest bilateral contract. You agree to sign over to us your immortal soul, payable on demand to bearer, and we in return will grant you a single wish. You may select your wish from any of the tempting possibilities pictured here, what are known as the 'House Packages', or you may prefer a programme tailored to your own particular needs – as long as your demands don't exceed what can be reasonably expected. We're not in business for our health, of course. Ha, ha."

Homer scrunched up his brow in a businesslike way. "I guess you're aware that I'm not exactly what you'd call a True Believer. As a matter of fact, I'm an atheist."

"Indeed, Mr Godwin, we *were* aware of that. And it is not a position entirely foreign to my nature. Your atheism makes no difference to *our* organization, which is essentially (I'm proud to say) democratic. Yes, extremely democratic."

"It seems to me that if I do have a soul, you must have a fair share of it already. I never heard of no atheists going to heaven. So I don't see ..."

"Sometimes we are just magnanimous. But let's waste no more time on such metaphysical twaddle, Mr Godwin. Let us get down to brass tacks. If you had a wish, sir, a single wish, for what would you ask?"

Homer burst into helpless tears. "Lotte ! Bring my Lotte back!"

"Just a stroke of this pen, Mr Godwin, and she will be yours." The young man went on to outline the other terms: a guaranteed minimum of ten years more of Homer's life; his wife given back, sound in mind and body, the same Lotte he had always known.

Homer took the proffered pen and in that moment the young man's glazen eyes deepened precipitously. He felt himself falling into twin whirlpools that drained off all the foulness of the universe. A coffee cup shattered in Homer's hand; he didn't notice.

"Excuse me, sir," the young man said, once more like himself, "for startling you so, but we're required to do that, you know. Try to put it out of your mind."

Homer signed the paper. The stranger said, "Splendid," folded it, and tucked it away in his black case. In the next room Lotte heaved a deep sigh.

She was sitting half-way up by the time he reached her side. He took her hand, warm, soft, alive. "Where in the world, Homer ...?" she asked in a trembling voice.

"You were ill," he replied, cursing his clumsiness. "And we thought ... It was a mistake."

Her nostrils crinkled. "Homer, have you left something burning in the kitchen?" It was Lotte to the life!

He rushed in to rescue the dry coffee pot from the burner on the stove. The young buyer had vanished. Outside an engine caught and tyres spun in gravel. Drawing the curtains aside he caught a fleeting glimpse of tail-lights. The sky had purpled, preparing for the dawn.

"Homer?" his wife called from the living-room. "Homer, something is wrong!"

He returned to her, grinning with an extravagant happiness.

"How'd I get all this make-up on my face? And where'd this flimsy dress come from? And there's *lacquer all over my hair*! I must look like a perfect floozy. How long was I asleep, for goodness' sake?"

"The doctor declared you dead Friday night. Now it's Monday morning. We were going to bury you today, but ... uh, you got well just in time."

"I should hope so! Do you mean to tell me, Homer Godwin, that that dirty old Jim Botsch has been dressing me, and handling me, and giving me baths? In that nasty downstairs parlour of his!"

"We had to, Lotte. We all thought –"

"You thought! You mean you *didn't* think!"

His grin broadened, with love and pride. No one could approach his Lotte when she got into one of her tempers.

"I sure am glad to have you back, honey. I sure am. I like to died of my own cooking."

"And I suppose the kitchen is a pigsty. I'll be days just cleaning up and putting things back where they belong." She swung her lower legs over the edge of the coffin, and he stepped forward to help lift her out. But as his hands gripped her armpits, her body stiffened and her face blanched beneath the thick make-up.

"What is it, angel?"

"I just thought – By rights *I can't be alive*! Jim Botsch must have filled me up with that embalming fluid, didn't he?"

"Yes, I guess so, but –"

"Then it's a miracle, Homer. God has saved me by a miracle. I've been raised from the dead! It's a modern miracle!"

Homer couldn't quite swallow this insult to his intelligence. "Oh, Lotte, here you go again with your superstitions. Miracles! God! Poppycock! It wasn't your God that brought you back to life – it was me and ... It was me."

"You! What could *you* do? What did you use – a sack of ammonia?"

"No, I dunno. I –" He scratched his neck with frustration.

"Seems to me then that there isn't any explanation possible but it was a miracle. God did it to show you the way."

"It wasn't no damned miracle. It was just the opposite. I sold my damned soul to bring you back to life. *I* did it, not God!"

"Oh dear oh dear oh dear!" Lotte's voice shrank into inaudibility. She wriggled back from his touch. "Oh, Homer, how *could* you ever do that? What a terrible, *terrible* thing to do – to sell your immortal soul!"

"I wanted you back. Lotte, I couldn't stand it. I never took much care of souls or such anyhow, so it's no great loss. Lotte. I just had to have you back."

"Not on those terms. I'm not *coming* back." She swung her legs back into the coffin.

"What are you doing?"

"I'm getting back inside this coffin and lying down the way God wants me, that's what. You had no right resurrecting me in such a sinful way, and I'm going to see that no good comes of your wickedness."

"Lotte! Lotte, what are you saying? Aren't you glad to be alive?"

"It's no use arguing with me, Homer Godwin. My mind is made up. I'm *dead*, and that's that." Lying back, she arranged her features into a mask of calcined sobriety, then pulled down the heavy lid.

Homer was still pounding on the closed lid when they came around in the morning. Jim Botsch dealt professionally with the widower's excessive, incoherent grief. He had never before had such an opportunity to demonstrate his more human gifts. Murmuring his usual consolations, occasionally interspersing soothing agreements with the man's crazed contention that Lotte was alive inside the coffin, he wrestled him into the back seat of the lavender Cadillac. They drove only part of the way to the funeral, then turned off on the road that led to the mental hospital in the next county. Homer, in the back seat of the car, sat absolutely rigid. Inside his head a movie was being shown.

The coffin descending slowly into the earth. Reverend Santesson dropping the handful of dirt, mumbling, turning away. The grave diggers filling in the hole with an efficiency approaching grace. The last clods tamped into place. At last the sound too small for the departing workmen to hear, Lotte's sigh of pious satisfaction.

This movie ran continuous performances for the next ten years.

THE DISCOVERY OF THE NULLITRON

RESULTS OF AN EXPERIMENT CONDUCTED BY
THOMAS M. DISCH AND JOHN T. SLADEK

Whilst attempting a verification of Drake's classical "Massless Muon" experiment (the experiment in which a massless muon was annihilated, producing, as Hawakaja had earlier observed, the supposed "isotron"), a new particle was observed, having a mass of 0, a charge of 0 and a spin of 0. This particle has been termed the "nullitron".

An Important Breakthrough
A first the nullitron was thought to be a neutrino – or massless, uncharged particle with a spin of $+\frac{1}{2}$ – but when the experiment was repeated using a gyroscopically-balanced nubium target in place of the old, fixed frimium one, the spin was calculated to be 0.

Though having no mass, the particle cannot be truly termed sub-atomic, for it appears to be about one metre in diameter, perfectly round and rather shiny. Its red colour can be explained by the well-known "red-shift" or "Doppler" effect, used by the fact that no matter from what vantage point the particle is viewed it seems to be retreating from the observer at the speed of light.

Whence the Nullitron? Whither Bound?
The nullitron can be produced experimentally only under the most favourable circumstances. A cyclotron one mile in diameter filled with alternate solid blocks of lead and quicksilver is useful but not essential. Of utmost importance is a willingness on the part of the investigator to discover them.*

With the discovery of the anti-nullitron a great leap forward has been made in the general area of investigation concerning the nullitron.

A Great Leap Forward
Like the nullitron itself, the anti-nullitron has a mass of 0, a charge of 0 and a spin of 0, but unlike the nullitron, it is green and cubical. The most careful measurements (obtained by passing the nullitrons and anti-

---

* The first nullitron was observed, in point of fact, on the isle of Ibiza, where the investigators had repaired for a brief holiday. For three successive afternoons, while sleeping on the beach, Mr Sladek had vivid dreams of swarms of nullitrons that formed into rings, biting their tails and eventually melting into butter. This proved to be the case.

nullitrons through a dense field of spinning neutrinos, upon which they have curiously little effect, or none) show that the cubical anti-nullitrons are exactly equal in volume to the spherical nullitrons. No satisfactory explanation has yet been offered for this phenomenon.

Theoretical considerations led to the inexorable if highly unlikely conclusion that nullitrons and anti-nullitrons exist everywhere in nature. Indeed, the universe can be said to be drenched with them. Due to the laws of conservation, however, they are rarely observable in their natural state, since the nullitrons cancel out the anti-nullitrons and *vice versa*.

Not Without Significance
This does not mean, however, that the nullitron is not without significance. On the contrary, the nullitron is known to be in constant interaction with all known sub-atomic particles. A nullitron can join a neutrino to form an anti-neutrino and with an anti-neutrino to form a neutrino. These interactions (and many more besides) are constantly occurring in nature, but (due again to the laws of conservation) can never be observed directly, only inferred.

Aside from their "colour", the nullitron family possess certain other "secondary" characteristics:

The sound of two nullitrons colliding from opposite directions is a *whirring* noise, very much like that of a defective electric fan (such as the fan to be found in the Las Palmas hotel in Ibiza). The collision of two anti-nullitrons, by contrast, produces exactly the same sound with the exception that the profile upon an oscilloscope shows the troughs of one pattern correspond perfectly to the crests of the other, and *vice versa*. The result, from an auditory point of view, is a perfect silence, which may account for the fact that the nullitron has waited so long to be discovered.

Uses of the Nullitron
In respect to taste, the nullitron, despite its striking red hue, has a distinct flavour of liquorice, while the anti-nullitron tastes like nothing so much as the unripe juice of the juniper. Further investigations are being carried out in this fruitful field and already manufacturers of dietetic foods have expressed interest in the possible commercial uses. The chief problem confronting industry is the extraction of nullitrons from their "potential field" in sufficient quantity.

Of the possible employment in warfare (and particularly whether a "nullitron bomb" is feasible at this point or in the near future) nothing can be said with any confidence.

Space, Time and the Nullitron
One of the most curious aspects of the nullitron was its relatively short life. In all cases observed the nullitron was instantly and utterly annihilated at the moment of its creation. This was not apparent during the early investigations, because the demolished nullitron is instantly replaced by another, identical nullitron, indistinguishable from its "parent" in all

respects.

The first task which presented itself to the investigators after the discovery of the nullitron was the splitting of the nullitron into sub-particles. This experiment consisted simply of catching nullitrons and hurling them with considerable force against a floor. While too little energy in the "nullitron beam" thus formed can cause a troublesome wobble, too much force will result in excessive bouncing – the by-now-well-known "Bounce Effect". This troublesome elasticity is most easily overcome by first embedding the nullitron in a casing of pi-mesons and then "letting Nature take its course."

While over seventeen thousand separate types of sub-nullitronic particles have been discovered by this method as of the time of this report, the difficulty in distinguishing between these different types was great, since all the different sub-types created by this method appeared to be identical.

Clearly, a more sophisticated approach was needed.

A Sophisticated Approach

The method finally arrived at by trial and error was as follows: While one investigator holds the nullitron in both his hands, the other investigator either sits upon it or strikes it a sharp blow with a molybdenum hammer. Two main categories of sub-null particles are thus produced: the "sit-upons" and the "others".

The "sit-upons" consist of isons (small, blue and round); nisons (smaller, two-dimensional particles of a curious rice-colour); and null-nisons (*extremely* tiny, orange, and of fanciful shapes).

The "others" are more varied, falling into two main sub-groupings: the isotrons and the phlogistons. The isotrons are medium-sized ovoid semi-massless particles which upon creation can be observed to tend immediately to the nearest light source and buzz about it until swatted or consumed by anti-isotrons.

Countless "other" particles were observed, ranging in size from 1/8 inch to the great phlogistons, which are fully 1,800,000 kilometres in diameter, though in mass equivalent to an electron. Only one phlogiston has been produced experimentally. This particle, being photophiliac, sped immediately towards the sun at an estimated velocity of 0.9 the speed of light.

A Possible Explanation of Matter?

The single phlogiston produced in this last, and definitive, experiment may eventually afford us an explanation of the nature of matter. On its collision with the sun, the phlogiston was annihilated, as well as the sun, and a number of interesting photographs were taken.

While it is still too early to begin speculating on this phenomenon, one may look forward to the day when, with a fuller understanding of the wonderful nullitron, we shall possess a new and more comprehensive explanation of the nature of our "solar system", if not of "matter" itself.

Danny's New Friends from Deneb

with Thomas M. Disch

Danny had wandered far from his parents' beach house, into the shady place where the little green creature was sitting.

"Hello," said the little green creature. "What's your name?"

"Danny. But I can't talk to you. Momma told me never to talk to coloured people."

"I ain't coloured. I'm green."

"Green's a colour."

"It ain't either!"

"It is so!"

They wrestled a while, but the green boy was tougher and Danny had to admit that green was no colour.

After he got his breath back, Danny asked him if he was a Martian.

"Naw – I'm just a *boy*. But if you want to know where I come from, I come from Deneb."

"Oh. How come you're green?"

"I ain't ripe yet, stupid."

They both giggled at the joke.

"How come *really*?"

"How come you're *pink*?"

"My Dad is pink. So's my Mom."

"My Dad's green. He doesn't want me to talk to pink people. He calls them savages."

"What are you doing here?"

"I came with my Dad and Mom. We're tourists."

"So are we."

They stopped talking while a jet went by overhead.

The green boy made an unhappy face. "I hate this place. I wanted to go to a gloopher ranch." He rolled over on his stomach and pulled up tufts of grass.

"I been to Disneyland," Danny remarked.

"Yeah? Gee whiz! What's it like ..."

"They got – oh, a Tomorrowland. That tells you what the future's like ..."

"Aw, I seen the future. It ain't nothing."

"My Dad says there's no future in the grocery business. He owns three stores!"

"How much money does he make?"

"A million dollars, I think. How much does your Dad make?"

"More than that. My Dad owns the Golden Gate Bridge."

"He does not!"

"He does so!"

"Prove it," said Danny cannily. He wasn't going to fight him any more than he could help.

"He bought it yesterday. A man he met on the street sold it to him for a zillion dollars. We're going to take it home when we leave."

The green boy thought he was so smart! Danny had one last trick up his sleeve. "Why does an elephant wear red tennis shoes?"

"What's an elephant?"

"An animal bigger than a house."

"Oh! You mean a *gloopher*. Last summer I was at a gloopher ranch. I got to ride on one."

"Weren't you scared?"

"No. It was a tame gloopher. Besides if it threw me, my Dad would tear it in little pieces and eat it all up."

"So would mine," said Danny. "My Dad was in the Marines and his arms are tattooed!"

"So are my Dad's." But Danny could tell he was lying.

"How come you got those funny carrots on you head?" Danny asked.

"They're not carrots, stupid. They're *feelers* for when it gets dark."

Curious, Danny took hold of the slender noodles.

"Hey! Let go – that hurts!"

"Hah-hah! I guess you think you're pretty smart, don't you?"

"*Leggo*!"

"Not until you admit green *is* a colour."

"Please!"

Suddenly it came off in his hand. Danny began to switch at the green boy with it.

"Ow, hey, give it back. Don't!"

"Nyah, nyah, nyah!"

"Give it *back*," said another very stern voice, and a big green hand caught hold of Danny's shoulder.

"Dad, he took my feeler and started hitting me with it."

The green boy was such a sissy that he was crying.

The big green man looked angry. "I leave you for one minute to pack the Golden Gate Bridge, and you manage to get into trouble. Didn't I tell you to keep away from natives?" He turned on Danny. "Now *you*, you little devil, give him back his feeler." He shook him roughly.

"I didn't mean to break it. I was just touching it and it came off."

He handed the feeler back to the green boy, who wet the end of it and restored it in place.

"I'm sorry," murmured Danny.

"Young savage!" growled the green boy's father. Then he tore Danny in little pieces and ate him all up.

MYSTERY DIET OF THE GODS: A REVELATION

WITH THOMAS M. DISCH

Have you ever become suddenly quite ill after eating a single slice of buttered whole-wheat toast? Does your skin crawl inexplicably every time you see gigantic displays of "fresh" tomatoes? You are not alone! There are millions of others just like you who feel the same helpless rage when they see self-confessed Darwinians poisoning the wells of Education with their fairy tales about the so-called "Descent" of Man. According to those know-it-all PhDs, the apelike hominids of the past were touched with some kind of magic wand – they call it Evolution! – and instantly they were transformed into today's useful citizens, poised at this moment on the very brink of Interstellar Space! Could anything be less likely? Who's kidding who, anyhow?

Now at last a few brilliant World Scholars are daring to challenge these fabrications. Erich von Däniken and others have established the basic groundwork of Truth on which others can begin to build: *viz.*, Our hominid ancestors were visited by "gods" from other planets, who mated with the apelike females (see Figure 1) to produce *Homo sapiens*.

Who were these extraterrestrial "gods"? Why did they come to Earth, breed a new race of intelligent creatures, and then mysteriously vanish? The answer is literally staring us in the face every time we sit down to breakfast, lunch, dinner, supper, and midnight snack. *Diet*!

What is more central to the very Mystery of Life than Diet? Who can deny that, as Albert Einstein probably said, "You are what you eat"? How true! Yet is it the *whole* truth? Perhaps we also eat what we are!

These two notions are but two sides of the same secret coin, as stated by William Makepeace Thackeray: "We have no wittles to eat, so we must eat *we*." (*Ibid.*) Is Thackeray really suggesting cannibalism? And if not, how shall we account for the great Jonathan Swift's "Modest Proposal" in his book *The Portable Swift*? There Swift suggests that the Irish poor should kill and eat their own children. And Swift was a Protestant Divine! Are all three of these renowned sages – Einstein, Thackeray, and Swift – just "joking"? Are they crazy? Or had they stumbled on a fantastic secret, which would eventually cost all three of them their lives?

Recently, scientists taught a species of worm to crawl through an elaborate maze. (See Figure 2.) Then they cut up these "educated" worms and fed them to other worms. The new worms, who had never seen a maze before, calmly threaded their way through it without one false step. (One cannot help but think of the legend of Theseus and the Minotaur

Ariadne.)

In the light of this all-important experiment, which we have never known one Establishment scientist to contradict, there is no need for theories of Evolution or the Transmigration of Souls to explain the origins of *Homo sap*. The truth is as simple as sandwiches: *The first diet of mankind was Man.*

Once one holds this key in one's hand, every door of History and of Ancient Legends may be opened with ease. Indeed, the most amazing thing is how long it has taken us to recognizethis obvious truth, which seems literally to be staring at us from every newspaper headline and advertising billboard that we pass on the street, until one's impulse is to grab people and *force* them to look at the evidence!

Only consider these facts: The mightiest of Greek "gods," Cronos and Saturn, are said to have devoured their own children. (See Figure 3.) Since time began, Australian aborigines have performed a rite wherein they cut themselves and offer their blood to their children to drink – *in order to make them wise!* There are also many well-documented accounts of human sacrifices and blood-drinking ceremonies among the ancient Aztecs. Can this be merely "coincidence"?

If more proof be needed, what of this? The Greek hero Atreus, the Primal Chef, killed the children of his friend Thyestes, *boiled them in a cauldron*, and served them up at a special banquet. As Robert Graves explains: "When Thyestes had eaten heartily, Atreus sent in their bloody hands and feet, laid out on another dish .... Thyestes fell back, vomiting, and laid an ineluctable curse upon the seed of Atreus."

This legend has often been misinterpreted as pertaining to some taboo against parents (more advanced species) eating their children (less advanced species, the so-called "Underprivileged"). Poppycock! Thyestes' illness was the result of his children being *boiled in a cauldron*. No human nervous system can absorb unlimited traces of iron. The fact that Atreus realized this is shown by his trying to atone for his original sin by bringing in raw, pure flesh as a second course. For, as the ancients knew, it is only in eating raw meat (ambrosia) and drinking fresh blood (nectar) that vital essences can be transferred from eaten to eater.

Thus, the Arawak Indians of South America eat their victims raw, as did the sages of ancient Poland, the so-called Vampires. The same Diet Secret was known as well to the Moggadil of ancient Wales, who feasted on the raw kneecaps of their enemies, thereby gaining their strength. It is a well-known fact, documented in the *Protocols of the Elders of Zion*, that the medieval Jews (sages who preserved the hermetic doctrines of the space gods) made ritual – and probably very delicious – meals on Christian babies. The physicians of Pope Innocent III prescribed for him a daily dose of the fresh blood of three infants. At this point the "coincidence" theory begins to look very lame indeed!

Many ancient texts tell us precisely how autophagy originated. Hesiod, the earliest of the Greek poets, is thought to have personally known the extraterrestrial gods. He speaks of their secrets guardedly, as a "fable to the kings, who are themselves wise." The fable tells of a hawk who catches a nightingale, saying to him: "I shall make a meal of you if I wish, or set you free." At the end of his "poem," Hesiod reveals his true meaning with this warning: "You kings, mark this punishment well, even you: For the deathless gods are close among men ... *On the many-feeding earth there are thrice ten thousand immortal observers set there by Zeus to watch over mortal men.* They keep watch on judgements and evil deeds as they move, clothed in mist, all over the earth." (*Ibid.*)

Could any words be plainer? We were the food of 30,000 (thrice ten thousand) alien invaders. However, we weren't always helpless nightingales, as the distinguished British scholar Sir James Frazer demonstrates in *The Golden Bough*. After noting that the Cretans, at the festival of Dionysus, "tore a live bull with their teeth," he goes on: "*We cannot doubt* that in rending and devouring a live bull the worshippers of Dionysus believed themselves to be *killing the god, eating his flesh and drinking his blood*." In clear English, the mortals who had been mere Ambrosia revolted! The eaten became the eaters, and the worm turned!

As a direct consequence, our 30,000 hawks were indeed forced to clothe themselves in mist (possibly produced by the evaporation of "dry ice") and flee from the suddenly much smarter nightingales. Some went to Mexico, where they instituted their culinary practices on a truly grand scale. The eminent anthroposophist William H. Prescott tells us that in 1486 AD, a year after the defeat of Richard III on Bosworth Field, at the dedication of the great temple at Huitzilopotchil, the prisoners reserved for the great banquet "were ranged in files, forming a procession nearly two miles long"! He asks – but neglects to answer – how the Aztecs could have dealt with this huge food surplus: "How could the remains, *too great for consumption in the ordinary way* [!?!?!], be disposed of, without breeding a pestilence in the capital?"

Archaeologists like Erich von Däniken have found the answer in the great Mexican pyramids. (See Figure 4.) Like those of Egypt, these gigantic edifices had a very practical purpose – *freeze-drying*! "This idea may sound Utopian," says Von Däniken, "but in fact every big clinic today has a 'bone bank' which preserves human bones in a deep-frozen condition for years and makes them serviceable again when required. Fresh blood – this too is a universal practice – can be kept for an unlimited time at minus 196°C, and living cells can be stored almost indefinitely at the temperature of liquid nitrogen. Did the Pharaoh have a fantastic idea which will soon be realized in practice?" (*Chariot of the Gods.* London: Souvenir Press, 1969, page 102. *Ibid.* **QED**)

The answer must be a resounding *yes*! The flesh of mummies is so well freeze-dried that it is still delicious thousands of years after it was put up! Think of the incredible know-how of those pharaohs – how expertly the unsavoury parts of the ambrosial bodies were removed, how the cavities were then stuffed with spices and neatly prepacked for the greater convenience of the "gods." What we would give today for just one of the recipes! The fact that sarcophagi depict the features of the deceased is no longer an enigma to bate PhD's (PhD = Phony Dumbbell!). After all, don't *we* label our canned beans, frozen broccoli, etc., with appetizing pictures? (See Figure 5.)

Of course, prepacked foods are never as tasty as fresh. Perhaps for this reason the gods left Egypt and Mexico and settled in the undersea city of Atlantis, somewhere near to the Shetland Islands. In the "legend" of *Beowulf* the human hero sets off in a submarine to pursue the "god" called Grendel's Mother. "For hours he sank through the waves. At last he saw the mud of the bottom and all at once the greedy she-wolf who'd ruled these waters for half a hundred years [i.e., since departing from Egypt] discovered him." Grabbing him in her claws, she carries him to Atlantis, which is described as "someone's battle-hall, where the water could not hurt him, nor anything in the sea attack him through the building's high-arching roof. A brilliant light burned all around him." As for the Diet of the Atlanteans, it's spelled out quite clearly, for this old chronicle begins with a description of the extraterrestrial Grendel "coming to Herot when Hrothgar's men slept, killing them in their beds, eating some on the spot, fifteen or more at a time, and running off to his *loathesome moor* [an obvious cryptogram of 'Atlantis' from which only the 'n' and 'i' are missing] with another such sickening meal awaiting in his pouch." This pouch may have been the trunk of a small powerful car, probably a Volkswagen. A diving expedition to the Shetlands would undoubtedly bring to light a true Aladdin's cave of wonders. In fact, Atlantis and Aladdin's cave are undoubtedly *one and the same*!

The one riddle remaining is: Why did Man, having tasted the flesh of the gods and grown wise, regress into the corrupt vegetarian practices of his ape forebears? We see in the Book of Genesis that eating roots, tubers, and fruit-pulp had always been a temptation for the first humans. When the serpent tempts Eve – poor half-simian creature that she was – with an apple (or, more likely, a banana), he says: "In the day ye eat thereof, then your eyes shall be opened, and ye shall be as gods."

How guileful! The serpent knew full well that a diet such as he is recommending would have just the opposite effect. We all know the tragic outcome of Eve's choice: Show an ape a banana and the rest, alas, is history. For one brief moment Man became a god – and then he slipped on the banana peel of his own deepest racial memories – and not just once but over and over again. First came the substitution of animal flesh for the real thing. Then the discovery of the abominable potato. After the rise of elaborate pastry chefs in the eighteenth century came the avowed vegetarianism of Percy Bysshe Shelley, George Bernard Shaw and Adolf Hitler. Bloodless poetry led to cynical plays and on to a world plunged into hideous wars. (See Figure 6.) *All because Man has turned his back on his own flesh and blood.*

Is it too late to reverse this age-old tendency? No, by changing yourself, you can still change mankind! Here are four simple rules by which you can lead a life that will make you healthier and raise your IQ at least 20 points:

1. Boycott fruits and vegetables in any form.
2. All cereal products – rice, wheat, etc. – are out!
3. Banish coffee, tea, water, milk, and other unnatural beverages from your cupboards and refrigerators.
4. Use only meat substitutes, such as beef or venison, when you have no other recourse.
5. Insist on a plentiful, spontaneous Diet of the "Food of the Gods" – *Nectar* and *Ambrosia*!

On the public level – talk to your friends and neighbours. Show them the evidence – bit by bit. Ask them to read *Chariots of the Gods?*. Then invite them to a dinner they'll never forget!

Finally, write to your congressman in Washington, D.C., asking for a return not only of the death penalty but of public human sacrifice. Let's make Thanksgiving a day to be truly thankful for by eating our own children, as did the original Pilgrim aliens.

If you want to *be* like gods, you've got to *eat* like gods. That's the Mystery of the Mystery Diet. It's still not too late for you to join the side of True Human Evolution and take your place in the great Garden of the Universe, where god eats god in an Eternal Cycle of glorious Diet!

It's up to *you*!

Suggested Illustrations and Captions

Figure 1. (Venus di Milo) *Caption*: "Neanderthal woman. Note stooped, apelike posture, heavy jaw and narrow pelvic girdle."

Figure 2. (Photo of topiary maze) *Caption*: "Maze."

Figure 3. (Goya's painting of Saturn eating his children) *Caption*: "Goya's visionary rendering of the first contact between the 'gods' from Outer Space and Mankind."

Figure 4. (Any Mexican pyramid) *Caption*: "When explorers first opened the secret chamber of this Aztec pyramid, a light went on inside!"

Figure 5. (Any string of hieroglyphics) *Caption*: "Papyrus scroll found in the mummy-case of Im-hotep, a supermarket manager of the IVth Dynasty. It reads: 'Contains 100% Government Inspected Ambrosia, with permitted preservatives.'"

Figure 6: (Crude "composite photo" of Shelley, Shaw and Hitler) *Caption*: "Three vegetarians!"

Transplant Your Own Heart

A DO-IT-YOURSELF GUIDE BY

Thomas M. Disch and John Sladek

Let's get one thing straight right away – *Anyone can perform the single act of surgery necessary for a heart transplant.* So-called medical doctors would like us to believe the contrary, of course. According to organizations like the AMA it takes years of tedious university study and a hospital full of costly equipment.

Don't you believe it! In fact the average man or woman with a high school diploma and enough manual dexterity to operate a pencil sharpener can successfully transplant any or all of his organs. "After a few weeks of practice," says one successful amateur, "switching hearts or livers becomes as easy as switching license plates on your ambulance."

And that's only the beginning. When you've learned the simple technique of auto-hypnosis, the way is clear to the most difficult self-operation of all – the whole-head transplant.

Two important rules
1. Don't listen to defeatists who say it can't be done. Remember, they said van Gogh was crazy.
2. Don't accept failure. Keep trying.

Naturally before you undertake to transplant your own organs, you'll want plenty of practice with the help of family, friends and pets. Most self-surgeons run into their first difficulties here. Rejection of the *concept* of transplantation is as common as the purely medical problem of tissue rejection. People are afraid of anything new and untried, and logical arguments won't work against fear. You may have to resort to the tested-and-true US Army method of simply choosing your volunteers. If the volunteer doesn't agree with your choice, it's just as well to have a can of chloroform and a strong assistant standing by.

Assume that you have your recipient ready for the table. You have a number of sharp knives and scissors, needle, thread and so on. you've put down a few newspapers to sop up the mess. Slip on your kitchen rubber gloves, tie on your spotless white surgical mask (optional, but it does impart an undeniably "distinguished" look) – and you're ready to start the countdown.

Eight rules for surgery
1. Tools: Be sensible. Don't expect perfect results with a clumsy

serrated breadknife. Keep all knives and scissors ultra-sharp. (Remember – it's the dull, rusty knife that will slip and cause a nasty accident.)
2. Be bold and decisive. Remember – you're not a barber – you're a surgeon!
3. Start small. Don't try to remove a whole heart the first time round. Start with maybe just the little pointy bit at the bottom.
4. Work from right to left, and top to bottom. When sewing up, this rule is reversed.
5. Safety first! Cut away from yourself. (Of course, this doesn't apply when operating *on* yourself.)
6. If the recipient should wake up during the operation, smile warmly and keep up a steady flow of conversation. If possible, get a shoulder in the way so he won't see what you're up to. Say you're sewing buttons on his shirt, etc.
7. Remember – alcohol and blood don't mix. Do your celebrating afterwards.
8. Trust in God to see you through.

Finding a donor is the next problem, and here's where an ambulance with false licence plates come in handy. If you can't afford that, get a stethoscope. Practice the technique of racing to the scene of an accident, listening for a heart-beat, and shaking the head gravely. Don't be choosy – anyone with a visible wound is as good as dead anyway.

If you can't find an accident, don't become discouraged. For beginners, practice with substitutes and simulations is a good alternative. Does your supermarket have artichoke hearts or heart-of-palm? Any old valentines in the attic? How about that greasy deck of cards you keep meaning to throw away – plenty of hearts in that.

The same principles apply for other types of transplantation. Every supermarket stocks a good supply of liver and kidneys – and what's more they're relatively cheap! Just warm them to body temperature (98° Fahrenheit, approximately) in a pan of water (don't fry or broil) and heigh-ho, heigh-ho, it's off to work we go!

One thing to bear in mind – the replacement parts should *not* be larger than the parts removed. A kidney-shaped coffee table, for instance, should not replace a kidney. Confusions or misjudgements of size and lead to trouble at sewing up time.

The whole-head transplant

Now that you've swapped a few hearts, lungs, livers, etc. you're ready for something really challenging. For a head transplant, we find that both literally and figuratively two heads are better than one. That is, two surgeons have an easier time subduing initial resistance. They can take turns at the arduous work of cutting through bone and gristle. Finally, teamwork brings out the sheer good fun of surgery.

One time, for instance, the authors of this article were doing a head transplant using Mr Disch's cousin (a pipe-smoker who had once complained of a headache) as recipient. The donor had been struck down some minutes earlier by an unidentified, hit-and-run ambulance.

While Disch removed the recipient's head and his billfold, Sladek did the same with the donor. Then we sewed on the new head in record time. We were just washing our hands before lunch when the patient began to complain of blindness.

Optical nerve damage was our first hypotheses. Sladek then opted for hysterical blindness while Disch maintained that Sladek's thumbs had slipped into the donor's eye-sockets during the head removal.

The real explanation was much simpler. Disch had turned the recipient's body over from a prone to a supine position, while Sladek had not similarly rotated the head. In short, the head was on backwards, so that as the patient lay on his back his eyes were pressed into the pillow.

We had quite a laugh about our little mistake. Disch's cousin was furious at the time, though by now he has come to terms with the rearrangement. Today, with the aid of two mirrors, he can light his pipe, shave, and otherwise live a completely normal life – *and* his headache is gone!

Rules for head transplants
1. Take special care with head-body orientation. Labelling heads and bodies *front* and *back* is helpful.
2. Rejection problems. Be sure donor and recipient take the same hat and collar sizes. Heads have been known to reject foreign bodies due to their outlandish metric sizes.
3. Save leftovers. Spare heads and bodies always come in handy during emergencies.

Surely it is the highest calling of all surgeons to ply the paring-knife and coping-saw on their own flesh and bone, following the immortal commandment of the Carpenter of Nazareth, "Physician, heal thyself!" Don't forget, though, in the enthusiasm of your first weeks of auto-surgery that you can have too much of a good thing.

Rules for auto-surgery
1. Use the buddy system, especially at first. Sure you can go it alone, but there's no reason to be ashamed of having a friend stand by, just in case. Anyone can pass out.
2. Don't overdo it. Auto-surgery is basically healthful and invigorating, but it does tax the system. If you've just done a kidney transplant, for instance, give yourself a week or two before trying open heart surgery.
3. *Don't* try and work without mirrors. There's no place in Medical Science for show-offs! *Do* remember: Left becomes right in a mirror, and vice versa. One of our colleagues now has a very tricky double left ear, from forgetting this simple rule.

Finally, a few words on the controversial subject of lobotomy. Both of us have enjoyed the benefits of lobotomization for many years. We feel that it represents a definite plus, both physically and spiritually. The lobotomized mind feels a profound sense of Inner Peace. Lobotomies were a normal part of life among the ancient Aztecs and Egyptians – why not in our supposedly "scientific" age?

Those who regard the operation as "disfiguring" might as reasonably argue that appendectomies should be abolished because they're a threat to the bathing suit industry! (Actually, as most of us realize, surgical scars are decidedly *arousing*!) To all such crepe-hangers we say – Poppycock! Let common sense and humanistic philosophy prevail: there is no form of auto-surgery that isn't worth trying out.

Few hobbies can be so inexpensive and so educational at the same time. Moreover, auto-surgery is health-giving, improves sallow complexions, is a good cure for depression, and gives you something to do with your hands.

So if you're still hesitating, our advice to you is – Dig in!

Sladek on Sladek

THE PROFESSION OF SCIENCE FICTION, 29: KIDS! READ BOOKS IN YOUR SPARE TIME!

Mainly I write science fiction in self-defence. It's one way of getting to grips with a peculiar world, a world that I find Astounding, Amazing and altogether a Weird Tale. I wonder how people unfamiliar with sf manage to find their way around in our world of Watergate and Jonestown, Khomeini and Haig, robot factories and vodka-cola, Manson and Moonies and the MX missile system. I deal with this stuff as I can, and if the end product looks like satire, look at the raw material.

In 1969 I happened to mention "President Reagan" in a novel, probably because Ronald Reagan had become governor of California and because, after Nixon, anything seemed possible. It's embarrassing to have one of your sillier predictions come true. I still can't get used to having a real President Reagan (played by Henry Fonda), much less his Secretary of State, Alexander Haig (George C. Scott). In fact I never did get used to having a President Nixon (Warren Oates).

The fact that our current President starred in *Juke Girl* and *Bedtime for Bonzo* does seem to fit in with the present age of childishness, in which otherwise normal adults collect comics, go roller skating, wear track suits and go to see movies about Popeye and Superman. I suppose it's disingenuous of me to comment upon this as though I were somehow above it, when it must be obvious that science fiction is getting a free ride on this boom in infantile culture. I just hope the free ride doesn't end with no one reading anything.

But in some ways I am outside the American, or at least the Cal-American culture sphere. For one thing, I haven't lived in America since 1965; people have to explain to me in their letters what they mean by tranquillity tanks or jazz dancing. I am still shocked to hear that the children of nice middle-class people I know have become addicts, had multiple abortions, joined mind-destroying cults or been murder suspects, all while still in high school.

One gets over shock, of course, and fashionable jargon is as easily learned as forgotten. And the cultural distance between Britain and America isn't so great: a constant stream of media-packaged Americas (from *Dallas* to the Valley of the Shadow of Silicon) flows across to us. The real barrier seems to be between my Midwestern childhood and what I glimpse of America today.

After a rough start, my childhood was spent with doting grandparents in a sleepy little town (pop. 4000) in the middle of Iowa. We were poor but not destitute, and it was one of those safe, secure, pleasant childhoods celebrated by Ray Bradbury, complete with hand-packed ice cream, rusty screen doors, waking in the morning to the sound of the milkman's horse ... I don't know why, unlike Bradbury, I've never felt especially lyrical about my home town. It could be because, much of the time, my home town was boring. That may have been one reason why I read a lot. Like most children who read, I read everything that came before my eye. I worked my way right through the local library's children's section, from Uncle Wiggly (adventures of an elderly rabbit) to the Hardy Boys mysteries, then moved to the adult section where I read things like a Jules Verne novel and the stories of Poe and O. Henry. At home I had cheap editions of a lot of "children's classics" like Robin Hood, Three Musketeers, *Huckleberry Finn*, Kipling's *Just So Stories*. Kipling's book and the Oz books really possessed me, not just through their prose but through their illustrations. Kipling did his own drawings, with so many details you could sit peering at or daydreaming over for mindless hours – he must have known everything about child psychology. Later I found a similar delightful jumble of detail in the comic *Smokey Stover*, which I read in Big Little Books. I was not allowed comics at home, so kept up with them at other kids' houses and at the drugstores. In various fits of reading I got hooked on, e.g., dog books or war adventure. And there was *Piang, a Moro Chieftain*, which impressed me so deeply that I can still recall some of the details and even the names of a couple of its characters. And there was a big anthology of "classics" bowdlerized for children by Charles and Mary Lamb, things like The *Iliad*, *Midsummer Night's Dream*, *Pilgrim's Progress* and *Robinson Crusoe* (now of course everyone recognizes that these were not genuine classics in the sense that the works of Hugo Gernsback and H.P. Lovecraft are classics). My grandfather brought home his own junk reading, which I also read: a stack of paperbacks every week, usually Westerns or sports stories (I remember Malamud's *The Natural* turning up; it seemed weird and sexy for a baseball story), also hardboiled detective items. He also brought home the *Saturday Evening Post*, which I always read from cover to cover: slushy love stories, C.S. Forester yarns, Ray Bradbury (I recall reading "The Veldt"), articles, cartoons, even ads for Arrow shorts (with limericks). My grandmother favoured *The Sacred Heart Messenger* and *Catholic Digest*, so I read these too; and when I was supposed to be doing the supper dishes, I was often down on all fours reading the newspapers put down to protect the linoleum.

At the age of thirteen I went to live with my mother and step-father in the big city, St Paul. The library there had sf anthologies and I remember reading a few Lewis Padgett stories. But my baptism into science fiction must have left my heel unimmersed because it didn't quite take. At the same time I discovered Steinbeck and the world of grown-up books.

I went to the University of Minnesota to become a mechanical engineer. This field began to seem, after a couple of years, like another stifling small town. The work itself was fascinating, but wasn't there more to the world? My fellow students seemed to believe there wasn't. Finally I got a job in the Physics Department, working for a real engineer. He was bored and unhappy, but making so much money that he couldn't quit.

After three years, I switched from mechanical engineering to English literature, having decided that I really wanted to spend my life writing. I wasn't yet sure what I wanted to write, only that it would be a lot more fun to be F. Scott Fitzgerald or Jack Kerouac than to design flanges for vacuum pumps.

I had been fiddling around with writing since before high school, turning out little pointless story-ettes, then poetry and attempts at humorous essays in the Thurber or Leacock veins (I thought). Majoring in English did open up my horizons; I realized for the first time that there were people like Fielding and Hawthorne and Ring Lardner – and for that matter, Chaucer and Shakespeare. I concentrated as much as possible on modern literature, and of course took English composition classes too. They were encouraging and I came out of them no longer wanting to be Kerouac. Now I wanted to be Samuel Beckett. A long, tedious and I'm sure most un-Beckettian novel commenced; I dragged it around with me for years, until I went to Europe and lost it, without regret.

About this time (the early Sixties) there was so much good writing and dazzling writing popping up everywhere; books which were as great a pleasure to read as the first chosen book one reads in childhood: Vladimir Nabokov, William Gaddis, Joseph Heller, John Barth, Thomas Pynchon, Harry Mathews, Donald Barthelme. Most of them veered towards science fiction, as did the newly-translated works of Jorge Luis Borges. Science fiction began to seem to me less juvenile, especially since my friend Tom Disch was now writing it. I began to hear about and read worthwhile sf by Philip K. Dick, Alfred Bester, Kurt Vonnegut, Walter M. Miller. When I began to write sf myself, Tom helped me a lot with criticism and market advice, and even lent me his agent. Tom and I collaborated on a few things, most of them juvenile and silly but fun to write. My first solo story to be published was "The Happy Breed", which is about people being juvenile and silly. A warning?

I see this article is turning into something like a senile browse through a family album. All I've really said about science fiction is that I'm not very familiar with the genre. If I had been, there are a few other ways I might have tackled this:

1. *Tips from a professional.* Type on one side of the paper at a time. Read the fine print in contracts. Meet publishers with a warm smile and a firm handshake (Ask yourself, "What is there I can find to like about this person?"). Enclose return postage. And remember, science fiction may not be much, but by God it's a white-collar job.
2. *Anecdotes of genre awareness.* The time I met e.e. ("doc") cummings. How it feels to own a complete set of *Stupendous* (1937-1949) containing the first published story of A.E. van Georgerussell. How I laughed when the FBI kicked in my door and some of my teeth, accusing me of stealing the military secret that $E=mc^2$. Acronyms I

have used: FTL, ESP, UFO, BEM, GBH.

3. *Literary insights (interior dialogue)*: What is science fiction, anyway? Why do you ask? No but seriously, what is sf? It's just what you think it is. That's cribbed from Jasper Johns. Yes, but isn't sf itself cribbed from Andy Warhol? Images of the electric chair – you could be right – but it's an answer itself implicit in the question, which is itself free-standing only if we set aside the question of Albanian political sf and confront the larger socio-economic problems, taking up the science fiction of William Jennings Bryan in the process. Well I say, cut the cackle and just tell a good yarn, start right at the beginning, have some more in the middle, and finish up at the end, what's so doggoned complicated about that? I won't answer that, since we haven't even begun to take up the distancing effect of space travel, the alienation of aliens, Orwell's aunt, this. This? This dialogue, it grinds on like the pointless gears of a Forster machine, only connecting, only connecting. Toothless you mean, surely? What about Ideas in sf, pretty controversial thought in itself, eh? Oh I don't know, Forster's "When the Machine Stops" has plenty of Ideas, reminds me of my own unwritten story, "MutAnts", by the way is this me talking or you? Why do you ask?

WRITING PLACES

Writing, it should go without saying, requires solitary confinement. The writer's immediate surroundings must exclude forest fires, screams from mental wards, head-banging music, cries of ecstasy, the anguish of infants, jet aircraft taking off and so on. While any of these distractions can be turned to some writer's advantage, the general prejudice is against them and in favour of quiet solitude. That is why noisy cities are clogged with writers, who avoid the quiet countryside as though anthrax stalked the land.

Yet writers who live in cities go on fondly imagining that the city is the last place they want to be. I too have indulged in the general fantasy:

*

About to begin a novel, I find myself locked away in a snowbound cabin. There is plenty of black coffee and I guess a supply of coarse wool shirts from Lord & Taylor, and maybe one or two absolutely essential reference books. But all of the noises, distractions and irritations of the city are far away, beginning of course with my family and friends. No mail can get through to me, not so much as a postcard from my dentist – certainly not bills, rejection slips, requests from New Zealand high school teachers for a complete bibliography of all my short stories by return mail, fan letters demanding that I explain some dumb joke or reveal my real name – this cabin is beyond the reach of postal services, telephone lines, rail, road or waterway. Unpredictable winds rule out helicopter visits, while a nearby magnetic mountain or something cuts off all radio and TV. The nearest library and the nearest good Indian restaurant are a thousand miles away. There is now nothing to stop me from rolling the paper in the typewriter, taking a reflective puff on my pipe, and beginning: *Chapter One*.

The fantasy has to end there to remain credible. In reality I would probably sit dazzled to snowblindness by the white page, or else turn to the reference books and look up "chapter" and "one". Then I clean the typewriter, then sit contemplating the strange paradox, my having to be alone to communicate. Surely there's an essay in that? Solitary confinement – or confinement in the other sense, to bring forth a literary child? Okay then, where's the child? Still a blank page.

It occurs to me that this fantasy owes something to the film *Young-blood Hawke*, starring I think James Franciscus and written I believe by Herman Wouk. As I recall, the writer in the film collapsed in the snow with pneumonia and nearly died, and he also lost some crucial pages of his manuscript. That probably says something about how Herman Wouk really felt towards this fantasy.

Okay then, I wander around the cabin until I find a cupboard door I hadn't noticed before. I open it. Inside is an old, dusty telephone and, to my surprise, it still works. I phone my wife.

"Would you get out the *Film Guide* and look up a movie for me, called *Youngblood Hawke*?"

"I thought you took it with you."

"No, no, I took only essential references."

"Look, I can't find it," she says. "You must have put it somewhere. How are you getting on?"

"Touch of pneumonia. Any letters?"

"The usual. Threat from the bank, urgent request from a Canadian high school teacher for a complete bibliography. And a postcard from the dentist."

"Did my agent phone?"

"Yes, he's just got back from the Monte Carlo Book Fair. Says he's got some Hollywood deal lined up, you're to phone him back immediately."

"Okay, but could you look for that book?"

"If I find it," she says, "I'll send it out on the snowmobile. I just found out they're starting a regular daily service."

I spend the rest of the day trying to reach my agent, who's at lunch. In the evening I phone my wife and ask her to bring our daughter and come skiing over.

"You're kidding, you wanted to be alone to work," she says.

"But I'm dying of pneumonia. Besides, I'm afraid of losing some pages of my manuscript."

"Some pages? Then it's going well?"

"Oh yes, yes." I turn my back on *Chapter One*. "But I'm lonely."

"And as soon as we get there, you'll say you want to be alone to work."

"You're right, of course." I hang up and go back to the typewriter, but it's getting late now. Make a fresh start tomorrow.

The rest of the week is the same. I divide my time between trying to phone my agent and cleaning the typewriter. The snowmobile brings daily requests for bibliographies and more rude fan letters. In a hidden cupboard I find a dusty old TV set; miraculously, it works. A bunch of old friends drop in, on their way to the new Indian restaurant that's just opened round the corner. I'll have to take my wife and daughter there, when they ski over.

My agent's secretary says he's away at the Rio Book Fair.

"Did he say anything about a Hollywood deal?"

"Hollywood? No, you mean *Holyhead*. There's a chance for you to give a lecture there, to the Holyhead Herman Wouk Society. What shall I tell them?"

"Tell them ..." I look out the window. The sky is filled with a wonderful light. The snow is melting and running down to nourish the good earth. "Tell them Willie Boy gives his regards to Broadway. Tell them tomorrow is probably another day, a day in the Human Work of

Herman Wouk. Tell them I'm going home! Home!"

*

Where was I? Herman's hostility towards his own hibernation fantasy is, I'm sure, shared by writers at large. Most of us, however ungregarious, resent having to shut ourselves away from the world in order to get work done. Most of us, however gregarious, resent having the world interfere with our work. In short, most of us are as full of resentment as a new shirt is full of pins.

Did Milton prefer *L'Allegro* or *Il Penseroso*? Yes and no. Coleridge and Wordsworth, were they keener on the spontaneous-overflow-of-emotions side of things than on the recollection-in-tranquillity side? It all depends. As he sat down to write his bestseller, Augustine no doubt prayed, God give me a quiet place to work, only not yet. If writers hanker for the country so much, why do they seem to cluster together in cities? Take for instance the 30 writers of science fiction interviewed by Charles Platt for *Dream Makers* (1980), all from the UK and the US.

	Number of SF writers	
Place	*Actual*	*Expected**
New York (Metrop. area)	10	1.3
Los Angeles (Metrop. area)	4	0.8
Chicago (Metrop. area)	1	0.8
Other US	9	20.6
TOTAL US	24	23.5
Greater London	3	0.8
Other UK	3	5.6
TOTAL UK	6	6.4
TOTAL (US & UK)	30	30
TOTAL URBAN	18	3.8
TOTAL NON-URBAN	12	26.2

* The 'expected' number of SF writers living in an area is just the area's share of the population (UK + US), applied to a sample of 30 persons. In other words, out of 30 persons drawn at random from the total population (UK + US), about 1.3 will live in New York, 0.8 in Los Angeles and so on. Anyone who says there can't be 0.8 of an SF writer hasn't looked at *Omni* lately.

Dreams in this case seem to be made mainly in cities, and in properly urban cities like New York at that. There are many arguable causes for this – one could say that for writers to live in a publishing centre like New York is not surprising, or that Platt (himself a New Yorker and author of *Twilight of the City*) has selected nearby interviewees – but it remains an odd statistic. We might imagine that science fiction writers flock to just those places where life is hardest: New York is not twice as big as Los Angeles but it gets twice as many writers. This despite New York's high rents, high-rise living, impassable traffic, street crime, intolerable weather, highly visible poverty, ugliness and dirt, civic bankruptcy and so on, all features not associated with Los Angeles. What has New York got? Art? Culture?

Without pushing the argument too far, I would guess that what New York really has to offer science fiction writers is high rent, high-rise living, impassable street traffic, street crime, etc. Some science fiction writers are a rare kind of oyster; they need some grit in the shell to get the pearl started; New York provides the grit. In such a place people move faster, talk faster, work harder. They set their sights higher. Science fiction writers in New York understand very well one of the great moving forces in science fiction: the desire to be elsewhere. I will not go so far as to propose there is a New York school in science fiction, but if there were, I think it would be characterized by a style that is aggressive, witty, cerebral and paranoid.

Los Angeles really has nothing like this to offer. It's hardly a city at all, more like a long smear of California coastline. No one can desire to be elsewhere if they already are elsewhere. In such a place people move slowly, talk little, work hardly at all. I would characterizea hypothetical Southern California school of science fiction as dreamy, solemn, peritoneal and mystical.

To outsiders, both New York and Los Angeles are incomprehensible. I've tried living in New York for a year and hated it. I've been in Los Angeles for a week and found it empty. It may be that a special kind of neurosis is required for tolerating either city.

My own brand of neurosis seems to suit me for life in London, just now. Its special features are of course invisible to me, though no doubt obvious to any outsider. But it's a wonderful place from which to write about the imaginary Midwest of my childhood on the planet America.

4-Part List

I saw a TV programme the other evening which told me exactly how to handle a mob like you. In public speaking, they said, the big secret is to have a three-part list and a contrast; so you say Friends, Romans, Countrymen – that's the three-part list, then you bring in the contrast – I come not to bury Caesar but to praise him. It's a terrible rule really, it reduced all the great speeches of history to a kind of inane game: never have so many owed so much to so few: government of the people, by the people, for the people. It reduces then all to a sort of 3:2:1. I for one don't believe it is that simple, I didn't believe it then, I don't believe it now and by thunder I never, shall believe it. It may be all right for Hitler, Churchill and Lincoln (this is the contrast) but it isn't all right for me.

Anyway, I have a four-part list for you. I found the four items a few years ago in a book by A.J. Ayer called *The Problem of Knowledge* in which he outlined four fundamental questions of philosophy concerning knowledge, which are: first of all, how do we know the physical world is real?; second, how do we know other people have thoughts and feelings as we do?; third, how do we know what the past was really like?; and fourth, how do we know that the entities of science (things like electrons and atoms) are real? It occurred to me when I read this list that these four questions turn up very frequently in science fiction. They also turn up in mental hospitals and they turn up in mystical religions and in pseudo-science cults, as I hope to show.

Well, how do we know that the physical world is real? After all, we only experience it through our senses and senses can be deceived. It is always possible that one is experiencing not reality at all but some artificial illusion, some dream or hallucination. Well, science fiction characters, of course, have often experienced all of these – Alice was only dreaming Wonderland. In Robert Heinlein's story "They" the entire world is made up of actors and stage sets, all for a one-man audience; New York is hastily put together when he visits New York; Paris is put together whenever he visits Paris and the weather is constructed according to what weather report he believes. In a Ray Bradbury story, astronauts are hypnotized into believing that Mars is Heaven and that the horrid Martians are their loved ones. In Stanislaw Lem's *Solaris* the illusion created by the planet seems so pervasive and complete it isn't possible to tell whether they are illusions or hypnotic suggestion or a dream. But I think no one has more consistently explored the possibilities of false reality than Philip K. Dick; and I think it is fair to say that most of his work is steeped in questions about reality. He often seems to be doing philosophy, including theology and ethics as he writes – or, I should say as he wrote. This is not going to be an eulogy for Philip K. Dick, I am certainly not the person to do it and I hope that confident scholars will have much to say about him. I should perhaps say that he died in March – I don't know if everybody was aware that he had died. To me at least it is almost the greatest loss that science fiction has had.

Anyway, my own favourite scene of his in exploring the reality of reality, if you like, is the scene in *Time Out of Joint* where a man on a beach goes up to an ice-cream stand to buy something and while he is standing there looking over the flavours, the entire stand, including the proprietor, sort of shimmers and disappears. There is nothing left on the beach but a slip of paper on which is typewritten "ice-cream stand". Well, I may have the details of this wrong, I haven't looked at that passage in fifteen years, but it is a kind of vivid image that stays with you for ever. It is one of the great shocking images of fiction, in fact, as powerful as the image of Robinson Crusoe gaping down at a human footprint. In both cases the reader is asked to enter the body of the observer character and look out through his eyes to get the full impact of the discovery, and the paradigms of reality collapse all at once.

In an experiment done a few years ago people were put in an analogous state when a small piece of their reality collapsed. They were shown pictures of playing cards flashed on a screen at very brief intervals and they were asked to name the playing cards; but mixed in with the normal cards were a few anomalies such as a red six of spades or a black four of hearts. When these came up people might make mistakes about them when they were shown briefly, but as they were shown for longer periods of time people became confused. Shown a red six of spades a subject might say, "Well, it is the six of spades all right, but there is something wrong with it, it has a red border." Some of them were very agitated and one finally said, "I can't make the suit out, whatever it is. I don't know what colour it is now or whether it is a spade or a heart. I am not even sure now what a spade looks like. My God!" Well, reality is after all a hypothesis we make and we continue to make and revise as we go along. I should say that Ian Watson's work deals with reality as a hypothesis which is limited only by our limited perceptions. I believe that one of the themes of his work is that perception causes reality or manufactures it and thus enhancing perception, whether through taking drugs or mystical enlightenment or being an alien, produces a correspondingly richer reality.

It is an interesting idea, carrying on from Bishop Berkeley who said that if no one saw an object it didn't exist and hence this was the necessity of God to watch all the objects that nobody else was watching. I think Ian Watson's work carries on from that, though certainly it is not limited by the Berkeley idea. But I noticed that in the Philip K. Dick example the story only gets remarkable at the point where he actually reads the slip of paper; the disappearance of an ice-cream stand, remarkable as it might be, might be explained as a mirage or a dizzy spell, but it is that little piece of counter-reality, like the wrong card colour, that upsets everything. It is an image designed to raise the hairs on the back of your neck as you read it, I think. This desire to play games with physical reality, let's say, to move the border a little, the border between reality and unreality, is not confined to science fiction. Part of the force behind occultism is certainly the same desire to have an alternative reality.

Recently Barry Singer, who is Professor of Psychology at the University of California at Long Beach, and some of his colleagues conducted an experiment in which they asked a student named Craig to develop a few simple magic tricks and present them to their classes. Now Craig would put on a blindfold and he would then use his fingers, or pretend to use his fingers, to read a three-digit number. He would teleport some ashes through the hands of the volunteer and he would do a bit of Geller-style metal bending. These were standard, easy tricks which he learned in minutes and which are, in fact, tricks in kids' books of magic. When he performed before six classes of college students, in three of them the professors told their students that Craig claimed to be psychic though they said that they (i.e. the professors) were sceptical. In the other three it was explained that he was an amateur magician using tricks. The professors made sure that the students understood that this was the case and made them write down the instruction to make certain that they understood it. After the performances, during which Craig said nothing at all about his own abilities, the students were asked to write down their reactions. Well, you may not be surprised to learn that in the classes where he was supposed to claim psychic powers, about eighty percent of the students thought he really was psychic, and this is a quote: "Many students gasped or screamed faintly during Craig's performance and were visibly agitated, and about a dozen students became seriously disturbed or frightened, filling their papers with exorcism rites, or warning Craig against trafficking with Satan." What might be more surprising is that even in the classes where students were told that these were stage tricks, over half those students still thought Craig must be psychic. People find it very hard not to believe in something like this, I think. We all enjoy the tingle at the back of the neck and to believe that it is only stage magic takes a lot of it away.

Well, the second point, how do we know other people have thoughts and feelings as we do? I have worded that badly; really, it ought to be how do *I* know other people have thoughts and feelings as *I* do, or how do you know; the 'we' already begs the questions. Anyway this is, as far as science fiction goes, the realm of robots and androids, animals and aliens. With alien stories the general assumption seems to be that they do have thoughts and feelings and the interest of these stories is often in exploring the differences, the anthropological distance between them and us; James Tiptree Jnr and Ursula Le Guin come to mind. But in general I suppose science fiction aliens are not really alien enough, they aren't *uncanny* enough either – they don't possess that mixture of strangeness and familiarity we associate with robots and androids.

Probably no one has explored that territory so thoroughly as Philip K. Dick, again. He seems to have shown that the uneasiness and uncanniness we associate with robots has something to do, perhaps, with the ambivalence of our feelings about other people. Other people are, in one way, objects; no one really cares about the thoughts and feelings of a bus driver or a street cleaner as such so long as the bus gets driven and the street cleaned. People you haven't met are objects, strangers are usually objects, and to many British people at the moment the people of Argentina, for example, are a mass of objects. People here are already suggesting nuking Buenos Aires, for example. This is not exactly consistent with thinking of the human beings that live there. Try imagining an Argentine resident getting up in the morning and brushing his teeth, worrying about how he is going to pay the gas bill this winter, or walking his kids to school, or something, and *then* talk about nuking them – the whole exercise becomes pointless, really. Once you admit that someone has thoughts and feelings, they have to be allowed to join the human community.

This duality works on us too – in *Do Androids Dream of Electric Sheep?* someone finds that in the absence of human company, "he found himself fading out, becoming strangely like the television set which he had just unplugged. You have to be with other people, he thought, in order to live at all." Well, as part of our attempt to understand this duality, humans have since before history made images of this. I believe the idea of the robot is one of the oldest and one of the most deep-set ideas in the human consciousness. It goes back to whenever children first had dolls which they knew weren't real babies, but all the same ... or to whenever grown-ups first made a statue and then fell down to worship before it, knowing it wasn't a god really, but all the same ... Well, the robot idea plays with this exactly in the same way. It is real but it isn't real. Prometheus was supposed to have made a man of clay and when Momus, the god of mockery, saw this creation he criticized it, saying that Prometheus should have made a door opening into its heart so that we could see its secret thoughts. Well, that's one of the oldest artificial man stories going and already the worry is "What is the robot thinking? What is it thinking about?" Legendary robots often seem to have a touch of madness, in fact. Talus, the bronze man who guarded the island of Crete from invaders, was said to heat himself up to a glowing heat and then embrace his victims. Legends always mentioned his grin, his hideous gaping grin. To move forward in time a little, when Friar Roger Bacon built his brass talking head (which he didn't build really but it is a good story anyway), what was it thinking? A servant was set to watch it all night in case it said anything of importance, and if it did speak he was to waken the friars. Late that night the head said, "Time is" and the servant deemed this unimportant. Later it said, "Time was" but again the servant didn't waken the friars. Finally, the head said "Time is past" and exploded into a thousand pieces, or so the servant probably said once he'd hidden his hammer and wakened the friars; I am sure he simply smashed the thing up so that he could get some sleep himself. One of the consequences of being alien and enigmatic is that robots historically get bashed a lot.

Albertus Magnus is said to have worked thirty years on an automaton servant made of wood, wax, leather, metal and glass. One day it saw his pupil Thomas Aquinas on the street and called to him by name. Aquinas replied by smashing it.

Well, moving forward again in time, Rabbi Löw of sixteenth-century Prague was said to have created a golem, a man of clay brought to life by magic. The magic works like this – the secret name of God is inscribed on a parchment and placed under the creature's tongue. This is the first program. When Rabbi Löw removed the parchment the creature would be inert again, and he did this on the Sabbath every week. But one Friday evening he forgot to deprogram it and the golem followed him to the synagogue and tried to force its way inside. Just in the nick of time he managed to deprogram it and prevented it from profaning the Sabbath. After that he put it away in the attic and never used it again.

Well, the golem in these stories is always a soulless, rudderless creature, a sort of unthinking automaton. And it was not long after this that Descartes, besides opining that he thought therefore he was, began to have opinions about automata. He said that animals were automata, lacking human free will. There is also a curious legend that Descartes himself owned an automaton girl named Francine whom he kept in a box. During a sea voyage in 1640 the ship's captain peeked into the box and saw Francine move her limbs. Convinced that this was the work of the devil, he threw the box overboard.

It was about this time, or not long afterwards, that Descartes' young contemporary, Pascal, invented the first thinking machine, or at least the first calculating machine. He set mankind on a course that led, I believe, to the computer and I believe will lead to the walking, talking, thinking and feeling robot.

About artificial intelligence I have little to say except that machines are probably going to get smarter and smarter until either they reach some limit, or else they don't. Likewise, the way they think is going to become more like ours, or more compatible with our way of thinking. Mentally, it must be obvious to everyone by now that machines are coming in our direction. People still argue about whether machines can reach our intellectual level or not; well, what is certain is that they are certainly going to try. That is to say that they will be made to try. If it is possible to make a machine indistinguishable from a human it will be done; so long as it can be done without costing more money than there is, taking more time than there is, and so on. We want robots of this kind just as we wanted wind-up automata, golems, homunculi, dancing toys, mannequins, talking dolls, marionettes, ventriloquists' dummies, and so on. Perhaps, like God, we need company in the universe.

I believe that UFO cults probably spring from a similar impulse – a strong desire to have company. In this case, the company *is* a god, ready to either destroy us or do us tremendous favours. But there are others who look instead for wild varieties of humans, yeti for example in the Himalayas, or Bigfoot in the California forests. Similarly, there is a great interest in teaching chimpanzees human language and communicating with dolphins, and so on. Finally, there are the attempts to communicate either by radio or by sending out decorated metal plates to the four corners of the universe. All of this, I think, points to a strong desire to find someone not human to talk to. Perhaps like the character in Philip K. Dick's story, we think it will help us to feel more real.

Another aspect of this has been making computer programs that seem to talk. One of these, created by Joseph Weisenbaum, is named "Doctor" and it imitates a psychiatrist, using non-directive therapy. Another, created by Kenneth Colby, is called "Parry" and it imitates a paranoid person. Inevitably, the two programs were brought together for a conversation, part of which goes like this:

Parry: I don't understand your motives.
Doctor: Why don't you understand my motives?
Parry: Shouldn't I be?
Doctor: Why do you say that just now?
Parry: That's just the way it is.
Doctor: Suppose that's the way it were not?
Parry: So?
Doctor: I am not sure I understand you fully.
Parry: You harp on the same questions too much.
Doctor: What does that similarity suggest to you?
Parry: I don't get you.
Doctor: Do you wish that you did get I?
Parry: It's about time you showed some interest in *my* feelings!
Doctor: Oh, I showed some interest in your feelings?

Well, it's easy enough to see in this "non-conversation" some of the flaws in these programs, but they both perform much better when used against human beings, and often humans talking to Doctor simply refuse to believe that it is only a simple program and not a real person that they are talking to, or communicating with by teletype.

Just now there seems to be an undercurrent of worry and even fear about the place of real people in the universe, if any. I don't know the cause, possibly technology, including cybernetics, but this fear does break out in films like *Westworld* and *The Stepford Wives* and no doubt *Blade Runner*. There are also things like cloning stories; still more duplicate people to worry about.

So much for that question, anyway. Third, how do we know what the past was really like? How do we know there was a past at all? We have our memories, but these memories are nothing but the firing of neurons in our brains and this pattern can be altered or erased. How about history before our time? How can we be certain about that? Well, by time travel, of course. Science fiction, as usual, comes up with the answer and in taking up time travel, science fiction has had to take up the entire burden of philosophical problems associated with time, especially time paradoxes;

the most popular would, I guess, be Ray Bradbury's "A Sound of Thunder", in which a time traveller goes back to the dinosaur age, accidentally steps on a butterfly and consequently changes our entire world. The opposite story has to be Alfred Bester's "The Men Who Murdered Mohammed" in which time travellers find it impossible to change anything by going back in time to kill someone – Napoleon, Hitler, Aristotle, Mohammed; the person remains unchanged but the time travellers themselves begin to fade away. And there are the hundreds of stories where people become their own ancestors, or kill their own ancestors, or would have. Science fiction also investigates subjective time versus objective time and, of course, time running backwards as it does in *Counterclock World*.

The most noticeable movement of today which I think questions the conventional scientific view of the past is, of course, Creationism, which has had amazing recent success in getting laws passed in certain American states to enforce the teaching in schools of Bible creation stories as science. The creationists' arguments are essentially that evolution is only a theory and that one theory is just as good as another and that therefore they want equal time in schools. Well, the reason why they have been so successful in pushing through these demands is that almost no one understands anything at all about evolution – and I include myself in the ignorant mass here. We merely have a few catch phrases like "survival of the fittest" or "natural selection" and a dim notion of a family tree beginning with protozoa and ending up with man. This feeble picture is easy enough for creationists to attack. One creationist pamphlet gave these arguments for dropping evolution – I am not going to give you all the arguments, just a couple.

1. Natural selection was Darwin's main idea as to how evolution happened; the fittest survive and the unfit perish. Fine, but where is evolution in this case? A certain rabbit can run faster or hop higher and may therefore live longer and produce more rabbits; this in no way implies that the rabbit or its offspring would be more fit for survival if it were evolving into some other animal. In fact, the opposite is true; any alteration in the rabbit's physical or mental characteristics would make it less, not more fit for survival. Natural selection cannot explain evolution. Nothing can explain how evolution happened because it never happened. That is a fact and anybody who says it isn't is being an unscientific fanatic.
2. Students, how many times have you seen and heard that scientists have proof for evolution in the fossil records, in the bones? Here is the truth, let any scientist come forward and deny it if he can; there is not one bone in the entire world that shows one animal evolving into another!

That's wonderful, isn't it – there is not one bone that actually denies evolution either! I think of these I prefer the theories of my Uncle Joshua who founded the Institute for Not Really Difficult Studies. In his Institute science is derived straight from the Bible; Uncle Josh is a creationist, of course, although he has much more powerful arguments against evolution. First of all, survival of the fittest. This pathetic idea, says Uncle Josh, is ruining the world. People everywhere are taking keep-fit classes because they believe that the fit survive, but do the fit survive? Look at Ronald Reagan, he survived an assassination attempt even, and what is he fit for really? No, the truth is that every single creature on this earth eventually dies, fit or not – nothing survives.

Second, Darwin's claim that the giraffe has a long neck because generation after generation of giraffes stretched up their necks to reach the leaves on the trees. Wrong. First of all giraffes don't have to stretch their necks because they are already very long, and secondly what about dolphins? They live in the seas where there are no trees at all.

Third, Darwin's theory is that man descended from the apes. The fact is that there are no apes, there never were any apes. The so-called apes we see in zoos are nothing but men dressed up in hairy suits. Uncle Josh has a picture of one such hairy ape costume and he will send copies to any interested group wishing to see this proof.

Fourth, the odds against evolution are staggering, says Uncle Josh; not only are they staggering, they are getting sick on the pavement and pissing in bus shelters and generally making a nuisance of themselves. But really, the odds against a horse evolving from a horsefly are ten to the five thousandth power to one; and as for evolving a world famous mezzo-soprano from a Rubik's cube – forget it.

The Bible also says that the earth does not move, so not only was Darwin wrong, D.H. Lawrence was wrong too.[*] Uncle Josh says that the earth is flat and the sky is about six hundred miles up. The sun, moon and stars go whizzing around under this sky roof and this means that there is no room really for astronauts. So astronauts have been faking all their moon trips. (Uncle Josh probably saw the same film on TV as I saw.) He says that the astronauts really go to a spot in the Nevada desert where they go floating around on wires and pretend to pick up moon rock before they come back to earth so that they can open up sports goods stores and go into politics. Uncle Josh says that the earth is not only flat, it is really the top of a large mahogany chest of drawers with brass handles. Earthquakes are only someone in a hurry to get out a pair of socks and slamming the drawer. His wife, my Aunt Lotty, says in that case why don't we smell furniture polish all the time? She says that God probably never intended to make the universe at all, only there was some of this material left over after God made some slip covers for the living-room furniture and it seemed a shame to waste it.

Anyway, enough of my uncle and aunt. How do we know that the

---

[*] And I'm wrong: it was Hemingway whose characters discussed earth movements.

entities of science are real? Well, like all four-part lists, I think this is almost going to turn out to have three parts. The fate of the entities of science (by which I mean electrons and atoms rather than Newton and Einstein) is not really that interesting. Science fiction naturally deals with science, and it is the rise of pseudo-sciences that reflects, I think, a deep discontent with our civilization. People are uneasy about science for a number of reasons. It seems to be, first of all, an indisputable authority – a sort of court from which there is no appeal. It produces terrifying weapons and profound changes in our surroundings. Not only is it an authority, it also seems in league with other authorities – government, military powers, multi-national corporations – helping them to keep their grip on things and people. Scientists are generally seen as cold, ruthless people; the kind of people who would turn the sun into a supernova just to get some good pictures. Well, all of this is obviously not true, but there is an element of truth in it that, I think, gives a great deal of credence to people presenting alternative science that is superior, morally superior at least, to the above kind. But often they seem to want to be part of the ruthless authority and actually seek scientific approval of their work.

It is also interesting to see cases where genuine scientists slip over into doing pseudo-science. I think one of the most notable cases in recent years is that of the psychologist Sir Cyril Burt, the undisputed leader in British psychology for about fifty years; in fact he shaped British psychology until his death (about 1970). The case for believing that IQ is largely inherited rested solely on evidence supplied by Dr Burt and a few of his colleagues. Burt had made a study of twins separated at birth and raised apart, comparing them with twins not parted, and the evidence showed clearly that IQ and heredity were linked. In 1977 it was found that his evidence was faked; some of the colleagues who had co-authored his studies had in fact not worked on them at all, and others were non-existent colleagues. There were numbers invented to fit the theory and, indeed, it looks as if he invented the separate pairs of twins There is currently no evidence to support the theory that IQ is inherited. There is no evidence against it either, it is simply not a theory.

By coincidence, Burt was also a strong supporter of telepathy and contributed article to a book called *Science and ESP* in 1967.

I think that pseudo-scientists are no strangers to this kind of fakery. By another coincidence, one of the leading researchers into ESP, Walter Levy, was caught by his co-workers faking his evidence in 1973. (I should put in a caveat here since I am going to speak about Professor Hans Eysenck and I don't want it to seem as though I am accusing him of doing any fakery.) Eysenck is the currently acknowledged leader of British psychology and has also been a supporter of IQ inheritance theory. He continued to support the idea after Burt's data was thrown out but I don't know if he still supports it. Earlier he was a supporter of ESP (in his 1958 book he says so) and he went on in 1977 to study the effects of the zodiac on personality, writing a paper in collaboration with an astrologer. The wonderful effects Eysenck found, however, were not replicated and finally he dropped that idea. Later he wrote a book which, at least reviewers claimed (I have not read it), stated that cigarette smoking had negligible effects on the lungs, cancer being largely caused by the genes instead. I have not heard much of that idea lately either. Although it is hard to keep up with all of Eysenck's latest innovations, it will be interesting to see where he strikes next; there are so many open fields in alternative science.

I should finish off speaking about alternative science by saying that I have written pseudo-science books myself, one particularly promoting the idea of a lost thirteenth sign of the zodiac. I cannot say that I want to carry on writing pseudo-science books because I don't suppose I quite realized its effects when I wrote this one. I have a drawer full of fan mail as a result of this book from people who were absolutely convinced by the idea and thought what a wonderful thing it was that somebody had found the lost thirteenth sign of the zodiac. These people all turned out to be born under this thirteenth sign of the zodiac, of course. Next, I think I'll try something a little less personal. If I do anymore pseudo-science books I may discuss something like the East or West Pole.

What I have been driving at here is that science fiction *is* pseudo-science in a sense. Having written some of each I guess I am in a position to compare them. I think their emotional content for both writer and reader is the same. I have been calling it the tingle at the back of the neck but it is more than a cheap thrill. It is giving one's mind over to large ideas about the way that the world works, to the tune of your own imagination, you might say. I understand this is the way artists and scientists function too. The trouble is that you cannot lose yourself completely in obsession and madness. The artist has to take a step back from his obsession and get control of it. The scientist has to tighten down on his imagination at some point and try to keep the idea within certain bounds, try to make it into a hypothesis which can be tried and tested in the real world. Maybe Prometheus had the same problem – how to steal the sacred fire from the gods and get it back to us without setting the world on fire in the process.

Science fiction, like any fiction, has to obey the general restriction: the play of ideas has to end up as more or less legible prose. It is identified as fiction, that is, not the real world. It is a lie which tells us about the world, as Picasso said of art, and any truths in SF are indirect ones; they are artistic truths, not facts. Pseudo-science refuses this kind of tightening down restriction or distancing; it refuses to play the game; in other words it masquerades as science. I have enjoyed writing it, but I don't think I want to write any more. I will stick to science fiction for a while; unless anyone wants to join my expedition to look for the East Pole.

How I Became a Science Fiction Master in only 15 Minutes a Day

Firstly I believe in dressing the part. You can't write science fiction wearing your ordinary everyday writer's uniform. Throw away the tweed jacket with leather elbow patches, the pipe and horn-rim glasses. Shave off that beard. An SF writer can only wear a beard if it looks weird enough.

The usual SF uniform includes a baseball cap with a NASA emblem on it, a T-shirt depicting some comic book superhero and plenty of buttons with obscure slogans on them ("QUARKS!"). If I can't get all this, I try to make do with a silver jump suit, red cape and fishbowl helmet – jet-propelled roller skates with silver wings on the side being an optional accessory.

The next choice is, how fast to write. SF is famous for authors who churned out novels in five days, short stories in five minutes and so on. Though no one in SF has so far surpassed Georges Simenon (who probably wore a rubber *pipi* bottle to save leaving the typewriter even for a moment) there have been many speedwriting legends. One prominent scientologist, I understand, back in the 1940s wrote on a special typewriter with extra keys for commonly used words like "inter-galactic" and "spunng". He also saved time by typing directly onto a roll of toilet paper. Even now there are said to be SF writers whose word processors can't keep up with them – after all, electrons can only move at the speed of light.

Since I write relatively slowly on a manual typewriter, I naturally envy those who can whip out half a novel while I'm trying to make up my mind whether "spung" has one *n* or two. Mostly I envy their money. I also envy the money of rich people who do not write, and I envy terrific athletes and those who understand modern physics completely. It always seemed to me that if I really tried, I might achieve partial success at least in any of these fields. I could maybe write a novel in fifty days, or make say half a million. Or at least understand one quark. But I spend all my time writing slowly. One *n* or two?

Next, how much science to put into my SF. Some writers argue that there must be plenty. I maintain that all is science, anyway. If someone drives a car in a story, that implies the principles of thermodynamics; if he rides a horse, that implies the evolution of horses; if he turns on a water tap, there's fluid dynamics for you. The hard science school might prefer it if we wrote: "He turned the tap and filled a 500ml beaker with hydrogen hydroxide ..." That seems unnecessary to me. Get the science out of our stories, I say, and get the people back in.

Only we can't overdo that, either. One mistake I try to avoid is letting my characters have lives of their own. Authors are always complaining that they create characters who "come to life" and "take over" the story. I say it's just a question of who's the boss. If any of my characters dared try any such rebellion, they'd very soon find themselves back on the street looking for another author, Pirandello maybe. Only once did one of my employees pull anything on me. In *The Müller-Fokker Effect* I invented a minor figure called President Reagan. This cagey guy waited until *after* the novel was published in 1970 and *then* he came to life. I'll make sure that it never happens again.

JOHN SLADEK COMMENTS

Most of my novels and short stories are set in the near future, in a recognisable America in which technology has either solved all of our problems or failed to solve any of them, or something else entirely has happened. Something else entirely is always happening in science fiction, I understand. My work is usually called satire or black humour, but it also reflects my preoccupation with certain themes.

I am endlessly fascinated by machines which can mimic or displace human beings. So a number of my characters are robots (such as "The Steam-Driven Boy") or computers or cyborg, or self-replicating machines (as in *Mechasm* [*The Reproductive System*]). This theme informs *Roderick; or The Education of a Young Machine*, first of a two-part novel which attempts to cover the entire "life" history of a robot learning machine, and efforts to assimilate him into human society.

A parallel concern is with dehumanizing processes – ways in which governments and other institutions, mistakenly modelled on machines, attempt to reduce their citizens or members to mechanical components. This is the argument of three novellas, "Masterson and the Clerks", "The Communicants" and "The Great Wall of Mexico", and of at least a dozen short stories, and it creeps into the novels, too. It seems almost as though machines, evolving rapidly towards a kind of mimetic humanity, are meeting humans on the way down.

People do of course escape the process of robotization, and one escape route is madness, another recurring theme. Most of the stories in *Keep the Giraffe Burning* seem to deal with mad people (as well as bad, sad and silly people) and how they succeed at their madness. As the title indicates, these stories are steeped in Surrealism; they are meant to blur the border between dream and reality.

That border is blurred by science fiction all the time. Science fiction, it seems to me, constitutes the right brain hemisphere of contemporary fiction (the dreaming part). My work, if it isn't buried in the hypothalamus or the hippocampus or something, is probably somewhere near the lobotomy scars.

Acknowledgements

The editor and publisher are enormously grateful to all the following for bibliographic advice, help and support during the compilation of this collection:

Mike Ashley, Ned Brooks, Michael Butterworth (editor of *Concentrate* and *Corridor*), Ruth Carruth and Patricia Willis of the Beinecke Rare Book and Manuscript Library at Yale University, William Hodges of the Bodleian Library, The British Library, The British Newspaper Library, Graham Charnock, CIX Conferencing, John Clute, Matthew Davis, Thomas M. Disch, Alistair Durie, Jo French, Lawrence Kestenbaum, Valerie Langfield, Hazel Langford, Frank Lessa, Anthony R. Lewis, Michael Moorcock, Charles Platt, Christopher Priest, David Pringle, Richard Mangan of the Raymond Mander & Joe Mitchenson Theatre Collection, Yvonne Rousseau, Edward James and Farah Mendlesohn and Andy Sawyer of the Science Fiction Foundation, Pamela Sladek, Sandy Sladek, Phil Stephensen-Payne and Chris Drumm (compilers of *John T. Sladek: Steam-Driven Satirist – A Working Bibliography*, 1998), Mrs V.C.P. Stonham, Keith Lodwick of the Theatre Museum, Peter Jolliffe and Marius Kociejowski of Ulysses Bookshop, Damien Warman, Tanaqui C. Weaver, and David Wingrove.

Notes on the Text

The Incredible Giant Hot Dog
The opening and closing sections were cut by *Escapade* magazine, so the story began with Joe Scharf and ended with "Consummation" (*Escapade*'s capital C).

The Lost Nose
25: The "Yes" option leads to a "No" continuation, and vice versa; whether this is an error or a Sladekian jape is unknown.

44: Much of the text is handwritten or typed on scraps of coloured paper gummed into the book: one such piece is missing here. To restore continuity if not total authenticity, the first paragraph was supplied by David Langford. Fred's ultimate noselessness in this story branch is indicated by a sketch which also shows a man with a hammer (suggesting the artisan) retreating into the distance.

The Marching Raspberries
References to the villain's "secret lavatory" are not typing errors but deliberately made authors' corrections on the MS pages where Disch or Sladek had originally typed "laboratory".

Publish and Perish
As published, Gleason's first directive about the apparatus was "Green wire to the red coil" – which makes better sense in context as "Red wire to the green coil" and has been so changed.

The Switch
As published (under the title "The Train"), this has Finley reaching the scene of his intended crime at 10:15 and working hard for eight paragraphs, after which "It was 10:15 ..." The first time has been adjusted for plausibility.

Original Appearances

4-Part List – *Vector* #112, February 1983
Alien Territory – *New Worlds* #195, 1969
The Atheist's Bargain, with Thomas M. Disch – *The Devil His Due* ed. Douglas Hill, 1967
Bill Gets Hep To God! – *New Worlds Quarterly* #5, 1973
Blood and Gingerbread – Cheap Street chapbook, 1990
The Brusque Skate – *Ronald Reagan: The Magazine of Poetry* #1, 1968
By an Unknown Hand – *The Times Anthology of Detective Stories*, 1972
Comedo – *Corridor*, May/June 1971
Danny's New Friends from Deneb, with Thomas M. Disch – *Mademoiselle*, September 1968
Dining Out – *More Tales from the Forbidden Planet*, 1990
The Discovery of the Nullitron, with Thomas M. Disch – *Galaxy*, February 1967
Down His Alarming Blunder – *Just Friends* #1, 1969
The Entropy Tango – *Foundation* #25, June 1982
The Floating Panzer, with Thomas M. Disch – sold to *Intrigue* magazine in 1965 or 1966, but not published there. Disch believes that this may have appeared in a companion magazine from the same publisher, perhaps *Bizarre*.
The Four Cows – *Riverside Quarterly* #8, March 1967
The Future of John Sladek – *Bananas* #7, Spring 1977
Goodbye, Germany? – *Bananas* #9, Winter 1977
How I Became a Science Fiction Master in Only 15 Minutes a Day – *The Science Fiction Sourcebook* ed. David Wingrove, 1984
The Incredible Giant Hot Dog, with Thomas M. Disch – *Escapade*, April 1966
In the Distance – *Concentrate* #1, 1968
In the Oligocene – *If*, July 1968, as by John Thomas
It Takes Your Breath Away – syndicated in various London theatre programmes produced by Theatreprint, 1974 (including *Play Mas* at the Phoenix Theatre and *A Streetcar Named Desire* at the Piccadilly Theatre)
John Sladek Comments – *Twentieth Century Science Fiction Writers* ed. Curtis C. Smith, 1986, and other editions
Just Another Victim – *Titbits* #4276, February 1968
Kids! Read Books In Your Spare Time! – *Foundation* #25, June 1982
[Killing is Easy – *Titbits*, 1968 – Sladek's own recorded title for a story apparently published as either "Just Another Victim" or "Timetable"]
Letter – *Just Friends* #1, 1969
The Lost Nose – written 1968-70, text first published as a Big Engine

chapbook to promote *Maps*, April 2001
Love Among the Xoids – Drumm Booklet #15, 1984
Love Nest – *Holding Your Eight Hands* ed. Edward Lucie-Smith, 1969
Machine Screw – *Men Only*, October 1975
The Marching Raspberries, with Thomas M. Disch – first published in *Maps*, 2002
The Misinterpreted Letter – *Just Friends* #2, 1970
The Monkey's Paw Effect (see Introduction) – *Just Friends* #1, 1969
Mystery Diet of the Gods, with Thomas M. Disch – *Swank*, October 1976
No Exit – *Ronald Reagan: The Magazine of Poetry* #1, 1968
Now That I'm Free – *Titbits* #4293, June 1968, as by Dale Johns
Page – *Just Friends* #1, 1969
Peabody Slept Here – *Men Only*, December 1974
The "Pelican" – *Just Friends* #1, 1969
Plastitone (artwork) – *Ronald Reagan: The Magazine of Poetry* #1, 1968
Practical Joke – *Titbits* #4312, October 1968, as by Dale Johns
Publish and Perish – *If*, June 1968, as by John Thomas
Radio Cats – *Drabble II: Double Century* ed. Rob Meades and David B. Wake, 1990
Reinventing the Wheel – *Interzone* #66, December 1992
Robot "Kiss of Life" Drama – *New Worlds* #216, 1979
A Section from the Adventures of I.E.M. – *region* #1 ed. David Morton and others, Summer 1963
Seventh Inning Stretch – *Ronald Reagan: The Magazine of Poetry* #1, 1968
Some Mysteries of Birth, Death and Population that Can Now Be Cleared Up – *Bananas* #13, as "Some Mysteries of Birth, Death and Population", February 1979
Stop Evolution in Its Tracks! – *Interzone* #26, November/December 1988
Sweetly Sings the Chocolate Budgie, with Thomas M. Disch – first published in *Maps*, 2002
The Switch – *Titbits* #4279, as "The Train", March 1968
Timetable – *Titbits* #4282, March 1968, as by Dale Johns
Transplant Your Own Heart – A Do-It-Yourself Guide, with Thomas M. Disch – *Transatlantic Review 60*, June 1977
The Treasure of the Haunted Rambler – *Holding Your Eight Hands* ed. Edward Lucie-Smith, 1969
United We Stand Still, with Thomas M. Disch – first published in *Maps*, 2002
Untitled and Untitled 2 – *region* #2 ed. David Morton and others, Fall 1963/Winter 1964
The Way to a Man's Heart, with Thomas M. Disch – *Bizarre! Mystery Magazine*, January 1966
Writing Places – *Focus* #6, Autumn 1982
You Have a Friend at Fengrove National – *Titbits* #4278, March 1968

EXTENDED COPYRIGHT PAGE

The Way to a Man's Heart copyright © 1966 by the Estate of John Sladek, Deceased, and Thomas M. Disch.
The Floating Panzer copyright © 1965 by the Estate of John Sladek, Deceased, and Thomas M. Disch.
The Incredible Giant Hot Dog copyright © 1966 by the Estate of John Sladek, Deceased, and Thomas M. Disch.
The Marching Raspberries copyright © 2002 by the Estate of John Sladek, Deceased, and Thomas M. Disch.
Sweetly Sings The Chocolate Budgie copyright © 2002 by the Estate of John Sladek, Deceased, and Thomas M. Disch.
United We Stand Still copyright © 2002 by the Estate of John Sladek, Deceased, and Thomas M. Disch.
The Atheist's Bargain copyright © 1967 by the Estate of John Sladek, Deceased, and Thomas M. Disch.
The Discovery of the Nullitron copyright © 1967 by the Estate of John Sladek, Deceased, and Thomas M. Disch.
Danny's New Friends from Deneb copyright © 1968 by the Estate of John Sladek, Deceased, and Thomas M. Disch.
Mystery Diet of the Gods: A Revelation copyright © 1976 by the Estate of John Sladek, Deceased, and Thomas M. Disch.
Transplant Your Own Heart copyright © 1977 by the Estate of John Sladek, Deceased, and Thomas M. Disch.

All other stories copyright © the Estate of John Sladek for the dates shown on pages 303-304, as previously published.

Lightning Source UK Ltd.
Milton Keynes UK
UKOW03f2231110214

226312UK00002B/284/P